Also by Ali Knight

Wink Murder
The First Cut

About the author

Ali Knight has worked as a journalist and sub-editor at the BBC, *Guardian* and *Observer* and helped to launch some of the *Daily Mail* and *Evening Standard's* most successful websites. Ali's first novel, *Wink Murder*, was chosen as one of the *Independent*'s Books of the Year 2011. She lives with her family in London.

Visit Ali's website to find out more about her and her psychological thrillers at www.aliknight.co.uk and follow her on Twitter @aliknightauthor.

ALI KNIGHT

Until Death

HODDER

First published in Great Britain in 2013 by Hodder & Stoughton
An Hachette UK company

First published in paperback in 2014

1

Copyright © Ali Knight 2013

A CIP catalogue record for this title is available from the British Library

ISBN 978 1 444 77713 0

Typeset by Palimpsest Book Production Ltd, Falkirk, Stirlingshire
Printed and bound by CPI Group (UK) Ltd, Croydon, CR0 4YY

Hodder & Stoughton policy is to use papers that are natural, renewable
and recyclable products and made from wood grown in sustainable
forests. The logging and manufacturing processes are expected to
conform to the environmental regulations of the country of origin.

Hodder & Stoughton Ltd
338 Euston Road
London NW1 3BH

www.hodder.co.uk

To my family, for all their love, support and ideas

Kelly spun the rickety display case round with her finger. The pamphlets about domestic abuse coasted to a stop beside her, a mournful child with huge eyes stared out of a black and white photo at her. 'Children are the real victims . . .' the headline said. She pulled her eyes away and caught the receptionist behind the desk opposite sizing her up, her jaw working some gum slowly from one side of her large mouth to the other, masticating over what problem had pulled Kelly in here.

Kelly shifted in her chair, the imitation leather squeaking under her thighs. The drone of stationary October traffic on the Euston Road filtered up from the street. The two women's glances collided again as if the space were too small for them to look anywhere else. Kelly pulled her beret hard down on to her head, trying to hide beneath it, trying to fight her feelings of failure.

The door across the small lobby opened and banged against the partition as a balding man in a pinstripe suit appeared. 'You next? Come on in then.' He held the door open for her as she walked across the poky lobby and into his office. He sat himself down at a desk in front of a shelving unit lined with law books that looked like they'd never been opened. 'How can I help you?'

'I want a divorce.'

He smiled on autopilot, small, irregular teeth poking from between his lips and leaned back, the chair groaning under his weight. 'OK. Let's just get some details down, shall we?' He reached for a pen and dragged a piece of paper across the desk. She looked out of the dusty window at the cluster of neon fast-food signs encircling King's Cross Station like Indians round a wagon train. He didn't go far for his lunch, by the look of the crumpled McDonald's wrapper in the waste bin by the desk. 'What's your name?'

'Kelly Malamatos. My husband's family was originally from Greece.'

'Can you spell that for me?'

She said the letters aloud. 'He's having an affair.'

He didn't even flicker, didn't look up. 'Well, these days you don't have to actually give a reason. We just work out a financial settlement and you can go your separate ways. How long have you been married?'

'Five years.' Get it down, get the money, get the next client in the door. There was no space here for the messy emotions built up over time. 'I really loved him, for the record.'

The lawyer looked up for the first time and gave her a small smile. 'There are few who walk up the aisle who don't feel that. But by the time they come through my door, it's a distant memory, if they can recall it at all.' He moved swiftly back to business. 'Now, does your husband work, or is he on benefits?'

'He works.'

'And you, do you have an income?'

'I make masks for theatre productions. It's not a full-time job. I take commissions when and where I get them.'

'So he's the main breadwinner.'

'Yes.'

'Do you have children?'

Kelly felt the tragic little pause she always had when asked that question, but she ploughed on. 'Two. My daughter from my previous marriage and we adopted a son together.'

'Uh-huh. What's your address?'

'We live in a flat above St Pancras Station, next to the clock tower.' She saw his eyes dart out the grubby window, stare across the Euston Road and up at the Gothic splendour of the huge station and hotel. 'In the penthouse.'

'I see.' He put down his pen and she caught him staring at her shoes. Footwear showed your income bracket more than any other item of clothing. He was rapidly reassessing the dark, nondescript clothes she wore. 'Well, you're in excellent hands. We'll see you through the process, make no mistake.' He leaned back, giving her his full attention for the first time. 'Tell me about your husband. What does he do?'

'He runs a shipping company. His grandfather started the business, his late father expanded it and now it's his. And before you think we're like Onassis, he's got money troubles. He had businesses in Greece that have been decimated by the recession.'

'And the mistress?'

'She's his PA.' Kelly picked a piece of lint off her black skirt. 'I guess you've seen it all before.'

The lawyer puffed up his cheeks for a second. 'Doesn't mean it hurts any less for you.'

'It hurts. But then it always does when your dreams die, doesn't it? I only care about one thing: custody of the children. That's more important than the money.'

He looked at her searchingly. 'It's unusual for a woman to think that the best she can do is get away with custody of her children. From where I sit, half of everything up there in that penthouse, half of every trust fund, half of every car in that underground garage is yours. It's my job to get you your fair share.'

She shifted uncomfortably on her chair. She had always been attracted to strong men, big personalities, but for every positive a negative came trailing in its wake. Strong men like her husband didn't like to lose. 'Christos will see this as a battle with one winner and he fully expects to come out on top.'

'Who has your husband appointed?'

'I haven't told him I want to leave yet.'

He looked surprised. 'The first thing you must do is talk to your husband. Tell him your decision.'

She gave a nervous laugh. 'I'm scared.'

He smiled again; a kinder, more confident face appeared. He leaned across the desk towards her. 'That's what the law is for, to achieve what you can't on your own, Mrs Malamatos.'

'I'd prefer it if you called me Kelly.'

'Remember, Kelly, you're a wife, you have rights. And one of those is the right to leave.' He was allowing himself to become expansive. 'After the love has gone, we appear.'

She turned away, anxiety chewing at her guts. She was in here, not a high-end Chancery Lane lawyer's office with fresh flowers and a college-educated secretary because this was nearest to the flat. Christos sometimes asked her to account for every moment of every day. His manipulation and control masquerading as concern had become more extreme as the years had come and gone.

'Millions have gone through it, just like you're doing. Once you emerge out the other side, it'll be a new start, a new you.'

Now he was resorting to platitudes and it annoyed her. She needed him to know that deep within her was a pounding fear of even being in this office. 'How long have you done this job?'

'I've been a lawyer for twenty-three years, for my sins. Been here in this building for seventeen.'

'I bet you've seen it all, every lying sucker, every cheating husband—'

He finished the sentence for her: 'spoilt wives, manipulative mistresses, violent kids. Nothing can surprise me.'

'You're very certain of yourself.'

'Believe me, in this business you get to see how dark human nature is, how extreme some people's suffering.'

She gave a small nod. 'I know all about that.'

The buzzer went on his desk and he pressed the button without taking his eyes off her. 'Not now, Bethany.' He grinned at her. 'Here's what you do. Tell him your decision, try not to get involved in an argument or recriminations. Try to keep it calm and rational. Then come back and see me and we'll get the ball rolling.'

'Tell me, are you married?'

'I'm divorced. Twice.' He looked a little ashamed and she warmed to him immediately. 'Dreamers and optimists tend to be.' He threw his hands up in a 'what can you do?' gesture. 'Let's get those details down, shall we?'

Ten minutes later he ushered her out of his office and past Bethany's desk and shook her hand at the doorway to the stairs. 'Come back as soon as you've told him.'

She nodded, but with every step down the narrow stairs her courage dimmed like a torch with a fading battery. Asking Christos for a divorce was a risk. But maybe now she knew he had a mistress, had Sylvie Lockhart to distract him, she could slip away. He spent twelve hours a day with the bottle blonde. She had short hair that tended to the spiky, like her character, and a big laugh. She wore high heels and patent belts, preferred loud colours and fashion extras that served no purpose such as zips on sleeves and bows on shoulders. Kelly suspected the American accent was emphasised to make her stand out, to be heard and seen. She was the complete opposite of herself, and that made the hurt lance her anew – Christos hadn't chosen a lover who was anything like his wife.

She stepped off the kerb of the Euston Road and heard the squeal of brakes, the siren of a horn and felt the wind caress her cheek as air was shoved aside by a heavy object inches away. A bus was silently coasting down the inside lane, a row of blank city faces staring out at her. She sharply told herself to get a grip and walked along until she could cross the road at the lights. Adrenalin fluttered through her body, mixing with the shame, the defeat, the anger. But none of these emotions was stronger than the fear.

2

She walked past a couple hand in hand outside the St Pancras Hotel, enjoying London on a loved-up city break. She looked away and headed down a side road past the brutalist British Library to a discreet smoked-glass door. The drill of large machinery competed with the hum of traffic. The whole area was being rebuilt and redeveloped into something shiny and new. The contrast to her rotting marriage was not lost on her.

She walked past a concierge who nodded coldly at her. Such was her level of paranoia about her husband she wondered if he was paid to spy on her, whether this man too had Christos as a boss. She rode up in the lift to their dedicated floor under the roof, to the flat he had chosen and despite her disagreement had bought anyway.

She walked into the bedroom off the corridor near the lift, saw his suit in its dry-cleaning wrapper on the bed. She hung it in the wardrobe. Christos liked things in the right places, he demanded order and routine. She caught sight of herself in her drab black outfit in the wardrobe mirror. It was as if the colour had leached out of her life with every year of her marriage. She tried to anticipate what he would do, how he would react when she told him, and she felt sick to her stomach. It seemed impossible that he would walk out of the house he loved, so she busied herself in packing a bag in case it got ugly, threw some clothes of hers and the kids' in. They might be leaving in a hurry.

She collected the kids from school, made a meal for them, watched them with a forensic eye. Change was upon them, but they were loved, they would adapt. They'd have to. She felt her heart soar with the possibility of being with them without her husband, how light that would feel, how free. And then she heard the lift doors opening and her husband walking up the wide curving staircase from the corridor below, the heels on his hard-soled shoes clicking across the marble of the living room floor and into the kitchen. The colours of the day dulled, the air seemed colder. Her shoulders tensed.

Yannis heard him coming, got down from the table and ran to give his dad a hug. Florence stayed where she was. He roughhoused his son for a while, picked him up and pretended to throw him across the room, which made Kelly flinch, anticipating an imaginary impact. He put Yannis back on his feet and came over to her, shoved a hand up the back of her skirt and pinched her arse. 'You look like a real slut in that. Where have you been today?'

She murmured something to him about language in front of the kids and moved away down the kitchen to put a plate in a cupboard. He stared at her, the dimples in his cheeks visible now. 'I'm starving. Why can't you make beef stew like my mum makes it? Eh, Yannis, why can't your mum cook beef?' He turned back to her. 'Have we got a T-bone in this bloody fridge? I want it with peas, not salad.' He thumped the kitchen counter with his palm and picked up his phone.

Half an hour later Christos was sitting opposite her at the kitchen table, sawing his steak into squares. Christos liked his table laid a certain way, with a placemat and a napkin in a ring, too many different types of glassware and classical music's greatest hits on low, as if a TV crew were about to arrive and start filming the perfect family dinner. He was picky and precise and chewed his food carefully, spearing his peas with the sharp tines of his fork so that each one burst, sending a tiny squirt of liquid across the plate. The scrape of metal on china made her spine jump unpleasantly. The children were downstairs in the den next to the main bedroom, watching telly.

'If you've got something to say, say it.' He could always anticipate what she was thinking. He tended to be one step ahead of her. Back in the early days she had been enthralled by that, now it was one item on the long list of things she didn't like. He put his knife and fork together, wiped his mouth carefully with his napkin and sat back, his hands gripping the table as if he were readying himself for a bar fight.

She listened for the kids, couldn't hear them. She took a deep breath, teetered on the edge of an emotional precipice and threw herself off. 'I know about Sylvie. I know you're having an affair.'

He didn't reply, but stood up, calmly moved his chair back and walked across to the percolator. 'Do you want coffee?' He hadn't even acknowledged what she'd said.

'No, I don't,' she snapped. 'I want a divorce.'

He turned round with a small china cup in his hand and sat down again. The cup made a small cracking sound as he placed it on the slate table. He picked up a sugar cube with the silver tongs from the bowl on the table and put it on his tongue, waited a few moments for it to begin to dissolve and then chased it down with a large gulp of coffee. He didn't take his eyes off her. 'What did you say?'

'I said I want a divorce.'

'Don't be ridiculous.'

His dismissive tone was making the anger swell in her. 'You're cheating on me with another woman.'

He tossed the cup back down on the table where it cracked in two. He didn't even flinch. 'You married me, you'll learn to make a life with me.'

A dying relationship was like cancer, she decided. The rot started slowly, hollowing you out and then it took over everything that used to give you pleasure, robbed you of your peace of mind, your happiness, the person you used to be. Christos's hair was dark and thick, he had long eyelashes like a child and skin that turned walnut brown in the sun. Once, she had thought him handsome, courageous and exciting. Now she just hated his guts.

'This is very simple. I've given you whatever you wanted. You're my wife and you're staying my wife.'

'We can come to an arrangement that suits everybody. The kids will be OK. They want to see their parents happy—'

'You think this is about being contented? Do I look like I'm joyful?'

'I'm sorry, so sorry.' And at that moment she really meant it.

'You're not leaving this marriage. You can't and I won't let you.'

'It will take some time to sink in—'

'I picked you and your daughter up from the gutter, gave you a roof and a life and opportunities, gave you that studio where you work, sitting pretty here with a view of London. Love doesn't pay the bills, Kelly, my grafting twelve hours a day does.'

'Please, Christos, don't make this into a financial battle. Let's try to salvage something for the kids. We don't have to let our failure be theirs.'

Now he got angry, fists opening and closing, a flush across his face. 'Failure? I won't even hear that word in this house. What's success, Kelly? I'll tell you what it is, it's an image I work very hard at. You think I can go into meetings looking like a pussy who can't control his wife? If I can't keep you in line, how can I run a successful business?'

She could feel the stopper on her rage beginning to loosen. 'I am not something you own! You don't control me!'

He got up from the table so fast he knocked the chair to the floor behind him. He walked away into the laundry room, a doorway leading off the kitchen where the bleach was stacked and the ironing board erected once a week by the cleaner or his mother. Kelly followed him in. They were far from the kids here, their marital mess wouldn't be heard.

He bent over and plugged in the iron, slammed it down on the board.

'What are you doing?'

He ignored her. 'You have to understand how this works, fast. If you try to leave me, I'll make sure you never see the kids again.'

'You don't mean that.'

'I always do what I say I'm going to do.'

The stopper blasted off her anger and she screamed at him now. 'How dare you even say that aloud!'

'Those kids are never leaving me and neither are you.'

'You can't stop me.'

'Try me. Nothing is impossible, Kelly.'

'I'll go to the police.'

'No, you won't. I'll have you classed as an unfit mother. Those pills you take for your panic attacks? You'll be lucky to stay out of a mental institution once I've finished with you. We're married until death us do part, Kelly.'

'You're having an affair. You're cheating on me!'

'Sylvie is irrelevant. This is about you – and me.' He spat on the plate of the iron and the water bounced away in crazy bubbles of heat.

'Christos, please.' She felt tears of frustration and heartache well inside her. 'There is no you and me. We don't know each other any more.'

'You don't know me? What a fucking joke. Of course you

don't know me – I protected you from the reality of what it costs to cling to wealth and power. You should thank me, not abandon me.'

'I've tried, I've really tried to make this marriage work, but I can't go on any longer—'

'Can't go on. You have no idea what you're talking about. You've survived the death of your child. I *know* you can keep going.'

He was right. She had survived the worst that life could throw at a mother. And as a mother she realised that she was programmed to do one thing above all others: protect her children. She had failed at that once before, she wouldn't again. She turned to the door. She was going to go downstairs, pick up the bag and walk out of the door with the kids. She would call his bluff, wait for him to calm down, but he whirled round with a force she hadn't been expecting and threw her to the floor. She was stunned, the breath knocked out of her. She lay on her back looking up, thinking here was the line that he had casually crossed and she had no idea what lay beyond it.

He picked up the iron, the tendons in his forearm standing proud like ropes. For a moment she actually looked round for the shirts, and then a second later she understood how bad it could really be.

3

Two Weeks Later

Kelly glanced at the security camera in the corner of the bedroom. The fisheye lens stared back at her, unmoving, like a bully at school. She looked away. Her image was being relayed and stored on tapes in 'security control', a machine that had been set up in the office. It collected images from fifteen cameras that surveyed every room, noting movement, the comings and goings of family life, butting in on secrets and confidences. Christos was paranoid about security, fearful that the world wanted to take away what he had worked so hard for. The flat had been built with a complicated alarm system and security cameras by the two lifts, one that led to the garage and the other that doubled as the front door, but the day after she had asked for a divorce a workman had arrived and installed nine more cameras, in every room, covering every angle. Now she was never more than seven steps from a camera. Christos said it was for her safety and protection, for the sake of the children, but he never explained why it was necessary or who she was to be protected from. She knew it was to keep tabs on her, and her alone.

She leaned over the dressing table and stared in the mirror, smearing foundation across her cheeks with jabbing little strokes. She paused and assessed. The coverage wasn't thick enough. She put on another layer then picked up an eye pencil and got to work. She could hear Florence and Yannis playing in the corridor outside the bedroom. They were racing scooters, scraping the small protruding bit of wall outside her studio and slamming into the entrance lift doors. Her mother-in-law, Medea, ordered them to put the scooters away. The cloakroom door banged open and shut and the padding little steps of seven-year-old Yannis faded. He had been dressed in a sailor suit by Medea, even though he'd wailed and protested at such a sartorial insult. But Christos wanted to parade their children in front of their guests and what Christos wanted, he got.

The doorbell rang, a harsh, penetrating sound. There would be a waitress waiting with a tray of drinks by the doors that were painted to look like the moulded oak of a grand country house but slid apart to reveal the lift. That was their lives all over, Kelly thought. Pretending to be something they're not, painted to give the illusion of something else entirely. Her hand shook as she brushed eyeshadow across one of her lids.

The flat was filling with chatter and laughter, the doorbell buzzing over and over. Undulating tones of excitement and admiration, the clack-clack of stilettos ascending the curving staircase. A small party for eighty, Christos had said. There would be champagne and canapés and staff.

A low, coarse laugh penetrated the bedroom door and Kelly scowled. Sylvie had arrived and was being greeted by Medea. Sylvie managed to bring out a warmth, a joy, even, in her mother-in-law that was beyond Kelly's talents. Kelly applied lipstick, decided on another layer and then brushed her hair. Sylvie was now chatting to Florence, bombarding her with questions. Florence's answers were inaudible. Her shy and quiet eleven-year-old daughter would be wilting under the scrutiny of adults she didn't know.

She took off her bathrobe and put on a plain black dress. She glanced out of the bedroom window, the skyline of Bloomsbury and central London laid out before her, the entrance to the hotel at St Pancras directly beneath them, the Euston Road far below, only the faintest hum of traffic audible through the double-glazed windows. A pigeon came to rest on one of the eleven black metal spikes that decorated the windowsill. Even this high up the Victorians hadn't scrimped on the Gothic splendour of the building. One of the bird's feet was contorted into a stump, lending it an awkward hobble. It looked too tired to bother to fly away. Kelly knew just how it felt.

Kelly caught Christos's voice from somewhere deep in the flat and she froze. She slipped on her black shoes and turned this way and that in front of the mirror, checking. The dress with its three-quarter-length sleeves and high neckline was a good choice. With her heavy make-up she could obliterate all traces of her former self – the person she had understood. For she had become one of those women whom no one understands unless they've been in the same situation – the ones who stay with brutal, controlling men because the fear of going is greater than the pain of staying.

She came out of her bedroom and closed the door, took a deep breath. She met Sylvie on the stairs coming down and was shocked to see that her nose was covered with a thick layer of bandage and gauze and there was bruising under her eyes. Despite her dislike of her rival, she needed to find out if she was all right. 'What happened to you?'

Sylvie smiled and made light of it, waving away her concern. 'It looks bad but it's nothing. I've got nasal polyps. They have to go in and dig around, it's disgusting. The worst thing is they cut them out but they grow back in two years. Gonna have to have it done again one day.'

'Is it painful?'

Sylvie made a scoffing sound. 'The bandages will come off in a couple of days.'

There was an awkward pause. Here they were, the wife

and the mistress, chatting away as if they were friends. Which they weren't. They were so, so far from friends they needed to invent a new word for enemy. But that didn't mean Kelly didn't act nice when the interloper was in her house. She might be fearful but she wasn't stupid.

Sylvie's mouth was moving and Kelly tuned back in. 'Medea needs a pashmina. It's freezing up in that living room.'

Kelly watched Sylvie as she turned right at the bottom of the stairs. She was doing all the running, thinking her efforts would pay off. She obviously didn't realise that Christos would never leave his wife. A crowd of people she didn't know pushed past, eyes on the top of the stairs. She followed them up to find about forty people in the living room. She paused, her eyes roaming over the guests. Their home was all about views, and the large, open-plan living room that ran the width of the building. They were high above the skyline here and had no curtains or blinds because there was no need. Through a series of pointed Gothic windows on the far wall, north London was revealed, the green spaces of Primrose Hill and Hampstead Heath; if she turned around, central London was exposed. The space was too large really, living quarters fashioned from a grand municipal building that didn't have the cosy or workable proportions of a home. The room was echoey and the acoustics bad, the floor was laid with gaudy marble tiles and the furniture had been specially commissioned to be large so that it filled the space. A grand piano no one had the skill to play stood in one corner, and part of the room was divided by a large aquarium in which brightly coloured fish swam on a never-ending loop from one end to the other. She saw Christos standing with his back to her and walked through the crowd that surrounded him. She linked arms with him and kissed him on the cheek.

'There you are!' He stood back to appreciate her fully. 'Doesn't my wife look beautiful?' He introduced her to some people who worked in his office. Kelly shook a bunch of hands and fixed on a smile. Sometimes you couldn't get away. And then it became a question of enduring. She put her arm round Christos's waist and pushed closer to him. We do what we must to survive, she thought. She automatically began to scan the crowd, looking for her children.

She felt a pull on her dress and turned round. 'Mum, I need to tell you something.' It was Florence, her pale eyes staring up at Kelly.

'What's the matter, Flo?' She took her hand and bent down low so she could hear her quiet voice.

'I'm hungry.'

'Come with me.' Kelly excused herself and they walked into the kitchen. The room was stacked with boxes of supplies for the caterers. They were in the end of the building here, windows facing full west where the stream of headlights on the raised motorway that sliced through London on its way to Oxford never ceased. Off the kitchen on the left were various storerooms and the service lift that stopped on the floor below at the far end of the corridor and then the ground floor. Caterers were loading canapés on to silver platters and uncorking champagne bottles. 'Do you want some cocktail sausages?'

Florence shrugged, pulling herself up to sit on a counter and swinging her legs. 'I don't know.'

Kelly guessed she had used her hunger as an excuse to get her mother on her own. She opened the fridge and scanned the contents. 'Do you want a cheese sandwich?'

She shrugged again. Kelly took that to mean yes and pulled out butter and cheese.

'There are lots of people here I don't know.'

'Same with me,' replied Kelly. 'Why don't you play with Yannis? Where is he?'

A squeal from the living room provided the answer. Yannis was being swung between Christos's legs, guests laughing indulgently as they scattered to avoid his whirling limbs. Florence shook her head. 'Can I watch a film?'

Kelly laid the pieces of cheese on a slice of bread, put another slice on top and cut through the sandwich. 'Your dad wants you here, you know.' She saw a look close to panic cross her daughter's face and she relented. Hopefully Christos wouldn't miss her. 'Come on then.' She put the sandwich on a plate and moved to the service lift, glad of an excuse to be away from the party herself. They came out of the lift on the floor below and walked past her studio and a spare bedroom where Medea sometimes took it upon herself to stay over. On her right was the door to the TV room. 'What do you want to watch?'

'*The Princess Bride?*'

'OK.'

Kelly handed the plate to Florence and her daughter flopped on the sofa, crossing her legs. Kelly was struck anew by how much her daughter looked like Michael, her late father, with the same upturned nose and pale skin. Florence's younger sister Amber had had the same profile, but she had been darker, taking more after herself. She hovered for a moment in the doorway, the noise of the party pulling her out. All I have left of Michael and Amber is in her, Kelly thought.

'Mum, Sylvie says you're going away.'

'What do you mean?'

Florence shrugged. 'She said you were going away at the end of the month.'

'Away where?'

'I don't know.'

'Did she say for how long?'

'I don't know.'

'I'm not going anywhere, Flo. Not without you and Yannis. Don't worry.' She managed a smile, though she was perturbed. 'Enjoy the film.' She shut the door, her mind a swirl of unpleasant conjectures.

She walked back up the stairs to find the numbers had swelled. She recognised almost no one, so exchanged pleasantries with a marooned-looking wife of a shipping broker. 'Have you met Christos before?' Kelly enquired.

'Just once,' she replied. 'At a dinner where he was the main speaker. He had the room enthralled. I can't quite remember what he was talking about, but he was very passionate.' She leaned over a crowd of heads. 'But goodness, do you know what's happened to his wife? She looks like she's been in a car crash.'

It took Kelly a few seconds to realise the woman meant Sylvie. She looked across the room to see Christos and his mistress side by side, meeting and greeting people, shaking hands. 'I'm Mrs Malamatos. That's Christos's PA,' she began and the woman's apologies at her mistake tumbled out one after the other. An easy error to make, thought Kelly. She could almost think the same herself the way Sylvie tried to insert herself into their lives; buying gifts for the kids, telling them their mother was leaving . . .

Yannis began to weave in and around the guests, a Lego model of a pirate ship in his hand. Christos bent down and pulled him up into his arms, pinching his cheek with affection. Kelly watched him hand his champagne glass to a passing waiter. 'Now listen.' When Christos talked people did indeed listen. He had a naturally loud voice and it commanded authority. Christos turned to a shelving unit behind him that jutted out into the room at ninety degrees. It contained the fish tank and a selection of large designer squares in which models of ships and tankers sat in glass cases. 'Yannis, which is your favourite ship?' Christos pointed at the five models and put Yannis back down on the floor. Yannis approached the cabinet and Christos beckoned the surrounding guests in closer.

Yannis squirmed with delight at being the centre of attention. He was so different from Florence, he thrived in the
limelight. Kelly watched as the group around Christos and
her son fell quiet, waiting for Yannis to answer. He pointed
at one of the ships. 'I like that one.'

Christos beamed. 'And why's that, Yannis?'

'Because it's the biggest.'

Christos laughed. 'Yes, it's the biggest. Do you know what
it's called?'

Yannis pointed his finger at the ship again. 'This is the
Saracen. One of the biggest ships in the world.'

'And what's this type of ship called?'

'It's a container ship.'

Christos looked like he could burst with pride. Kelly heard
some of the women sigh. Yannis put his finger on the glass
showcase that held the *Saracen* inside it. The model was more
than a metre long and every radar post, porthole and anchor
chain was crafted in great detail. Every container of the many
that sat piled high on the deck had the brand name of the
shipping company etched on it.

'And what's so special about this ship?'

'It's got an engine that makes it go fast.'

'Yes it has, Yannis.'

'And it's unsinkable.' He jumped up and down on his short
legs.

Christos turned to his guests. 'This ship is the triumph of
man over his environment. In the past, when man crossed
the oceans he had to wait and he had to pray. His livelihood,
his very life, were at the mercy of the wind, the currents and
the ocean. There were so many hurdles on his voyage. Time
and tide used to wait for no man – we used to say that you
couldn't swim against the tide. But that's not true any more.
We have tamed nature, beaten it into submission with tech-
nology. We control it, not the other way round. The *Saracen*

is powerful enough to ride out a hurricane – it is unsinkable. I would like to propose a toast, to the *Saracen*, to Malamatos Shipping, to our power to face down our competitors, and to the future of this company – to Yannis here!'

The room roared its approval, glasses rising towards the lights in the ceiling. Kelly dug her fingernails into her palms to keep herself under control. Her eyes had come to rest not on the ships in their glass cases, but the fish tank, with its little stream of air bubbles that rose to the surface and disappeared. Amber and Michael had not had the air they needed. They hadn't been able to swim against the tide . . .

She retreated downstairs to the ensuite bathroom and splashed water on her face, concentrating on calming herself till the panic attack faded. She needed a pill for the anxiety that was beginning to dance up her spine, that threatened to burst through the top of her skull. She wasn't proud but sometimes those pills were the crutch that got her through the days, that made it all seem better. They were also the threat that Christos held so effectively over her head. The reason why she was still here suffering the indignities thrown her way by his mistress. Why she lived in fear of the man she had once loved.

Why had Sylvie said to Florence that Kelly was going away? Where was she supposed to be going? She redid the mask of her make-up and dragged herself back to the party. As she climbed the stairs she met Sylvie coming down again. 'Did you miss Yannis and Christos's speech? It was a blast. Your son holds a room just like his father.'

Christos will never leave me for you, she thought. How she hated this woman spouting her superficial platitudes. Christos doted on the children, that much was clear. They had tried for children of their own for eighteen months with no success until they had discovered his low sperm count. They had adopted Yannis soon after and the subject was never mentioned again but she had always been made to feel that the fertility failure was hers rather than his. Even Medea had once alluded to it as her problem.

She went back into the room, walked towards Christos. 'Hey there.' She turned and was blinded by a camera flash. She grabbed the man's arm with so much force he actually winced.

'No photos. There are to be no photos. Delete it now.' She couldn't even manage a smile. 'Please.'

4

Kelly was dragged from sleep the next morning at six thirty by the drilling of the doorbell. She staggered from bed, confused at who could be calling so early. Christos was in the shower so Kelly answered the door. A woman stared up at her through the video camera. 'This is Customs and Excise at the Port of London. We have a warrant to search your property. Can we come in please?'

Kelly typed in the code to work the lift and ran into the bathroom to tell Christos. She pulled on a pair of jeans and a top and came back out into the corridor and stood staring at the lift doors, straining to hear the faint clanking as it rose towards her. Two seconds and they would be here. The shower fell silent. Kelly swallowed, mentally checking where the children were: Yannis was pulling on socks in his bedroom opposite her, Florence was upstairs, probably slurping milk from a cereal bowl. Before she had time to process what this visit might mean, the lift doors opened. Four people were suddenly in the foyer as Christos emerged from the bedroom in a towelling robe, his hair glossy with water.

A young woman who wasn't yet thirty stepped forward. 'Mr Malamatos, my name's Georgie Bell. I'm a criminal investigation officer at Customs and Excise. We have a warrant to search your property for evidence of suspected customs fraud.' She handed Christos a piece of paper. 'Your offices are also being searched—'

'What fraud?'

'A shipment of Brazilian rosewood was found when your ship the SS *Sea Shuttle* docked at Silvertown on the 3rd of October. Your company is listed as the shipper and owner of the goods. We had a tip-off the wood was on a banned list and the accompanying paperwork forged. This has now been confirmed—'

'Who's the tip-off?'

'Anonymous. Mature Brazilian rosewood trees are on a list of banned materials that—'

Christos didn't let her finish. 'This is about wood?' He sounded incredulous. Kelly didn't hear the rest as the rage that was always pulsing just beneath the surface in Christos burst out and he began shouting about taxpayers and scroungers and drug dealers and terrorists. Kelly stood back against the corridor wall and put her arms around Yannis's shoulders. The boy had emerged from his room and was staring, open-mouthed.

Georgie Bell was saying that anything they took away from the flat would be logged and returned as soon as possible. She would need to take Christos's mobile phone and any portable devices. She was unfazed by the big man shouting; in fact, Georgie looked like she was enjoying herself. Kelly noticed that the three men with her took a good look at the size of the flat and stared at the view out of the master bedroom window. A moment later they began to shuffle deeper into the flat to open doors and look in rooms. Christos angrily left a message with someone before he handed over the mobile, a damp patch of shower water collecting underneath him on the carpet.

Georgie tried to open the door opposite Kelly, next to the lift. 'What's in here?' she asked.

'That's the office,' Kelly said.

'Can you open it for me, please?'

'I don't have the key, my husband does.' She felt shame

lance her that parts of her own home were off limits to her.

Georgie's brown hair was tied back in an efficient ponytail with what looked like a rubber band. She had a big mouth that suited her face and when she spoke Kelly could see there was an attractive gap between her front teeth. 'Is the office always locked?' She smiled at Kelly in an open, inviting way.

Kelly shrugged, her mind churning over how Christos would react to this intrusion. With a control she didn't feel she asked Yannis to go upstairs and get his breakfast. She watched him retreat up the stairs to the kitchen and then turned to Georgie. 'Do you want to start in my studio?' Georgie held out her arm for Kelly to go first. Kelly opened the door next to her bedroom as Christos watched her from the corridor. 'It must look chaotic to you, but it's very well ordered to me,' Kelly said. Her small talk was a way of keeping a lid on her nerves.

The middle of the room was dominated by a large trestle table on which lay a half-finished papier-mâché mask, paint pots, brushes and tubes of paint. There was a paint-spattered office chair on wheels, and a dressmaker's dummy stood in the corner by one of the windows. A sewing machine sat on a chest of drawers in the other corner. Opposite the windows along the wall was a series of deep shelves that held bales of fabric, piles of newspapers, prototypes of mask models, 'look books' and scraps of papers that were inspirations for designs.

A man probably just a few years older than Georgie came into the studio. 'I'm Mo Khan.' He nodded towards the view. 'It must be hard to work when you could look at that all day,' he said, staring out of the window.

Kelly didn't reply. The view was south from this room, the morning still and sullen. She could see the London Eye where Christos had proposed and she had cried with joy and accepted. To the left were the fantastical pointed tips of the

Royal Courts of Justice, as remote and unhelpful to her current situation as Sleeping Beauty's fairytale castle, surrounded by thorns. Kelly knew all the weight of the law and people's good intentions were on her side, the police, the courts, women's refuges, social services. And it all meant nothing. They couldn't stop the fear, they couldn't stop Christos exercising his power and using his money. The law worked too slowly to help her escape. She had visited her doctor for depression, she had been prescribed pills. It would be too easy for him to make her look like an unfit mother. And the fear that pressed down every waking hour was that he would take away her children. She had lost one child for ever; she would endure anything to cling to the remaining two.

'This is quite a production you have here.' Georgie was looking round the room, assessing, judging.

'I make masks and sometimes puppets for theatre shows.'

'That sounds interesting. Did you train in that?'

Kelly swallowed, keen to steer the conversation in another direction. 'I'm largely self-taught. Papier-mâché is my speciality. It's great for making larger masks as it's light yet strong and you can build it up really well. It's very flexible too. That's why I keep so much newspaper in here.'

'Do you have a laptop?'

Kelly shook her head and saw Georgie looking at the blinking green light in the corner.

'There are a lot of cameras in this flat.'

'I want to protect my family.' Christos's voice seemed to boom as he entered the room.

'From what?' asked Georgie. She turned towards him, her large eyes holding him in a steady gaze.

Kelly gripped the edge of the trestle table, torn between fascination that this woman could so casually defy Christos and fear that it would end very badly for her. She didn't know what Christos really did in the course of his business, but she had been given a glimpse. Six months ago he had taken her with him in the car one evening to the docks. He'd had a meeting with someone. He had ordered her to sit in the car with the driver and he had got out with another man. They had met a third, younger man and had walked partly round a corner. A conversation had begun, which after a couple of minutes had turned into a lot of shouting that had ended when Christos had picked up an iron bar and pummelled the young man across the shoulders and then around the head. Christos's friend had laughed. The young man had crumpled to the floor and stayed there as her husband and his mate had walked calmly back to the car. Christos got in next to her, the tangy scent of sweat and adrenalin rising from him and lifted a hand to her head. He let out a strangled groan, every sinew in his neck standing to attention. Kelly knew then that Christos, far from being a man who couldn't control his violence, was someone far worse: a man who could choose exactly when to maim and when to stop. He had lowered his hand. He had great reserves of self-control – and he had let her know it then.

'When you've got money, lots of people want to take it from you,' Christos said now.

'Do they?' Georgie looked genuinely puzzled. 'There's only one group who can legitimately take money from your business and that's Revenue and Customs. That's us. If anyone else is trying to take your money it's a matter for the police and they will help you.'

Christos smiled, looking incredulous. He had a very good smile and Kelly wondered how Georgie would react to it. 'How long have you been doing this job?'

'Not long, but I intend to do it for many years.' Georgie's voice was flat London with hints of Essex in it. She had no wedding ring, Kelly noticed, and was wearing lace-up brogues and black trousers with a turn-up. She had an easy grace to her movements and Kelly figured she was sporty, but she looked too urban to be someone who strode across a moor in walking boots, too substantial and bold to be a dancer.

'If someone your age is leading this investigation it's obviously not an important case. I've got nothing to worry about.'

Georgie remained calm. 'We need to get into the office. Do you have the key, Mr Malamatos?'

Christos was still in his bathrobe, his legs wide apart, a pair of calves as thick as Henry VIII's protruding from the bottom.

'I've got it here. I've got nothing to hide.' Christos's bathrobe was loosely tied at his waist. He put his hand in its deep pocket and as he did so the cord undid itself and his towelling robe fell open. Kelly felt the visitors tense to waxwork dummies. 'Oh, look at that,' Christos casually said. Georgie and Mo were treated to a full frontal view of her husband, his dick hanging thick and heavy. Georgie looked like she wouldn't react, then Kelly saw a deep blush start at the woman's neck and spread over her cheeks. Christos was proud of his big cock and he was trying to rile and humiliate the young woman with it. A moment later, Christos retied the bathrobe. He pulled the office key from his pocket and held it up, his eyes never leaving Georgie's face.

Georgie had to step towards him to get the key, her cheeks aflame. 'After you, sir.' Her voice was neutral, those telltale cheeks the only giveaway that he had riled her. Christos wasn't smiling now, his face was hard. He left the room abruptly and Georgie turned to Kelly. Their eyes met and for a glorious second Kelly hoped that this young girl could be her way out – before despair rushed back in and she discounted the idea.

They left Mo searching the studio and walked to the office. Christos opened the door and entered with Georgie, who instructed two men to look through it. Kelly watched from the corridor. She had rarely been in this room. It was Christos's private space, where he retreated for certain phone calls, occasionally where male visitors with three-day stubble or the dark, tanned skin of the newly arrived from foreign climes came. The walls were lined with shelving containing photographs of dead family members and idyllic, isolated beaches of Medea's homeland, and a few books. Facing the door was a large, dark wooden desk, empty except for a second phone line, a computer and a pen in a holder. The room smelled faintly of the furniture polish Medea used to buff the surfaces to a sterile shine. At right angles to the desk sat a green filing cabinet. Christos unlocked the cabinet and an officer slid out the top drawer.

The passports were in the cabinet.

She'd noticed, only once, about seven months ago. They'd come home from a holiday in Greece. The plane had been delayed and they were all tired and as she hurried the kids into their beds she had come out of their room to see the office door bounce against the run of shelving and begin to swing shut on Christos. In the three seconds before the closing door cut him from her view she had seen him pull the passports from his pocket and put them in their resting place. She had bent instantly to untie her sandal. Better if he didn't know she had seen.

'Mr Malamatos? What is this machine here?'

'It stores the recordings from the cameras. They're backed up on disk.'

'We'll need to take them.' Georgie's cheeks had returned to a normal colour, she was trying to reassert her authority.

Christos wasn't interested any more, he had his victory and the woman was just a nuisance now. He pressed a button and the green light on the camera nearest Kelly went black. The security system was off. She heard the home phone ringing and a moment later Florence called out from the top

of the stairs that Sylvie needed to talk to Christos urgently.
Kelly watched Christos walk out of the office and past her
in the corridor to enter their bedroom. The nearest landline
point was on the far side of the bed. He had to get round
the king-size to the phone – twelve steps at least and then
back out into the corridor.

Kelly was halfway across the office before she even realised
what she was about to do.

Georgie was leafing through the filing cabinet as she
reached it. She turned, surprised, but didn't stop her as Kelly
shut the top drawer with a confidence she didn't feel and
opened the one below it, hearing its screech above the
battering of her heart. She prayed the noise wouldn't bring
Christos running; he knew people were in here. She reached
in and pulled out the passports, not pausing to discard the
one she didn't need. Georgie looked at the passports in her
hand and carried on searching.

'What are you doing?'

Kelly froze, and turned. Yannis was standing in the doorway,
his palms pressed into the door frame on either side of him.

'I'm helping the officers. Now get your school uniform
on.' She shoved the passports in the back pocket of her jeans.
Yannis didn't move as Kelly crossed the room towards him.

'What's going on?' Christos stood behind Yannis in the
doorway, the portable landline to his ear.

Kelly wondered if she could find her voice. 'The number
of times I have to nag this boy to get ready for school . . .'
Kelly trailed off, walking past both of them and up the stairs.
She felt Christos's eyes boring into her back. The passports
were a brick in her back pocket. Three steps, two steps, one
step. She prayed Sylvie's charms were enough at this moment
to distract him sufficiently for her to get up the stairs and
away. When she got to the living room her strength failed
her and she had to sit on the sofa and let her heart return

to normal. She saw the light above the camera in the corner of the room turn green.

A few moments later she heard someone jogging up the stairs and Georgie appeared. She began walking around the room, assessing, forming opinions. 'We won't be here for that long.' She opened the lid on the piano and glanced inside, looked over and smiled at Kelly. 'It seems like a big intrusion, but by this afternoon it'll be like we were never here.' She stopped by the fish tank, put her hands in the pockets of her trousers and leaned in to look more closely. 'I've got a goldfish at home.' She tapped the glass, trying to get a reaction from the fish. They ignored her. 'I have to make sure the lid's always on, otherwise the cat would get him like that.' She clicked her fingers as she said it. 'What's this boat at the bottom here?' She was looking at the vessel half submerged in the stones at the bottom of the tank.

'It's a model of a competitor's ship.'

Georgie turned round. 'You're kidding, right?'

Kelly's laugh came out as a high-pitched squeal, bordering on hysteria. 'No, I'm not.'

Georgie was obviously someone who found laughter contagious because she joined in. 'That's very revealing,' she said, shaking her head. Georgie had a warm, open face; you could chat to her if she sat next to you on a bus. Kelly saw Georgie watching her before her attention was taken by something else. She cocked her head. 'What's that noise?'

Kelly looked up at the beamed ceiling. 'It's pigeons. They're in the roof. This building was derelict for nearly fifty years. When they began the renovations, there were thousands of them living up there and in the clock tower at the end of the building. They had to get a specialist team in to remove their droppings. Pigeon shit is highly toxic.'

Georgie was nodding. She tapped her chest. 'I heard it's bad for the lungs.'

'They cleared them all out, mended the roof, but they wouldn't stay away. It drives Christos mad. If even a small hole remains, they get in.' She paused. 'Once they're in, they can't find the way out. They're there till they die.'

There was a small pause. 'Trapped,' Georgie said, almost to herself. 'Dying, trying to escape.'

Kelly looked at her and felt something pass between them. She watched as Georgie's smile faded and a frown appeared in its place.

Georgie made a movement to come towards her and then stopped, uncertain. 'Can I help you? Are you OK? Here.' She pulled out a business card and handed it to Kelly. Kelly put it on the arm of the chair, staring down at the mobile number.

No one can help me, Kelly thought, no one at all. I'm all alone. She heard the heavy tread of her husband on the stairs. She turned away from Georgie and stared out of the windows at the teeming life of the city below her.

5

Georgie was standing in Angus Morton's office waiting for the big boss to arrive. She was on her feet because the piles of paper on his desk had mated with those on the shelves and produced more piles that now occupied the two chairs this side of the desk. She saw that the wastepaper bin was now on top of a further pile. She wondered if Angus was turning into a hoarder; she'd seen a TV programme once where a house owner had to crawl through a two-foot gap to get into any room, such was the level of clutter. She was imagining Angus digging through layers of paperwork when she heard him walking down the corridor, the sound of more papers slapping against his thigh.

He had rolled the pile in his hand into a tube and as he said hello and sat down behind the desk he used the papers as a baton to thump out a finale to the tune in his head. 'How did it go this morning?'

'Good, good,' Georgie lied, feeling like one of those idiots in *The Apprentice*. Angus had recently promoted her and she sometimes wondered if he'd done it for his own amusement – to see her grey-haired, pot-bellied colleagues mutter into their pints of bitter. She'd only joined the force a year ago, and still felt she had a lot to prove.

Angus was in his late forties with attractive salt and pepper hair. He was a big, tall man but moved with a surprising grace that she found mesmerising to watch. She hated herself that she fancied him, that she was an office cliché – he was nearly twice her age, married and with kids. It was so inappropriate it was laughable, which was exactly why she wanted it so much. She felt the familiar blush beginning to creep up her neck and forced herself to control it. She would die a thousand deaths if he found out how he populated her night-time thrashings in her tiny single bed back home.

She turned round as Mo arrived.

'Here, Georgie, I got you a coffee.' Mo handed her a take-out from the café near their offices. 'And a side order of sausage.' He laughed and handed her a paper bag.

She stood there with the items in her hand and glanced at Angus. He was making no effort to hide his smirk.

'You know you can take it further if you want,' Angus said kindly. 'Make a complaint against Christos Malamatos.'

Mo was getting into the swing of it. 'I mean, it was huge! Down to his knees!' He made a gesture with his hands like he'd caught the biggest fish of his life. Angus's smile was broadening. She heard a snigger from over her shoulder and Preston entered. Preston had a perma-tan and a suit that was a lot too shiny for Georgie's taste. 'You don't see one that size every day—'

'I do,' said Preston, and laughed at his own joke.

'It's not a problem, really, let's just forget it,' Georgie said. Fat chance. She felt her cheeks begin to flame again. The story of how she'd had an eyeful would be round the force like food poisoning round cousin Gary's wedding. They would rib her about this for years to come, undermining her struggles to be taken seriously and left to do her job. At that moment she hated Christos Malamatos.

There was a long pause as they waited for Preston to pick up a pile of paper from a chair and put it on the floor, wipe the seat with his hand and sit down, unbuttoning his jacket carefully as he did so.

'So, impressions?' Angus asked.

Mo took the lead. 'The flat's unbelievable, like a fancy Fort Knox. You can see the whole of London from up there. There're video cameras everywhere. You can't get out of the flat without typing in a code and you can't let anybody in without doing the same. You can't get in or out of the flat unless the person who programmes it wants you to.'

'Are the offices the same, Preston?' asked Angus. Preston had led the team that had gone to the Malamatos shipping offices.

He kept them waiting a good while as he thought about an answer. 'No. They have standard office security, that's all.' He paused, a sly grin widening across his tanned cheeks. 'Ooh. What's he hiding?'

Georgie spoke up. 'The office at the house was locked, but there was only standard security on the laptop we took.'

Angus thumped his paper baton on the desk. 'OK, so what have we got? An anonymous phone tip-off about illegally harvested Brazilian rosewood which is shipped to London using fake export licences. We've got a whole can of it impounded here that came off the ship mentioned by the source. We're looking for patterns: we need to know how much we're dealing with and what the scale of his operation is. Now, before you think this is only wood, it's not girls or guns or drugs—'

Preston let out a sarcastic cheer and Georgie wished that Angus hadn't smiled. His flashes of childish inconsistency punctured her fantasies of him. She didn't think he'd like to know that behind his back they called him Anguish. Preston added insult to injury by looking across at her and winking.

'The margin on illegal tropical hardwood is better than drugs – think about that,' Georgie added, giving Preston her best dagger stare.

'Indeed,' added Angus. 'This guy's not a pusher on a street corner, but he could well be making more money than one.'

'Jungle hardwood is called green gold, I heard,' Georgie added. 'For all we know we might have ourselves a rosewood kingpin.'

'We know the rep this guy's got, right?' said Preston. 'He's a proper wrong'un.' He exchanged a look with Mo. 'There was that allegation about GBH that was made by someone working here last year, but then the guy dropped the charges and left the docks. Word was that he had been leaned on.'

'You think that's bad?' Mo began. 'About three years ago, there was that potentially huge case involving the Ecuadorian government, wasn't it? And the whistleblower ended up drowned at Gallion's Reach?' The men in the room nodded as they remembered. 'An open verdict was recorded, but you know the bar talk—'

'Well, you don't,' interrupted Preston with a grin.

'No, I don't personally, since I never go in pubs, but you get my drift. We're dealing with a right fucker here, pardon my French.'

'You need to make sure you follow proper procedure on this,' said Angus. 'I don't want him wriggling off the hook with his clever lawyers if we find anything that can implicate him. This "Deep Throat"' – Angus raised his fingers in a quote mark – 'also claimed that Christos was moving other stuff. So if there *is* something else coming in in those cans, we need to know about that too, and I suggest we try to find out who this tip-off is and get him some protection; he's going to need it. Oh, and by the way, the line was so garbled we think the tip-off was using a voice changer, so it could in fact be a woman.'

The team nodded and Angus thumped his desk with the rolled-up paper, as if bringing the meeting to a close.

'Sir, there's something weird at that house.' Georgie sensed them stilling as they turned towards her. She feared they were waiting for her to say something ridiculous.

'What do you mean?' asked Angus.

'Well, I mean . . . Just hear me out. It's a hunch, I guess.' Damn, that had come out all wrong. She could see Preston leaning back in his chair, luxuriating in her every fuck-up so soon in her new job. 'They've got two kids and lots of money, but they live in a flat with no garden, right on a busy road. The windows don't ever open, there's an air-conditioning system. Why aren't they living in a nice house with a garden in . . . I don't know, Chelsea, St John's Wood?'

Angus shrugged, flicking through a pile of paper to find something he needed. 'Maybe they like city living.'

'OK, well, that's my point really. She works at home, does the artsy thing and makes masks, yet they're right next to King's Cross, one of the biggest construction sites in Europe. It's all noisy and chaotic. Fine behind the double glazing, but once outside, not a place for kids. I've got a friend who's an estate agent, and he says that it's women who choose houses, you're always selling to the wife. But my point is *he* chose that flat – he's the boss. And you can grow to hate your boss.' Angus frowned and looked alarmed. 'No offence, but maybe our anonymous tip-off came from the wife.'

Preston made a sucking sound on his teeth. 'Don't overstate it. These wives are up to their necks in it, just like their husbands. They're always family affairs.'

Georgie was about to argue this point vehemently with Preston but her eye was caught by the receptionist outside Angus's office gesticulating at her.

The receptionist opened the door. 'Sorry, Georgie, but there's someone downstairs for you.'

Georgie frowned. 'Who is it?'

The receptionist looked stricken. 'I think it's your dad.'

'Are we quite finished?' Angus was staring at her.

'Sorry, sorry.'

'The only way to find out for sure about the wife is to talk to her,' Angus continued, 'find out if there's something about her we can use—what's all that shouting?'

'Excuse me,' said Georgie, leaving the room in a hurry.

Georgie was already at a near run as the sound of shouting rebounded off the stairwell. She flew down the stairs two at a time, finding her dad beginning to tussle with a security guard in the entrance. 'Thank you, I'll take it from here.' She grabbed the back of her dad's jacket and pulled him through the swing doors and up against the side of the building, panic beginning to build. She didn't want him further out in the car park or her colleagues would have a stadium view from the windows upstairs. 'It's eleven thirty in the morning, what the hell are you doing?'

'I kept telling them that I needed to . . . why were you not here?'

'Where's Ryan?'

'That fucker has gone off and I couldn't get the fire started, it's freezing in the house, why weren't you here?'

He was leaning heavily on her, the sharp tang of spirits clinging to him.

'Tell me you didn't drive, please tell me . . .'

'Drive? I couldn't find the bloody keys, could I? Where did you put the keys?'

She tried to lead him down the side of the building, painfully aware that if anyone saw them it could be ammunition loaded and stored by her colleagues such as Preston to use against her in the months and years to come. She needed to get her dad to the road and into a taxi as soon as possible.

'Where are you taking me? I'm alone on the bloody anniversary, no one thought about that, did they?'

Georgie stopped and stared at him. 'It's October, Dad. Mum died in April—'

'See, six months. Your brothers didn't remember . . .' He started to keen and stagger about as she pulled out her phone. Three dockers walked past, ogling her tawdry domestic mess.

She made a call. 'Ryan, where the hell are you? Dad's here at work, I need you to come and get him, or get Karl or Matt to come. Right away.' How ironic. She was the only one in the family to have a job, but she was the one left to pick up the pieces, the one Dad fell apart with. The only woman left in the Bell family, the family of bloody bell ends.

'I feel sick.' He burped loudly. 'She wouldn't have left me like this, no she wouldn't.'

'You're not really going to be sick, are you?' Oh, please God, not here, not in front of the new life she was trying to forge. She felt shame for her father's weakness and sorrow for the grief and injustice he still felt so acutely. Thirty-two years of happy marriage before cancer dragged her mother from him. 'Dad, today is difficult I know, but I have a job, I have to work, you can't keep turning up like this. It doesn't help me. Dad? You listening to me?'

He was quiet now, staring at the side of a large warehouse as men in yellow reflective jackets reversed a fork-lift truck. 'You done well, girl, getting a job here.'

'Dad!' He had turned to look at her now, the usual feral glint back in his eyes. She leaned in close to him, squeezing his arm. 'Don't even think about it. This is where I work. There will never, I mean *never,* be any knock-offs, any special deals . . .'

He smiled at her, his grin crooked. 'But you're a Bell.'

Georgie heard the squeal of brakes on a badly driven car behind her. She faced round to see Ryan's Rav 4 swerve to a stop. Her brother opened the door and got out. He was five years older than her and three times as big. The day was cold but he wore only a tight black T-shirt and jeans. No point in spending all those hours body-building in the gym if no one could see the results of your efforts.

'Ryan, get him home and get him a coffee. Honestly, he can't come here—'

'What's got into you two? I thought someone had died from all the messages I got.'

'Someone *has* bloody died – your mum.'

'It's six months today,' Georgie added.

Brother and sister looked at each other. 'Dad, you can't do this every month,' began Ryan. 'You can't mourn—'

'I do this every minute of every day, I'm mourning every second.'

'Dad, I didn't mean that . . .'

Georgie looked at the ground to stop the tears. Her dad's grief, still so raw, was painful to witness. Conflict chewed at her. She loved her family, but she felt the familiar pull of disappointment and frustration with them. She had chosen to tread a different path, and she had never told them what a battle it had been. She had wanted to be a police officer, but that would have been a step too far, a betrayal they wouldn't have tolerated. She had settled on customs instead. She was aware that her family was all she really had; no job was worth alienating all of them.

'Look at all this stuff, Ryan.' Her dad was nudging his first-born, nodding in the direction of the miles of warehousing and stacks of containers, egging him on. Ryan winked at Georgie, who swore under her breath. Here they were, sniffing round her job, wondering if there was an angle they could exploit.

'Take him home.'

Ryan groaned. 'I've got to go to the gym, see Shelley, I'm so busy today.'

'Busy!' Ryan had never had a job, not a legal one anyway, yet he always claimed to be busier than her. Georgie saw Mo coming out of the entrance to the office. 'I have to go, Dad, you dragged me out of a meeting. You can't come here when I'm at work. You have to phone first.'

'At least Ryan thinks of the family. Family's important to him.' His voice was rising, the drink setting him off again. 'He knows when the heart's been ripped from a family.'

'Please, Ryan, take him home.'

Mo came up to them. 'Georgie, Angus is asking for you.'

'Mo, this is my dad and my brother Ryan.'

Georgie was acutely aware of the miasma of spirits clinging to her father. She hoped Mo was standing upwind. Mo smiled and said hello and the two Bells stared at him, her dad swaying uncertainly as the silence stretched.

'OK, I'll see you tonight, Dad.' She turned and walked away with Mo. The silence was so painful she had to break it. 'Sorry about that.'

'Sorry about what?'

'My useless fuck-up of a family. I've got two more brothers who are even worse.'

Mo turned round as the Rav 4 roared off and up the ramp to the road. He smiled at her. 'Your bro's got a sick car.'

6

It was the middle of the afternoon, the dead time before Kelly's evening rush dealing with kids and chores. Medea had come round to cook Greek dishes in Kelly's kitchen, spattering flour across the floor and leaving trails of honey on the surfaces which the kids got on their sleeves. Now her mother-in-law was sealing a series of Greek dishes in clingfilm, mummifying them in layers to be freed at suppertime. Their remains sat in the fridge for days afterwards, staring up aggressively, demanding to be eaten. Normally Kelly was irritated by Medea's thoughtless intrusion but today they had had an OK chat and had even laughed with each other. She felt emboldened. Maybe she could use Medea to get Christos to change his mind about letting her leave. She watched her mother-in-law wipe the kitchen surfaces and miss a large drop of honey, making Kelly wonder how bad her eyesight was becoming.

'There's a special bond between a mother and her only son, I can see that.'

Medea nodded, lifting the toaster to clean underneath.

'You love him very much, don't you? You want only the best for him.' Kelly moved closer to Medea, the two of them side by side, working in the heart of the home. 'He deserves a life with someone else, someone who can make him happier than I can.'

Medea didn't turn her head.

'It would be better for the children if we separated.' Kelly grew bolder; her argument had not been rejected so far.

Medea took the cloth she had been holding and began to fold it in half, creating smaller and smaller squares as she went. 'It sounds to me that you're being very selfish. You can't just walk away when things get tough.'

It was as if she had slapped Kelly. 'Medea, he's got a mistress.'

'Don't be ridiculous. He's married to you.'

'He's having an affair with Sylvie.'

Her mother-in-law's face contorted like she'd tasted something bad. 'If he is, then that's partly your responsibility. You need to think about what you're not giving him, what he's seeking elsewhere. To love and to serve are in your marriage vows—'

'I don't believe what I'm hearing—'

'There are a lot of pressures on a powerful man. You need to support him, help him through. You need to think about the family name.'

'We need to think about the happiness of our children.'

Medea had folded the square as tightly as possible and now was unfolding it, reversing her actions. 'Where were you living when you met Christos?'

'In a flat in the Elephant and Castle.'

'Did the paper peel? Could you smell the stale cigarettes from other flats, Florence looked after by whoever came to hand so you could wash dishes and serve?'

'I loved him so much. I have tried and tried to make this marriage work—'

'You think that a few years down the line you can walk away? Abandon the man who saved you, who pulled you from the gutter and placed you up here? Who gave you everything you wanted? Look at yourself, girl, if you're in a cage, it's a golden cage.'

Kelly tried to keep calm. 'You know him better than anyone, Medea. You know in the long run this is the only solution.

At the moment he flatly refuses to consider a separation.
Please help him to see sense.'

'You need to find your sense of duty.'

That was it. What Kelly had given up to do her duty! She
didn't see her mother or old friends, couldn't visit her home
town. She had faced down injustice and it had cost her nearly
everything . . . Kelly could control herself no longer. 'You
shove duty down my throat so hard you make me want to
puke. He's a brute and you know it. You can cover your ears
and shut your eyes but I know you hear it and you see it,
what he does to me!'

Medea was unmoved. 'My husband was a very religious
man. A union was sacrosanct to him. A marriage would be
lifelong, whatever hardships were thrown up along the way.
What he believed, we believe. Union, family honour, stability,
they are more important than the whims of a girl from
nowhere.'

Kelly had a memory of the arguments she used to have
with her own mother about Michael, about how he wasn't
good enough for her, that he was a wrong'un. Her mother
was keen to stop her daughter repeating her mistakes. She
hadn't seen Mum in years; the aftermath of the trial made
it difficult, her fear for Florence meaning she had been scared
to go back home. And now she was broken and she didn't
know how to get back in touch. 'I may be no one from
nowhere, I may have had no money but I know what's right
and what's wrong. You've raised a psychotic brute and you've
blinded yourself to it.'

'How dare you talk about my son like that!' Medea threw
the cloth down on the side.

'Let the children grow up in a happier home. As a mother,
make him let me go. I beg you.'

'You'll be on your knees begging a long time. Only God
can free you from this marriage.'

'Please, Medea, help me!'

'I was married for forty-five years, Kelly. Long years. I nursed my husband through the cancer at the end. I emptied those bowls of blood, stood by him as he moaned in pain. I did it. I endured. I took pride in my service to my marriage. I put the lives of others before myself. There is a glory in the selfless life . . .'

Kelly couldn't take any more. She slammed her hands over her ears and let out an incoherent wail in the kitchen, the frustration and the horror of the many potential years to come bubbling from deep inside her.

'Do that, if it makes you feel better. Take your pills. But he will never let you go.' And Medea turned and began the never-ending and ineffectual wiping away of the stains.

7

'Can we play planes?' shouted Yannis, jumping up and down and pleading. Florence joined in, their faces staring up at her. Kelly smiled. Medea had gone home, and the bitter aftertaste of their argument was washed from her mouth by her children. They were just back from school, the time of day she liked the most, particularly on the days Medea didn't come fussing into their lives, and before Christos got home. After the commotion so early in the day and after the customs officers had left, Christos had gone to work and she had spent a long time wondering where to hide the passports in a way that couldn't be seen by the relentless green light in the corner of every room. She had decided in the end simply to leave them where they were, in her back pocket.

'Come on then.' They bundled into the kids' bedroom and Kelly lay down on the floor, her legs stretching up towards the ceiling. She grabbed Yannis's hands and put the soles of her feet on his stomach and lifted him into the air. He squealed with delight. 'Arms out wide, make a plane,' said Kelly. He purposefully stuck out his solid little legs rigid behind him, jutting his chin forward purposefully. 'Turbulence,' said Kelly theatrically and began to jiggle her feet as he protested at being bounced up and down. 'Coming in for landing,' she said and lifted her legs behind her head so that Yannis could roll over on his hands and land with a thump on the carpet behind her head.

'Again, again,' he shouted.

'The planes are stacking. Yannis, Florence first.'

She laid one leg straight out on the floor and the other up towards the ceiling. Florence was slim and light, and took off on Kelly's one raised leg, arching her neck and flinging her arms wide, graceful as a swan, her stomach a taut drum on the sole of Kelly's foot. Kelly looked up at her daughter hovering, eyes closed, before she started jiggling her leg and Florence crashed to the floor. Her children shrieked and Kelly's heart soared. Her children were happy; they were loved. She sometimes had her happy moments. Maybe she should endure it all for the sake of the children. Get some therapy, maybe try to make it through the day without feeling the crippling fear, of her husband and of the past . . . She glanced out of the kids' bedroom and saw the office door, bolted shut. As if. Even if she wanted to put the passports back, pretend she'd never done it, the door was locked and she couldn't.

'Again, again,' shouted Yannis as he clambered on to the bed to launch himself at her. Yannis was in the air above her now, making loud revving noises when the lift door slid apart and Kelly instinctively dropped her legs, Yannis clattering to the floor in an untidy heap.

Christos was home. The game and everything else was instantly forgotten as she searched his face for signs she might be in danger, that he might repeat what had happened a couple of weeks ago. She tried to anticipate what he might do or say. She mentally ticked off with a flash of panic whether she had done everything in the right way since he had left this morning. After all, today had started with a surprise and that had thrown the routine out. She had laid out the newspapers, put his clothes away just as he liked. Was there cold water in the fridge? God, had she forgotten the water? She sat up in a hurry. 'How did it go at the office? Is there anything you need help with?'

They were playing the charade of the happy family. He shook his head, one hand holding a briefcase and the other smoothing back his hair. He still wore his tie. She allowed herself to breathe out. Still wearing the tie was a good sign. When he got frustrated he had been known to rip it off and whip the furniture with it, before moving on to other things. But he seemed keen to see the children, who gave him a hug. 'I've got a call to make,' he said. 'I won't get my phone back until tomorrow; it's unbelievable what an inconvenience it is.' He made to leave the room, then turned back. 'If customs come by again and ask you questions, you tell me, OK?'

She nodded and tried to swallow the saliva draining into her mouth. The threat hung heavy in the air. They were to stick together, through anything. 'Do you want me to make you some dinner?' she called after him. There was no reply. She thought very hard, trying to concentrate through her chattering fear. No reply meant yes to food. She sank back down to the floor on her back to calm herself for a moment.

'Mum, what's that?' she heard Florence ask.

Kelly opened her eyes. Florence was sitting cross-legged on the bed, staring at her stomach. Her baggy black shirt had rucked up around her waist and her trousers had worked their way down low on her hips and her daughter was staring at her stomach. Kelly yanked her shirt back down. 'It's nothing.' Florence was silent. 'I accidentally splashed myself with boiling water when I was making tea. It looks much worse than it is.' She had the sensation of staring down at herself from above, unable to recognise this woman who lied to her own daughter, who made light of her searing injury, who was so broken and cowed.

She followed Christos out of the room, as obedient as a dog to its master, and was blindsided by what he said next.

'I had a call at the office from Yannis's school today.'

'You did?'

'It seems he's been in trouble again.'

'That's strange, they didn't mention anything to me when I went to pick him up. What did he do?'

'Threatened a teacher or something.'

'Threatened?'

'He probably brandished a ruler, you know what kids are like.'

'I don't understand—'

'What's to understand?' he said, irritated. 'It's simple. He's been misbehaving.'

'No, I mean, they didn't phone *me*.' She paused, knowing she was entering dangerous territory by bringing it up. 'They normally do if there's a problem.'

'I am their father.'

'Yes, but often you're busy, in meetings. I would have thought they would have contacted me.'

'They want to see us tomorrow.'

'Tomorrow? But it's Saturday.'

'The older boys have Saturday school.' He gave her a look like something was her fault 'It must be important to call us in then, but I'm too busy, you'll have to go on your own.'

'OK.' She paused. 'There's something else, Christos. The night of the party, Florence said something about me going away. Sylvie told her I was going away at the end of the month. I didn't know what she meant.'

The home phone began to ring. Christos turned away so she couldn't see his face. 'She must have got that wrong.'

She tried again. 'Florence doesn't usually misinterpret things.'

'I don't agree. She's a bit like you, a bit of a fantasist.'

She watched him walk away into the bedroom. So that was how this was to be spun. Christos and Medea would make her out to be unhinged, belittle her sufferings.

'Mummy?' It was Yannis, calling for her.

She turned back into the children's room. 'Come on, let's fly to the clouds and back.'

'I don't want to fly any more. I want to kill Barbie. Die, Barbie, die!' He picked up Florence's old toy and banged her head against the bedpost three times before Kelly yanked the doll from his hand and placed her on a high shelf beyond his reach.

8

Kelly woke with a start, heart pounding from a bad dream. In the half-light her youngest daughter Amber was climbing on to the foot of the bed in her Winnie the Pooh pyjamas. Amber turned and sat cross-legged and smiled at Kelly, her dimples huge in her little face. Kelly's heart soared and she blinked. The end of the bed was empty. Her daughter wasn't there. She wasn't in Southampton, the man next to her wasn't Michael. She could feel Christos's leg with its scratchy hair, lying heavy on her thigh. She forced herself not to whimper. Christos didn't like it when she cried for her lost family. She was now the wife of a man she feared, in a flat with no air in a city she didn't like. She felt she was lying not in a bed but a box, with a heavy black lid that was sliding slowly over her.

She wriggled out from under Christos's leg and got out of bed, the tears slipping silently down her cheeks. She walked through into the bathroom but didn't turn on the light, she didn't want Christos to wake. She began ticking off hiding places for the passports. She knew Medea searched the house under the guise of cleaning it and cameras covered the areas that Medea didn't. At the moment the passports were still in the back pocket of her jeans, tossed casually on the chair in the bedroom, but if they were found she could be in very great danger. She was under no illusions as to the violence her husband was capable of.

She opened the bathroom cabinet. The panty pads were

still in their opened box. Her eyes rested on the third in on the left. Wrapped inside the mint-green cover was the one cashpoint card she had managed to apply for and hide a few months after Christos had started to question every bit of spending she'd incurred on their joint account. She walked soundlessly out of the bedroom and across the corridor to the children's bedroom, sandwiched between the lift and the stairs. The green light on the bottom of the hall camera pierced the darkness.

There were ample bedrooms in the flat, but the children preferred to share. She took pleasure in how close they were, half-brother and sister. She had never had siblings, it had been just her and Mum. Yannis had thrown off his covers and lay sprawled the wrong way round on the bed. His checked pyjama top had ridden up, exposing his stomach. She watched the line of sweat on his hairline as he snuffled and snorted in his sleep, his mouth working through his dreams. She sat down on a small armchair and pulled up the blind that covered the window. The view this side of the flat was north, over the wide stretch of train tracks from St Pancras right below her, the tracks of King's Cross Station to her right, snaking and curving away through north and east London. At this hour, just a touch before dawn, the railway was still moving, lights coming and going. The inky black crescent that was the Grand Union Canal, which ran to Birmingham and the heart of England, bisected the railways, and she spotted the faintest winking red light of a cyclist heading north past the side of the British Library. She didn't know all the destinations served by those trains, all of the north of England and Scotland, Paris and Brussels and places further afield. They were a tantalising glimpse of all the places Christos wouldn't let her go. Those trains could take her back home to her mother, to her old life, if only she could go there.

Sometimes Christos changed the code on the lift so she couldn't get out. He would take the children to school and leave her there, shut up like a princess in a twisted story, invisible in her tower. The first time he had done that she had ranted and railed, the second time less so. Now she endured. On those days she would sit here in the children's bedroom, her head resting on the double glazing, and she would stare for hours at the lives of others beneath her, feeling invisible to the entire world bar her children.

She missed the beach. She used to race Michael on beaches near their home, her husband just beyond her fingertips, his shouts loud and free, his long legs thumping across the sand and his heels leaving deep holes when he suddenly changed direction. But now those memories felt so distant they were less substantial than a dream. She had met Christos when the foundations of who she was had been hollowed out. Kelly knew that her identity was buttressed by her children, family and friends, but these had been stripped away, leaving behind a teetering façade overlain with grief.

Christos had picked apart what was left. Now he was smothering her to death, slowly erasing the other facets of her life that didn't revolve around him or the children. The fact that Yannis and Florence needed her was what stopped her disappearing altogether.

She stared out, trying to summon the belief that she could live through Yannis and Florence – that it was enough. She still clung to her job. Christos let her work doing what she loved and before she had met him that hadn't been possible, she had had to spend long hours as a waitress to pay the bills. Yannis twisted in his sleep and threw out an arm. A mother's love is boundless. A mother would die for her children. She endured the life she did for them and she prayed that they would never know the dark side of that life.

She shifted in her chair and put her hand on her stomach,

feeling the undulations of the scar tissue through her T-shirt. A shaft of anger pierced her; the old defiance was still burning there, the old Kelly was buried under the layers of grief and shame. She knew what was right and wrong. She watched a train snake away from King's Cross, wobbling as it picked up speed. The passports were a piece of good fortune that she had a duty to use. Since Christos would never give her or the children up voluntarily, she had to run, and run far. She thought about Lindsey, her friend from when she worked as a waitress. Lindsey had gone back to the country a long time ago, but Kelly had her email address.

She heard a faint shuffling out in the corridor. It sounded like someone walking around. Maybe Christos was up. She stood uncertainly and came out of the bedroom into the dark corridor. She stared for a long moment into the deep shadows, the flat silent, the faintest hum of night-time traffic outside. Christos had never hurt the children. Yet this didn't give her comfort, it was the thing that terrified her most: that put her and her children in the greatest danger. She turned with a heavy heart back to her bedroom. She had read about mothers attaining superhuman strength to save their children – women able to lift cars off bodies, break down doors with their bare hands. Because the day he laid a finger on one of them would be the day she was taken away from them, because it would be the day she murdered him.

9

Georgie watched Mo log on to Google Maps to find the address on the paperwork that was attached to the container of rosewood. She was surprised to see it was almost within walking distance. Mo used the zoom feature to expand a square on a map of east London. The river's irregular, pale blue expanse was flat and calming, so unlike the real thing. Mo played around making the map smaller and larger.

'I've always thought zooming in makes it look like a slow-motion bomb drop,' Georgie said.

Mo swivelled round with mock seriousness. 'Careful – I don't want you to report that.'

'You're safe, there's no one to hear you today.' Georgie gestured round the half empty office. It was Saturday morning, and a skeleton shift were at work. 'Come on, West End boy.'

Mo reached to the back of his chair for his coat. 'You're on, East End girl.'

Differences attract, Georgie felt. Working with Mo was one of the highlights of the job. He had been in the service a year longer and was three years older than her but he didn't mind being paired with her in the least. The third son of Afghan immigrant parents, he had an ability to let insults and setbacks bounce off him without a care. He was never without his iPod buds shoved in his ears and as they got in the car – he let her drive – he belted out their favourite song of the week: 'East End Boys, West End Girls' United over the Pet Shop Boys was a good way to start the day.

Even though the address was in walking distance along the dock, they needed to negotiate a warren of streets that were dead-ends or blocked off or one-way to get to their destination. Eventually they found Casson Street, a faded Victorian terrace and a set of low-rise fifties council blocks, some in the process of being dismantled, that ended in a dead-end by the river. The new shopping complex loomed over the housing. The end of the street also housed a children's indoor play area that, Georgie assumed, you could walk to from the newly built shopping centre, enjoying the fine view of next to nothing bar the grain silos on the opposite bank of the river as you did so. In ten years she knew her commute to work would be longer as the docks were pushed further east, the pressure on property prices driving trade further downriver. They'd be laying cobbles over the expanses of tarmac and installing fancy floor-level lighting here in a few years. She parked and they got out. A St George's flag hung from a council balcony; a minaret of the local mosque poked over the terrace.

'We're looking for number four.' They walked along to the play area and a grinning clown's head stared back at them.

'That's number three, I think,' Mo said. They both turned round and looked across the road. 'And that's number four.'

'Or that's where number four should be.' They crossed the road and walked on to a gravel space between a three-storey estate and another building. Weeds broke through the rough ground, puddles reflected the sky. Whatever had stood here years before had probably been destroyed or damaged in the Blitz, and nobody had got round to rebuilding. Part of an ancient chain-link fence still clung to the edges of the space, but the pretence of keeping anyone out had long since been abandoned.

'How disappointing,' Mo said flatly.

Georgie walked into the middle and looked down at the

large truck tyre marks in the mud. 'What do you think the chances are that anyone in these flats here has seen anything?' she asked Mo.

He paused for a moment. 'Oh, nil to zero.'

Georgie looked around for CCTV cameras. You could always hope. The shopping centre would have them, but out here was unlikely.

'I don't get it,' Georgie said. 'Why does anyone need a whole shipping container worth of wood? For a floor, you'd use Indonesian plantation wood, you wouldn't run the risk with this stuff, would you?'

'And guitar makers don't need this quantity.' Mo stood quite still, thinking it over. 'It must be a cover for something else. The question is, what?'

Georgie thought for a moment. 'You're looking at this the wrong way round. The question isn't what is he really shipping into London? The question is how is he hiding whatever it is, so we can't find it?'

10

Across town in the solid comfort of Marylebone, Kelly sat on a chair outside the headmaster's office and watched the morning sun slide across the parquet. It was so quiet here, so different from her own memories of school. The headmaster's door opened and he came out. 'Mrs Malamatos? Please come in.' The headmaster was in his late fifties and wore thick glasses and, even on Saturday, an academic gown. She stood and he ushered her into his office. 'This is Mrs Weaver, who deals with pastoral care of our children. She really understands the pressures on parents these days.'

A large, big-breasted woman with short blonde hair leaned across to shake Kelly's hand. 'I've got three of my own,' she puffed and raised her eyebrows to the ceiling, inviting Kelly to agree. Kelly said nothing.

Yannis sat on a chair next to the headmaster's desk, his legs too short to reach the floor. 'Please, take a seat.'

The room smelled of damp; a large clock that looked like it dated from 1940 loomed over them. 'We need to have a talk about Yannis, Mrs Malamatos,' the headmaster said. 'And the next steps.'

'Please, call me Kelly.' He smiled at her vaguely, as if she were shifting in and out of focus. 'What do you mean, next steps?'

'I'm afraid your son's behaviour has fallen below the high standards we expect of pupils here.'

'And it's not the first time, is it, Yannis?' added Mrs Weaver.

Kelly looked at her son. He sat on his hands and looked at the floor. Christos had been to this school. She knew early on that Yannis would be sent here too. The prospectus had shown a series of solid Victorian buildings and narrow courtyards on its heavy paper and there were long paragraphs about discipline and boundaries and the highest academic standards. She had seen pictures of serious-looking boys wearing protective goggles doing science experiments. She looked at Yannis, the weight of being in the headmaster's office on a non school day hanging heavy on him.

Kelly had tried to explain to Christos that she thought their son needed a different kind of school. A nurturing, protective place, where the boys and girls would grow sunflower seeds on the windowsills and there were lots of drama productions. Christos had said no. He demanded competition, rigour and results. She had wanted only love for Yannis, space for him to dream, and as the years had gone on she had had a dream of her own, that maybe his school could be a relaxed place where she could chat to other mothers as they clustered in the playground at home time. Somewhere she could dare to make a friend. But here the school, with its high fees and cramped urban site, was full of au pairs or nannies speaking languages she didn't understand, and the mothers who might have been her friends jumped from their four-by-fours and harried their offspring, car keys waving in their palms, worried that today they wouldn't avoid the traffic wardens who hovered over the easy pickings on the double yellows outside the gate. Her relationships were of the most superficial kind. She felt invisible here, too.

'I have to be honest with you, Mrs Malamatos, if this school didn't have such a long-standing relationship with the Malamatos family, we would have to think quite carefully about whether we could still have Yannis attend,' continued the headmaster.

'What did he do this time?' asked Kelly.

'He punched Mrs Inskip,' said the headmaster.

Kelly felt a vein twitch behind her eye. 'I'm astonished that he did such a thing,' she began, but Mrs Weaver was already talking over her.

'As I'm sure you're aware, Mrs Malamatos, I've had a long chat with your husband and I think we can put some things in place that might help Yannis with his behaviour.'

'Chat with my husband?'

Mrs Weaver smiled. 'I understand things have been a bit . . . challenging at home, and in those situations a strong sense of routine can really help children to feel more, adjusted shall we say.'

Kelly felt the temperature in the room drop ten degrees. 'I don't know what you mean. What issues at home?'

'Yannis and I had a conversation and he was talking about how much he loves animals, horses in particular.'

Kelly looked at her son's sad and confused face.

'And I and your husband hit upon an idea that I think it might be useful to try. There are horse-riding lessons in Hyde Park, not far from the school here. The children also have to learn the discipline of mucking out the stables and caring for an animal. A long-term project such as that can have a really positive effect on a child.'

'You spoke to Christos about this earlier?'

'Yes.' She smiled. 'He was enthusiastic.'

Kelly knew she needed to be careful here. She couldn't be seen not to be at least considering the idea. 'It seems to me that you're rewarding bad behaviour. That would send the wrong message, surely.'

'This would be after two days' detention.' Mrs Weaver's smile hadn't wavered. Kelly wondered if she could keep it up for an entire term. 'And then we could start the morning horse-riding. Working in a stables is not for the faint-hearted.'

Something about that sentence struck Kelly as wrong. 'This would be once a week, right?' Kelly asked.

The headmaster took over. 'It would be every morning—'

Kelly shook her head. 'It's a nice idea, but I'm afraid it just isn't practical. I have my daughter to get to school and that's in north London.'

'Mr Malamatos had a very good suggestion. Sylvie Lockhart, his PA, can take Yannis in the mornings – she's a great horse-rider, apparently – and then drop him here at school before going to work.'

Kelly felt like she had been slapped. 'No, I don't think that would work at all.'

The headmaster raised his hands. 'Why don't we try it for a month or so? Because the purpose is to improve your behaviour, young man,' he said, turning to Yannis.

Kelly felt the anger mushrooming. They had decided all this without her. Christos hadn't even bothered to mention it to her. And suddenly here was Sylvie, presumptuous enough to think she could slide from her husband's bed into their family routines – take her son to school. Well, it wasn't happening. 'This is all very well, but no. Sylvie doesn't need the distraction from her job. I will deal with it at home and make sure that Yannis doesn't do something like this again.'

The headmaster looked unconvinced, but he turned to Yannis. 'What do you say, young man? Are you going to make sure your mother and father don't have to come into the school again? Are you going to follow their good example and never hit anyone again?'

For the first time in the meeting, all eyes were on her son. He looked up at them, his bottom lip jutting forward in a little pout, a frown of confusion on his face. 'But—'

'Don't start a sentence with "but", Yannis,' interrupted the headmaster.

Yannis swallowed and Kelly thought he might cry. 'When Daddy gets angry . . . When Daddy and Mummy . . .'

Kelly stood, reached over and grabbed Yannis's hand, yanking him to his feet. She saw Mrs Weaver start back and fold her arms over her big breasts. Kelly's fear at what Yannis might unwittingly reveal about what Christos did, here, in Christos's old school . . . it didn't bear thinking about. She had to cut this conversation dead at all costs. 'I've changed my mind. We'll try it for a month, if that's what everyone wants.'

'I think it's worth a try,' Mrs Weaver said carefully.

Kelly was too ashamed to argue or to answer back. She needed to get out of this claustrophobic office as quickly as possible; she was losing the ability to breathe, feared she might have a panic attack.

She marched Yannis along the vaulted corridors to the exit. The swing doors sucked closed behind them. She bundled him into the car, mute. She sat gripping the steering wheel so hard she felt she would pass out with fury. Her son had seen. At some point, he had watched what Daddy did to Mummy. She had to save him from what he saw. Shame at how she was aiding and abetting what Christos did almost crushed her. Parents shaped their offspring as surely as a modeller shaped clay. Yet Yannis was being moulded into something foreign to her – picking up and absorbing the worst traits of her situation, and she was letting it happen. If she didn't get him out he would become an image of his father and all that brought with it.

'Mummy? I'm sorry, Mummy.'

She turned to look at Yannis sitting in the back of the car, saw his attention caught by something on the seat next to him. He picked up one of his favourite toys, a model of a container ship. He began bouncing it along the seat, tossing it as if it were in a storm. 'Daddy says this ship will be mine when I grow up.'

11

The Wolf glanced once at the stopwatch and then yanked hard on the chainsaw's starter cord. The noise of a powerful motor bursting into life assaulted his eardrums and he held firm as the saw juddered to attention in his sinewy arms. He bent low and began a slicing action at the top end of the great mahogany trunk, stripping the one-hundred-foot tree of its branches with firm, aggressive strokes. They thumped dully to the forest floor as he worked his way along the tree to its base. He wasn't wearing ear muffs, he liked to be surrounded by the noise of the chainsaw and he wanted to be able to hear the man's screams when they reached a pitch that was higher than the motor.

The man was tied to the length of the trunk, ten feet away from him now. Out of the corner of his eye the Wolf could see him writhing as the chainsaw's teeth moved closer.

Five branches away from the man's head the Wolf glanced up at the stopwatch, forcing the whirring blade through the thick branches, forcing it back upwards as the yellow dust of the trunk flew around. The resiny smell of freshly cut wood hung in the air. All the branches were off now, lying like felled soldiers at his feet. He started on the massive trunk, pitting the teeth against the densest and heaviest part of the tree. He bent his knees low, the strain spreading across his back as he pushed down on the blade. The adrenalin was pumping through his body, driving him to work faster. It was hard, physical work, the humidity high and bugs the size of dessert spoons buzzing. He had to keep the correct angles; always working away from himself. He had seen what those machines could do to a human body. A chainsaw didn't cut flesh, it shredded it. Each of the many teeth cut its own path, flesh exploding from the wound like streamers from a party popper. Sweat was running from his pores under his safety shirt, heavy with layer upon layer of string to tangle in those vicious teeth and save your limbs. The man was screaming fully now, his mouth a dark hole in the cloud of wood dust, his eyes dark pricks of terror. He cut the trunk a few inches above the guy's head and jumped across him to chop the last, biggest and heaviest slice below the prone man's feet.

He turned off the machine and silence slammed against him, underpinned by the sobbing and gasping of the man on the tree trunk. He looked at his stopwatch. Four minutes, twenty-seven seconds. He was panting hard as he unhooked the heavy machine from the harness hanging at his side and pulled his goggles on to his forehead. He yelled something incoherent, the adrenalin and the smell of the tree fuelling a cocktail of mad joy in him. There was something else, tangy and salty. He looked down at the quivering man, a dark stain of urine spreading across his trousers. A sense of freedom and power overwhelmed him. A lumberjack used to working in the Amazon could fell and chop a giant rosewood or mahogany tree in less than two minutes. He had been used to it once, but he was out of practice now. He wasn't going to be too hard on himself.

The Wolf leaned close to the man. 'Which ship is it on?'

The man was trying to say something through his sobs, words tumbling too fast from his dry mouth. It sounded like 'I don't know'.

The Wolf picked up the chainsaw again and the man screamed, tears carving a pale line in his wood-dust face. 'It's on the *Saracen*. I heard that—'

'Be more specific. Where on the *Saracen*? There are hundreds of containers on that ship.'

The man started moaning again, begging for his life. The Wolf looked across the hillside at where the brush had been cleared, the smoke from the burning blocking out the sun. The big trees were still left here, a line of fifteen hardwood trees a hundred feet high, bursting up through the forest canopy. The third tree in towered at least twenty feet above all the others. Its trunk was thicker, its branches higher, its reach wider. An exceptional specimen: a wolf tree.

'Tell me now or I'll shred you.' The man had only strength to whisper. The Wolf leaned in and listened for a few moments, drew back and stared down at his captive. You could make a series of cuts in a trunk until it was so finely balanced that you could push over a 500-ton tree with a little finger. It would hit the ground with such force it would obliterate anything in its path. Trees spend centuries growing, and can be cut down in a couple of minutes. People were the same. Christos had been untouchable for nearly ten years, but now he finally had some information he could use. The Wolf just had to get everything into the right position, use his little finger and push.

He yanked on the starter cord of the chainsaw, the man writhing and screaming with a final desperate intensity. The party poppers of skin rose high in the air. The Wolf cut him right across the middle. It would have been kinder to cut off his head.

12

Kelly returned home with Yannis, but after being back for only a few minutes the doorbell rang on the service lift. She checked the video monitor and swore silently. Jason, a production manager who had commissioned her to make the masks and some of the props for his latest play, and Salvatore, his assistant, were downstairs on the garage level.

'Kelly, you ready for us?' asked Jason. 'I've got the van here for the props.'

She had forgotten. They had left a message saying they would collect on Saturday, but she had not remembered to call them back and change it. Christos was at work and Flo at a friend's house but Medea was sitting like a fat toad in the flat. She would tell Christos that two men had been here and that could be bad. 'Hi, guys. Come up.' She said it loudly as she pushed the raise button on the car park barrier so the deaf old witch would hear. She had nothing to hide, her voice suggested. She walked calmly down the long corridor into her bedroom, throwing a baggy old sweater with a glue stain on the front over her T-shirt. She walked into the bathroom, grabbed a flannel and scrubbed off her make-up. She was pleased to see her skin turn pink under the abuse. She came out into the corridor and saw Medea standing there waiting for her. 'Collection,' she said.

A few moments later, Jason and Salvatore came in. Jason

was in his late thirties with a quiff of brown hair and glasses he kept pushing distractedly up his face. He was tall and rangy and had a very good smile, which, she had realised the last few times she had met him, he turned on her with increasing intensity. The silly idiot, didn't he realise she was trying to put him off for his own good? Salvatore was in his twenties, exquisitely beautiful and gay and spoke with a strong Italian accent.

They followed her into the studio. 'Skeletons for a Mexican Day of the Dead parade,' said Kelly. 'They'd be great props for Halloween.' She gave Jason a look. 'I haven't let my children anywhere near them, I promise.'

'It's such a joy to come here,' said Salvatore, eyes darting round. 'You should *see* some of the hovels out east we have to go to, eh, Jason?'

Jason shrugged. 'Yeah, like my flat.' Jason looked to Kelly and they shared a smile. She couldn't help it. She was nervous when work people came here, but she also treasured their meetings; it was a brief glimpse into a world that was fun and where she had her own identity.

'It's lovely to see you both.' Kelly walked around a giant ghoul that was leaning against the wall near the door and over to the trestle table where three masks were sitting. 'The masks are still not ready, you know,' she began, but was interrupted by the door opening and Medea appearing. She introduced the two men to her mother-in-law and Medea went away to make tea.

'Don't worry, I know they're not finished,' Jason said. 'I really would be too hard a taskmaster if I judged before they're ready.' But, unable to resist, that's just what he did do, moving forward and picking up the first of the masks on the table. He turned it in his hands, nodding and assessing and gave the outer shell a hard rap with a knuckle. He gave her a knowing look. 'Just testing.'

'It's as strong as wood, Jason,' she answered, pride flaring inside her.

'It has to be. Ninety performances minimum, assuming the critics don't maul us.' He paused. 'It's beautiful.'

'Say Day of the Dead!' Salvatore held up his smartphone and took a photo.

'Oh no, get rid of that,' Kelly urged.

'Why? You're surrounded by skeletons and ghouls, it looks perfect.'

'Still, I don't like having my picture taken.' She frowned as Salvatore shrugged and began fiddling with his phone. She watched Jason's long fingers shaping and feeling the smooth outline of the mask. She came towards him and took the mask, held it up with her fist inside and turned one side to her visitors. 'Smiling.' She turned the far side towards them. 'Scowling. I made the nose big so each side obscures the other.'

Jason nodded. 'One side good, the other evil, each aspect present in every character.' She could see that he liked it.

Salvatore came over and put on the mask. He turned side-on to them and began creeping about in an exaggerated manner. Then he turned around suddenly and the transformation was profound. From a grinning, happy face to a grotesque, angry tyrant in less than a second.

'I've used reflective white paint here and here.' Kelly pointed to the cheeks and parts of the brow.

'It's lovely, really lovely,' Jason said. 'Move your head more, Salvatore. Is there too much movement?'

Kelly nodded. 'I can build it up more at the back of the neck so it's more solid. I'll make it more comfortable too, and I'm going to line it.'

'We need to be able to pull the masks upwards and away.' Jason threw his hands in the air above his head. 'It's a change of scene direction.'

Kelly considered this. 'I could put magnets on the top. Industrial grade are very strong yet small and light . . .' She tailed off as Jason groaned and closed his eyes, running a hand through his thick hair. 'You still getting your headaches?'

He nodded. 'I'm fine and then bam, suddenly it arrives. I've tried all the usual treatments, hypnotherapy, acupuncture, cranio-whatever. Something's misaligned.' He shook his head.

'Is that even a word?'

'It feels like a word and it suits my problem.' He gave a sigh. 'I'm getting so desperate I'm trying a new treatment on Salvatore's recommendation. You film yourself sleeping. You attach a small fitting like a light bulb to your light in the ceiling in your bedroom, say. It's motion-sensitive, so it films you as you sleep, gives you an idea what's going on in the dark hours. If you move too much in your sleep, if you are always on one side, that type of thing. You can interpret whether you're disturbed subconsciously, apparently. I might be sleep-banging my head against the headboard all night for all I know.'

'That'd give you a headache.'

'Quite.'

'And what have you found?'

'Nothing unusual so far. You need to do it for a week at least to get a good idea.'

'It's fascinating,' enthused Salvatore. 'I've spent hours with it. I realise that I love looking at myself. I'm vainer than I thought.'

'You're not vainer than I thought,' Jason added. They laughed easily. 'I'm desperate so I'll try anything.' He looked at Kelly. 'The Sleepchecker camera. I recommend it.'

The door to the studio opened and Medea came in bearing a tray with teas on it. She had added Greek pastries as well. Jason came forward and got all interested in them. 'Did you cook these?' He made Medea describe what was in them and listened intently to her replies, leaving Kelly desperately wishing he would ignore her. He was being too polite, he would make too much of an impression, Medea would begin to wonder why. If Medea was in the flat on the rare times she had visitors, she would offer drinks and food, her generosity a cover for her spying. She would report back to Christos later, but Kelly would take her comforts where she could. She was acutely aware that Christos could stop her working whenever he pleased. Finally Medea left with the tray and she relaxed a bit.

'I can have the masks finished this weekend, magnets included.'

'They're not needed until next week. Why not bring them in on Tuesday? That's the day the PR department wants to do a supplement to the programme with the "behind-the-scenes squirrellers", so to speak. You get a nice photoshoot.'

'Oh.' Kelly looked embarrassed. 'I'm terrible with pictures, I really hate them, you know. It's just not for me.'

Jason stared at her, unconvinced. 'Oh, I don't know, I think you'd brush up well.'

She felt herself flush. He had this way of dishing out compliments that made her feel good, which made the tired and untended cells of her body crave for more. And that made her hate him.

'Take the credit, you deserve it. There'll probably be cheap white wine, you know the drill.'

Kelly stood firm. 'I'm sorry, Jason. I'll email through a biog, but I won't do any pictures.' She picked distractedly at the fraying hem of her old sweater.

'You'd get more work, you know.' Here he was, dangling the dream of money she could earn doing what she loved. He had no idea how unachievable it was. How his castaway comments pierced her to the core.

'No.' It came out harsh and offensive.

'Salvatore, what can I say?' He looked hurt for a moment but he recovered quickly. He held up a finger and waggled it at her. 'We'll start to wonder what you've got to hide.'

'Then again,' said Salvatore, 'you're so much more alluring with something to hide.'

Kelly felt the sweat spring up on her back.

13

Sylvie pulled on her bikini bottoms and pinged the ties at her hips. She looked out of her changing cubicle at a slice of the Hampstead Heath Women's Pond. The water looked murky and drab. She shook her shoulders and slapped her thighs. Not the Jersey Shore in July. She knew Kelly would be arriving soon. She knew her routines off by heart. They weren't difficult to learn, she didn't have the imagination to vary them. Sylvie's disdain for her rival came back with full force. All that money and status and she still wasn't anything more than a retiring mouse. She could mess with her mind in here today, and, really, why the hell not? Sylvie thought of all the oxygen pools and personal trainers across the capital that Kelly could have chosen to keep her tiny body in trim, and here she was, opting for a pleasureless dunk with the lesbians of north London.

Well, anything the mouse could do, she could do better. Sylvie bent forward to stretch her hamstrings but decided against touching the floor with her hands. Too many pubes wriggling in the cracks in the tiles probably, if the women in here were anything to go by. But she would never make the mistake of underestimating Kelly. Christos chose her and married her – a woman with the baggage of grief and a kid but no money to sweeten the deal. She must have had something else. Kooky was alluring, Sylvie needed to remember that. She put her hands on her trim waist and bent sideways as an old woman emerged from the next cubicle wearing an ancient black swimsuit and a woolly hat. Sylvie was as much fascinated as she was horrified. She watched her wobble away to the dock and silently climb down the metal stairs into the water. The pond was fed by an underground stream, greeny black and kinda greasy. Sylvie didn't care. She had undergone far greater discomforts to get where she was and to get where she was going she would endure even more. She wasn't prissy or squeamish, she could get stuck in, make no mistake.

She heard the door bang and stepped back into the cubicle. Kelly had arrived. The door to the next cubicle opened and closed and she heard the little sighs and rustles of a woman disrobing inches from her. Sylvie felt her heart beat slower. It was illicit and exciting, listening in on her rival's private moments, to garments being shed from folds and crevices. She heard the door bang and knew Kelly had gone out to the pond. She pushed her shoulders back, chin forward and followed her out. It was surprisingly quiet out here in the middle of the Heath, the odd plop of hands breaking the still surface of the water or twigs falling from the trees. The lifeguard's chair was empty.

Kelly was in a wetsuit, standing at the end of the dock, swinging her arms around to warm them up. Her long dark hair cascaded down her back. Silhouetted against the water she was casually beautiful, like a black mermaid plucked from some watery depths. Sylvie felt a flash of hatred for her. Some people didn't deserve the gifts they were given. Not to cultivate and protect the natural bounty that chance and a bunch of genes had given her, not to appreciate the fortune it had saved her in treatments and surgery meant Kelly was a fool and not deserving of her respect. She was also weak – the old crones in here weren't insulated with rubber against the cold and neither was she. That weakness was why her husband had been easy to pluck.

She watched Kelly spend a moment stretching her neck

from side to side before she turned and climbed down off the jetty. She looked vacant, lost in some other place. As Kelly began to strike out for the middle, Sylvie walked to the end of the jetty, took a deep breath and dived in.

It was fucking freezing. So biting cold she was astounded her poor heart could still beat. She struggled to the surface, unable not to gasp. She saw Kelly front crawling to the rubber ring in insulating neoprene and used her anger to fight off the paralysis brought on by the arctic water. These mad English bitches! She gritted her teeth and struck out after her. With every stroke she got angrier and angrier, her panting not warming her. Kelly turned in a lazy swirl and headed back, passing Sylvie as she went. As they came level Kelly finally saw her and came up short, gulping in some of the murky water. She made a small coughing sound that made Sylvie smile. Behind them a woman screamed as her skin made contact with the water.

Sylvie saw Kelly swear and her mouth contract in an unbecoming line. She watched Kelly swim away faster. Sylvie ploughed on in the debilitating cold for the ring, touched it and turned. She was doing breast stroke now, it was too cold to get her head under. Kelly was nearly at the dock and turning again for another lap. 'Bring it on,' Sylvie muttered and began to swim after Kelly, determined to overtake her, but she hadn't reckoned on Kelly being such a good swimmer. She liked that it was more of a battle than she had been expecting. They were both swimming hard now, Kelly front crawling ahead with a good technique and the right equipment. Sylvie toiled on, her feet and hands numb. She saw Kelly turn at the ring and head back; she dug deep and sped up further, feeling ridiculous, dragged far from her comfort zone. The lizard in the hat was already limping back to the changing rooms.

Sucked under by the cold water, Sylvie felt the indignities

of playing the waiting game, of being the mistress, an object of pity and scorn, always waiting and hoping he would leave his wife. Well, she wanted to shove their pity down their fucking throats. The cold bit down and she powered on, gaining slowly on Kelly ahead of her. What women did for men, what she did! Agreeing to take the little whiny one horse-riding! The anger inside her began to warm her up.

Kelly reached the jetty and turned again, passing Sylvie for another lap. She had a look of triumph which made Sylvie mad. Real mad. She began to front crawl, head under the water, going all out to catch up the wife ahead. She was going to win, it just required more effort. She got to the ring and had gained a few metres; she powered on. She was stronger, faster, more agile, more determined than her rival. Of that she had no doubt. The outcome was already set. She was level with Kelly's feet, the jetty a few metres ahead. They were locked in a race as important as an Olympic final. She gave a last push, her muscles and tendons straining, her heart burning, as they reached the jetty at the same time. Sylvie grabbed a hold on it, gasping with the cold and the exertion.

A wave of water slapped her in the face, Kelly planing it with her palm at her. 'Stay away from me, stay away from my kids.'

Sylvie swooshed the water back. 'I'm not going anywhere.' She reared up and dunked Kelly's head under the water. She felt her rival flailing as she let go.

Kelly flew up out of the water and tried to slap Sylvie round the face. 'Why did you tell Florence I was going away?'

'Because you are.'

'You'll be waiting for ever, you stupid cow, he's never going to leave me.'

Sylvie laughed. Her emotions changed in an instant – now she was enjoying this. She liked it when she got under people's skin, when she made them show their hidden selves. 'Wouldn't he like this? Us fighting over him?' She dunked Kelly's head under again.

'Ladies!' The lifeguard was above them on the dock. 'That's enough. Out. Now.' She bent down and grabbed at Kelly's hand and half pulled her out of the water.

'You bitch,' Kelly spat down at Sylvie.

'Stop it!' shouted the lifeguard. 'This is a nurturing place for women to come. Peaceful. Leave your arguments at the door.' They always called upon the sisterhood to protect them, thought Sylvie; they conjured it like some holy relic, something that could ward off evil.

Sylvie watched Kelly stomp away to the changing rooms, her wet hair spraying angrily. She climbed out via the stairs. She didn't feel cold now, she felt energised, her skin bright red and burning. Pleasure and pain were often chasing each other, fluid as emotions. What she felt so strongly one moment, what consumed her completely, could be ditched by the next. Kelly disappeared into the building. Sylvie felt her obsession with her begin to drain away as surely as the brackish water drained off her toned limbs. Kelly had nowhere interesting to go and no one interesting to meet. The battle was already won.

14

Kelly didn't dismiss the Hampstead experience so quickly. She was not that kind of personality. It churned in her stomach like a badly digested meal, anger and outrage mixing and parting. She stomped down the paths of the Heath towards Camden, swearing to herself she was angry enough to kill Sylvie. The cheek of her. To follow her to her sanctuary, the one place she could feel at peace, where Amber and Michael were somehow closer to her. Sylvie had no idea of the layers of memory and pain she had intruded on so heartlessly. It was her or Sylvie, this situation couldn't continue. The bag with the wetsuit banged ceaselessly against her legs as she went. The usual bracing post-swim high didn't materialise as she hit the road at the bottom of the Heath. Nothing would change. Nothing could change. She felt tears of helplessness prick her eyes and she was ashamed. Oh, how she had changed from the feisty twenty-something who had taken on the bad bits of the world and lost herself so spectacularly.

She trudged on, hardly knowing where she was going. She ended up in Camden when she passed a Spystore. Jason's conversation came back to her as she stared in at the window. A moment later she went in and bought the Sleepchecker camera he had raved about. Christos had installed a video system that had cost thousands to keep a check on her. She'd buy one for £39.99 and see if it could help her find a way out.

She threw the packaging away in the shop. Medea searched

the bins – even sometimes the hoppers in the underground garage – for evidence of what she had been doing, or planned to do. This was to be her little secret.

When she got home Christos was watching golf and the kids shouting and laughing in their bedroom. She walked to the store cupboards by the kitchen, and checking the angle of the security camera, put the Sleepchecker in a lightbulb box and took it to the bedroom. She got the stepladder from the cupboard near the back stairs and set it up under their bedroom lampshade, unscrewed the light bulb and inserted the camera and made a show of turning the switch on and off. She climbed down, feeling like she'd won back a little of herself.

The feeling didn't last long. That evening she put the kids to bed and began tidying up the kitchen after their meal. She had been civil and compliant to Christos all day, keeping quiet about the indignities dished out by Sylvie earlier. She retreated to the bedroom once she'd finished and Christos followed her, holding a glass of wine. He put it down on the bedside table and she took a big swig and lay back on the bed. Another day dawdling to its close, Kelly thought, with none of her compromises resolved. Then he said something that surprised her.

'You don't sing any more.' He lay back on the bed next to her. 'I love it when you sing.'

Kelly said nothing. The memory was almost too painful. When she first met Christos, she had been a singer, someone who expressed her emotions through the power and range of her voice. Someone who felt great joy when she sang. Her desire to do it had withered with the years she spent with him.

'You know why?' he continued. 'You look like an angel when you sing.'

'That's silly.'

'It's true. Most people never really look. They think they do, but they don't study a face, a person. When you sing you go somewhere else, a place no one can follow you to. It's fascinating to watch. I never get bored of looking at you, I could do it for ever.'

He ran his hand up and down her thigh, up and down again over her knee and shin. He had a way of touching her that was just right. He reached down and took tight hold of her ankle, held her instep. She felt herself relax, her cares begin to float away. He could love all of her, right to the extremities, like no one else she had known.

He kissed the tip of her nose. 'My darling Kelly.'

In rare moments he was like this: he was the man she had fallen in love with, who could take her away from the pain of her dead husband and child – a man who could work a miracle such as that. She wondered whether Sylvie knew they still had sex. She guessed not. For a second, triumph thrilled through her at the thought of the mistress swallowing the lies about a sexless marriage. She rolled on to her side and he kissed her. She kissed him back.

He was a good kisser. Despite everything, she was still a physical person, she liked to be wanted and occasionally she desired the man she feared and hated. All the lines of right and wrong were blurring and she didn't know how to pick them apart. Christos rolled on top of her and she opened her eyes. She saw the ceiling light and shame lanced her. Her spy camera would be recording everything. She hadn't thought that through and felt embarrassed. She tried to push him off. 'No, not now.'

'Come on, Kelly, let's play.'

She could feel his erection hard against her stomach, on her scar. It didn't hurt. He ran his hands across her breasts, began kissing her neck. He pulled her arms above her head and ran his strong hands up and down them.

'Kelly, I'm sorry.' He was thrusting against her on the bed, his head in her neck, nuzzling. 'I hurt you and I didn't want to do that. I love you.'

Those words that always softened her scarred heart. He put his hands under her bum and yanked her further up the bed, his heavy weight full on her now. 'I want you to lie back and do nothing.'

He rolled over so he was underneath and she was astride him. He peeled off her top and undid her bra, massaged her breasts and undid the zip on her trousers. He rolled back over again and sat up, pulling her trousers off in one expert yank. He began to vary the speed and intensity of his touch. She was panting, her limbs writhing with pleasure across the bed. Her hand flew out and knocked the wine glass on the bedside table where it clattered into the lamp base and broke, falling to the floor.

Kelly didn't care. His face was between her legs, licking, sending darts of pleasure up her back and across her stomach. Her tired and untended soul longed for and needed it. She heard his zip coming down and his erection probing for its home. He slammed into her and she cried out with pleasure, they were moving hard against each other and his head was in her neck again, mumbling, 'I'm sorry,' over and over again. Her eyes were closed, the sensations strong and persistent. He was moving faster, she was bucking against him, floating away to a nice place for a few fabulous seconds, her cares forgotten.

She came twice, long and loud, some tears squeezed free with the intensity of it, and he followed her a few seconds later.

He rolled off and stood up, full of energy now as she lay sated on the bed. She saw him through teary distortion looking at her stomach. 'We could get you some plastic surgery for that, tidy it up a bit.' He patted her on the leg and walked through into the bathroom.

Kelly lay still for a moment, stunned. She sat up, anger swamping her ecstasy. The bastard. He had caused that scar, that searing pain and fear, and now he was blithely trying to erase it from their history, from her body, as if it was no more important than a cap on a tooth. Fury replaced her anger.

Through her tears she saw a fluttering movement outside the window. A pigeon was on the wrought-iron decoration on the windowsill, beak nudging through a dirty city wing, a stump in the place of one of its feet. She felt a forceful hatred for that deformed bird and wanted to kill it. Yesterday she had seen the same pigeon and had wanted to hold her hand out to it through the glass. Now she felt as stunted as that poor, sad air rat.

Christos was in the bathroom, the shower on. Her outrage was wild in her. She grabbed the broken wine glass off the floor, a pool of dark red like a bloodstain spreading through the carpet fibres by the bed. She held the glass by its stem like a dagger and ran into the bathroom.

He was in the love shower. It was what the workmen had jokingly called it when they installed it. Shower heads at either end of a large rectangle, big enough for two. They had never shared it. Too much day-to-day monotony to be able to make it special enough, too much water splash. The fancy double shower now had a cheap white curtain at the entrance to stop the water spraying the bathroom floor.

He was humming, unaware, the drone of the water unceasing. She felt her breath coming shallow and fast, she was watching herself from high above, as if she were already dead. She could see his outline through the curtain. She was inches from his naked body, moments away from slashing that curtain and freeing herself from the brute behind it. She raised the broken glass to her shoulder, her whole body shaking with anger and purpose. She could already see the blood draining away down the plughole as she imagined stabbing again and again at his neck.

She took a step forward and felt something squish under her foot. It was one of Florence's socks, blue and mauve stars balled up and discarded on the floor. Kelly paused, the curtain shivering. Florence had already lost her father and her sister. If Kelly did this, she'd go to jail. Florence would have no one.

She retreated back the way she had come, dropping the glass in the waste bin in the bedroom and collapsing down on the bed. A few moments later she heard the scrape of the curtain sliding open along the pole and Christos came back into the bedroom, his face pink with heat and self-satisfaction.

'That was nice, wasn't it?' he said with a grin.

15

Georgie put her right hand behind her and felt for the small bag of chalk attached to her right hip. The moisture in her sweating fingers was absorbed in an instant. She could feel the sharp stone of the narrow ledge under her left foot, the thin rubber soles of her climbing shoes gripping every inch of her foot. Her right foot was as high as her right hip, her body flat against the vertical cliff face. The nylon rope with its red and white pattern snaked away past her cheek to the top of the climb.

She took a deep breath, her eyes fixed on the small groove in the wall above her. She tried to haul herself up, the echoing, early morning sounds of the Victorian water pumping station fading away. She was absorbed in her own private conundrum, her mind empty of everything except getting to the top. She was on the hardest climb at the centre; her arms and legs were beginning to shake, muscles and veins standing proud of her skin as they tried to flood her body with more oxygen. Her fingers couldn't find a grip in the groove, the angle was too steep, the rock too shiny. She knew she had to retreat to her former position.

Climbing was a puzzle that had to be solved; brute force and strength would only get you so far. The very best climbers – and her mentor had told her she could be one of the very best – used their brains, not their muscles, to get to the top. It was about shifts in position, working through a maze of tiny protrusions and indentations almost invisible to the naked eye to defy gravity and get to the finish. Changing the angle of an ankle, starting with a different leg, crossing arms over in the right way meant you could climb an overhang or impossible-looking rock face.

Georgie climbed when she wanted to relax, when she wanted endorphins to flood her body and take away the petty stresses at work, the major stresses at home. She balanced on her right leg and swung her left over to a further point. This buttress was thinner but longer, allowing her to get the whole length of her foot on it. It changed her body position subtly, and allowed her to approach the rock face in a new way. She often wondered why she loved climbing so much, but she knew the answer: it was one of the few places in her life she could actually have space around her. She thought of home, to the tiniest box-room carved off the main bedroom that was all the space she had to call her own, where trying to go out in the evenings involved tense pacing and waiting for the bathroom door to open and racing in before one of her three older brothers barged her out of the way to spend hours primping and preening themselves. Getting ready for work was easier; she was the only one up early, the only one of the family with a PAYE number.

She'd been a mistake. Mum and Dad often told her, with a smile that showed all their love and, until Mum got too weak to lift her arm, a ruffle of a hand in her hair. A fourth – and a girl. There was no room in the house, precious little room in their lives. Old habits clung on; she wondered if they'd called her Georgie because it was easier to stick with boys' names. She was simply the last and littlest of the Bell gang and expected to tread the same path.

She dabbed more chalk on her fingers and completed the rest of the climb, swung her leg over the top and stood, staring down at the blue crash mats far below. But she didn't want to follow that path, working for her dad, the suffocating weight of her family on her. She just needed to endure home for six more months, then she would finally have the money to get her own place, carve out a new life at arm's length from her family. At twenty-eight she could make a start. Work was the solution and the salvation. Pity she was the only one in her family to think it.

She paused for a moment, letting her breath return to normal. The exercise eased her frustrations, her lack of privacy. Hard economic realities kept them all at home, but it wasn't only that. Duty had kept them there through Mum's long illness, and grief after she'd gone. She turned to abseil to the ground. It was seven thirty on Monday morning; it was more private showering here than at home.

Four hours later she had Kelly's name in the computer and was left scratching her head. There was precious little information, which was frustrating. There was nothing filed under her married name, no record of where she grew up, no arrest record. She typed Kelly's maiden name into the computer. 'Access denied' came up across the screen. She hadn't been expecting that.

Mo came over with a pile of printouts. 'I've got her mobile phone records. Why are you so interested in the wife?'

Georgie didn't answer. She glanced down the printout of Kelly's mobile phone use for the past three months. The last month's stretched to barely half a page. Again, unexpected. 'Mo, if you had loads of cash and were young and good-looking, what would you be doing? No offence or anything.'

He laughed and sat down. 'I wouldn't be here with you, that's for sure. No offence.'

'None taken.'

He scratched his chin, warming to the idea. 'I'd be seeing the world, getting out and about.' He paused, his eyes glazing over. 'I'd go to Vegas.'

She was surprised. 'That's not very Muslim.'

He roared with laughter. 'Not very Muslim! If I started a list of non-Muslim things we'd be here all day.'

'OK, point taken.'

'I'd go to New York too, though I'd be too scared to get out of my seat to use the toilet on the plane in case they got suspicious of me even standing in the aisle. Before you know it, I could be in Guantanamo or somewhere.'

'You're from Cricklewood, Mo, not Kandahar.' She grinned. 'The only crimes you'll be committing are crimes against fashion.'

'Ouch. Any more of that and I'll make you listen to my dad's sitar music—'

Georgie was in the swing of it now. She started singing: 'Come with me, I've got the keys to my Dad's MPV . . .'

'I'll put all seven seats down for her, make her feel special,' added Mo.

They both laughed. Mo sat back, thinking. 'You need money to travel.' He paused. 'You know, that's the thing about poverty, it keeps you indoors. You've got no money to go out, so you have to stay in.'

Georgie looked back down at the few phone calls Kelly had made. Poverty stunted friendships, too. No money to go out, no money to have fun. The bill was at odds with the opulence of the house they'd visited. Georgie made a note of that. She came from a family where things that didn't add up were things that were worth looking into. Kelly Malamatos merited her attention. She got up and walked towards Angus's office, glancing back to make sure Mo wasn't watching before she adjusted her bra strap, checked there was nothing horrid stuck to her teeth and tightened her pony tail. Miracles might happen and he might one day notice her . . .

Angus was trying to fish a tea bag out of a mug and balance it on a pen to get it to the waste bin somewhere at his feet.

He glanced up as she entered and the tea bag plopped on to a pile of paperwork on his desk, splattering at least five forms. Angus swore.

'Sorry,' she said, as he picked up the paper and slid the tea bag off, she presumed into the bin. Why she felt the need to apologise for his irrational way of making a cuppa she tried not to dwell on.

'Yes?'

'I need to run something past you.'

Angus licked the tea off the end of the pen and nodded.

'I've got a file on Kelly Malamatos here, but there's hardly any information at all. If you type her into the computer it says access denied. What's that mean?'

'Don't get overexcited. It could mean something or it could mean nothing. The file's been lost, it's a computer glitch' – they both nodded – 'she's working secretly for the security services . . . I have no idea, and unless I'm told otherwise by my boss, I've learned to stay away from that sort of thing. Get yourself tangled in that kind of politics and . . .' He shuddered. 'You sure this is a fruitful line of enquiry?' Angus reached behind him for a pint carton of milk.

Georgie ploughed on. 'Well, that's my point really. What I did find is that she lodged a complaint about domestic violence by her husband a year ago but then didn't want to pursue it. We should talk to her, dig a bit deeper.'

'Your tip-off theory. So bring her in.'

'I think it might be better to meet her on her own turf. Mo and I could follow her and make an approach—'

Angus put the carton down fast. 'Ever hear of budgets? This investigation can't justify the kind of surveillance you're suggesting.'

She wasn't going to be beaten. 'You said yourself that you suspect what we found in that ship is just a fraction of what Christos might be smuggling. If it's true then it makes sense to make a proportionate effort. You mention politics, but I bet a high-profile environmental prosecution is just the good news the PRs are looking for. Better than airport queuing times.'

Angus looked up at her, his eyebrows raised.

She felt her spirits soar, he was listening intently. She might have a fantasy about wanting him to fancy her, but even more than that she wanted his respect. 'A rosewood kingpin.' She shrugged. 'It makes a change from a drugs bust.'

She could see him mulling it over. He was part of the new guard in the service; stories that garnered good publicity were catnip to him.

'No overtime, no night shifts.'

Georgie nodded.

'And no rocking boats.'

She smiled at him and left him to his tea.

16

Now Georgie and Mo were waiting for Kelly to come out of her apartment. They worked out that she would appear at some point to collect her children from school, or return with them to the house. But a woman who looked so much like Christos she had to be his mother had come back with the children after school.

Georgie was growing frustrated and irritable. She felt cooped up, she was sick of the endless cans of Tango Mo drank and nothing was happening. It looked like they might have missed Kelly altogether.

'Woman walking a dog, ten points,' Mo said, pointing at the far pavement. 'So it's two hundred and ten plays ninety.' They were playing the points game as a way to pass the time. 'White van with writing in the dirt on the back, thirty points! I'm murdering you.'

Georgie drummed her fingers on the steering wheel with irritation.

'What's a couple kissing worth?'

Georgie made a face. 'Let's take points away for that.'

Mo sipped his fizzy drink. 'I doubt there's a romantic bone in your body. Why's that, eh? You know I could fix you up with one of my brothers if you liked. They drink alcohol and try to fuck beautiful women like you and they're not "angry", like me.' Georgie gave him a withering look but it didn't stop him. 'Why don't you have a boyfriend? I don't get it, I really don't. All I'm saying is: you ever feel like company, I've got a queue.'

Georgie tried to smile. She could never get beyond two dates. After that they tended to want to come back and see where you lived. Meet the in-laws. Be made to squeeze in between the body-building bulks of Karl, Ryan and Matt on the settee, listening as they lionised the Krays, made bad jokes about the police, talked a little too knowledgeably about institutional visiting hours. The men she fancied would – and should – run a mile. She had a flash of seeing Anguish on her couch at home and shuddered.

'OK,' Georgie said. 'A couple kissing is a hundred points and an instant win. Hugging doesn't count.'

'You're on.'

They were interrupted by the garage door opening and the nose of a black Audi inching out. They both craned their heads to see who was driving. 'That's her,' Georgie said.

They followed as Kelly drove east towards the City and then along the A13, turning off towards the river. Ten minutes later she was turning into Casson Street.

'Is she going where I think she's going?' Georgie looked at Mo in disbelief.

They followed Kelly into the parking lot of the children's play area. They watched her go in with her son.

Georgie unbuckled her seat belt. 'You stay here.'

Mo nodded.

The play centre was huge, with a café near the entrance and a second storey that catered for children's parties. In the after-school rush the noise level could compete with a nightclub. A carpeted area ran under a series of nets of varying heights where children dangled and squealed and colourful slides, some twisting, burped children out on the carpet. There was a pit filled with plastic balls, rope swings and distorting plastic mirrors, and high netted walkways that ran above Georgie's head and disappeared into tunnels.

Georgie was impressed, wishing she had been taken to

something like this when she was a child. Then again, her brothers would have started a fight and they would all have been ordered to leave. She watched Kelly help Yannis off with his shoes and he ran off into a tunnel. The rear of the play centre backed on to the Thames. Through a series of windows Georgie could see the dull flatness of the water and an expanse of dock.

She watched Kelly queue at the café, buy tea and a packet of crisps and sit at a table near the equipment. Georgie picked up a newspaper that had been discarded and watched her. Kelly didn't move or pull out a phone or read; she sat staring into space. She finished her tea and started chewing through the polystyrene absent-mindedly, leaving bite marks in the cup. All around her, women jiggled babies on their knees, laughed and gossiped with friends or yakked on mobiles, but she looked all alone. Occasionally Kelly caught sight of Yannis and waved at him. Ten minutes passed.

Kelly got up, threw away the cup and walked to the toilets. Georgie followed. The toilets were empty apart from the two of them. Georgie wedged her foot against the exit to stop anyone else coming in and waited for Kelly to finish. The cubicle door opened.

'Kelly Malamatos?'

Kelly whirled round at her name, knees bent, ready to try to fight off an attacker.

'Afraid of something?'

Kelly didn't answer; her eyes were two dark pools watching her. She looked like a cornered animal.

'It's Georgie Bell. Can we have a chat?'

She looked nervous. 'Do I have a choice?'

'Yes. You can walk out of here at any time, but I hope you won't. This way I don't have to make it official.'

'In here.' Kelly walked into the disabled toilet and Georgie followed. 'What do you want?' She'd calmed down now, was smoothing her hair and adjusting her clothes.

Georgie leaned against the sink. 'Tell me where the wood goes.'

'I have no idea.'

'You'll have to do better than that.' Kelly didn't move. 'It comes here, Kelly, right next door to here. About twenty yards from where you've parked your car. Care to say anything?' She saw Kelly go pale. 'Why do you use this play area? There are others much nearer your house.'

'I've got a studio at the docks near my husband's offices. I need to pick up something from there after I leave here. I was familiar with this play centre because my husband has organised fundraising events here before. His charity offices are across the street.'

'What's the charity?'

'The Lost Souls Foundation. It originally helped children of sailors who'd died at sea.' She wiped a strand of hair from her face. Georgie saw her hand was shaking.

She was lying. Georgie felt the frustration that Preston was going to be proved right in the end: she was in it with her husband. 'Someone delivers the wood to that vacant lot over there and someone else picks it up. Who picks it up, Kelly?'

'I don't know.'

There was a pause. Georgie crossed her arms. 'You need to think about what's more important to you, your kids or your husband. If you're found to be withholding information or lying, you could be looking at jail. You'll be separated from your kids. It's your choice.'

'Choice.' Pinks spots appeared on Kelly's cheeks. She took a step across the toilet cubicle. 'You don't have a husband, do you? Or kids? Of course you don't. You talk like you can separate them, like eggs. They're all tied up together, one messy, tight little ball.' She screwed her fingers together, twisting them over and over each other. 'I don't know anything.'

Of all the defences, that was the one that riled Georgie the most, the 'I don't know' lie. She had heard her own mother use it more than once when their house had been raided by the police. She'd stand in the cramped hallway, shouting as the police marched through, doing their jobs, doing the right thing, Georgie realised now. As her mother lied. As her dad lied. As Karl and Matt gave each other looks, Ryan bundling out the back door and over the fence into the night. The bonds of family made people lose their moral compasses. 'I looked you up, trying to find out about you. But there's hardly any information on you at all. That always gets me to wonder. Everyone has a trail, but you, you have nothing at all. Where did you grow up? Where did you go to school?'

'What does it matter to you?'

'It's as if you don't exist. Who are you, Kelly Malamatos? Come on, throw me a titbit. Tell me something about yourself.'

'There's nothing to tell,' Kelly hissed.

Georgie smiled, but there was no warmth in it. 'You're just a loving wife and mother, right? Kelly, I'm an East End girl. I grew up near these docks where your husband makes all that money that keeps you in a penthouse and your children at fancy private schools. Don't think we don't all want a slice of that. I know all about wanting to get out, Kelly. So don't give me that helpless woman routine. No woman wins the rich man, actually *gets* the ring on her finger, without a lot of calculation. You're harder than you look.'

Kelly took another step towards her so that she was very close in the cubicle. 'One thing's for sure, you have no idea how hard I am, to survive what I've lived through.' She pulled herself up tall. 'Ask his PA about the business, she's fucking him. Ask *her* to share the pillow talk. He tells me nothing.'

'So all is not well in the Malamatos marriage?' Georgie saw something shift in Kelly's face. She had been trying to goad Kelly into a revelation, but she'd gone too far.

'Stay the fuck away from me and my kids and keep the fuck out of things you know nothing about.' Kelly was livid, her eyes blazing as she opened the door and it slammed against the wall as she left.

Georgie swore silently. She had wanted to get Kelly onside, and her big mouth and the problems about her own family had got in the way and made it all worse. She walked back to the car and got in.

'How'd it go?' Mo asked. 'I just saw her marching her kid across the car park ahead of you.'

'I'm afraid I really didn't do that very well.'

'You rubbed her up the wrong way?' Mo shook his head. 'That'll be a first.'

Georgie caught his sarcasm and shook her head. 'Shit. I think she's lying, but I don't know about what.' She sighed in defeat. 'Come on.' She nodded across the road to a tired Victorian building. 'Let's go.'

Mo began to get out of the car, then pointed across the car park and punched the air. 'A couple kissing. Instant win!'

17

Georgie and Mo crossed the road to number 1, Casson Street, and walked up the three steps to the dusty front door. Bars covered the lower windows and a succession of broken venetian blinds could just be made out behind the thick dust stuck to the dirty windows. A panel with more than ten doorbells on it faced them. One had 'Lost Souls' written on it in a neat hand.

They rang the bell and waited, the door buzzing open after a few moments. The building had probably once been a grand Victorian ballroom but was now cut up with miles of plasterboard into a warren of corridors, with office and fire doors every few metres. They spent the next few moments pulling and pushing and holding open doors that swung hard against shoulders and feet as they battled to the back of the building. They followed a dark corridor round several right angles until Georgie lost her sense of direction completely.

They eventually found a white door with opaque glass in the top third and a bell that was half hanging out of the plasterboard. It worked, though, and the door was opened by a short, middle-aged woman in a shalwar-kameez and a headscarf who introduced herself as Anila. Georgie asked if she and Mo could come in.

Anila didn't smile but she wasn't unfriendly either. She beckoned them in to a small office. 'How can I help you?' she asked.

'How many of you work here?'

'There are just three of us. I'm one of the directors along with my colleague Fazhad and our assistant Julie. Julie's off sick today and Fazhad is out on a visit.'

'What does your foundation do?' asked Georgie.

'We're a small charity. We do what we can to improve the lives of families who work the ships or are affected by them.' She waved an elegant hand out of the window. 'Ships bring a host of problems, I'm afraid to say – prostitution, drugs and unwanted babies. Part of what we do is adoption. The fathers find the attractions of places like Vietnam and Thailand very compelling. It's hard to keep them here. We work closely with social services finding families for the unwanted babies of men who've "run off", let's say. We raise funds locally and through benefactors.'

Mo was nodding. 'I hear you, sister.'

Anila bowed her head towards him.

'The thing is,' Georgie began, 'we've impounded an illegal shipment of tropical hardwood at the port of London that was going to be delivered opposite the Lost Souls Foundation, to that vacant lot.' Anila looked blank. 'It's a Malamatos shipment.'

Anila shrugged helplessly. 'I'm afraid I don't know what you're talking about.'

'You've never seen what comes in to that lot opposite?'

'The lot? We don't face it.'

All three of them looked out of the dirty window. The view was uninspiring to say the least: a high brick wall with green stains from a constant stream of water that trickled across it. A lone plant clung to the brickwork. The drilling from the big machines building a new wing to the shopping centre made the floor vibrate.

'Tell me what Mr Malamatos does for the charity.'

Anila smiled. 'No charity can survive without money, and Mr Malamatos has been very generous in providing that support to us. We couldn't continue our work without him. He has a talent for fundraising at charity events.'

'Does his wife get involved?'

She shook her head. 'She's not involved in the day to day running and she's not a director, but she helps with the Halloween party we have every year because she's a mask maker.' Anila changed the subject. 'It's not the grandest of HQs by any means, but it's convenient. We're in this building because the play centre down the road is a good place to hold fundraising events and to organise days out for the children we're supporting. And it's cheap.'

Georgie began to walk around the small room.

'We've been running for forty years now, we've helped hundreds of children, placed tens of children with new families.'

Georgie had come to a shelf that held certificates and photos. She picked one up and turned to Anila. She tapped a finger against one of the faces. 'This blonde with the short hair. Who's she?'

Anila smiled. 'One of the directors here. She's been a huge asset over the last two years. She's been invaluable, has really taken the fundraising to a new level. I asked her once how she was so successful. "I have the balls to ask, and if that doesn't work, I demand."' She smiled. 'It's a skill not many have.'

Georgie put the photo of Sylvie back on the shelf.

'We're having a fundraiser for Halloween at the play centre on the 31st. It's nice to bring a bit of joy.'

Something struck Georgie. 'How often do you hold charity events there?'

Anila thought for a moment. 'About every six months.'

'When was the last one?'

'Just a moment.' Anila consulted a diary and sat back. 'May 3rd. They're quite grand affairs. Guests get a tour of the

docks – Christos takes them – so they can see where all the
problems stem from, the scale of the business waterside,
before they are brought back to the play centre for a party.'
She smiled as if remembering a private joke. 'Christos said
that watching poor children play was the easiest way to get
rich women to open their purses. It was more than enough
compensation for having to come all the way out here to east
London.'

'Have you got a guest list?' asked Mo.

She nodded, printed out a few sheets of paper and handed
them over.

'Have you ever seen any trucks or vehicles in the lot opposite?' Georgie asked.

Anila sighed and shook her head. 'Never. It's only ever
used when we do the charity events. Then all the catering
vans and the set people take it over. It looks like a gypsy
encampment then.'

18

The next day Kelly sat in the chair by the lawyer's large desk. The same law books sat on the same shelf, still unopened, but Mr Cauldwell had greeted her with great warmth and had scolded Bethany into bringing coffee straight away. They sat chatting almost as if they were friends.

'You look tired, if you don't mind me saying. It's been nearly three weeks now since I saw you, are you ready to move on to the next stage?'

She changed the subject. 'How's business?'

He screwed up his face. 'It's the worst I've ever seen it. In a recession as deep as this, people have to stay together, they can't afford to part. It's caused some pretty horrendous situations, I can say.' He looked at her searchingly. 'So, did you tell your husband about wanting a divorce?'

'No. A divorce isn't possible, it turns out.'

He splayed his hands in disappointment. 'Oh.' He puffed out his cheeks. 'Well, I'm glad to hear you made up with your husband.'

'No, you're not.' She paused and pulled something out of her bag. 'We haven't made up, either.' She handed him two pieces of paper. 'I wrote this. I want you to keep it.'

'What is it?'

'My will. In case something happens to me.'

He raised his eyebrows and took the papers. 'Of course. May I ask, are you ill?'

'No. I'm in perfect health – whatever he might say.' She

took a sip of coffee, then stared at her cup, surprised. 'This is good.'

He frowned. 'Why wouldn't it be? Bethany used to be a barista at Caffè Nero.' He looked down at the sheets of paper. 'Let me have a look at this.'

She watched him as he read through her words. He was calm, methodical. She warmed to him even more.

After a few moments he put the papers down and gave her a level look. 'These are quite . . . extreme allegations.'

'Do I strike you as a hysterical kind of person?'

He shook his head. 'Quite the opposite.'

'Do you believe what I've written there?'

'Every word.'

'I think he's going to kill me. I want to make provisions for my children.'

'So you say.' He adjusted his bulk on the chair, holding the papers as if they were an unexploded bomb. 'I strongly urge you to contact the police.'

She gave a thin smile. 'They act after the event, as you know.' He didn't disagree. 'I want custody to go to my mother.'

'At a trial, rest assured all your wishes will be taken into consideration.'

'And if there isn't one?'

'Isn't what?'

'A trial.'

He paused and stared at her for a moment, drumming his fingers on his lips. 'I'm not going to sugarcoat it, he is their legal father, it would be difficult.' He paused. 'We need to witness this.' He pressed the intercom. 'Bethany, get in here.'

The door opened and Bethany poked her head in. 'Yeah?'

'Bethany, sign here.'

She did so, added the date, then left the room. Kelly stood up. She had to get back before she was missed.

'Is there another copy of this?' he asked.

'No.'

'I'll keep it safe, then.'

'Do you read the papers, watch the news?'

'I'm addicted. All human nature is there. It makes my job easier, understanding the depths to which people will go to get what they want.'

'I need you to keep an eye on the press. He's an important person. The death of his wife, so young and healthy, will be news.'

'Again, the police are your best option.' She didn't reply, watching him glance out of the window and up at the Gothic spires of St Pancras Station, wondering for a moment at the man who lived there. 'I liked you from the first moment you walked in here. I'll keep an eye out for you. You've got a lot about you. One day I predict you'll come through this door and I'll get you the divorce you want so badly. The freedom you deserve.' He came round the desk and shook her hand, holding her last will and testament in the other. 'Good luck, Mrs Malamatos. One more thing.' He hadn't let go of her hand, was almost clinging to it. 'Don't run. In my experience, that makes it worse. Don't think running will free you or the children.'

19

That evening Kelly sat listening to metal forks against china, the chinking of glasses as they were set down too hard on the unyielding slate table in the kitchen. Every few moments Medea scraped her chair across the marble floor, moving with the evening sun, wanting every last ray to drill into the leathery skin on her face. The house had so many hard, brittle surfaces, echoing like the inside of Kelly's head did. The sounds were like the clanking of huge metal chains, scraping and rubbing against each other . . . She felt the panic rising in her and she tried to focus on Christos's mouth and the way he ground his teeth together as he ate, the way small globules of food would cluster at the corners before he wiped them away.

'These are good stuffed peppers,' Christos said, nodding as he chewed through one. Kelly murmured her agreement, realising that this would be the last time she would eat her mother-in-law's food. This was their last meal together. This was a day of endings: she had gone to the lawyer and Jason had come round and collected the masks that she'd finished. He had revved away in the van with hardly a backwards glance. She had waved after him, a tear cresting, realising he was the closest thing she had to a friend. She would miss him.

She glanced at the clock. Six twenty-three. She had memorised the time of every train that ran to Exeter via Tiverton Parkway, knew which Underground train they needed to take to get to Paddington Station. They would be in danger for no more than three or four minutes.

'Eat your pepper.' Christos pointed his fork at his son.

Kelly was unsure how she could swallow, her heart was doing a crazy jump round her ribcage. The passports were like a huge brick on her backside, so heavy and obvious they felt. She poured a glass of wine from the bottle Christos had opened. He was faithful and respectful to the memory of the country of his parents, but he drew the line at Greek wine, calling it vinegar with syrup thrown in, and drank expensive French red instead.

Walking away is what Medea had claimed she wanted to do. As if leaving a man like Christos was that simple. Just off you go and shut the door. Kelly took a swig of wine. It tasted like blood. The degradation had been bit by bit, almost unnoticeable, as if she had put her hand in a pan of cold water and it had been heated slowly and inexorably until it had reached boiling point and her body was a writhing mass of pain.

'Daddy, I want to see where you work,' Yannis said.

Christos put down his fork. 'Now there's an idea. I'll take you to the docks some time. It'll be your business one day.'

No, it won't be, thought Kelly. She caught Florence looking at her. She often had no idea what her daughter was thinking, what those big pale eyes really saw. She might need to be prepared for some pretty tough questioning from Florence once they left.

'Daddy, Mummy said we can go and get ice cream after dinner. Can we?' Her daughter looked up at her father.

'I brought baklava,' Medea said flatly.

Yannis made a face.

'There's a new place I saw that's just opened on Judd

Street,' Kelly said. 'I thought it was worth a try. Do you want to come?'

Christos stopped chewing and Kelly wondered how she could breathe.

'No. I can't.' He paused. 'You go.' He turned to his mother. 'The pastries will keep. Bring me back a scoop of chocolate, will you?'

Kelly smiled, not least because Medea's mouth had puckered to half its usual size. 'Medea, do you want anything?' The vigorous shake of Medea's head didn't surprise her. 'Do you want sprinkles, Christos? They might do something good like sprinkles.'

She cleared up the kitchen after their meal, careful not to seem in a hurry. 'Put your shoes on, kids,' she called, and walked into her studio, the city light bouncing against the props and masks and throwing phantom-like shapes up the walls. She opened a drawer and scooped out an envelope of photos of Amber and shoved them in her bag, feeling the camera burning into her back. It was a danger taking them, it would alert them sooner that she had really gone, but she had to take the risk. She picked up a sweater as she left and walked into their bedroom. She glanced at the photo of Amber as a baby in the frame on the dressing table. *Goodbye, little one.* It would be the first thing he'd notice was missing. She was leaving this life with only the clothes on her back so that she could still be there to bring up her remaining children. Her eyes stayed dry.

She walked into the ensuite bathroom and casually threw the wrapped panty pad with its cashpoint card hidden inside it into her bag. She came and stood by the lift and waited as Yannis put on his shoes. 'We ready?' She stood by the door to the lift and punched in the code.

'Yannis?' Christos was walking down the stairs as she

turned, the lift sliding open behind her. 'Why don't you stay here with me?'

Four steps, three steps, two, one. He was standing right next to them.

Yannis looked up at his father. Kelly bit her tongue till she tasted blood. She had to pretend it didn't matter if he came or not. 'Daddy . . .' Yannis was rocking from one foot to the other, teetering between options.

'I want Yannis to come with us,' Florence said.

His sister pushed him into a decision. 'I'm coming, I'm coming.' He jumped up and down, the pull of chocolate greater than the attractions of his father.

The lift door began to close behind them and Kelly stuck out her foot to bounce it open again. 'See you later.' She turned to go.

'Just a minute.'

She turned back to him, her heart in her feet. He came close, put his arms around her and squeezed her tight. A wave of panic hit her as she realised he might feel the passports in her pocket. She pulled away and backed into the lift. As the doors began to close he blew her a kiss. And then they were gone.

She stared at herself in the mirror as the lift plummeted downwards. Terror and defiance were etched on her face. In the lobby, a caretaker she didn't recognise nodded at her lazily as she took her children's hands in hers and headed for the smoked-glass door.

They walked left out of the door towards the Euston Road. There was a side entrance to the station near them to the right, but she couldn't be sure Christos wasn't watching the security camera that guarded the exit. She tried to hurry the children to the corner. They would be out of sight then.

They rounded the corner and she started running.

'What are we doing?' Florence asked.

She didn't answer, jogging through the front entrance of St Pancras. She saw a cashpoint and jammed in the card, taking out her daily maximum amount of £1,000. Then she ran with her protesting children to the Underground.

'Where are we going, Mum?' Florence asked once they were on the train to Exeter, heading west.

'Somewhere by the sea,' she said.

'Is it warm there?'

'Not at this time of year. We're going to see a friend of mine. An old friend.'

Two hours later the train pulled up at Tiverton Parkway and they got out, a blustery wind blowing down the platform. The few other passengers melted away and Kelly stood in the darkness, unsure what to do. She saw a figure in a denim jacket and a curl of cigarette smoke, heard the scrape of her high heels. 'Lindsey.'

'Hello, Kelly.' Her voice was rasping and flat and she flicked the cigarette away and gave her a hug. 'You sure you want to do this?'

Kelly nodded.

'Let's get a shift on then, it's a long drive.'

20

Nearly four and a half thousand miles away, and five hours behind Kelly, the Wolf was still in the bar in Belém he'd entered at eleven that evening. A girl was next to him on the bed in an upstairs room, but he wasn't sure it was the girl he'd started out with. Her long dark hair fanned out across rumpled pillows and twisted sheets. He could hear Thomas Jefferson, nicknamed 'President', captain of the *Saracen*, talking and laughing behind the paper walls in the room next door to him. His hangover was beating percussion in his brain, and he had lain here quite long enough, the woman pushing him down whenever he tried to get up. But it was time to get to work. It was good to start a voyage with a bellyful. It brought good luck, the Wolf believed. It would help the fourteen-hour shift he was about to start in the heat pass quicker.

He tried to sit up and the woman moved to pull him back down again. 'Enough, enough, I've got work to do.' He stretched and scratched and glugged down some water.

'President! All hail the President!' he shouted and heard swearing and groaning in reply from the other side of the wall as he bent to pick up his T-shirt. He pulled it over his head and the sour odour of old sweat hit him. Most of his gear was still on the ship; this had been only a three-day stopover – he'd shower and change later.

The woman had her pants on now, had snapped back into business mode. 'You owe me more. You've spent an hour extra.' She had stepped towards the door to block his exit.

He held up his hands, smiled. She'd played a fast one but he wasn't going to condemn her for that. A woman who had her eye on the money was someone straightforward, someone he respected. 'Fair dues. You don't miss a thing.'

'No, I don't. Where you going, anyway?'

'London.'

She put her hands on her hips, swaying to one side. She had a mole on the corner of her lip which had attracted him last night. In the morning light it still looked cute. 'One day I leave here and see the world.'

'I'll tell you something for nothing, the world's all the same.'

'I've got a passport, you know. I'm not staying here for ever.'

Young dreams that would fade and die. He gave her the extra money and banged on the wall to hurry the President along. He opened the door and half ran out, sliding down the banister to the ground floor. He didn't bother to say goodbye.

The President half fell down the stairs after him. 'You're a bad, bad man, you know.' The President wiggled his finger at the Wolf and shook his head as they stepped into the tropical heat outside. 'God, that's one hell of a hangover.'

'That's why you love me. Come on.'

They walked down a rubbish-strewn alley and out to the quayside. It was busy in the early morning, because the day would only get hotter. A mile-long stretch of docks and wharves, gantry cranes, thousands of men from all over the world, permanent or just passing through, moving the goods that oiled the world economy – and the other items that never turned up in a balance sheet: the guns, drugs, contraband cigarettes, women, children . . .

The *Saracen* was registered in Cyprus, flying an Argentinian flag, staffed by a crew from six nations and operated by Christos Malamatos, resident of London. It was taller than a twenty-storey building, as big as a small town, with giant smears of rust that ran down its huge sides to the water. The gantry cranes used to load the containers were so high off the ground you couldn't see the operator. As a merchant seaman it was the Wolf's floating home for a sixty-seven-day stint, and he was on the last leg now, seven days across the Atlantic to London with forty thousand tonnes of cargo on board – some more precious to the operator than others.

The Wolf stopped walking and stared up at the ship. 'You carry on, I forgot something.' He left the President and headed back to the bar. The best plans were simple. He took the stairs two at a time and opened the girl's door without knocking. She was efficient, already stripping the bed, and had tidied up the bottles. She looked surprised, was still young enough to find life a shock. In a few years that too would be gone.

'What's your name?'

'What do you want it to be?'

He laughed. 'It's in your passport, unless you're a lot cleverer than I thought.'

She smiled back, a broad mouth and black eyes bright with calculation. 'Luciana.'

'That's a pretty name.'

'It is, isn't it?'

'Fancy seeing the world?'

21

K elly woke in a small room, shafts of sunlight piercing the gap between the flowery curtains. She could hear kids playing outside, their voices rising and falling on the wind. The window pane rattled in its warped frame. She pulled on her clothes and opened the bedroom door, heard the clattering of plates in the kitchen, the tinny tones of a radio.

'You slept late. You must have been shattered.' Lindsey was in faded pyjamas and a big wraparound sweater, her dirty blonde bed hair poking up at odd angles. She poured water into a giant mug that said 'Sports Direct' and handed her a tea. 'Strong, milk, no sugar. Don't worry, Steve's gone to work. There's no one to answer to.'

Kelly came over and gave her a hug, staring over her shoulder at the kitchen door that gave on to the garden. A broken swing was swaying in the wind, a kid's tractor and some old farm implements were stacked in the corner of the weedy lawn. 'It's perfect.'

Lindsey picked up her cigarette packet and opened the door and they went out. Yannis and Florence were pushing one of Lindsey's kids on an old tricycle. The lawn gave way to a field and then another and then some low farm buildings and in the distance the Atlantic.

'Damn wind, can't light my fag.' Lindsey had her back turned, hunched over with a clicking lighter. Kelly felt a fresh wind, straight off the ocean, pushing back her hair. They walked to the edge of the garden where the potholed drive wound away and two old cars sat rusting by a garage. 'I swapped the bright lights for this. You're lucky it's not raining. It's always raining here.'

'This is a lovely place, Linds. I can see why you moved back.'

'You're having a laugh.' She inhaled, regarding her old friend. 'You look even thinner, you old cow. You must have been pretty desperate to come all the way to deepest Devon to get away.'

'More than you know.' Kelly turned her face to the sun again. 'Oh, to have the wind in my face, to breathe, you have no idea.'

'It went that wrong, eh?'

'As wrong as it can.'

Lindsey sighed. 'He use his fists?' She took a deep drag on her cigarette when Kelly didn't answer. 'I told you at the time he was too good to be true. Didn't I tell you?'

Kelly started to nod. 'But tell me how a woman in my situation was supposed to refuse.'

Lindsey let out a half laugh. 'You weren't, that's the point. He could have who he wanted. He could have had any of us in there. Still thinks he can, by the sounds of it. He wants all the choice and none of the responsibility. We all dreamed of escape, Kel, you actually did it.' She inhaled again. 'Remember when he laid out that map of that ship on the table? My God, he saw you coming.'

'Oh stop, Linds.' She almost laughed. They had both been working that day when Christos came in to buy a coffee. He used to tip well, they had all noticed. Then he had laid out a plan of a ship, and the siren call of the sea, of her old life, had brought her over.

You like ships? She had seen his dimples then as he smiled.

More than you can know.

Come closer, let me show you the biggest ship you've ever seen.

She had glanced back at Lindsey, saw her bulging eyes behind the counter urging her on, the look that said, *Live our dreams for us*. And she had discovered, serving him coffee that day, that she still had the capacity to flirt, to put her looks and her charm to work once again. She still wanted fun and adventure, to believe that all the heartbreak and loss had not ended her life, but thrown it in a new direction. How she had loved him then. And how, only five years later, she hated his guts.

'The kids look good,' Lindsey said. 'Happy.' The kids began rolling around on the grass before running into the house.

Tears pricked at Kelly's eyes. 'They are all I've got.' They both sighed at the small pieces of good fortune each had been handed.

A cat came alongside and jumped on a low wall, its bushy tail wafting through Kelly's fingers. 'How many of these have you got now?' Kelly asked.

'Just the two.'

'You're destined to end up a cat woman.'

'With just two? They hardly keep the boredom at bay. She had kittens recently, so sweet they were, racing all over the house and up the curtains. We gave them away – see how good I am? But she still looks for them.'

'Looks for them?'

'Yeah. She wanders round the house mewing, calling for them. She searches everywhere, but her children aren't there.' Lindsey took a final drag on the cigarette, then flicked it away and glanced back at Kelly. A second later it dawned on her what she had said. 'Oh God, Kelly, I'm so sorry, I didn't mean to upset you. I didn't mean – oh Kel, I'm sorry . . .'

'It's OK, I know you didn't mean anything by it.'

Lindsey looked stricken. 'I'm so sorry. Jesus, I'm a stupid insensitive cow sometimes . . .'

Kelly hugged her friend. 'No, you're not. Not at all.' She saw Lindsey wipe away a tear. 'I won't be here long, Linds, just today while I get my money out. I didn't dare to keep it in the flat in case he found it. You've got a lot on your plate and not much space.'

'Where are you going to go?'

'It's better if you don't know. Really, it's better. I need to get to a bank, is there one nearby?'

'I can drive you to the village, there's a post office. Will that do?' She looked at her watch. 'You slept late. It's shut at lunch, but opens afternoons.'

'We'll leave this afternoon if you can drive us to the station.'

'If that's what you want.' Lindsey gave Kelly the look she used to give her when they had a difficult customer in the bar. 'Men,' she spat. 'What fuckers they are.'

Kelly smiled. It was good to see her old friend, to hang out. 'So what do you do when you've got a few hours to spare and a beach nearby?'

Lindsey urged Kelly to go and stretch her legs. 'Take the path at the far end of the garden and it'll take you down to the beach. I'll feed the kids. I used to deal with twenty covers at a time at the restaurant, remember?'

Kelly said goodbye to Florence and Yannis and followed the path as it wound through dripping woodland and then cut down a cliff to a pebbly beach where the breakers pulverised the sand. The wind was stronger here; the high tide line held a broken plastic bucket and part of a wetsuit. A dog walker came past, smiling. Kelly began to walk away from the path into the wind, feeling freer and lighter with every step. She walked further than she meant to, and it took her longer than she had imagined it would to get back to the path. She speeded up; she didn't want to leave her children for too long.

When she got back Lindsey was in the corner of the garden

furthest from the house, trying to get an old lawnmower started. 'If I don't mow it I get no end of grief from Steve. You'd think he'd lift a finger.' They fiddled with it together for a while, swearing and laughing, enjoying the autumn sun on their faces as the kids played in and out of the back door, running round the side of the house. This is how life should be, thought Kelly. Normal interactions, an ebb and flow to relationships, a give and take . . .

She saw Lindsey turn towards the house; something had caught her attention. Kelly looked up. The faint thrum of an engine. A car. Two black Audis came fast up the drive and pulled to a stop by the broken-down hatchbacks. The children ran towards the cars, intrigued and excited.

She saw Christos get out of one, Medea the other.

Kelly sprinted across the garden, the wind whipping away her cries. Christos was hugging Florence. Medea had picked up Yannis and was folding him into the first car.

She was halfway across the garden now, rounding the broken swing, hollering and shouting. Florence turned to look at her mother as she sat down on the back seat next to Yannis, half in and half out.

'Let go of the kids.'

Kelly slammed at full pelt into the side of the car by Florence and began pulling on her daughter's arm. Medea came round and stood in front of her.

'We're going home, this is ridiculous.'

'No, we're not.'

Yannis put his hands over his ears, trying to block it all out. Medea pushed Florence's legs into the car and tried to shut the door as Kelly fought with her.

'Get in the car, Kelly.' Christos was right by her, holding her arm.

She let out a sob and at that moment Medea slammed the door and walked around to the driver's seat. 'No.'

Lindsey ran towards them, her own kids ordered into the house. She was pulling her big sweater round her for protection. 'Leave her alone or I'm calling the police.'

Christos dragged Kelly to the second car, her feet scoring deep marks in the gravel as she fought him. She saw Christos's driver at the wheel.

'Take your hands off her, for God's sake.'

He threw Kelly into the back seat and slammed the door, then turned towards Lindsey. He came close to her as she began to back uncertainly away from him, and whispered something in her ear. Kelly had righted herself and saw Lindsey's face freeze like a statue for a moment before it crumpled into sobs. Christos walked to the far door and got in to the car. 'Go,' he said.

Lindsey's hands were shaking, tears coursing down her cheeks. 'You sick fuck!'

'What did you say to her? What did you do?' Kelly tried to open the window, jabbing at the button.

The first car had driven away, crunching out of sight down the drive. Kelly howled in pure fear. Without her children, all she could feel was the fear. As the driver pulled away, Lindsey began to run along beside the car. Kelly splayed her fingers on the glass; Lindsey was saying something to her as they picked up speed. 'I'll pray for you,' she was mouthing, and then Lindsey and the house disappeared from view.

She turned in the seat to Christos, who was calm, staring ahead. 'How did you find me?'

'It's not like you have many friends, Kelly. She was the only one left, and I have a trace on your phone.'

'I hate you. Every time I see you I hate your guts.'

'I don't care. It doesn't matter if you hate me. You really think that love has to be returned? How naïve. You remember, Kelly, the rules I work to: nothing is impossible. What matters is that I chose you, and I work very hard in life to get what

I want. We are a family, Kelly, no one breaks the bond of family. However far you run, I will always find you. I'll never let you go.' He pulled out a small black box that looked like a pencil case. He opened it with a click and pulled out a hypodermic syringe.

'You're not—'

She couldn't finish what she'd started saying, because he'd jabbed the syringe hard into her thigh and was emptying the contents into her leg. The last thing she remembered before she blacked out was him stroking her hair, almost tenderly.

22

Ricky Welch was sitting in his armchair by the window that gave on to the back alley of a house in Southampton. He was trying to read the paper, but one of the dogs was trying to squirm into his lap, trying to nudge him to take him for his morning walk, and was knocking the pages around. It had been easier to read a big paper in prison; there were no distractions, no pets or wives or Dawn's nieces and nephews to knock into you. It was the only advantage he could think of. He'd read a lot inside, it had changed him, given him perspective.

Dawn was on the phone to her sister, yak yak yakkety yak. It amazed him how much women could talk. She'd only seen her two days ago and they'd talked for six hours solid, the childcare for Sally's kids hardly puncturing the flow back and forth. It always struck him how much she laughed, her voice pealing away upstairs, at the theatre, in the khazi even. Men just sat in silence together as a rule, compared betting slips. He knew this all too well, had lived it for eight years. He tried not to let his mind travel back there, tried to block it off before it made him bitter. Dawn had suffered too, had a capacity for forgiveness he knew he didn't possess. She had stood by him, loyal till the end. Many would not have.

He pushed the dog off his lap and it started humping his leg. We were all beasts in the field in the end, programmed to procreate. He stood and shook him off as Dawn made a 'down, boy' motion with her hand and rang off from her sister.

She bent down and picked up the dog, nestling her face in its stomach. His wife had a mass of blonde curls that were beginning to be flecked with grey. She'd put on weight over the years, rounding out from a buxom blonde into a less defined, more maternal shape. A shape that was deceptive. He felt the pity he had for her return with force. She put a brave face on it, but she was also sadder, her mouth turned down. We get the face we deserve, he'd read somewhere. That wasn't true. Dawn hadn't deserved her lot.

'That was Sally,' Dawn said, as if he couldn't recognise her sister on the phone. 'She wants to go to a show at the Mayflower in the New Year. I'll get the tickets; we'll all go.' She walked over to the boxy computer on a table at the side of the room and switched it on. It made a sound like a helicopter taking off. 'I'll show you.'

She didn't patronise him or get irritated at the things he couldn't do or didn't understand. The world had turned in eight years, leaving him reeling. His wife had always loved the theatre, but she used to go without him. Back then he would scoff, but he had changed. It was funny how years of incarceration could expand a person's horizons. Now they went together. She brought up the website for the theatre and clicked on *The Day of the Dead*. 'Have a read. I'll get the dogs' leads.'

He wasn't sure why he had to read it, his wife's opinion and passions were good enough for him. He floated through culture, whether high or low. She'd insisted on framing his Open University degree certificate – Sociology and Social Sciences – but had then hung it in the toilet. He was never sure whether she was having a laugh at his expense. He glanced through the photos of the actors and the production staff, the mask makers . . .

It was her. Plain as day, it was the woman who had told the lie, the monstrous lie that had stolen years of his life. She was sandwiched between a skeleton and a table, in a room with pointed windows. He felt a rage well up like he hadn't experienced since it first all happened, unstoppable. She had stolen Dawn's life too. He looked at her name. Of course, she had changed it. But she hadn't changed her face. It was an unusually fine face, a face many would covet.

Through the windows and down the inglenook, up from the floorboards and through the soles of his feet, came the deep drawn-out note of a ship's horn in the harbour. He heard it ringing in his ears as it faded away. It was calling him, a siren call of danger, but maybe also of answers. Ships had been his life once, until he'd gone down for murder. He felt capable of it now. He picked up his jacket and walked out of the front door, the blustery morning wind trying to shove him back into the house, back to sanity and reasonable behaviour, back to the straight and narrow. He could hear Dawn talking to the dogs in the kitchen, her soft inviting voice not enough of a pull to keep him rooted to the spot.

23

Kelly woke disoriented, remembering in a flash her struggle in the car with Christos. She was in her own bed at home, the flat hollow with quiet. She ran her tongue over her teeth. None was missing or loose. She sat up tentatively, but no jarring pain from a fresh injury slowed her rise. She lifted a shaking hand and felt her face, her eyes. There was no swelling or bruising. She knew from the silence in the flat that the kids were not there. She picked up her mobile, charging by the side of the bed. There were no messages. She glanced at the date, confusion scratching at the inside of her skull. She'd been dragged into Christos's car on the afternoon of Wednesday 23rd of October, now it was late morning on Thursday the 24th. Nearly an entire day had been erased from her memory.

She got out of bed fast, alarm beginning to pierce the fog of tiredness and confusion she felt. She was wearing her old jogging bottoms and a top. She headed for the kitchen, adopting her old habits as she had no better ones to replace them with. She dragged herself up the stairs, feeling a hundred years old. As she crossed the living room, she could hear the swishing, sliding sound of slippers on tile. Medea was in the kitchen, loading the fridge with her hermetically sealed dishes in clingfilm.

'Sit down, I'll get what you need,' Medea said to Kelly, not bothering even to look at her, her face and neck buried in the refrigerator.

'I don't want anything,' Kelly replied. The thought of pushing food past the great knot of disappointment in her throat was too much for her. Medea decided she didn't like the dolmades on the middle shelf and moved them to the bottom shelf.

'Are the kids at school?'

Medea nodded. 'Just have a little plate. Sit down and have a little plate. It'll settle your nerves.'

'I should get ready to go and get them.'

'Sylvie's doing it. She's taking them to the Trocadero as a treat.'

'Sylvie?' She hadn't believed it was possible to feel worse, until she heard that name. 'She doesn't have to do that.'

'Christos has to work, I am old, you were . . .' She waved a hand as a substitute for airing something that was too despicable to mention. 'You should be glad she stepped in and volunteered to take them after school.'

Kelly sank down on a chair, staring dully at the view of west London through the window. The city looked hung over, a long traffic jam clogging the flyover heading west. Still to be in this flat, with the same objects, the same restrictions, the same toxic relationships . . . Her heart couldn't take the pain.

'Here. Have something.' Medea put a plate in front of her and pulled back the clingfilm. It made a squeaking sound as the food was revealed. There were four types of dessert – some deep-fried, others soaked in honey, cloying in their sweetness. She sensed Medea drawing a shawl round her shoulders and huffing. 'You're so suspicious all the time. I'm only trying to help. You need energy. Eat. You're too thin.'

Her irritation began to build. This wasn't Medea's home, yet she came and went as if it were. Kelly would eat what she wanted to, when she wanted to. 'I don't . . .' Her voice died away as she heard a precise tread across the marble of the living room and Christos came in.

He looked at her and Kelly felt fear wash down her back. Their cat and mouse game was over, but all its deadly conse-quences were still to come.

'So you're awake.' Fear had closed up her throat and she couldn't speak.

'She's spurning my cooking,' said Medea.

The old bitch, thought Kelly. She looked down at the pastries, picked one up, put it in her mouth and began to chew. She forced it down her throat. 'It's very nice.'

Christos took a step towards her and she speeded up her eating. Medea took the plate away. It was like she was in a mental institution, except the wall between the inmate and the jailer was invisible. Kelly felt the heavy sweets were ready to come back up again if she didn't use iron will to keep them down. Panic began to sing through the fibres of her being. 'I need to see the kids.' She stood sharply, her desire to be with them rising in her like a wave cresting a sea wall.

'They'll come back later,' Christos said.

She put a hand on the kitchen table to steady herself as dizziness threatened to overwhelm her. There was no mention of her escape attempt. It was being wiped clean from the family history, as if what she had done, what she had planned for so long, had never really happened. That was more terri-fying than Christos flying into a rage. Kelly could feel the strength drain away from her legs as she sank back into a chair.

Christos was about to turn away but when he saw the look on her face, pulled out a chair and sat down next to her. She just managed to stop herself shrinking back as he reached out a hand for her shoulder. 'Why is it always so difficult, eh? Things will all work out.' She couldn't control the shiver that ran down her arm. He reached forward for the zip on her old hooded sweatshirt and began to do it up. She could feel the fabric tightening over her breasts and up to her throat. It took all her reserves of self-control not to cry out. She felt that he was going to keep on zipping, right up over her mouth, nose and eyes, as if he were closing her up in a body bag, a cadaver to be wheeled away.

24

K elly went to get dressed. She had to try to get through the day, be ready for the kids when they got home. She put on some make-up, staring at a face in the mirror she didn't recognise. She looked different, yet she couldn't understand how exactly. Fear? Fraying nerves? There were many reasons. She caught a glimpse of the bedroom light reflected in the mirror.

Medea was still in the kitchen, Christos had gone out. She dragged the stepladder from the cupboard next to the service lift and set it up under the lampshade. She unscrewed the light bulb and Sleepchecker camera, then picked up her bag. She left the flat and headed to an internet café, sat down at a computer, plugged in the SD card and began to watch, keen to see what had happened since she had installed it.

The recording was black and white and motion-sensitive, with no sound. She had three and a half days to look through, from Sunday afternoon to this morning. She fast-forwarded through the night she nearly stabbed Christos in the shower, barely able to watch. The twisted passion she showed then was beyond her now. The next night she was in bed alone, turning this way and that, hugging a pillow for company as though she were trying to find a place of refuge in the large bed. The next images captured were of Christos moving back and forth through the bedroom, often on the phone. That was the night she had run. She watched his body language for a moment, playing the tape backward and forward. He didn't look stressed, he was in control.

Medea trudged through the film occasionally, a cloth slipping over surfaces as she cleaned and poked about in drawers and shelves. Then her husband was carrying Kelly to the bed, fireman-style over his shoulder. She was out cold from the drugs he had given her in the car. He laid her down on the sheets and Medea came in and covered her over.

Tears sprang to Kelly's eyes for her comatose body, being carried and pushed about. She had lost her free will completely. She felt outraged on behalf of the woman on the screen. Mother and son were in the room, chatting calmly, but she couldn't make out what they were saying. Then Medea left the bedroom and Christos took a notebook from his pocket and bent down and examined the insteps and soles of Kelly's shoes and began writing in the book. She frowned, not understanding what he was doing. He put the notebook away and came closer to her, fast asleep on the bed. He pulled something – a pair of scissors – out of his pocket, leaned over and cut off a lock of her hair.

Kelly reeled back, mystified. Why had he taken her hair?

She went home, put the camera back inside the lampshade and dragged the ladder back to the storage cupboard. Her eyes fell on two suitcases neatly stacked at the back. She didn't recognise them; they were from the era pre-wheels, when a person's items were lugged across concourses the world over, shoulders and necks protesting. She walked back down the corridor, the silence of the house, its absence of people, pressing down on her. She stopped by the door opposite the TV room – the bedroom with an ensuite bathroom. She pushed open the door and walked inside.

It was the smell that hit her first, the distinctive aroma of sandalwood mixed with orange. It was the smell of Medea, already leaching into the plaster and settling like dust on the carpet. Kelly walked leaden-footed into the room. The bed had an old-fashioned bedspread on it, with blankets and sheets – Medea didn't use a duvet. At the end of the bed was a nightstand with a small black and white TV on it, half covering a lace doily.

Kelly threw open the doors of the inbuilt wardrobes. The faint smell of mothballs drifted out. She glanced along the rows of clothing: a fur coat, hermetically sealed in its dry-cleaning wrapper, summer dresses, several pairs of slippers; clothes for all seasons. Medea had arrived, and she wasn't going anywhere soon. She had slipped seamlessly from her flat near Primrose Hill to the Euston Road. The spy had been sent in to watch her more closely. She felt as if she were lying in the black box again, the lid slowly closing over her, cutting out the light. She ran to her bathroom, opened her bottle of pills and swallowed two.

Twenty minutes later her panic attack had subsided, so when she heard the movement of the lift and realised her kids were coming home, she felt prepared. A few moments later the lift opened and they piled out, but they looked embarrassed to see her. They shuffled and examined the floor as she wrapped them in awkward hugs. She ignored Sylvie, who stood proprietorially in the doorway, a large bag filled with gaudy plastic toys in her hand.

'Kids, cut it out, your mom's not been well.' Sylvie studied Kelly as she bent over and reached out, pleading with her kids to respect her, forgive her, love her. As if blood bonds alone were enough. Sylvie had been pretty convinced this afternoon that they weren't. It was interesting to see how easily a child's mind could be turned with a few cheap bribes. How easily their affections could be bought. The young one was already sorted; he was as malleable as his pudgy skin, squeally and demanding with his own needs. Narcissism started young. The daughter was more of a problem. She was a watcher. Sylvie would need to be careful. If Florence ever made a scene, people would listen. She needed to spend some time thinking up clever ways to pander to her. Ways Florence wouldn't expect. Then again, how hard could it be? An eleven-year-old couldn't know the base nature of the world. She would be undone by her need for love, the social pressure to feel wanted, to feel *it*.

Wait, were those tears in Kelly's eyes? Of course. Her failed escape attempt would have brought her low. She must feel like shit. After all, Kelly was stuck in a marriage that was beyond repair, she had a dead kid and husband and needed a pile of pills and who knew what crap to get through the days. But here was the thing about Kelly, she never looked like shit. Because with a face and body like that, no one could believe that you could suffer.

Sylvie dug her nails into her palm so hard she nearly drew blood. Kelly was a winner. She had won the great race of a woman's life; she was more beautiful than 90 per cent of the bitches out there. She hadn't had to scrabble for the scraps left after the desirables had had their pick. Sylvie watched Kelly hold her son's head in her hands, her fingers entwined in his hair. Kelly's nails were short and unvarnished, she'd probably never bothered with a manicure. Kelly didn't sit in salons inhaling acetate fumes and listening to hip-hop bullshit about women workin' it, or waste hours of her life staring at the bitchy Korean girl in the mask because there's fuck all else to look at. Good looks got you a free pass from having to maintain, from having to buff and wax and starve. And in its wake came allure, and choice, and power.

And Sylvie wanted that. She wanted it badly.

She studied Kelly as she ran her untended fingers down Florence's arms, engrossed in her children.

You've got your looks and your kids. I'll take them from you. Just you watch.

Kelly knelt in front of Yannis, holding his uncertain face close to hers. 'Everyone gets ill once in a while, Yannis, even your mum. But I'm fine now.' She took his hands and shook them in hers, trying to pull him out of it. She forced herself to stay calm, she could win this battle, she was their mother, after all. He didn't answer. She looked at Florence, standing taller next to him. She got up and smoothed down her daughter's hair. 'I'm going to make you your favourite meal. No one makes a spaghetti carbonara like your mother.'

The children looked at each other and smiled, smiles that seemed as bright as a thousand suns to Kelly.

25

The *Saracen* began to rock in the ocean swell. To the Wolf it was like riding an elephant, a rhythmic rising and falling as the ship powered through the Atlantic. The sea turned darker blue as they moved off towards the ocean depths. The wind freshened. The sun was lower in the sky now and not as strong. The rest of the crew had their shirts tied round their waists but he kept his on his back to keep the rays off and the skin cancer at bay. As the swell deepened the ship began to creak, the engines a constant low-level rumble beneath them. He watched the white boats (anything smaller than this beast of a vessel was dismissively called a white boat) scurry out of their way. Container ships were an expression of pure power, they threw their weight around. A bit like their owners. If the *Saracen* hit something in its way, you wouldn't even feel it.

He picked up the portable chiller cabinet of steak and walked through the doorway to the leeward side, where the rest of the crew was setting up the barbecue. It was a ritual that crews often performed before they hit the big ocean. There was a crew of fifteen aboard the *Saracen*, under the President's command, but there were always a few stragglers paying for rides home and company men doing company stuff as well. The only women present were two squat Indonesians in flip-flops and sarongs. They were threading lamb chunks on to kebab sticks, wiping away the sweat on their brows with their wrists. Luciana was stashed away in his cabin. The President was pissed at him, but the Wolf had paid for her and as long as she didn't show her face and upset the crew the captain was happy to live with it.

The gang was assembling around the barbecue with the grateful air of those for whom a long shift has just finished. Before leaving port they worked non-stop to load the ship, returning to regular shifts only when out in the ocean. They all wanted the overtime, all craving the extra cash. What the Wolf could earn with his brawn and his hands was never quite what he needed and way less than what he desired. He popped a top off a beer and tossed it over the side into the vast garbage can of the Atlantic.

The President came out and introduced a young man he had with him, Jonas Wyman. 'He's a paying passenger so treat him kindly, boys. I've told him to stay out of your way.'

They raised their beer bottles to Jonas in a tired welcome.

'Where you from?' the Wolf asked.

'London. I'm travelling home from South America. I was supposed to start college in October. Guess I've slipped by a couple of weeks.'

'Gap year stuff, eh?' the President added indulgently.

Jonas nodded again. 'I thought I'd see the world by travelling across it.'

'Well, this is what you see,' said a Pole, throwing his arms out around him. 'Water. Nothing but water.'

They laughed, but the Wolf was taking a long hard look at Jonas. He was thin with pitted skin and looked older than a student at the end of a gap year. He felt holes would open up in that story pretty quickly if he found some leverage.

Jonas came forward again and asked if he could help.

'Yeah. Chop this salad.' The Wolf handed him a knife and some tomatoes. 'You been on a ship before, Jonas?'

He shook his head. Christos would be keen for any extra income, the Wolf felt. When he'd boarded he had noted that the angle of the gangway was steep, steeper than he had ever seen it. The ship wasn't full. The recession was biting; they were carrying fewer containers, lifting the ship out of the water and lowering the profits. Christos could be hurting.

'You worked on ships for long?' Jonas asked.

The Wolf took a swig of beer. 'Years.' He said it like there had been too many.

'I guess it's a very different kind of life.' Jonas was getting cocky, thinking he wanted to talk to him.

'It can make you rootless.'

'Does it make you start to wonder where home really is?'

'This monster of a thing is my home for now. This ship burns about two hundred and fifty tons of fuel a day. I think of people back home stressing about their light bulbs, and I laugh. This animal takes a mile and a half to stop. But you gotta get those red kidney beans to the vegetarians somehow. Perhaps if they knew how it got to their supermarkets they'd stop pretending they enjoyed them.' He skewered the meat with a fork and held it over the barbecue for Jonas, almost as a challenge. 'How do you like your steak?'

'Rare.'

The Wolf smiled. Jonas had an unpredictable look that he responded to. 'You'll go far.' They stopped talking and listened to the satisfying sizzle of burning fat.

Even with such a big, powerful machine as this there was always a chink. The Death Star came to mind, an empire destroyed by a small, old-fashioned jet. The Wolf took a deep glug of beer and felt the bubbles catch at the back of his throat. Even the strongest outfits were vulnerable if you knew how to strike them.

A sullen-looking man who had a stink of the company about him had just come outside and was standing nearby. The Wolf understood at once. Here was the guard, pure and simple, for the cargo.

The sun dipped lower behind the bridge and cast this side of the ship into shade. The Wolf looked at the shadow the hundreds of containers threw far out into the ocean. If he played this right he would be coming home for good. He was sailing into London, the beating heart of Christos's empire. A small, old-fashioned jet.

26

George coasted her bike down the ramp into the station car park. She was in a bad mood: on her journey in she'd noticed both her lights were missing – her brother Karl had taken them and not returned them and she would have to cycle home in the dark. It didn't help that a sports car, reversing aggressively to fit perfectly into one of the parking spaces, nearly clipped her front wheel as she came down the ramp. She skidded to a halt and shouted at Preston. 'You nearly knocked me off.'

'Calm down, calm down.' He said this in a pantomime Scouse accent which infuriated her. The fool was born and bred in Dorset. 'You on the rag, Georgie?'

She was so angry she wished she'd knocked into him and scraped his car. She locked her bike to a railing and looked at the Thames, its grey expanse visible between a series of grotty Portakabins and the squat brick customs offices. This far downriver the Thames was as wide as a sea. Today the wind was warm, gusting hard, blowing straight from the Caribbean.

A customs officer's job was to stop banned goods coming into the country. Unless they were lucky, or smugglers were stupid, the most effective way to do that was to work on information given to them – tip-offs. To search a container ship properly for its secrets would take weeks, long weeks where the bananas rotted and the grain sprouted and the electricity bill for the refrigerated units ramped up and the insurance claims spiralled. Trade had a momentum and an importance all of its own. They weren't even cogs in a machine, they were 'flies on the arse of the great beast mammon' as Anguish liked to say from behind his piles of paper.

She had been proud when she'd got the customs job; she could turn it into a career. She'd be the first person in her family to have one. She'd been here a year after her training period and was beginning to get a feel for how things worked. How rumours circulated. How good or bad internal affairs were at rooting out corruption.

Her dad and her brothers laughed when she got the job. They constantly talked about how people down here were on the take, supplementing their state salaries with private contributions, insisting that people had been bought. 'Human nature, you can't argue with human nature,' her dad had said.

No, Georgie thought as she pulled open the door and took the stairs to the first floor, you can. She wanted to believe that you could be good and get on; she was determined to prove her family wrong. Not all people were liars. Mo waved at her from his desk and made hand gestures suggesting Anguish was in a bad mood. She nodded to show she understood. She saw Preston swaggering down the corridor behind her.

Mo came over. 'Anguish wants to see us. He's got something to show us.'

'What does that mean?' Georgie took off her reflective jacket and put down her bag.

Mo shrugged. 'The more he bigs it up, the more unimportant it is.'

She smiled. When they discussed corruption Mo would joke that no one ever dared bribe him, they thought that he was too angry, and anyway, he knew where the plutonium was already.

Angus came out of his office and beckoned them over. 'Come and see the mess we've got outside.'

They followed the boss out of the side of the building and along the dock towards a faded red container placed far away from any storage facility, marooned in a sea of tarmac.

'What's that smell?' Mo asked. Something in the container had gone bad, that much was clear.

'You really want to know? I'll show you.' They walked a bit further on. 'You can't get any nearer,' Anguish said. They were standing with their hands or shirts over their noses and mouths. 'Twenty tonnes of rotting New Zealand lamb. The refrigeration connection failed on ship. One of the worst cases I've seen.'

'That's disgusting,' Mo exclaimed. 'You know how if the heating fails in an office and the temperature falls below a certain level, you can have the day off? Can we do that for smell?'

Anguish gave him a withering look. 'If I was being mean, I mean really mean, I would make you guys search it.'

'If that was pork, I'd be excused,' Mo argued, voice muffled through his shirt sleeve.

Georgie didn't dare breathe. The stench was making her stomach heave. This must be how human flesh smelled. It was a marvel how quickly it transformed and corroded.

'Now let's get back inside and you can tell me what's happening with the Malamatos case.'

Mo looked at her with pity as they trailed back to Anguish's office. Angus sat down behind his desk and stared at them, his bad mood radiating towards them.

'I don't think the wife is the tip-off. She told me pretty convincingly to eff off,' Georgie said.

'Charming.'

'The charity he runs and that the mistress – but not the wife – is a director of, is opposite the drop for the wood.'

Angus looked up at her in surprise.

'I've talked to the residents near the drop point and they

say that there are never trucks pulling up and switching trailers. I drew a blank there,' Mo added. 'But the only time there's activity in that yard is every six months when there's a charity event and caterers and prop companies deck out the play centre and park up next to it. Perfect cover for another lorry to pull in and a waiting flatbed to drive away.'

Angus steepled his fingers. 'So we think they're doing deliveries every six months?'

Mo and Georgie nodded.

'When was the last charity event?'

'Early May. Their next charity event is Halloween – and one of Christos's ships is docking here the day before: the *Saracen*, coming from Belém, northern Brazil,' Mo said.

'But if they're shipping it every six months, why did we find this stuff two weeks ago? It breaks the pattern.' No one had an answer. 'We'll have a good rummage over the *Saracen* when it arrives, of course.' Anguish threw up his hands. 'I don't get it. Why is this stuff being imported into London? The market for illegal hardwood is China.'

'There seems to be nothing hidden inside the wood, and anyway, you'd use cheap pine to hide stuff, not something illegal to start with,' continued Mo.

'We're looking at a hell of a lot of wood,' added Georgie.

'So we've still got nothing.' Angus's voice was flat. He rubbed his forehead, trying to smooth away the tension lines. 'If Christos *is* hiding something on the *Saracen*, we'll find it.' He nodded his head towards the tonnes of rotting meat outside on the dock. 'I've even seen that used before. Smugglers might think they're being original, but nothing is a surprise to us, absolutely nothing.' He paused. 'But find me something, get this thing moving. You're not the only ones with a boss.'

They left his office and Georgie told Mo she wanted to have a look at something. She walked along the quay to one of the customs storage facilities, stacked with impounded goods from all corners of the globe. She had a quick chat with the man organising crates at the entrance and went to look at Christos's container of logs. They were unsawn, still with their bark. Each trunk was about two metres across, giant, jungle-fixing trophies. She was looking at one of the most magnificent things the earth produced. Cut down in its prime and stacked in a cold metal box in a warehouse. What a waste. She hoiked herself over the first trunk and began to walk into a space along the side.

'Ever seen what a weight like that'll do to your bones?'

She turned too quickly and banged her head on top of the container. A man in his fifties with a serious weight problem and too little hair stood behind her. 'Come out slowly. The whole thing's unstable. Logs like that'll crush you to death.'

'I just wanted to have another look. It's beautiful stuff.'

He blinked at her as if she had started talking Bantu. 'I've got imitation Gucci jackets, fake Sony PlayStations, a ton of knock-off Marlboros, and you want to look at wood.'

She jumped down from the logs and held out her hand. 'I should have introduced myself. Georgie Bell, Customs and Excise, from up in the offices.'

He didn't take her hand. 'One of the new ones.' He said it without affection.

She put her hands in her pockets, pulled herself taller. If he wanted to play it this way, that was fine by her.

She saw that nearby was a small table where another man close to retirement sat on a swivel chair, a copy of the *Sun* in his hands. She could see a portable radio through the steam from two teas rising lazily in the warehouse draughts.

She ignored the first man and bent to look closely at the grain of the rosewood end-on. She traced a finger across it, the whorls and circles of life rough from where the teeth of the chainsaw had chewed through. The man didn't move away.

She stood up, heard the banging of boxes being moved further across the warehouse. A young man was stacking crates in a corner by himself. He was the only one wearing the regulation safety hat. 'Do you have a copy of the reports that were done on this wood?'

The two men looked at each other. 'You've got those in the office, no?' the first one said.

'Can't you find a copy here?'

He shrugged. 'I could, but . . .'

You're too bloody lazy to, thought Georgie.

'You can get them when you go back upstairs.'

The man sitting by the table yawned as he turned a page of his paper. Now Georgie got angry. Laziness was an unforgivable sin in her eyes. 'You read that page already. Or can't you read?'

Both men looked at each other and burst into sniggers. 'Feisty!'

The man turned the *Sun*, held up page four, pretending to read. The topless Page 3 teenager grinned through newsprint at Georgie.

'Why don't you two just fuck right off?'

Their smiles got broader, they held up their hands in mock surrender. 'Can't you take a joke?'

'Yeah, don't get so touchy . . .'

'She's a new recruit who likes smelly boxes.' The two men roared.

'You take orders from the office, right?' Georgie said. 'I want to see the dog handler's report on this wood.'

'It's already been done.'

'Do it again.'

They weren't laughing now. The one holding the *Sun* had

turned deadly serious. 'Run along back to the office, little girl, this is where the big boys work.'

'And I want the density check done again. I'll come back in three hours.'

She left the warehouse, glancing briefly at the silent young guy by the crates. The word 'bitch' seemed to float on the drifting currents of air behind her.

27

It was strange for Ricky actually to talk to the woman who'd put him behind bars. He'd got her number from the London theatre and had just phoned her up. They were courteous with each other, amiable. Ricky found he quite liked lying, pretending to be someone he wasn't. He'd had to act tough to survive the worst that jail threw up, but he hadn't been forced to change who he really was. Dawn's passion for make-believe had meant convincing Kelly that he was a prospective client had been straightforward. He could talk the talk without struggle.

She didn't offer to meet at her house, that would have been too much good fortune for Ricky, and he knew life wasn't like that. She had a studio at the docks where she kept the large-scale pieces – a Chinese New Year dragon that was never used, a collection of Janus masks, two extra white rabbits from an *Alice in Wonderland* production. She talked a lot. Too much, Ricky thought. You revealed your weak spots if you talked a lot. Her location was interesting too; she couldn't stay away from the big ships. Her husband had worked at Southampton docks before he died, along with her kid. A boating accident, his lawyer had said.

The studio was bigger than he was expecting, next to a row of low offices and a car park. He sat in the car and watched the doorway. She came on time, wrapped up in a large black coat and wearing a black beret. She unlocked the door and it banged shut behind her. Fifteen minutes later the pay as you go phone on the passenger seat rang and then beeped with a message. She was wondering where he was. An hour later she came back out the door. She had waited a long time for him, but then maybe others had got lost trying to get out to the docks. She walked to an Audi and drove off and he followed.

When she pulled into the underground garage at St Pancras he spent some time staring at the upper levels. She lived in a building with gargoyles on it. There had been a time when he had aspired to that, had felt that big and brash was how you judged worth. He had fancied himself a player, skimming off from deals at the docks, imagining his influence growing not steadily and slowly, but in leaps and bounds. Someone had plotted his fall, someone else had been there to move in when he was removed. That's why he had been so full of rage, spouting about getting his contacts to kill the witness who had seen him, about getting his crook's version of justice. How counterproductive. It had forced her into witness protection; they had obviously thought him dangerous enough to carry out his threats, and his shouty nature had cost the state a fortune and changed her life for ever.

But he had changed, too. His rage had died. He had taken a long look at himself and it had been hard. What he had been doing was illegal, after all. A lot of people did get hurt. He had become a model prisoner, whatever that was, got educated, took down the tension among the long-timers, encouraged the youngsters to keep going. His years inside had been catastrophic for his finances and that used to make him angry, that Dawn had to scrimp. But now he was less interested in clock towers and gargoyles. He preferred to read, do his Open University courses, work with young offenders, walk the dogs, listen to talk radio.

He had a greater capacity to change than he would ever have imagined. A life unexamined is a life unlived, he'd read somewhere. But he still had curiosity. He wanted to know, to understand why.

He drove away.

Kelly was alone in the flat. She was on edge; the man who'd rung about a potential job hadn't shown or called, and she was nonplussed. She went into the bathroom and popped open her bottle of pills. She would take just one more today, just to keep the anxiety at bay.

The bottle was empty. She actually saw herself, as if disembodied, turn the bottle over and shake it, trying to make the small white pills reappear. She felt panic begin to climb her spine. She forced herself to think. She took two yesterday. Was that why there were none left? She couldn't remember. A total blank.

She took a deep breath. Practical steps, think practically. She would go to the doctor's, get a repeat prescription. She went down in the lift, five, four, three, two, one second. She opened the lobby door and stepped out into the street. The sun was struggling to break through the cloud cover, but she found it too bright none the less. She felt a headache beginning its rhythmic thump. She turned right and under a grand arch into St Pancras.

The station was rammed with people pushing trolleys teetering with suitcases and holdalls to trains and away to taxi queues. The walls were lined with more bags, stacked high on top of each other. What was all this stuff that got carted through life? she wondered. The other day she had left with just a handbag for her and her two children; these people couldn't last two days without baggage they couldn't physically carry.

In the main concourse a group of students was exploiting Halloween. There were ghouls and ghosts holding a high banner with a pumpkin drawn on it; two women dressed as witches danced and cackled nearby. They were shaking their charity collection buckets, and the chinking of the coins against plastic sounded like the grinding of heavy chains . . . Kelly took a deep breath and focused on walking forward. The crowd was large here; she turned this way and that, searching for a faster route. She looked over her shoulder and caught the face of a man in a fishing hat, who was staring at her as they moved past one another. Ten years fell away in an instant. He looked like Michael, was it Michael? Kelly whirled round, searching for the hat. She had to see him again, had to understand that her mind was playing tricks, that it wasn't – that it couldn't be – him. A ghoul was near her shoulder, the clanking of the charity bucket by her ear. 'Hand over your pennies, or the dead will haunt you!' One of the witches let out a mock scream. The ghoul put his hand on her shoulder as she saw the man in the fishing hat beyond the line of taxis outside the station. She ran after him, the hollering of a ghost chasing her out. She crossed the road and headed into King's Cross Station. The concourse was being rebuilt, drills clamouring away unseen. A sign proclaimed that the enlarged and improved station could handle forty-five million passengers a year. There was a new roof soaring above her, making people look tiny in the huge expanse.

She stood in the concourse of King's Cross among the thousands of commuters, residents, tourists and hustlers of a big city rail terminus. She saw the sign for Harry Potter's Platform 9¾, the platform that didn't exist, half a baggage trolley fixed to the wall as if disappearing into the brickwork. Two grinning children were having their picture taken beside it. She hunted with her eyes, scanning thousands of faces to find Michael, all similar and none of them the one she wanted. It seemed as if a tide of humanity were rushing past her, hundreds and hundreds of faces, and then the iron will she'd used to keep a lid on her emotions for all these years began to slide away. She started to look for Amber. She was rotating on the spot in the huge station, faster and faster she turned as the crowds pressed past her, little children everywhere, little girls with their hair in bunches, young girls with balloons, young girls dragging on their mothers' hands. And the panic and the loss rose and rose until like a great wave it crashed over her and she was collapsing on the new floor of the station and she was screaming Amber's name, screaming for her dead daughter and her lost husband, hollering for them, her voice louder and more insistent than the drills and the cranes and the cement mixers that were transforming the place into something she didn't recognise. She sensed children being dragged away from her, bystanders gawping, people averting their eyes, lest she infect them with her madness and her grief.

After a few moments a woman in a Network Rail uniform and a policeman came and hurried her away to wait for an ambulance.

28

Kelly sat on the back step of an ambulance parked outside King's Cross. She was beyond calm now, deadened by her outburst, her tired limbs leaden, her throat sore. A paramedic was taking her blood pressure, checking her pupils. She rested her head against the hard metal of the door as he tapped her arm, trying to bring her round, like she was a faulty appliance that needed a nudge to get started.

She stood up uncertainly, apologised for taking up their time and moved away. She headed for the doctor's for a repeat prescription and an hour later had her replacement pills. She wanted nothing more than to get into bed and go to sleep, but when she got home and came out of the lift, someone was already there.

Sylvie heard Kelly come back in to the flat – the mid-afternoon amble round doing nothing much must be over. She didn't bother to call out, Kelly would find her soon enough. She continued to hunt through the bureau in the living room for the papers that Christos had ordered be found. Like *now*. She pushed one drawer shut and opened the one below it. It was an ugly piece of furniture that she would be glad to see the back of when she moved in here. She'd commission something special for this corner. She tried to sort through a heap of junk. Was there anything this wife actually did? She certainly didn't clean out drawers. With pleasure, Sylvie heard Kelly's high and reedy voice, pleading to know what Sylvie was doing in her house.

She turned casually and saw Kelly standing at the top of the stairs clutching the banister, dark-eyed and wild-haired. She looked like she'd shrunk, even from when she'd last seen her. 'Oh hi, Kelly. I'm just looking for something.'

'Get out of my house.'

The empty threats were tedious. Just a lot of hot air. 'Don't worry, I'm going.'

'You think it's OK to come into my house and start digging around in stuff?'

'I'm picking up some papers for Christos.'

'Where did you get the keys?'

'Your husband gave them to me.'

'You can give them back to me.'

Sylvie shrugged and handed them over. She wasn't interested in Kelly any more. In fact, she bored her. Kelly had put up a fight; her running with the kids and quite a stash of money had shocked her and Christos. He had been unaware of the money Kelly had collected *and* the passports. Sylvie had noted that he didn't have the greatest eye for the details, but then *she* did, so it wasn't an issue – and she had insisted they now watch Kelly a lot more closely – but that problem had been dealt with and it was nearly all over, bar a little unpleasantness.

'He'll never leave me, you know, never let me go. He'll never give up the children.'

Sylvie smiled. The wife was clutching at straws. She came towards Kelly and sighed. 'Maybe that's what you hope. Maybe you think I'm stuck in the mistress trap, hanging around to wait and please.'

'I don't care what trap you're in.'

'After all, why would he want to let you go? Tragedy has defined you, put you on a pedestal that no one can knock over. We always want what we can't get, ain't that the truth?' She couldn't resist, was close enough to Kelly to put out a hand and clasp her chin with her palm, as soft as a cat's paw. Kelly didn't pull away. Her eyes were large and brown and bloodshot, transfixed by Sylvie, as if she were seeing her for the first time.

'Has he hit you?' Kelly asked. 'Tell me, has he ever?'

'Jesus, Kelly, of course not! You need to see the doctor again—' But she had clearly made up her mind, had the vanity to assume what befell her must happen to all of her sex.

'You need to know what he's like, what he does to women—'

'Sshh.'

People tended to do what you wanted, if you just told them in the right way. Kelly was silent as Sylvie ran a finger along her jawline, still so firm, the skin smooth. She had always been fascinated by skin, the way it held everything in – yet what festered inside tended to pop out now and again. Skin to skin with Kelly was as close as one could ever get. She felt as if her fingers were merging with Kelly's face, the tiny hairs crushed by her palm. How she would love to have skin like that. For an intense second she wondered how much softer the skin on Kelly's inner thigh would be, or in the crook of her elbow. 'You're fucking beautiful.' Sylvie sighed. 'Beautiful people are so alluring, don't you think?'

The spell was broken. Kelly staggered backward. Sylvie noted with detachment that she nearly fell down the stairs. 'You sound just like him.'

This angered her, Kelly's misreading of where the power lay. 'You got that wrong, honey. *He* sounds like *me*.' She turned to pick up her bag, annoyed that she had been riled by her. She popped the handles of her orange bag over her shoulder and watched Kelly twisting with discomfort and outrage that she was here in her house. For the first time ever Kelly looked dishevelled and old, her padded black coat had a mud stain on the front, left from a clinging child's rain boot or a football kicked in anger. How low women had to stoop to live the dream, how much children made you give. 'Why do you have to wear those dark clothes?' she snapped. 'Can't you mix it up a bit?' She shook her head with frustration. She walked past Kelly, down the stairs, consoling herself by bouncing her fingers on the banisters as she went, in just the way she had seen Kelly do it.

29

Georgie was waiting for Sylvie to arrive at the Customs and Excise offices. She was late for their afternoon meeting, and Georgie was getting annoyed. It wasn't like she had to come far, Malamatos Shipping offices were nearby. When she finally arrived she was ushered in and sat down on a swivel chair, swinging her legs slowly from side to side. The gaudy pattern on her tunic showed up the drabness of the surroundings.

'Thanks for coming,' began Georgie. 'This is an informal interview. Do you enjoy working at Malamatos Shipping?'

'What is this? A happiness survey? It doesn't matter if I love it or loathe it, it's my job, and I do it the best I can.'

'Would you say it's a happy place to work? Are the staff contented?'

'If they don't feel lucky, they should. The recession is hammering shipping, like everything else. They should be thankful they have a job.'

'How long have you worked there?'

'Three years.'

'As Christos's PA?'

She nodded.

'So you work pretty closely with him, don't you?'

'Of course.'

'You're a director of his charitable foundation, is that correct?'

Sylvie nodded, not taking her eyes off Georgie. 'I've been doing it for two years.'

'It's an extra responsibility on top of your job?'

'Yes. It's voluntary and unpaid.'

'Did Mrs Malamatos ever want to get involved, that you know of?'

Sylvie made a dismissive sound. 'I doubt it. I'm sure it was just *too* much for her. After all, keeping house and looking after a couple of kids takes up so much time. Or maybe she just thought she was above it.' The sarcasm was dripping from her.

Georgie frowned. 'So Kelly was never much involved in the charity?'

'That pill-popping wreck's no good to anyone.'

Georgie glanced at Mo, who was twisting his watch strap round and round.

'You'd think his wife would lift a finger, but in the end I did it. And I enjoy it.'

'How often do you visit the charity offices?'

She thought for a moment. 'A few times a year, for meetings.'

'Have you ever seen any trucks in the yard opposite the charity's office? Any unhitched trailers?'

'I wouldn't remember.'

'The thing is, the shipment of illegal Brazilian rosewood that has been found on your employer's ship had a destination that has an address opposite your charity, Ms Lockhart.'

'I know nothing about that at all. The charity helps disadvantaged children – Christos has donated a large sum of money over the years.'

'Do you have the dates of when the meetings took place?'

Sylvie wasn't fazed. 'Of course. I'll refer to them myself, since I'm a meticulous record-keeper. I don't have to get anyone else to look it up for me.'

'If you could get that information to us, and let us know when Christos attended those meetings too.'

'You know this investigation is going nowhere. It's a dead-end.'

'That's not what the evidence shows so far.'

She shrugged. 'Someone is trying to bring Christos down. They want to muscle in on his business.'

'And who might that be?'

She gave Georgie a look like she was something unwelcome on the sole of her stiletto. 'Anyone. Everyone. Shipping is facing tough times. People think it's all Onassis and hanging out on yachts on the Riviera, but margins are tiny, risks are high. Christos has succeeded because he's been focused and cleverer than the competition.'

'He's got big debts actually.'

Sylvie snorted. 'Show me a successful businessman who hasn't. It's how money is made. If people have been badmouthing him it's because success makes people bitter. It makes them want to take a slice.'

'Is your affair with him taking a slice?'

She didn't even blink. 'An affair isn't illegal, last time I looked, or any of your business, for that matter.'

'But it must make it easier to overlook practices that other people might find unacceptable.'

'Such as?'

'Containers dropping out of sight, so to speak. Mistakes in labelling—'

'I've never seen such things, or participated in them.'

Georgie heard Mo sigh. They weren't getting anything here. 'If you could get us those dates, that would be great.' She stood up. 'Anything else you'd like to add?'

'No.' Sylvie turned and walked out of the room without bothering to say goodbye.

Mo let out a sharp breath which had too much of a hint of admiration in it for Georgie's liking. 'Now that is one ballbreaker, so help me God.'

'Yes,' added Georgie. 'You have to have pretty big balls to have an affair with Christos Malamatos.'

Mo grunted. 'Bigger than mine.'

Georgie frowned. 'What about the wife? She strike you as having—'

Mo shook his head. 'Just the opposite. Men like him, they marry the meek ones and fuck the high-maintenance nightmares.'

'Maybe,' Georgie said, not sounding convinced. 'But in the war of the mistress and the wife, the wife has kept the man.'

'Maybe he loves her.'

She shook her head. 'It's not that. She must be a ballbreaker who doesn't look like a ballbreaker.'

'See?' said Mo, throwing up his hands. 'I've said it before: there is not a romantic bone in your body, G. Why are you frowning?'

'We need to talk to the wife again. There's something she's not telling us.'

'Anguish isn't going to like it. I'm not going in there with you when you tell him.'

But Georgie's mind was made up. 'Call it women's intuition, if you like, but I'll get something out of her.'

30

Georgie had to cycle home at the end of the day in the rain; she was cold and soaked by the time she got back. She had to chain the bike to a lamppost. Ryan's car was in the garage and there was no extra space to get the bike in as a new bag of golf clubs was blocking her path. She came in the front door, shaking water from her like a dog emerging from a lake.

She flopped down on the couch next to Ryan, pushing aside a PlayStation console and a *Nuts* magazine, dropping her wet bag on the floor, moving it so it didn't get too close to the gas fire belching out its drowsy heat and causing rivulets of condensation to stream down the ill-fitting windows. Matt popped his head out of the kitchen at the back and did a double-take. 'Bad day at the coalface?'

She grunted. He disappeared and a moment later reappeared, wordlessly holding up a can of beer. She nodded and he tossed it across the room at her. She couldn't resist a smile. She took a long gulp of beer, kicking off her shoes and lying back for a moment, relishing a Friday night relax. She didn't even have the luxury of a full weekend to look forward to, she was working again tomorrow. 'Whose are those golf clubs?' She saw Matt and Ryan exchange looks. 'For Christ's sake, don't tell me, I don't want to know.'

'Then why do you ask?' Ryan asked, head down, killing zombies.

She groaned in frustration.

Ryan, without even looking at her, threw his console on the floor, pulled her to him, his bulky arm round her shoulder, and squeezed her as tight as he could. 'Moody G, I see.'

She fought him off, but not very hard and a moment later was snuggled into him, laying her head on his shoulder. 'I'm tired.'

'Uncle Ed's coming round.'

She yanked her head off his shoulder. 'Oh God, no. I can't take that, not tonight.'

'Oh, give him a break. You know Dad likes it – he brings him out of himself.'

'I wish you . . . I wish . . .' She tailed off, head sinking back on the couch. Her dad and brothers were hapless, slip-sliding over the line between right and wrong, skating on thin ice with rules and regulations. But Uncle Ed was over the line. Too far over, and he couldn't get back.

'I'm going out,' she said, but the front door was already opening and loud voices were crowding the living room. She pulled her wet shoes back on.

Dad and Uncle Ed came into the lounge. 'Hi, how was your day?' Dad asked, heading for the kitchen.

'G. How's my girl, eh?' Uncle Ed came towards her slowly, arms outstretched, luxuriating in his welcome. Seconds later she was face down in his camel coat, being held there by his strong hands for so long that she eventually had to pull away.

'I'm just on my way out.'

'Not so fast.' He sat down in Dad's recliner and pushed the footrest up. She was presented with the scored soles of his shoes, the Blakey's wearing away on the heels. 'How's your job going?' He was looking at her, his cold blue eyes unflinching.

Ryan shook his head. 'I can tell by her body language. Not good.'

'Mmm. That so?' They were talking about her as if she weren't even in the room.

Matt's head came round the door to the kitchen. 'Whisky, Uncle Ed?'

He held up two fingers in reply.

'I don't want to talk about work, not when I've just come home.'

Uncle Ed smiled, his very white, capped teeth a hard line in his mouth. 'If you ask me, it's a man causing you trouble. Always is, in my experience. What's the guy's name who's making you lose your beauty sleep?'

Dad came and slumped on the couch so she sat down again next to him, Ryan squeezed in on her other side. She didn't reply, trying to tell by the smell how many her dad had had in the pub.

'Come on, give us something to talk about,' Uncle Ed added. 'To speculate and gossip about. People are losing the art of conversation.' He stared at Ryan, head down to his phone. He didn't pick up on the hint.

'It's a shipping guy we're investigating, that's all.'

'Well, of course it's a bloody shipping guy.' He turned and laughed easily with Dad. 'What do I look like to you – stupid?' She saw Dad draining the can of beer, placing it carefully on the carpet by the couch. He opened another. 'How long you been there now? A year?' She looked away, trying to block him out. He gave a sharp shake of his head, as if thinking things unsayable. 'They're taking your best years, G. Before you know it, you'll be old and cranky like your dad here, with nothing to show for it.' He took the glass Matt had brought in to him and took a long sip. 'You wear that to work, do you?' He pointed the glass at her flat, dark lace-ups, her rain-soaked Gap trousers. 'You need make-up, a bit of voom. Now Ryan's Shelley—'

Georgie stood in a hurry. 'Thanks for the life coaching, I'm off out now in the freezing cold and wet.'

They crowded round, the men of her family, her dad

pulling her back to the sofa, Ryan offering a run for fish and chips.

'I'm just saying, the dice is stacked against you doing your job—'

'And he knows all about stacked dice, doesn't he, Dad?' she shot back.

Uncle Ed folded his hands round his stomach and smiled. 'Come on, what's his name, this shipping guy? Got a phone number? If you've got a number I can try something.'

'What's this *something* you can try?'

'Listen in on his messages, see who he's been talking to—'

'Oh stop.' She actually laughed out loud. 'You want to hack his phone? Are you seriously suggesting that?'

Uncle Ed swirled his whisky. 'I help you, you can help me down the line.'

'Just so we're clear, it's against the law, I can't use anything you find anyway, and I'd lose my job. Got it?'

Uncle Ed's contentment became Buddha-like.

Ryan sat forward on the couch. 'You can listen in on what other people are saying on their phones? How d'you do that then?' He stared at his phone as if it might provide the answer on the screen.

'Not what they're saying, their messages. You can listen to messages.' Uncle Ed turned back to Georgie. 'Remember, that dice is never going to roll you a six. Not without a little Uncle Ed help.'

She stood up again. 'But you're not my uncle, are you, really.' She moved to the door in silence. His leg shot out from the recliner to stop her going. Her family members were statues, Uncle Ed's eyes were hard and menacing. She'd said the unsayable, charged into dangerous territory.

'They're bent down there, bent as a two bob note.' His voice was low and quiet, thick with menace.

She said nothing.

'Back in the seventies, oh I remember, don't you, Vic?' He swung his glass towards Dad. 'The stuff we lifted off them ships.' Dad was nodding, staring glassy-eyed into his beer. 'All unionised then. Not a squeak unless you were carded. Not like now. Everyone for theirselves now.' He gave her a pointed look. 'Remember, G, there's always gotta be inside help. Your shipper's got someone on the inside. That's your Uncle Ed's advice. To beat them you got to be like them.'

She stepped over his leg and out of the room. 'I think I'd rather let him get away with it.' But she said it quietly enough that she was sure he wouldn't hear.

31

Mo was sitting at his desk, Tango in one hand, ear buds in the other, trying to offer Georgie some advice. 'I heard what you did at the warehouse for impounded goods yesterday, pulling rank on the lazy old-timers. You need to be careful. They work for customs, but they're dockers at heart. They can make life difficult.'

Georgie disagreed. 'My dad and my so-called Uncle Ed were dockers; they're not scary, they're fucking eejits.'

'Even so, you need to watch it. Don't be naïve. Imagine running an investigation with that lot trying to block you at every turn. It's hard enough as it is.'

They were looking at the records for May, two weeks either side of the landing date for the last visit of the *Saracen*. Checking the records of hundreds of containers on trade that never stopped. The docks were operating 24/7, 365 days a year. It was methodical, boring work, but Georgie was convinced they would get there in the end. Trade always left a trail. It might be a needle in a haystack, but if you looked hard enough, a needle glinted in the sun.

'Thanks for the concern, but I can take care of myself. Now we should look for consignments being delivered to potential shell companies, companies that don't exist,' Georgie suggested, keen to move on from their disagreement.

'Whatever.' Mo didn't look up. He was still in a bad mood with her.

It was hopeless. She threw her pencil down and went to

get some fresh air, standing in the car park in a patch of sun watching the cranes as they inched across the sky. She saw the two men from impounded goods walking away from the warehouse up to the pub. She looked at her watch. It was five to twelve; they were breaking for an early, and no doubt long, Saturday lunch.

She noticed that the young guy she'd seen with them moving crates in the warehouse was in the car park, pulling a tyre from the boot of an ancient Astra. She walked over. 'Can I help?'

He had the jack under the chassis and was wheeling the tyre over. 'I don't need no help.'

'What's your name?'

'Lukas.'

He was Polish. 'You been here long?'

He shrugged and didn't look at her, attaching the wrench to the lug nuts and yanking hard.

'I'm up in the offices.'

Still no answer. He had two of the nuts off already and was straining on the third.

'Sometimes they need a good kick.'

He glanced up at her and stood for a moment and she saw him scan the car park behind her, checking who was there. He didn't want to be seen associating with the wrong people.

'Come on, how long have you been here?'

'Four years.'

'You like your job?'

'It's a job.'

'How about your bosses? Do you like them?' She smiled.

He gave her a curt nod. He was being cagey; he'd learned to be careful.

'You can grow to hate your boss.'

He looked up at her but didn't answer.

'Here, let me help you.' She held out her foot. 'You hold the wrench and I'll stand on it.'

She held on to the car and put a foot on the wrench. 'You left family behind in Poland?'

'All of them.'

'You've come a long way to get on. Made a lot of sacrifices.'

'We all must work. There's no other way.'

She lifted her other foot off the ground and held on to the car. 'You know, I realised something the other day. There's no English phrase for the American dream. I find that strange, considering what I see.' She bounced up and down on the wrench but it didn't budge. 'How do you find England? London?'

He was staring at the wrench and made a gesture for her to get down. He aimed a forceful kick down on the metal. The nut moved.

'Chatty, eh?'

He said nothing.

Georgie wasn't about to give up, his silence only made her keener to press on. 'How old are you?'

'Twenty-seven.'

She glanced around, they were still alone. 'Tell me, how many promotions you had in four years?'

'None.' He moved the wrench to the last lug nut and stamped again and the nut slipped. A few moments later the wheel was off. No promotion in four years, in a service understaffed and with recruitment problems.

'Lukas, you can change this situation. You don't have to remain the underdog. Those men you're working for, how many years have they got left? They're five years from retirement? Ten? It comes quicker than you think.'

He was listening now, turning the wrench slowly to do up the lug nuts with the new tyre in place.

'If you want to get on, you need help. From people like yourself, and that means people like me. Not like them.'

He straightened and was now taller than her, the jack a heavy weight in his large hands.

'If you see or hear anything you don't like, about goods going missing or rumours about certain containers . . .' She trailed off, letting what she'd said sink in.

He walked slowly round to the boot and put the jack in it.

She followed. 'When the baton is passed, you want to make sure you're in a position to take it, before it's grabbed by someone else less deserving.'

He picked up the dud tyre as if it weighed nothing and put it back in the boot and slammed the door shut.

'Think about it. We can help each other. One underdog to another.'

He didn't reply. He didn't say a word, but he was looking at her, his expression impossible to read. He wiped his grease-stained hands on his thighs and locked the car and walked away back to the warehouse.

32

The weather at sea had changed with dawn, the blue sky and harsh sunlight replaced by a high band of white cloud and a cooler wind. The waves were crowned with white spray, the ship ploughing relentlessly onwards. The Wolf had done his four-hour shift and was coming to the end of his break. He was on the bridge with the President and Jonas. He was telling their new traveller all their worst stories, and Jonas was lapping them up.

'And then there was that time I was in Pakistan, stinking hot it was, and there was an armed guard at the end of the gangway telling us we couldn't get off the ship in case we were kidnapped and filmed having our heads cut off and posted on the Internet and I said, "Fuck that, I'm a merchant seaman, I'm fucking hard." And I got off the ship and I went looking for a drink. I'm fucking looking for a beer in Karachi!'

They laughed. 'It's a shame we're not going to Singapore,' added the Wolf, warming to his theme. He could feel the manic energy rising in him on the crest of the beer and the stories, his need to impress and his desire to have a good time.

'Stop ribbing the guy,' said the President.

'We can go to the mall.' He paused. 'You can visit the four floors of whores. There's a place at the mall in Singapore called the four floors of whores.'

Jonas shrugged. 'I've been there already.'

The Wolf cheered and slapped him rather too hard on the arm.

The President called Jonas up to where he was sitting. 'This is our course.' He pointed at the computer screens in front of him. 'This is our GPS position and this is the weather.' The Wolf noticed the tight concentric rings like a pinwheel covering most of the mid-Atlantic and touching on the shores of North Africa.

'There's a storm coming.'

The President nodded. 'Enjoy the weather now, Jonas, it'll get bumpy later.'

'Is that a big storm?' asked Jonas.

The Wolf slapped him on the arm again. 'Not for this great monster of a ship. That's when the fun begins.' He looked out of the bridge window at the containers, stacked end to end and high above the sides of the ship.

The President was more circumspect. 'If they're not lashed down good and tight they can go over, and what can be lost can be incalculable.'

The Wolf made a show of pumping his biceps. 'But with these muscles on the job it's no bother. Come on, I'll take you for a cycle.'

Jonas looked astonished. 'What do you mean?'

'The ship's so big we get around it by bike.' He wanted to keep Jonas close, find out more about him. His story didn't stack up. He looked and acted poor but travelling home on a ship was much more expensive than taking a flight. It was also a better route to try to get something back to England without anyone checking the contents of luggage too closely. The Wolf had noticed the old army rucksack on the floor of Jonas's cabin, how he carefully locked the door behind him as he left.

Jonas followed him down the steps of the bridge and along the tight corridors, down clanging metal stairs and past the cabins.

'Did you sleep OK?' the Wolf asked Jonas.

'I was out like a light.'

I wouldn't trust you as far as I could throw you, the Wolf thought. On a ship as big as this, it was too much of a temptation for a thief not to have a good look around, see what could be snatched. He wouldn't put it past Jonas to be light-fingered.

'How was your night?'

'Quiet,' the Wolf lied. He had known Luciana would probably be fun, but she had been more useful than he had imagined. She had spent a long time last night massaging the fingers on his right hand, trying to get the feeling back in them. Using the chainsaw a few days ago had brought on vibration white finger, the repetitive stress injury that had taken him out of the lumberjack trade in the first place and put him on ships.

He looked down at the index and middle finger of his right hand. They were a pale, waxy colour, the blood drained from them. He looked away.

Ten minutes later he was cycling with Jonas through a narrow walkway between a high canyon of containers. It was gloomy and cold down here, the sun never penetrating. 'There's a tamper-proof seal here' – he showed Jonas the plastic circle with the line of numbers on the door of each container – 'and a twist lock system keeps the containers in place.' They rode along to the prow of the ship and stood looking north over the Atlantic. The wind had picked up and was blowing strongly now, pushing the Wolf's hair away from his face and sticking his T-shirt to his chest.

'What's inside these containers?' asked Jonas.

The Wolf stared back at the wall of metal behind them. 'All the riches of the world, my friend.' He paused. 'And all its sorrows. Some say if you stand here on a still night you can fancy you can hear the shouts of those trapped inside. The ones who paid or hid to get a better life, inside the cans.'

'You're yanking my chain.'

The Wolf shrugged as they walked along pushing their bikes, like a couple of ten-year-olds in the park. 'The world is brutal and tough, people will do a lot for a better life. But you try hiding in the corner of one of these monsters, walled up behind other crates, for weeks at a time. It would eat at your sanity.'

'This one is missing.' Jonas had stopped by a battered pale blue container, whose door didn't have a security seal. The Wolf swore softly, knowing the captain would have to be told, forms filled out. He made a note of the four-digit code written on the side of the container and they walked on.

'Have you ever found stowaways?'

The Wolf paused. 'Just once. It was a bad business.' He paused and picked away some peeling paint on the rail with a fingernail. He stared out across the ocean. The vast expanse of nothing tended to make people contemplate. This had been a problem that had frayed his nerves when the Wolf was first on the job, but he had become de-sensitised to it over the years. 'People disappear on ships, Jonas. It's the Wild West out here, the usual rules don't apply.' He turned his bicycle round and grinned. 'Come on, let's get you back to safety. You know the one advantage of cycling on a ship? You never have to lock your bike, cos no one can steal it.' He looked Jonas straight in the eye. Jonas's eyes flitted to his for a moment and then looked away.

33

Kelly could feel the manic energy pulsating from Christos as he paced the living room. He was putting her on edge. Twelve steps across to one bank of windows, swivel, turn, twelve steps back. She moved silently past him to pick up a discarded cup on the coffee table and glanced at his iPad. Before the screen switched to black she saw a weather chart of the Atlantic, large concentric rings radiating out from a tight centre. A storm at sea.

She moved into the kitchen to get out of his way and glimpsed Medea placing some papers back in the bin and closing the lid. She had been rifling through its discarded contents again. She could hear the loud drone of the TV from downstairs where the children were watching cartoons.

Her husband came in after her. 'Sit down.'

She wasn't going to disagree.

Medea walked over to the far counter and picked up a pile of papers, walked back slowly to the table. Kelly bit down her irritation. It was all an act; the woman could sprint if it was to her advantage. 'I've got the brochures,' Medea said to Christos.

The vein began to twitch in Kelly's eye. 'What brochures?'

'Have a look,' said Medea. 'You need to study them and then we can all make an informed decision.'

Kelly felt the floor slide away from her. She caught a glimpse of a large Edwardian building set in landscaped gardens on the cover of one of the brochures in her mother-in-law's hands. She was going to be shut up in a madhouse, walled up in a psychiatric facility, like a Victorian melodrama where a wife who had become inconvenient was stored, never to see the light of the world again.

'We think the children should go to boarding school.'

So this was how he planned to punish her, through the children. 'They are not going to boarding school.' She saw Christos and his mother exchange looks. Kelly felt the anger beginning to flare inside her. They'd already decided. It was another sign that she didn't exist. 'Yannis is only seven years old.'

'He's been getting into trouble at school,' said Christos.

'Lots of children get into trouble at school,' Kelly answered. 'You can't send him away so young.'

'Hush, child,' said Medea.

'Stop calling me a child – I'm a grown woman.'

Medea narrowed her eyes at Kelly and took a deep intake of breath. 'Be careful, Kelly. Children need a calm environment. Shouting is bad for everybody.'

Kelly gripped the sides of her chair to stop losing control. The hypocrisy was breathtaking. This, from a woman who had never lived further than a mile from her son, who was still living with him when he was nearly fifty, like an East German Stasi spy, noting, judging and condemning.

Kelly knew defiance wouldn't work so she tried to reason with them. 'They are so young. Just wait a few years till we know more about how their characters are forming, then we can make the decision.'

'This needs quick and decisive action,' Christos said. 'They will have the benefits of some of the finest schooling available. How can you not want that for your children?'

'This is too soon, they are too young. They need the love and guidance of their family.'

'After what's happened, I think this is the best for everyone,' Medea added.

Kelly picked up the brochures and scanned the front pages. One of the schools was in Somerset, the other in Yorkshire. He'd chosen well, they were miles apart. It would never be possible for her to collect them both without him knowing beforehand . . .

Put the children far away and she had no reason to run. Put the children far away and she would never be missed by anyone. They were the last tie making her real. He would, and could, make her disappear.

'I think they should start at the beginning of November.'

'But it's October 27th!'

'The schools are amenable to them starting right away, halfway through the term. That way they'll be fully adjusted to it by Christmas.'

It couldn't be. She began to beg. 'Please, Christos, I won't run away again, please don't send them away.'

'Yannis is acting up, and Florence, she's so silent, too withdrawn for a child of her age. A change of scene will bring her out of herself,' Medea said.

'She is not withdrawn.' Kelly was getting exasperated. 'When did you go and see these schools anyway? Why was I not consulted?'

'Sylvie went to take a look at the schools,' Christos said.

'Sylvie. Does Sylvie have children?'

'Hush, child—'

'I'm not a child.' She turned to Christos. 'You send your PA, who has no children, to choose a school for them? It's a bloody insult. They need their mother.'

'Kelly—' Medea was too close to her now, her sandalwood perfume cloying.

'And you, you talk about childrearing like you made a success of it – look at the monster you raised!'

Medea slapped her across the cheek. Not hard, her arms were old and her aim poor. 'A dog from the street will always be a dog from the street.'

Kelly got up from her chair, her anger in full flow. Christos grabbed her arm to stop her. He was looking at the door; the children were standing there. All five of them were frozen in a horrid silent tableau of twisted relationships.

'Mum?' It was Florence, her voice straining to be heard in the large room. 'You said you were going to drop in to the theatre this afternoon and give out the Halloween invitations. Can we come?'

Kelly had to take the time to sit back down and collect herself, shame and anger and disgust battling through her. 'Yes, of course. Go and put your shoes on and we can go.'

They hovered for a moment in the doorway and then retreated.

'Kelly.' Christos was looking at her. 'You can only take one.'

'One what?'

'One child. Not both. You can see my point of view.'

She paused for a moment to let what he was saying sink in. 'You're telling me I can never take both my children—'

'Never.'

She could hear the scratching and cooing of the pigeons trapped in the attic. She could feel the panic beginning to lap around her chest.

'And the school thing has already been decided. They'll go after Halloween. Medea will take them. No point in hanging around once a decision has been made. Sylvie can arrange the details if it's going to stress you.' He paused. 'And one more thing: I want you to tell them they're going away. Now.'

34

'There's something I need to talk to you two about,' Kelly said. 'Something important.' The kids were upstairs in the kitchen, popping olives into their mouths and crunching through breadsticks. They had their shoes on to go to the theatre but they wouldn't be needing them now. She stood in the doorway for a moment just watching them, trying to hold on to every second of the calm before the storm. There was a vivid red sunset beyond them, a strong wind pushing clouds at speed past the windows, throwing shadows fleetingly across the kitchen.

The kids didn't answer, their mouths were too full of food. She pulled out a chair and sat down. 'I need to talk to you about school.'

Yannis groaned.

'Your dad and I . . .' She tailed off. They were still now, sensing the struggle in her voice. She swallowed. 'Your dad thinks you should go to boarding school. That it would be a really great opportunity for you both if you went to boarding school.'

She'd said it. She tasted something on her tongue like ash. She dragged her eyes up from the table to look at them. They glanced at each other.

'What's boarding school?' Yannis asked.

'It's a school in the country where you go and stay with lots of other children and you get a fantastic education.' She was trying to keep her voice upbeat, trying to believe what she was saying herself. 'There are lots of fields and green grass and you can play outdoors loads and make lots of new friends. You can still do your horse-riding, right at the school too.'

Yannis was looking excited, but his joy was punctured by Florence.

'And we have to sleep in a dorm every night and we no longer live with you.' Her voice was cold.

'It's like a sleepover?' Yannis asked.

Florence scoffed. 'No, stupid. You sleep there every night for weeks and weeks.'

'Florence—'

'Will you be there too, Mummy?' Yannis's face had clouded now, his confusion evident.

'No, I won't. I will be here at home, but I will come and see you very often, whenever you want, and at weekends.'

'So you won't be there with Florence and me?'

'No, not all the time. There will be other people who will look after you. But also, Florence will be at one school and you will be at another one. Dad's picked schools that best suit your characters.'

'But I want to be with Florence.'

'I'm afraid that's not possible, Yannis.' He was trying to process what this meant, and she could see he didn't get it. 'You'll have so much more freedom at boarding school, it's a much better place than the city—'

'We went to Lindsey's place. But that wasn't better.' Florence was staring at the floor, her face closing down.

'Yeah, Lindsey's place wasn't better.'

She needed to get this conversation back under control. 'It's hard to imagine what it will be like until you're there.'

'I don't want to leave my friends.' Florence again.

'You can still see your friends in the holidays and you'll make new ones too.'

'Do we have a choice?' she asked.

'It really is for the best.'

'It's the best thing for you, you mean.'

'What do you mean by that?' Her daughter was tracing her finger in a random pattern on the tabletop. 'Look at me, Florence. What do you mean by that?'

She did look at her. The pale eyes stared back at her, but they didn't show confusion or hurt. They showed pity. 'We have to go away because you're ill.'

'What makes you say that?' She could feel the anger beginning to thump its way through her skull.

'You're not well, in the head. You can't look after us.'

'There is nothing wrong with me at all. Who said there was?'

'Dad said you would deny it.'

Kelly opened her mouth and then shut it again. She was teetering on the edge of a world that made no sense, where the more she protested her point of view, the more something else was inferred or believed. 'Look at me, Florence, look at me.' She reached across and put her hand over her daughter's. 'There is nothing at all wrong. I love you both, more than anything; boarding school is a great opportunity that many families would kill for. It will take some adjusting to, that's all.' Kelly pushed the school brochures that she had in her hand over the table towards them. Florence wouldn't touch them. Kelly saw a tear roll silently down her perfect cheek. 'Flo . . .'

She watched her daughter trying to hold back the tears. 'I'll go, but only if it makes you get better quicker. Granny said she didn't think it would, but you have to promise me you'll get better.'

'Mummy! Are you going to die?' Yannis could evidently feel the emotional cross-currents in the room, but he was too young to understand what they meant. Tears were beginning to crest on his bottom lids.

'I am not going to die. There is nothing wrong with me.

It was your dad's decision to send you to boarding school. Medea is a silly old woman who really doesn't know what she's talking about. You mustn't worry.'

A large cloud slid across the low sun, plunging the room into early evening cold. 'Do you have any other questions?'

She saw her children looking at each other, cutting her out. She got up from the table and left the room. She walked on autopilot down the curving stairs, into her bedroom and into her bathroom. She opened the cabinet and pulled out the bottle of pills. She gulped down two, feeling the wash of shame lap at her as she did so. Two really pulled her away from herself. It was just what she wanted right now.

35

The next day Georgie rang Kelly but her phone was switched off and went straight to voicemail. There was nothing left to do but go and call at the flat, so she took a pool car and drove into central London. She was sitting in a queue of traffic in front of St Pancras Station, waiting to turn right and park outside Kelly's flat, when she saw Kelly walking east past her on the other side of the road. She pulled a U-turn when the light went green, prompting a crescendo of horns from all directions and tried to follow, but Kelly had crossed four lanes of traffic to the other side of the street and was standing outside an Underground entrance, looking behind her. Georgie thought she was about to enter but she turned and began walking again, cutting down a side street.

Georgie swore. The traffic she was caught in flowed away from Kelly on a long one-way system round some Victorian buildings, cutting Kelly from view. By the time Georgie had waited at several red lights and driven back round, Kelly was nowhere to be seen. She hung a right into a side street and began looking for her.

Kelly felt like she'd been awake all night. She had spent many hours on the chair in her children's room, staring at them as they slept. The idea that in only a few days this room would be empty, that their bags would be packed and they would be gone, was a pain she was unsure she could endure. She had already sat in a room where a child should have been, where

Amber should have been sleeping, where that child's breath would never be again. She couldn't repeat that, would not let that be repeated. She would fight Christos in the courts for custody of their children, for a right to live a life without abuse.

In the morning she got the kids ready for school, tiredness overwhelming her. It was best that they keep their routine, she decided, much as it pained her to see them leave for the day, but she also had somewhere she needed to go. She let Sylvie take Yannis horse-riding and then took Florence to school, came back and parked the car. She got out and walked down the side of the building to the Euston Road.

It was when she had crossed the road and was approaching the Underground that she felt she was being followed. A man in a dark suit with heavy stubble crossed the road with her at the lights. She glanced behind her and he looked away. The lawyer's office was nearby, but she walked past it and round the corner. The man followed. She picked up speed and turned another corner into a square with a football pitch encased in green fencing. He was still behind her. She held her bag tighter against her shoulder, her discomfort increasing. The square was quiet, no one was out and about on a cold day in October. He wasn't trying to hide what he was doing. She walked a whole circuit of the square, her anger building in her. Then she turned and ran at him. 'What are you doing? Leave me alone.'

He put up his hands. 'I'm employed to follow you, to make sure you're all right.'

'Bullshit. I'm calling the police, this is stalking,' she hissed.

'Really, Mrs Malamatos, it's just my job. Christos wanted me to make sure you're OK. He's worried about you.'

'Leave me the fuck alone.'

He shrugged his shoulders. 'If you call the police, there'll probably just be someone else here tomorrow. Try not to think too much about me, I'm just doing my job. I can stay further back if you'd prefer.'

She stomped off, but what he said had an absurd logic. There would be someone else here tomorrow, and the next day and the next. She turned around and headed back to the lawyer's office, making no attempt to hide where she was going.

She came to the door of Mr Cauldwell's offices, opened it and climbed up the stairs. She pushed open the door and stopped, confused. She must have the wrong floor.

She looked around. Bethany's desk was still there; a thin layer of dust covered the veneer. The chairs were gone. She ran through into Mr Cauldwell's office. It was bare, the law books taken from the shelf, the filing cabinets half opened and empty. The only trace of him was a McDonald's wrapper in the bin.

I'll be here for years, he'd said.

Not unless something or someone made him leave – in a hurry.

She went down a floor to another office, was buzzed in, and asked the receptionist there when the lawyer upstairs had left and why. The receptionist called an Indian manager out of a back office and they decided between them that he had left last week. No, the lease wasn't up, he hadn't said goodbye. No, he had left no forwarding address or number with them.

Returning upstairs, Kelly picked up a pile of unopened mail on the lawyer's floor. She ripped the envelopes and found normal day-to-day correspondence, even cheques. She sat down on the narrow steps with the hard blue carpet, stunned. Christos had done this, of that she had no doubt. He had frightened him away with just one visit. In twenty-three years Mr Cauldwell had never come up against anyone as determined to get what he wanted as her husband.

She felt the last threads of hope begin to unravel, her night-time vigil and determination fading to grey. The futility of her efforts to get out pushed down on her so heavily she feared she would stop breathing. She came out of the building and sat down on its shabby steps and wept. The man sent to follow her stood politely a good distance away and waited calmly for her to finish.

36

Georgie spent a good few minutes driving round the back streets south of St Pancras, not seeing Kelly anywhere. She was frustrated by one-way streets, blocked-off pedestrian access and cycle paths. She swung a right back on to the Euston Road and spotted Kelly sitting on a doorstep, sobbing. She pulled over and waited, unsure what to do next.

After a few moments Kelly took a deep breath, dried her eyes and stood up. She looked around and spotted Georgie sitting in the car. She froze, and then casually turned full on to her, mouthed something Georgie didn't catch and walked to the kerb and stuck out her hand for a taxi. A man standing a short distance away came to the kerb too. A few moments later Kelly and the man both got in a taxi. Intrigued, Georgie pulled out into the traffic and followed.

The taxi headed to Oxford Street and parked down the side of a small shopping centre. Kelly and the man got out and went inside. Georgie put her customs sticker in the window of the car and rode up the escalator a few shoppers behind them and watched Kelly enter a gym on the top floor. The man waited outside; he obviously wasn't a member. Georgie went up to reception and showed her ID to the manager and he let her in. She followed Kelly into the changing area.

She walked towards a bench facing a row of lockers and could see Kelly from a corner starting to take her clothes off. Georgie thought she was changing for a class, but she didn't put on sportswear; she wrapped a towel round herself, speared a pair of flip-flops with her toes and headed for the sauna.

Georgie stripped and scrabbled around in her bag for change for the locker, and then realised with a jolt of embarrassment that you didn't have to pay for them. She stuffed her clothes in hurriedly and picked up a towel. It was midmorning, the changing rooms empty before the lunchtime office crowd descended. Georgie glanced around and pulled at the thick sauna door.

It was gloomy inside, the faint smell of pine and sweat not unpleasant. Kelly was sitting on the top shelf near the steam source, the hottest part of the room.

'I take it you want to talk to me?' Kelly said.

'Yes. But you make it difficult.'

Kelly shrugged. She looked exhausted, with dark rings under her eyes and her shoulders slumped.

'Who's that man waiting outside?'

'The guy Christos has following me. When I got in the taxi I thought he might as well come with me, it's partly my money that's paying him, after all.' Her attempt at wry humour was lost on Georgie, whose questions were piling up.

'Your husband has you followed? Why?'

She gave a little irritated shrug of her shoulders. 'He's paranoid. He wants to know what I do all the time, who I see.'

'But why?'

Kelly rubbed her eyes with her fingers and let out an exasperated groan. 'Because some men are just like that. But there are always places a man can't go.'

Georgie felt the heat beginning to make her scalp itch. 'You were upset earlier. Care to share?'

Kelly wiped a hand through her hair, which was damp with steam. 'Share with you? You've threatened to take my kids away.'

'About our last meeting, I'm sorry, I felt maybe we got off on the wrong foot—'

'You're lucky you came into the toilets at the play centre to talk to me, otherwise I wouldn't have given you the time of day. There was probably someone watching me that day too.'

'Why is there so much security in your flat? What's he hiding?'

'He's not hiding anything. He's keeping something there.'

'What?'

'Me.'

'Why?'

'Because I'm desperate to leave. But a man like that, he decides, he has to be in control. So I can't go, certainly not with the children. Now he's punishing me through the kids, he's sending them away and I'm really worried he's going to do something to me when they've gone.'

Georgie saw the tears beginning to form. 'But you're married, you have rights—'

'You only say that because you've never been in my situation.'

'But the law is on your side.'

'He's just threatened my lawyer in such a way that he's abandoned the practice he had for twenty-three years. I'd just left his offices when you saw me earlier.' She was getting agitated again.

'I'm the law, I can help.'

'No one can help me.' She jumped to the floor in a sudden burst of energy, yanked her towel away and stood defiantly before Georgie. 'Just take a look at what it's really like.'

The sauna was narrow, and with Kelly standing, Georgie felt the shock of forced intimacy, of having to see a stranger's naked body. Her face was only inches from Kelly's pubic hair, but something caught her eye. And then she couldn't do anything but stare. Even in the gloomy light of the sauna, the white puckered skin on Kelly's stomach was impossible to miss, the tracery of lines and twisted skin that showed a burn.

A woman's history is written on the skin of her stomach, but Georgie wasn't looking at the folds and sags of impending old age or a lifetime's battling with body image, the welts of stretch marks from her pregnancies, a scar from where a baby might have been yanked. The burn had a definite outline, starting wide by her pubic hair and tapering to a point below her belly button. Within it were two lines of small circles of unburned skin that made the shape understandable, which told the real story.

The mark left permanently on Kelly's skin was from an iron.

'He did that to you?' Georgie's tongue felt huge and dry in her mouth.

'That burn took about twenty seconds. It will last a lifetime. The law takes about three months, then there are appeals, and more appeals and then my kids don't know me any more, and I'm in the nut house or the cemetery.' She turned away and in contrast to the violence inflicted on her stomach Kelly had a small dolphin tattoo low down on her back.

She turned back to Georgie again, her voice full of conviction. 'One day he's going to get rid of me. He's going to take me out on one of his ships and put me in the world's biggest grave – the ocean.'

'Are you the tip-off?'

'What?'

'Someone's phoning us, feeding us information about his illegal business activities.'

'He never shares his business with me. He thinks it's beneath him. He's got Sylvie for that.' She gave a bitter little laugh. 'You must think I'm sick in the head. How did I end up here? Such a doormat. You know there's no word for what I am. No word for the person I've become.'

Georgie tried to reassure her. 'You're in a relationship with a very violent and controlling—'

'No, I don't mean that. There's no word in the English language for me. For a mother who's lost her child.'

'I'm sorry, I don't understand.'

'England has some of the biggest and most dangerous tides in the world, do you know that?'

Georgie was nonplussed. 'No, I don't.'

'Neither did I, until my child died in one.'

'Your child?'

Kelly was somewhere else now, her eyes glazed, her voice low. 'I grew up in Southampton. Poole, near Southampton, sits on one of the biggest natural harbours in the world but it has a tiny entrance, like a huge bottleneck. All the water has to be pulled in through the bottleneck, and back out. The current's so strong there it'll pull you over at ankle height. The ferry across the entrance has to be attached to chains.'

Georgie had been there once, on a school trip to the Isle of Wight. She remembered liking the azure water of the south coast, so unlike the greeny-grey sludge of her native Thames.

'We were out in a friend's boat, my first husband Michael, Florence was four and Amber was two. The fog came down, thick and fast. We heard a distress call from another boat and we went to help. Its engine had broken and it was drifting fast in the fog so Michael tried to get on board to help the man in the other boat restart the motor. If boats get too close to the ferry they can be pulled right under it. I was at the front of our boat, steering, the girls were sitting in the middle, and Michael was trying to get from the side of our boat on to the deck of the other, but he slipped as he tried to climb out and he fell in. I had my hand on the wheel, looking behind me and Amber, puffed up in her life jacket, leaned right over to see where her dad was. I was screaming at her to get away from the side, but before I could reach her she toppled right in after him. And then they were being pulled away, so fast they were pulled away from the boat and I was desperately trying to follow their life jackets in the water, chasing after them in the boat, and I could hear we were so close to the ferry. And I lost them. The broken boat was carried right out to sea past the ferry. The guy was fine.' She paused. 'But neither Amber nor Michael was ever found.'

'I'm so sorry.' Georgie underwent a very rapid reassessment of Kelly.

'After something like that, I don't trust my own judgement any more, I'm overprotective of the kids, I'm a mess.' She leaned forward and looked Georgie straight in the eye. 'But I want to bring him down, before he decides he doesn't need me at all.'

'Tell me everything you know.'

'That's the problem, I don't know anything.'

'Does he keep papers at home that we wouldn't have found when we searched the flat? Do you listen to messages on the phone?'

'The cameras stop me looking.' She paused. 'Anything incriminating would have to be in his office. That's the place in the flat I can't go.'

'We looked there,' Georgie added with a sigh. She thought for a moment. 'The tip-off said something important was coming on your husband's ship, the *Saracen*. It's docking here in London in two days.'

Kelly sat up. 'On October 30th?'

'Yes. Why is that important?'

Georgie saw her pause, thinking through some problem. 'Sylvie crowed to my daughter that I was going away at the end of the month. Christos is sending the kids away to school on November 1st, his mother's going with them. He's clearing the decks of everyone. Why?'

Georgie looked at her. 'We need to find out what's on that ship, Kelly.'

But Kelly was thinking something else. 'Where am *I* supposed to be going?'

37

Georgie left the gym first and drove back to the docks. Stuck in a long queue on the Highway in Wapping, she pushed in the cigarette lighter and waited for it to pop back out. She touched the end of her finger with it. Less than a second later she had drawn it away, the pain of the burn lingering unpleasantly. Georgie spent the rest of the journey thinking about what women would suffer for the sake of their children.

In the evening Georgie wanted to go to the climbing wall and Ryan gave her a lift part of the way. They chatted about Dad and other family, about a neighbour trying to build an extension who was having problems with a busybody in the planning department of the council, according to Ryan. Georgie instinctively took the council's side, but decided it was best not to tell Ryan that. She wanted their journey to be pleasant and relaxed, Kiss FM was blaring, and it was good to have a catch-up with her brother.

They were stationary at the lights when Ryan made an announcement. 'We've got something for you – me and Uncle Ed.'

She was confused. 'What are you talking about?'

'A phone message. Want me to play it for you?'

He was looking triumphant and sly, the two commonest Bell traits. She became alarmed. 'You didn't do what I told you not to the other night, did you?'

'Yeah. It works a treat. If you have the number you can

get in to their message service – if they've never put in a security code or changed the factory default. He hadn't, probably because he rarely uses it, like most people nowadays—'

'Who's *he*?'

'Your shipping guy.'

Georgie was horrified. 'You broke into the message service of Christos Malamatos? How did you find his number?'

'You left your bag by the fire when you stomped out. You're always so moody these days, G, we all think it. So Uncle Ed looked through your papers. Malamatos sounds Greek. Is he?'

'For fuck's sake – I told you not to do that. What were you doing rooting round in my bag?'

'Oh, come on,' added Ryan. 'We're trying to help. Do you want to hear the message or not?'

'No, I bloody well don't. It's illegal.'

'That's not true though, G, is it? I know you want to get on, you don't want to be stepped on all your life, just like we don't.'

She knew he meant the rest of the Bells. Everyone doing what they could to live a little better, dream a little bigger. She had the same blood running through her veins. It was what she wanted, too. Ryan was waving his phone in front of her face, teasing her with it.

She switched off the radio. 'Play it.'

He pressed a button and put it on speaker. The automatically generated computer voice said, 'A message was left on Saturday, 19th October at 6.35 a.m. The caller withheld their number.' Then a bunch of noises and a man's voice, slow and deliberate. '1824 is no.' There was the sound of the phone being put down.

'Is that it?' She couldn't keep the disappointment from her voice.

Ryan was indignant. 'What did you want? A murder confession?'

'I suppose.'

'Who phones at six thirty in the morning? Everyone says their name when they leave a message, even if it's me phoning you. You know, the moronic "Hi, sis, it's me, Ryan" – as if you don't recognise my voice. But this message? It's code, must be, and people only use code when they've got something to hide. You took his mobile and iPad and stuff when you searched the place, didn't you, so no one would have been able to contact him. This is the old-fashioned way.'

Georgie thought for a moment. They had gone to Christos's flat the day before the message, on Friday the 18th.

'Play it again.'

They both hunched over, listening in. 'What can you make out about the voice?'

'He's disguised it. It's impossible to know if he's young, old, it's too short a message to reveal an accent. It's just a man, that's all.'

Georgie nodded. 'Which is why he risked leaving the message.'

Ryan played it again.

'What's that noise at the end?' There was a scrapy-tappy sound just before the call was cut. 'Play it again.'

The pitter-patter scraping, then the clunk of the phone going down.

Ryan shrugged. 'Sounds like Shelley when she taps her shellacs on the bar.' They both listened again to the short message, frowning at each other. Then Ryan smiled. 'You see, you can't resist, G. It's human nature to want to know.'

Georgie shook her head. 'You are not to do that again.'

'The thanks I've just had,' said Ryan, 'I'm hardly going to

go out of my way. But it's still a useful trick to know.' He put the phone away in his pocket.

'It's against the law, Ryan. That should matter.'

Her brother shrugged and roared away up the bus lane.

38

The storm was building in intensity, the slate-grey sky throwing flurries of rain at the windscreen, the ship careening down wave troughs and cresting skywards. The crew had worked for long hours, battening down everything that could move and cause damage. The Wolf was sweaty under his waterproofs and went back to his room to change. He found Luciana naked on the floor of the cabin doing the sun salute, the TV blaring. 'You OK?' he asked. 'Not feeling sick?'

She didn't even open her eyes as she pointed her perfect bum at the ceiling. 'Never better.'

He smiled, came out and swayed down the corridor to Jonas's door. It was closed. He was probably knees to the lino and head down the toilet, wishing he'd flown cattle class back to Heathrow. Sometimes these storms lasted for weeks, not days. He paused, wondering whether to knock. The door next to Jonas's opened and the company security guy came out.

The door banged shut with force behind him as the ship listed. The Wolf narrowed his eyes. 'That's not your cabin. What are you doing in there?'

The guy drew himself up, quick to anger and quick to pull rank. 'It's none of your business,' he shot back. He wasn't prepared to be grilled by any old deckhand.

The Wolf was having none of it. 'Cabins are off limits. So unless you tell me what you were doing in there, I'll be forced to enter and take a look myself.'

The guy looked at him like he was something that had got trapped in the grooves of his shoe. 'I'm moving cabins. I threw up in mine.'

The Wolf relented. You couldn't expect everyone to adjust as well as Luciana had to being on board.

'I was in number 23. I'll enjoy knowing that you'll be the one to clear it up.' He walked away down the corridor as the Wolf stared at his retreating back, his fists opening and closing.

He went up to the bridge where the captain and the first mate were. The Wolf could see the rings of the storm on the weather chart had tightened, like a noose round a convict's neck. The President was watching the might of the storm through the toiling windscreen wipers, standing with his legs wide to counteract the listing.

'It's going to be a cracker,' said the Wolf.

'Yes, stronger than we thought. Force 9 at least.' The President looked grey and tired.

'Should we have moved around it?' The Wolf would be surprised if he said yes – the ship could ride through hurricanes without too much bother and this storm wasn't that big. Yet.

'We could have tracked further south, but that would have delayed us several days.' He let out a grin, keeping the atmosphere light. 'Let's show our guests what this ship can tolerate.'

Their conversation stopped as the President took a call. The ship moved down a wave and they felt their feet and their stomachs lift. Spray hammered the windows and the white of a wave hit the prow.

The Wolf was surprised to see Jonas come on to the bridge. 'I expected you would be calling God on the great white telephone.'

'Me, I feel great.'

'I'm glad you're OK, seasickness can be really bad.'

The President was trying to explain to whoever was on the phone that the storm was fast-changing and unpredictable. But it sounded like he couldn't get a word in edgeways. From the tone of his voice he was only a shade away from apologising, something the Wolf found surprising. He was captain of the ship. You stood by your decisions and defended them. You were in control. The President turned to the Wolf and rolled his eyes. He was being leaned on from on high. 'Of course, I'll—' Another long pause. 'The cargo is fine,' he managed to say, before being cut off again.

Jonas was talking to the Wolf, but the Wolf wasn't listening. 'Who's that?' he mouthed at the captain.

The captain covered the mouthpiece with his hand. 'Head honcho, checking everything's OK. He's spending too much time looking at weather patterns. He's getting stressed.'

'The owner?'

The President nodded, the phone still to his ear.

A pen rolled across the bridge before the President caught it and clipped it back in his breast pocket. In this weather anything not tied down found a life and energy of its own. The Wolf looked out through the rain at the hundreds of tonnes of cargo surging north-eastwards to London. Christos was stressing about his ship in the storm. The contents had better have been fixed down securely inside those cans, or things would be damaged. He smiled.

'Wolf, do you want to play ping-pong?' Jonas was leaning on one of the rails with his elbows, completely unconcerned about the weather.

He shook his head. 'It doesn't work with this listing. I've got a much better game. Come on.' A feeling close to joy surged through him as he jumped down the stairs of the bridge and out into the corridor. 'You can't do this on dry land.' He took Jonas to a staircase of nine steps between the accommodation floors. 'Here's the challenge. How do you walk down those stairs without touching any of them or the walls?'

Jonas thought for a moment and then shrugged, stumped.

The Wolf grinned. 'Watch this.' He waited for a few moments as he felt the ship list to one side. 'Here we go!' The ship hit another huge wave and rolled back sideways, the staircase tipping up, becoming more horizontal with the lean of the ship. The Wolf took a long stride at the moment he judged the ship to be as far over as possible. Right then he staircase was at less than a twenty-five-degree angle and one long step could bring him to the bottom of what would be an impossible drop only moments before. A second later he was at the bottom of the staircase. 'See? Walking on water. Now you do it.'

Jonas laughed nervously, his hand gripping the stair rail. The ship was leaning the other way now, the staircase an almost vertical drop. The Wolf could see Jonas's hands were white where they clutched the rail. The ship rebalanced and began to careen back the other way.

'Get ready,' shouted the Wolf.

The Wolf saw Jonas take a deep breath and shout as he jumped along rather than down the stairs. As he landed he was screaming with exhilaration at the altered angles.

'Now watch this. You can jump up them, too.' The Wolf waited till the top of the staircase had tipped down with the ship's movement and jumped back up to the top stair.

'Man, that is better than an acid trip!' shouted Jonas.

You'd know, thought the Wolf.

39

For Kelly every remaining moment with her children was precious. It was Tuesday and they should have been at school, but she kept them home on the pretence that they needed to pack and organise. Also, being indoors served another purpose, she wasn't followed by Christos's men. Now Yannis was on the kitchen floor playing with Lego and Florence was opening cupboards and pulling out ingredients.

'Mum, I want to make cake batter and eat it all.' Florence tried to extricate the mixer from a crowded shelf.

'Let me.' She pulled out the Magimix and set it on the counter. She needed to treasure these normal moments with her children. Suddenly a memory flashed before her and she smiled. 'Do you remember, Flo, when Amber put Daddy's watch in the cake?'

Florence turned towards her, her face a triumph of rediscovery. 'Yes! "Watch cake, watch cake".' Her daughter laughed.

'What?' Yannis looked up, not understanding.

'Amber would have been about two and you were four, Florence. We were making a cake. Amber was standing on the chair by the stove, and Flo and I kept saying that when the cake went in the oven we would have to keep an eye on it to make sure it didn't burn. Dad took off his watch so Florence could tell us when the big hand got to six and then a little later we came back to the stove and we couldn't find the watch anywhere—'

'Yeah! Yeah! And we were hunting all over the place for it

and Dad was getting annoyed and eventually the cake came out of the oven and Mum cut it and in the middle was Daddy's watch.'

'That's right,' continued Kelly. 'Amber had put it in the cake. She turned her little face to me and she said, "Watch cake, watch cake." It must be one of your earliest memories.'

Florence nodded, looking at Kelly with her pale eyes. 'I see her, you know. Sometimes I see her.'

'So do I, honey, so do I.' Kelly burst into tears. 'She lives in you, a little bit of her is in you always.' She sat down on a chair because the strength in her legs had drained away. Her children came and put their arms around her, the simple uncomplicated acts of love from those who were young.

'Well, this is an affecting scene.'

Kelly pulled away sharply. Christos was in the doorway to the living room; she'd had no idea he was even home. Her love for her dead daughter was chased away by a visceral hatred for the man blocking a doorway in her home.

'Florence, it's important to remember to live life for now. You've got Yannis here, you'll always have Yannis and me.'

'And Mummy,' said Yannis.

Christos turned to Kelly. 'Yes, you'll always have Mummy.' But the way he said it sent a shiver down her spine. He turned back to his son. 'You know what happened today? Someone gave me a polo mallet. Ever heard of polo? You play it on horses, just like you're doing at Hyde Park in the mornings with Sylvie. Come on, I'll show you.'

Yannis could sense something much more exciting than Lego was at hand and jumped up and ran out of the room and Florence followed. Kelly felt a part of her heart going with them.

She thought about her conversation yesterday with Georgie in the sauna. She needed to try and find something to use against Christos, but it felt like an impossible task she wasn't capable of executing. Yannis's shouts filtered through from the living room.

There was one thing she could do. She went down to the bedroom and put on a jacket, pulled at the armchair in the corner of the bedroom and dragged it under the lightshade. She was too short to reach the ceiling light, so she grabbed the stool by the dressing table and, balancing precariously on that, could just reach to unscrew the Sleepchecker. She didn't care that she was being filmed by the green eye in the corner, she wanted to know what Christos had been doing while she had been sleeping. She threw the Sleepchecker in her bag and left the flat, heading through Bloomsbury to the Internet café. The man following her kept a discreet distance behind and waited in the street outside.

She settled down at the computer and watched the grainy images. There were five nights to look through. Thursday night she was recovering from being drugged, and she moved a lot, twisting and turning and thrashing in her sleep, the video a stop-start journey through the dark hours. Christos in contrast slept easily, jabbing a hypodermic into his wife's thigh not seemingly troubling him. On Friday's video she saw Sylvie walk into shot and lie a dry-cleaning bag on the bed. It was soon after this that she had discovered Sylvie in the flat after her collapse at the station. She was taken aback, Sylvie had put Christos's dry-cleaning on the bed just like she did. That evening she was comatose in the bed while Christos worked for at least two hours on his laptop. He got up in the night to go to the toilet.

Saturday night there was little video; she and Christos must have been sleeping soundly. At one point the camera recorded them both turned away from each other, still. Something struck her. The camera was motion sensitive, so why was it recording now? She rewound and watched the video again.

Nothing, bar a fleeting shadow to the right of the screen. She watched it again, couldn't make out what it was, but it must have been big to trip the motion sensor.

Sunday night Christos was in bed alone. She was in the kids' bedroom, processing the revelation that their father wanted them to go to boarding school. In the grey light of early dawn she saw herself come back into the room and crawl under the covers, defeat lying over her more fully than the duvet.

The video reached last night. Her husband seemed to have an untroubled conscience by the little tossing and turning he did, most of the night he was unmoving in the bed. She watched herself sleeping on her back, mouth open, saw that Christos was also asleep. The timer running across the bottom of the screen showed 3.55 a.m., the deepest time of night. The moment when an enemy attacks. Michael had told her that. They were both still, why was the video recording? She rewound and played the film again. And glimpsed a pair of legs walking through the edge of the shot. She flinched. The legs weren't Medea's, they were too thin. This body was lither and younger, tight trousers clinging to the calves. What the hell was happening? The legs stopped moving and walked to her shoes, lined up under the window. It was then that Kelly realised the woman was barefoot. The woman slipped on a pair of her favourite stilettos and walked out of shot towards the dressing room. She was sure now, the swaying walk in high heels had made it so: Sylvie.

Kelly got to her feet. This invasion could not stand. Did Christos know? Medea? The questions were coming too fast to process. Then something happened that made Kelly sit back down with a gasp. Sylvie reappeared at the other side of the bed, her side. She was still in the stilettos. Sylvie came up to the bed and leaned over, staring at Kelly, looming over her in the dark. Sylvie moved her head as if examining her from different angles. She was unhurried, her movements lazy and sure.

After a few minutes of scrutiny, Sylvie turned and put the shoes back, exactly where she had found them, and walked in the direction of the door. Kelly stood again, grabbed the memory card, and ran.

40

The storm was in full force, hurling everything it had at the *Saracen*. The waves were crashing over the prow of the ship, throwing spray far into the air. The crew was in a state of suspended animation, waiting, waiting for the weather to break. The temperature was dropping fast; the Wolf had already added layers of clothing. felt the cold fingers of the seas around Europe, the chill of an English autumn, reaching out to grab him.

He was scrubbing rust off a door lining with a coarse wire brush and a chisel, his hands chapped and red with cold – he preferred work to idleness in a storm – when he heard the President talking in hurried tones to some of the crew nearby. 'Up to the bridge, now.'

The President rounded the corner. The look on his face told the Wolf something was serious. 'You too, now.'

The Wolf dropped the brush on the floor, put the chisel in his pocket and they walked up the stairs. The entire crew was there on the bridge, including Jonas and some other travellers.

'The company employee is missing,' said the President. 'He's not in his cabin, he's not been seen for eight hours. Unless we can locate him imminently, we're looking at a man overboard.'

The Wolf heard someone swear in Polish. They all knew what man overboard meant. In a storm this severe, if you went in you survived less than two minutes.

The President outlined who was to look where on the vast ship, to see if the missing man could be located. The meeting didn't last long and the group broke up, keen to bring this unsavoury situation to a conclusion one way or the other. The Wolf walked away, rounded a corner and jumped down the flights of stairs to the accommodation deck, running to cabin number 18. He didn't have much time. The door was locked. He knocked. No answer. He knocked again, then inserted the chisel's thin end into the lock mechanism of the door, and turned.

41

The numbers 'one eight two four' had set up shop in Georgie's brain and weren't going anywhere soon. She tried fiddling round with the numbers, checking them against consignment numbers on shipping bills of lading, the unique BIC code that every container had, but drew a blank. She felt bad that she couldn't brainstorm with Mo, but she was far beyond legal here and no one else could know what she was doing. She discovered 1824 was a UN number for sodium hydroxide, a substance that the United Nations had classed as dangerous for international transport purposes. Sodium hydroxide, more commonly known as caustic soda, she noted, was used in the production of wood and paper pulp. But why would Christos be pulping prized rosewood? She checked the paperwork for the *Saracen* and there was no record of any sodium hydroxide being aboard.

She repeated the message to herself: *1824 is no.* The voice was emphasising the no, the negative, but that still didn't help her.

She put her ear next to the table and tapped the top. She was listening to her fingers, trying to test Ryan's suggestion that the sound on Christos's voicemail might be something to do with fingernails. She could approximate the tappy sound, but not the scrapy bit that preceded it. She began to stroke the table.

'If you're looking for something hard to caress, I can oblige.' Preston was grinning down at her, a cup of tea in his hand.

'Ha ha.' She scowled as she sat up.

'Anguish wants us in there now.' He nodded towards the boss's office.

Georgie followed Preston and Mo into Anguish's office for a post-lunch update on the case. Mo began. 'The cans are logged as coming in, going out with the delivery companies and arriving. We're seeing if anything's slipped through the system. We're about halfway through the paperwork and computer records for the dates we're looking at.'

'OK, keep going with that,' Angus said.

'I spoke to the wife again,' Georgie added. 'I think she's keen to help us if she can, but she doesn't know very much. The truth is she's terrified of Christos, he has her followed everywhere—'

'That's way outside our job description,' Angus said dismissively. 'She needs Women's Aid or something.'

Preston smiled in a self-satisfied way. 'If you play with fire, you're gonna get burned.'

'What's that supposed to mean?' snapped Georgie. After what she'd seen on Kelly's stomach yesterday, it was the most inappropriate comment she'd heard in a long time. She didn't feel she could tell them about the burn, it felt private, not something Kelly would relish her revealing to a room of men.

'You know exactly what it means,' retorted Preston. 'Christos is as dodgy as hell, we just haven't found the evidence yet. We know it, so does she.'

Georgie was getting angry and decided it was better to stay quiet.

'We could check the lorries that park up at the play centre? They're coming tomorrow to set up for the Halloween charity party,' suggested Mo.

Preston frowned. 'Why? We thought originally that the wood was being shipped every six months, but we've found no evidence for that. It could just be a one-off after all.'

'Oh, so you're prepared to assume Kelly is guilty with no evidence, but you don't want to pursue a good lead because of a lack of it.'

'Guys, please.' Angus held up his hand. 'Preston might be right.' Angus combed the back of his hair with a rolled-up piece of A4 before banging himself lightly on the head with it, thinking. 'To search the lorries by the play centre we'd need a warrant and I'm not sure we have cause to get one.'

Georgie persisted with the Kelly angle. 'Christos is clearing the decks at home, sending the children away as if he's planning for something big. His wife's suspicious of his every move.'

'Suspicious?' Angus leaned forward, pointing the roll of paper at her. 'The wife's a dead-end. Keep on task, Georgie, don't let other agendas distract you from the case.'

She sat back as if he had slapped her.

'We still don't know why there's so much wood.' This was Mo. 'We need to find a use for this wood. And why is it being sent in its raw state? It's cheaper to cut it at source and then send it without the bark – machine-planed it fits in the can better anyway.'

'I agree it doesn't make much sense at present,' conceded Angus.

'We've interviewed Christos's PA,' Mo added. 'She's also his mistress and on the board of the charity he supports, the charity that's opposite the yard where the wood goes. But we've checked out her story and, well, we've got nothing.'

'Maybe we've got this the wrong way round,' Preston said. 'Why are we trying to second-guess what they're using the wood for? All that matters is that someone wants it and someone is prepared to pay for it. It's that simple. End of.'

Angus gave her a look as if to say, 'Why didn't you come up with that?' To Georgie's immense irritation, she had no answer.

42

Kelly ran back to the flat. She would show Christos what she had found on the Sleepchecker. As the lift doors slid open she could hear raised voices upstairs, could sense stress in the air.

She took the stairs two at a time and came in to the living room to find Sylvie there with her family, following Christos as he paced around on his phone. 'I want a word with you,' she spat. She wanted this woman out of her home, *now*.

'It'll have to wait,' Sylvie replied, without even looking at her.

'I'm not waiting,' Kelly shouted.

'Mum' – this was Florence talking now – 'someone's gone overboard on the *Saracen*.'

'The seas are huge, there's no hope of finding him,' added Medea.

Kelly was brought up short by this news. 'My God, that's terrible. Who is it?' she asked.

Christos thanked someone on the phone and rang off. He looked livid, panting with shock and adrenalin. 'One of my employees. He's been with me for fifteen years. I can't bloody believe it!'

'How did it happen, when did it happen?'

Sylvie was wringing her hands together. 'That's what *we* want to know.' She was looking at Christos. 'Is this some kind of hit? You can't just fall overboard, even in a storm.'

'I'm so sorry,' Kelly added.

'What the hell is going on aboard that ship?' Christos was shouting at no one in particular.

'We'll just have to wait for news, there's nothing more we can do till the ship arrives tomorrow,' Medea said, trying to placate her son and his lover. 'The captain's still doing a full search. The coastguard's been informed, a search helicopter has been sent—'

'It makes no sense!' wailed Sylvie.

The news was indeed bad, but she couldn't help feeling that Christos and Sylvie's reaction was extreme. They didn't seem to be showing much pity for the man himself or his family. She wondered what Georgie would make of the news.

'Daddy, you said you'd show me how to use the mallet.' Yannis was tapping his father on his leg.

'Not now, Yannis.'

The boy started whining.

'I need to talk to you, Sylvie,' Kelly said.

'What?' Sylvie was frustrated and her mind was on other things.

'I want to swing the polo mallet—'

'Shut up, Yannis,' Sylvie said.

'Don't you dare talk to my child like that,' Kelly retorted.

Sylvie realised she'd been too harsh and relented. 'OK, look, *I'll* show you.' She had aggression in every movement, the look of a woman with a plan gone awry. She took a chair from the kitchen and placed it on the living room floor near the fish tank, then took a stool and balanced it on top of the chair.

Christos looked up. 'What are you doing?'

'It'll work, just watch. I'm showing Yannis how polo is played.' The polo mallet was on the coffee table. 'Come on, Flo, help me hold it.'

'He'll fall off,' said Florence, matter-of-factly.

'No, he won't,' said Sylvie, getting irritated. 'It's just a bit of fun.' She tried to hoik Yannis over the stool.

'Are you sure that's safe?' asked Christos.

Yannis took the mallet and tried to hold it up but his grip was poor and it fell to the floor.

Sylvie pulled him off the stool. 'Stand here, Yannis. Hold the bottom of the stool and I'll show you how to swing the mallet.' She climbed on to the high stool. 'You know how you're learning to sit up tall in the saddle when you go horse-riding with me?'

Kelly wanted to spit at her.

'Well, it's the same when you play polo. Hand me the mallet.' She almost snatched it from Yannis's grip. 'Now you swing right round with your arm. You need to put all your effort into it, that's how you play. Like this!' Sylvie straightened her arm and swung the mallet right round, just as Christos shouted out something that sounded like 'No!'

Sylvie's arm flew round at great speed behind her and upwards, straight into the fish tank. The mallet hit the glass panel of the fish tank at its moment of maximum force and bounced out of Sylvie's hand, clattering away. Everyone froze. Across the room, Kelly could see the small chip in the glass. For two full seconds they held their breath, then the first crack, an inch long, crept slowly across the glass, followed by a sharp noise like ice giving way on a frozen lake. Another crack snapped, much faster now, across the glass from where Sylvie had hit the middle of the pane, to the bottom corner and then Kelly heard Christos shout something incoherent as the glass panel exploded and a thousand litres of water came cascading from the shattered tank across the living room floor, the force upending the chair and stool that Sylvie was sitting astride and sending her skidding across the marble floor, her screams mixing with those of the kids. The water swung under Medea and she fell with a thump that sent her glasses skittering away under the grand piano. Christos dropped his iPad in the current flowing past him, and tried to chase it. The water started barrelling down the stairs. It rushed over Kelly's ankles, pondweed catching on her shoes. Flashes of tropical fish darted this way and that, gasping their last breaths. She saw the model of the competitor's ship coast away under the furniture. She bent down and picked up the iPad, the concentric rings of the tightening storm over the Atlantic lasting for a few more moments before the screen snapped to black.

Sylvie was screaming, her features wild and stricken as the extent of the damage spreading through the house began to dawn on her.

Kelly felt a thrill of victory as she watched the other woman on her knees, her expensive boots ruined, desperately trying to scoop up tropical fish as they swam past, water lapping up against the far corners of the room. Sylvie might be worming her way into the family, pleasing Christos in bed, ingratiating herself with the children, wandering through Kelly's bedroom at night, but she was still an outsider, she wouldn't know how much that fish tank meant to him. Kelly was pretty sure that Christos and Sylvie never talked of anything so mundane as the fish.

And then Kelly started giggling and found she couldn't stop. She could feel Flo's shoulders heaving with delight as she too became infected, and then Yannis also, until they were screaming with laughter. The flat and its expensive contents, its showy trinkets and crushing memories were being destroyed by the woman who had so much desire to keep it perfect. It was a rare and beautiful moment of joy.

43

Kelly felt hysterical. She hadn't laughed like this, sensed this release for many months. Medea was trying pathetically to mop with a bucket, and the kids were still screaming and running around, swishing the currents of water with their feet. Kelly felt the tears flowing over her cheeks, the laughter pouring out of her. Sylvie was moaning and ineffectually running this way and that, Christos was shouting instructions at no one.

Something in Christos snapped. 'Stop laughing. All of you stop laughing.' He shouted it loud and harsh, the flush of red on his neck and face impossible to ignore. They all fell silent and looked at him, his chest heaving. He gazed around the ruined room, and then he looked up at the ceiling. Kelly could hear the faint cooing, the persistent scratches above their heads. 'Those pigeons.' The tendons were straining in his neck, his fists were clenched tight. 'Those fucking pigeons!'

A strangled noise came out of his throat and he splashed across the room to the kitchen, the sound of heavy furniture sent flying, hard things rebounding off surfaces. The women stood frozen where they were, too rapt or terrified to move, until he re-entered the living room, a black object in his palm that Kelly only realised was a gun when Sylvie screamed. The next instants were a chaotic scene of smoke and dust and falling plaster as Christos began shooting at the ceiling, screaming and firing as the wailing women threw themselves on the children or under tables. 'I'll teach those fucking pigeons! They never give me a moment's peace!'

Kelly grabbed her children's hands, keeping low and running to the stairs, but Medea was already occupying them, crouched down and shouting at her son. In Kelly's rush she slipped in the water and Yannis's hand slid from her own. The noise was terrific, reverberating round the marble floors and walls, plaster and dust raining down on the sodden floor. Christos didn't stop, firing again and again and again until the bullets were gone and the harsh clicks of the spent gun were all that could be heard. Then he swore and hurled the gun hard across the room. It bounced and rotated and skidded into the corner under a window.

Kelly realised she was flat on the floor, pondy-smelling water soaking into her clothes. The silence after the chaos seemed deafening. Kelly dared a glance upwards, braced for a toe cap or a pair of hands round her neck.

She saw Sylvie had her arms out towards her husband, tears in her eyes. 'My love, stop. We're nearly there, so nearly there, Christos.' He glared at her, a sheen of sweat on his face. 'We agreed we'd do this. After all our work . . .'

He shook his head. 'I can't—'

Medea broke in. 'That's enough. Control yourself, Christos, there are children here.'

'Women. The bane of my life, a coven of women!' He walked away into the kitchen and they heard the clatter of something being swept off the table.

Sylvie set off after him but thought better of it. Kelly tried to stand. She was shaking all over. Medea was attempting to calm the children, who were whimpering. Kelly looked at her; the shock on her mother-in-law's face was plain to see. The gun had been as much a surprise to Medea as it had been to herself. It dawned on her that she had been living in a house with a loaded gun in it. Christos must have hidden it well, customs hadn't found it in their search.

Sylvie and Kelly faced each other. 'Nearly where?' asked Kelly. She stood up taller. 'So nearly *where?*'

Sylvie had a dusting of plaster in her hair that made it look grey and aged her fifteen years. A hard look of hatred had formed in her eyes. The fiasco with the fish tank was probably the first thing that had seriously driven a rift between the husband and the lover, so it was turning into Kelly's fault.

'I will win, Kelly, make no mistake,' she spat.

'There's nothing you can win. Don't you understand?' Kelly found it in herself still to laugh. 'He's married to me, remember. And despite what he might have said, he's never going to let me go.'

A harsh sound came out of Sylvie's mouth at that. 'No, he'll never let you go. He'll never love anyone as much as he loves the lonely and beautiful—'

'Mummy?' They were interrupted in their battle by Yannis, standing next to the grand piano, his bottom lip quivering. Kelly ran towards him and hugged him tight, trying to soothe away his sobs. He held something hard and spiky in his hand that poked her in the stomach. She pulled away and looked down. It was the competitor's ship.

'Don't worry, Yannis, it's over now. No one will hurt you. We can repair the fish tank, it was an accident.'

She felt someone coming closer; Sylvie was wading across the room towards her, her mouth a tight line. Sylvie opened her mouth to say something, but the words died on her lips. At that moment the streams of water, pulled down through the building by gravity and the Victorian gaps and fissures in the brickwork and beams, hit the electricity cables and the fuse box and the power shorted and the alarms went off.

44

Ricky had booked in to the hotel two days ago, and was still getting used to the way the wealthy lived. He'd asked the receptionist for an upper floor, the higher the better. He wanted to be close to her, to have a room right under where she lived. The receptionist had huffed and puffed and turned to consult an electronic board and tapped at the screen with nails that were too long. He'd asked for a single and discovered that there was nothing as straightforward as a single or a double any more, rooms were Superiors, Super Kings, or Club Queens. He had not a clue what she was talking about. In the end, since everything seemed to be masquerading as something else, he took the cheapest room on the top floor that overlooked the railway.

He had spent hours wandering the hotel, getting a feel for how it all worked, the service lifts, the staff shift changes, the plain doors down the side of the building where the workers hung around and smoked. There were conference rooms and lobbies, different cafés and restaurants. His old habits were beginning to reassert themselves: a desire to understand how an organisation worked, where the weak spots were, where the angle was.

Now he was having an early evening whisky and ginger in the bar when he saw two maintenance men hurrying across the lobby to the service lift. No one hurried in this hotel unless there was a reason. It unsettled the paying clientele. But these two weren't thinking about disguise. He downed his drink and followed. He watched the lift climb to the top floor.

He took the next lift and arrived at the top floor only moments behind the maintenance guys. They were talking in the doorway of one of the rooms. He walked over. 'What's the problem?'

'Oh, nothing serious.' The guy was probably lying, but Ricky wasn't going to condemn him for that. 'There's a flood from the penthouse upstairs. Fish tank's exploded, or something. We've got complaints about water dripping into the hotel rooms below. All in a day's work, I suppose.'

They all instinctively looked up at the ceiling, expecting to see something.

'What's that noise?' Ricky asked.

'Their alarm, probably. The water's shorted the whole place.'

Ricky left the workers there. As soon as he hit the stairs, he began to run to the ground floor.

45

It was the smell that hit the Wolf first, the unmistakable odour of a novice at sea – the tangy notes of vomit, of stale food, someone enclosed in a small space for too long, and not enjoying it. He stepped into the room and the door swung shut behind him with a precise-sounding click. A woman was lying on the bed, the sheets rumpled beneath her. Magazines were discarded on the floor and there was a bucket nearby. She had her eyes half closed but they widened with fear and surprise when she saw the man who had entered. She began to scrabble further up the bed away from him.

Her big round belly had pushed her jogging bottoms below it and her T-shirt above it. They stared at each other for a couple of seconds before she gave a little scream and the Wolf, in a delayed reaction, put his hands up as an apology.

'I just want to talk, just to talk. You speak English, yes?'

'Yes, of course I speak English.'

She was young, her hair very dark and straight and hanging long behind her. She was pretty in a simple way and wore no wedding ring.

'What's your name?'

'Isabella.'

'How old are you?'

'I'm twenty-two.'

'Can I get you a drink of water, juice?'

She shook her head.

'You'll need something sweet to make you feel better. Bad weather at sea.'

'Why are you in my cabin?'

'Why are you going to London?'

'You first. Why have you broken into my cabin?'

'There's a situation on the ship.'

Her eyes widened with surprise and he could sense that fear wasn't far behind. 'What do you mean?'

'We've got a man overboard. Your man.'

She looked like she was going to cry. 'I want to see the captain.' She was getting agitated.

'The captain is looking for a man presumed dead and steering a ship with millions of pounds of cargo on board through a severe storm. He isn't going to see you. Instead, you've got me.'

She didn't answer.

'When we dock, Isabella, there will be customs and police.' He paused to let that sink in. 'No one wants to be asked a lot of awkward questions, considering what's in there.' He stared at her swollen stomach and she shifted uncomfortably under his gaze and pulled her T-shirt down over the bulge. 'I just need to know why you're on this ship. Don't get me wrong, I'm not going to hurt you. I just need to know.'

'I'm going to see my family.'

'What family, exactly?'

She crossed her legs and looked defensive. 'My family.'

The Wolf took a chair and sat down. He was taking his time, there was no need to rush. 'You need to tell me who your family is.'

'I don't have to tell you anything.'

The Wolf looked at her and the ship emitted a low groan like an animal in labour. 'I think we both know that you do.'

He leaned back in the chair as a flurry of water hit the porthole. 'Neither of us is going anywhere. We've got hours and hours to go like this. Let's at least distract ourselves. Tell me your story.'

46

The women had to concentrate on the strictly practical and get the alarm turned off. Medea and Sylvie hurried downstairs to the fuse box and the emergency numbers. They didn't want the security service to come and see the state of the living room ceiling and what had caused it. Kelly splashed over to the far end of the room and picked up the gun from under a window. It was heavier than she had expected, and colder. She put it in the pocket of her tunic and felt it stretch the material with its weight.

Sylvie took control of phoning the alarm company, finger jammed in one ear so that she could hear.

The system was state-of-the-art, extensive enough to fit Christos's ballooning paranoia, and hence impossible to understand. Christos was staring at the fuse box next to a set of blinking security lights, flicking switches randomly, turning a key back and forth to no effect, his lips moving but no one able to hear what he was saying.

Medea was hurrying about like a nineteenth-century midwife, back and forth with towers of towels and tea cloths to soak up the water, and when she ran out of those, with sheets and blankets.

The caretaker's face appeared in the monitor by the lift as he explained that the hotel manager had been round as the alarm was disturbing the guests and water was coming in to some of their rooms – even some at the highest tariff – and then the screen went snowy and then black. Kelly looked up at the bullying green eye in the corner. It had gone out.

The children were standing, mute, watching events unfold with wide eyes. Kelly took them into her studio, where two streams of water were making their course down the walls by a large mouse effigy. She hugged them tight, a smile on her face. They couldn't talk because the alarm was so loud, so they just held each other, their warm limbs round each other, their hair tickling her face and neck.

Then, as suddenly as it had begun, someone down a phone line must have given the right set of instructions to Christos, who pushed and pulled the right buttons, and the alarm went off, the silence rushing in on them all like an avalanche.

She came out into the corridor. Christos was there, his trousers wet to the knee, his cowlick sweaty. 'Get the kids out of here. Take them out for food or something.' Medea turned to the children and hurried them along with her hands in a wheeling motion. Kelly wasn't allowed to take both of them out at once so she leaned back against the wall. Let them sort it out.

Sylvie and Christos were getting ready to go out, too. 'We're going to the office to try to find out what the hell's happening on that ship.' They used the lift, still working as it ran on a different circuit to the flat, and five minutes later Kelly was left alone. She felt high, a feeling she hadn't had since she smoked a few joints on the playing fields near her old school. She came down to the lobby and leaned over the caretaker's desk, a Cheshire cat grin escaping. 'Whoa, that was some evening!' She couldn't keep the giggles in. 'Everywhere, it went!'

The caretaker expressed his condolences and they talked of repairs and electricity blackouts. 'When the maintenance guy gets here I'll send him straight up,' he said. 'You don't want to be in there in the dark. Kids and all.'

She stepped back in the lift and as she got out in the flat her phone rang. Maintenance were fifteen minutes away, stuck in traffic; she listened as all the usual excuses about roadworks and nose-to-tail this and that flowed over her. She didn't care anyway, she could just be in her own home thrillingly unobserved for a few minutes. She wandered the ruined flat in the deepening dusk, seeing how the brown stain of the water had seeped down the walls of Medea's bedroom and had pooled on the towels she'd jammed into corners. It was dripping through a light fitting in one of the toilets, the stair carpet was a sodden mess that she squelched up.

The living room furniture had a tide line a foot deep on the corner sofa and armchairs. She could still hear the cooing of the pigeons, louder now with the holes in the ceiling. There was a smell of wet dust, rotting vegetation and soaked fabrics.

She wondered whether to light a fire, try to make the place cosy, begin to dry it out. It would throw out a bit of light too. The fireplace was an aggressive black tube suspended from the ceiling that stopped two feet short of the floor in a bulbous shape in the far corner of the living room, diagonally opposite the piano. It was one of the few bits of the flat that hadn't been touched by the flood. Kelly walked over but realised that while the fire was fine, the wood and its basket had been washed to the far end of the room. Part of the high tide had beached a flotsam and jetsam of household detritus against the wall.

She gave up, and, flopping back on the corner sofa, watched the lights of the city intensify as the last of the day drained away. Hampstead Heath remained a stubborn irregular black square in the view.

Her husband and his lover didn't always have it all their own way. She picked up her phone and called the number she had memorised from Georgie's business card. Georgie answered after four rings, sounding harassed. 'Yes?'

'It's Kelly Malamatos. Someone went overboard on the *Saracen* a few hours ago.'

'We just heard. Who is he?'

'An employee who's worked for the company for fifteen years. They're stressed. Really stressed.'

'OK. Got that. Kelly, does the number 1824 mean anything to you?'

'I don't think so. Should it?'

'Not necessarily. Never mind. Thanks.'

She put the phone down and heard the bell on the service lift. The maintenance men were here to bring order back to the chaos, to flood her world with light she didn't want. She dragged herself upright on the sofa and ambled through to the kitchen. The bell rang again before she was halfway across the room. 'All right, all right,' she muttered to herself, slowing down in protest at the way whoever was at the bottom was bullying to be allowed to do their job. She pressed the intercom. Snow and crackle on the monitor. 'Can you hear me? It's broken, I think.'

She heard something that sounded like 'Just about.'

She pressed the button to allow them up to the kitchen level.

Ten seconds later the lift pinged to announce it had arrived. She pressed the button and the door slid open. 'Have you got a torch? You'll need a torch.'

The shadows were deep now, it took those extra few seconds for faces and features to become distinct; it took that little bit more effort to see the details. Somewhere in Kelly's brain she registered that the man stepping out of the lift towards her had no bag and that he was going to have to go all the way back down to the garage to get it and she would be kicking her heels up here. The next thing she thought was that the baseball cap was strange, a touch too casual, this company usually had men wearing uniforms with a logo on the shirt pocket. The last thing she thought before panic took hold and adrenalin flooded her body, blocking out everything else, was she was glad her children had gone out – she loved Medea at that moment for saving their lives.

The man stepped into a shaft of light thrown through the kitchen windows from the city where she had made her home. Eight years folded back on themselves. Ricky Welch, the man from Southampton was here, in her flat, right now.

'Hello, Kelsey.'

It had been so many years since she'd heard that name, it sounded almost quaint, a glimpse so precious of the person she used to be that even when it came from the mouth of her killer, it was briefly enjoyable.

She turned and with a small gasp sprinted round the kitchen table and across the living room to the stairs. She threw herself round the wide curve and half rolled into the dark corridor at the bottom. She was up an instant later, careening into the wall and sprinting down the long corridor to the service stairs. She could feel him behind her, had no time to look back, as with every stride the panic was building, there was no way out. Christos had the key, she knew there was no way out of that door.

Her hands slammed into the hard wood of the door to the stairs. She yanked down on the handle once, then she tried up, forward and back. It didn't budge, as she knew it wouldn't. The service lift was on the floor above, she was trapped. She turned, her hands still on the door and watched him slow down in the corridor now, walking towards her.

She pulled Christos's gun out of her pocket and fumbled to get it the right way round. She felt ridiculous – she'd never fired a gun, never even seen or held one until half an hour ago. She took up a stance she had seen on American cop shows, legs apart, elbows stiff, pointing in the general direction of his chest. 'Get out.'

He stopped walking. 'Why did you set me up?'

'You're a lying piece of shit who clubbed a man to death.'

'Why did you lie at my trial?'

She took a step towards him, feeling bolder now. 'I *saw* you. You ruined my life with your threats of how you would kill me if I told the court what I *saw*, and now you're here to carry out those threats. How did you find me?'

He took a slow step towards her.

'Get back.'

He didn't move. She remembered his height, the muscled forearms and tattoos that poked out beneath the close-fitting white T-shirt when she had picked him out in the line-up, the earring, the darting eyes. He was grey now, his bulk and strength wasted away, his jacket making him look more like a university lecturer than the longshoreman he had been. Only the eyes showed he was the same man, careful and watchful, waiting for the right moment to pounce.

'I like the theatre and so do you, apparently. That was your mistake. To think you could go on to create another life and leave the old one behind, that you wouldn't have to pay. A photo of you in this very flat was online.' His voice had the slight south coast burr to it that hers had once had.

The picture Salvatore had taken here in her studio. She was astonished. Salvatore must have ignored her none too polite demands to erase the photo. She cursed inwardly. He had handed it to the PR department and from there it had come to the attention of the man wreaking vengeance in front of her. 'I did nothing wrong. unlike you.' She shouted it out, panic making her voice rise into a scream.

'You're coming with me.'

She tightened her grip on the gun. 'I'm going to kill you before that happens—'

He made a sharp step towards her and she gave a little cry and moved back. He took another step, close enough to touch her now. Her momentary power had slipped away. He reached up with a swift motion and grabbed the gun. 'I want to show you something.' He punched the button on the service lift.

'You need to enter the code to get out.'

'So enter it.'

'No.'

He paused for a beat. 'Enter the code.'

'What are you here for anyway, revenge? You going to kill me to get back at me? You're not man enough to admit you killed an old man for money, that you intimidated me so I had to leave my life and start a new one. You've already lost.'

'I want an answer to my question, why—'

'I *saw* you.'

'It wasn't me. You saw what they wanted you to see.'

'You're a liar.' Kelly felt her anger quelling her fear. She was in the right. The air conditioning was off, no appliances were humming, it was so quiet she could hear just the white noise in her head and the sound of the service lift arriving at their floor, waiting for them to step in, once she'd entered the code. Then she heard a new noise – the louder clanking of the lift at the other end of the corridor as it began to rise from the plush front lobby. It sounded hideously loud in the hermetically sealed apartment and she involuntarily turned her head towards it. The children were returning to the safety of their home.

She saw him register the panic on her face. He grabbed her wrist, understanding that the power was swinging back into his hands with every metre travelled by that lift. 'I suggest you type in the code.'

She didn't hesitate and typed in the numbers with shaking fingers. The service lift doors began to open. Kelly stepped in, desperate to be gone now, but he pulled her back out, still holding her wrist. 'I spent years inside because of you. I want you to beg for forgiveness.'

In the darkness Kelly could see the red light above the lift doors, far down at the end of the corridor, blink on. She had seconds to spare before they opened. To keep her children safe, she caved in. 'I'll do anything you want.' She stepped into the lift again and he came after her.

Tears misted her eyes. At the far end of the corridor, she saw an expanding rectangle of light as the doors opened and Yannis ran out, just as the door in front of her shut completely and they began to plummet to the garage.

47

Georgie was at Broadcasting House just north of Oxford Street, being collected from reception by Joel Flannigan, a sound recordist at the BBC. The BBC press office had found someone for her to talk to within hours of her calling. Joel had wanted her to email over the recording she wanted help with, but she was cautious and made excuses and insisted on coming in person once her shift was finished. Since it had been illegally obtained she didn't want a record of what she was doing.

Joel was young, had a beard and wore a T-shirt bearing a Banksy image of a kneeling young girl holding a bomb. He took the stairs three at a time, hands thrust deep in his trouser pockets. He led her along corridors and into a small windowless room that looked like the bridge of the *Starship Enterprise*.

'Wow. This is technical.'

'It's a piece of cake really. Take a seat.' He sat down in a swivel chair and put his ankle on his other knee, tapping out a tune on his raised leg with his fingers. 'How can I help?'

'I want to know if you can tell me anything about this recording I've got, where it might have been taken, what the noise at the end is.'

He nodded and leaned forward, took her iPhone and plugged it into his system and hit the play function. They listened to '1824 is no'. He paused. 'Short.' He raised his eyebrows invitingly at her. 'All very cloak and dagger.'

'Maybe, maybe not. You hear that weird noise at the end though, right?'

Joel adjusted some knobs and played the message again, much louder. Georgie heard the hiss of static and the strange pattering noise and the louder clunk of the phone at the end. Joel was now tapping his top lip with a finger. 'OK, let's start with what I do know. The sound we can't identify yet is about three to five feet away from the phone, I'd say. It doesn't resonate like a large sound that is far away, it has a tone like a small one close by.'

Georgie nodded. 'What kind of phone is that anyway? Can you tell?'

Joel smiled. 'You betcha. We've got a file just of different phone sounds.'

'You have?'

He reached across to a bank of CDs in a rack behind him and pulled one out and inserted it into a machine. 'Try this.' He pressed play and Georgie listened intently. 'Pretty similar, yeah? Your phone's got a receiver, probably connected with a wire, you can hear the old-school clunk-clunk as it's put back in the cradle. We use these sounds a lot in radio shows like *The Archers*. They're good ways to end scenes with the over-fifties.' He grinned.

'Yes, you're right.'

'With a mobile the recording just stops, and a hands-free is a different tone again, so is a cordless. So I'm thinking it could be an office extension phone, or something recondi-tioned from the seventies, maybe?'

'Yeah, interesting.'

Joel played Georgie's recording again, nodding and adjusting volumes. 'It's inside, I'd guess. There's little background inter-ference. No traffic noise or drilling, no birdsong.'

'Is it a car phone?'

He considered that for a moment, but shook his head.

'That sounds a little different again. And you'd hear a low-level background noise, but only if he was driving, I guess. So a stationary car is a possibility. There're also no squeaking chairs, no rings on his hands knocking together. No computer noise either. He's somewhere quiet.'

Georgie nodded. 'And then we have this noise at the end.'

'Yup.' They both leaned in, as if being closer to the equipment might produce an answer quicker. 'I can't identify it off the top of my head.' He thought for a moment. 'I can try to replicate the sound at the end, then we might get some idea of what is making it,' he suggested.

Georgie watched him, fascinated, as he ran his fingers along the library of CDs, pulling out several. 'A lot of our stuff is digital now, but we're still using these guys too. Let's do something fun, since you came all the way from east London to here. I'll play a sound, we'll see if it matches the one we're trying to replicate and you see if you can tell what the sound is. OK?'

'You're on.' For the next ten minutes Georgie listened to a random collection of noises, none of them similar to the one they were searching for. She failed to identify a cup rolling on a table, a food mixer slowing down, sheaves of paper being fed into a photocopier, a telex machine and someone sitting in a saggy sofa. She got a bath emptying and someone typing, but thought a coffee percolator was someone weeing. By the end of Joel's experiment they were both laughing. 'God, I was rubbish.'

'It's much harder than most people realise to pinpoint a noise.' Joel leaned back and let out a groan. 'This is very frustrating. I can't place it. Leave it with me and I'll keep thinking, maybe I can turn up something.'

'What can you tell me about his voice?' Georgie asked.

Joel made a pained face. 'Not really my area. It's high because he's disguising it and the message is short, that makes it much harder. The police have experts who can decipher huge amounts from a voice, but I do background sounds. Sorry I can't help you further.'

Georgie nodded. 'It's OK. By the way, does 1824 mean anything to you?'

He shrugged. 'Something to do with Beethoven?'

'That's 1812.' She said it before she realised that he was having a laugh with her.

'Remember, this kind of thing can begin to send you mad. You'll be waking up in the night, dreaming of 1824. If I come up with anything I'll give you a ring.'

'You do that,' she said and got up to go.

'Wait a sec, have a listen to this.' He pulled a CD from his library and inserted it and pressed play. She heard the sound of liquid being poured into a glass, the hiss of fizz, the chunk of ice and the glass being scraped across a bar. 'Fancy one?'

Georgie smiled. 'That's very kind, but I'd better not.'

Joel shrugged his shoulders. 'It was worth a try.'

Georgie nodded. Joel Flannigan was a nice guy.

48

Ricky held Kelly's arm as he got her out of the lift and into his car. He tied her hands together with cable ties, did the same with her ankles and fastened the seat belt. He was calm and quite gentle, which made it worse, because she knew he was going to kill her. No other outcome was possible. He didn't seem bothered about the CCTV and that worried her too. He wasn't even trying to hide what he was doing. He started the car and exited the garage, stopped at the red light, and then turned right on to the Euston Road and began to drive west.

Ricky occasionally glanced at her as he drove. Eventually he began to talk. 'I've only got one question for you, why did you do it?'

She began to shout at him. 'You had no alibi. You had motive. I *saw* you kill that man. The police thought you were such a threat to me that I had to change my identity and leave my home town, go into witness protection. They were right. Eight years later, you've tracked me down, tied me up and you want me to believe that you're not a violent psychopath – I'm supposed to believe that you didn't do it.'

He said nothing, following signs for the M3 motorway. He drove at no more than seventy-five mph the whole way to the south coast. Now they were parked in a lay-by on a rise overlooking Southampton. Southampton Water was like a black smudge across a mediocre watercolour below them.

'It's interesting how the other facts back up what you saw,' he continued. 'You've used them to convince yourself you saw me.'

'Oh, please.'

'I got a phone call that day, on the phone in the warehouse. I was supposed to meet a guy who wanted some stuff doing. That meeting happened at just the time you were walking by the front doors, looking into a dark interior. Were you already fucking him then?'

'Who?'

'You're not dumb so don't act it. Your husband, Malamatos.'

Kelly frowned. 'I didn't meet him till years later. That day I was bringing my first husband, Michael, a sandwich.'

'Did you often do that? Hurry on down to his work with lunch?'

'Sometimes.' She paused. 'Well, once before.' She paused again. 'He asked me to come that day.'

'Who did Michael work for?'

'The docks.'

'Who else?'

'How dare you speak ill of the dead.'

'Who else?'

'I don't know.'

'You sure, Kelsey? Think about it. Because him calling for you to bring the sandwich put you in the right spot at the right time to see me.'

'This is bullshit.'

'The star witness at my trial, a beautiful young mother, a promising singing career but nothing too immoral – catnip, you were.'

She sat up straight and looked at him.

'Once upon a time I was the go-to guy. But I was taken out. You know what happens when there's a vacuum? Something always rushes in to fill it. Your husband has an interest here at the docks. He bought part of an operating company six years ago.'

She was having none of it. 'You expect me to feel sorry for you? You're a violent crook who's kidnapped the woman you threatened because she told the police what she'd seen. I'm supposed to sit here, tied up and *understand* you? Just get this all over with and let me go join my dead husband and kid!'

There was only one way this could end. If he let her go he would be headed back to jail before two hours were out, police crashing through his door, witness protection officers surrounding her house. The thought of Sylvie bringing up her children flashed before her as she tried futilely to yank her wrists apart.

'You see the streetlights on the square down there?' He pointed out of the window. 'I first went joyriding round those streets when I was twelve. I glassed a man in the Crown when I was seventeen. He needed thirty-seven stitches. You know now? I can't even remember what the argument was about. I can't remember, but he still has those scars. He looks at them every day. I deserved to go to jail for all those things I did when I was young, for all the people I cheated and the violence I inflicted. I served my time in prison, just not for the right crime.'

She got angry. 'Lucky you. I haven't been able to come back here for eight years. I did the *right* thing and you ruined my life.'

He shook his head. 'I want to show you something.' He drove into the town, past old landmarks that whispered to her, the turning up to her old school, the sign to the hospital where Amber had been born, down to the streets near the dock and then out again further inland where the terraces gave way to cul-de-sacs and thirties' housing. He parked.

'You make a sound now and I will kill you.'

He pulled a penknife from the glove box and cut her ankle ties. He came round and opened the car door, took her arm and walked her along the pavement to an alley between two houses. It was dark here; she heard him scrabbling around and moving what looked like an old milk crate. He made her stand on it and from up there she could see into the garden and kitchen window of a neatly kept thirties' house. A woman with blonde curls was sitting in a chair, the flickering light of a TV bouncing off her face. She had three dogs round her, two lying on the rug on the floor and one in her lap. She was playing with its ears, nuzzling into him now and then, while chatting on a mobile clamped to her ear.

Ricky stood up on the milk crate next to Kelly.

'That's Dawn. My Dawn. I love Dawn as much as you love your children. You say I deserved to go to jail, and I did, but not for something I didn't do. Not for murder.' He grabbed her neck tightly, forcing her face towards the window. 'Look at that woman. She stood by me, all the years I was inside, she believed in me, and she waited. She never missed a prison visit – she used to bring cakes she'd made in for the screws. They'd make a show of not accepting it, against the rules it was, but I'd see them sharing it out later. Always managed a smile for me all those years she must have been hurting, all those years that were draining from her life, a life put on hold for me. Look at her!' She could feel the hard top of the fence pushing into her cheek as he gripped her tightly. 'Look at her. What does that woman look like she wants? What is that woman in mourning for?'

Dawn had put her mobile down on top of a book now; she was beginning to stand, picking up the dog on her lap and talking to it as she gave it a hug and put it on the floor. She stretched and turned lazily to the back window, the frown lines deep between her eyebrows, the tired lines round the eyes catching the dancing TV light. 'That woman wants a baby. She's forty-two. She's never going to get her baby. She's the victim of what happened that day, just as much as you are.'

They both looked back through the window at Dawn, staring now into the middle distance, twisting a lock of hair round a finger, sadness at permanent rest on her features.

'It was critical to the case that you saw me. Someone organised for you to see me. Who was it?' He yanked her head round, so their faces were inches from each other.

'I don't know. You must have friends at the docks, you must be able to find out that way.'

'That's just it. The only names I've heard are your husbands'. Your dead husband and your new one.'

He took his hand off her neck and she breathed in the cold air so quickly it burned her throat. She staggered forward off the crate. 'That can't be. They didn't know each other.'

'How did you meet Christos?'

'I met him in a restaurant.'

'How sweetly run-of-the-mill. You both sat down at the same table? Reached for the sugar at the same time?'

'I served him. You'd managed to turn me into a fugitive from my own life, remember? I was working a dead-end job.'

Ricky barked out an approximation of a laugh. 'You hear a lot of tales inside. It's the one thing you can still do inside, talk. It confirms what you already know – life is about what you've got to trade, whether you're conscious of it or not. You were young, a pretty face, a nice singer. But you had somebody else's kid, no money, no connections and a bucketful of grief. It doesn't add up, Kelsey. It's not a trade. And a man like Christos, he trades. It's in his blood. It's what he does. He makes deals. So you need to ask yourself, what's the deal here?'

'He loved me. That was the deal. After everything I'd been through I deserved a bit of that.'

'Did you get it? Well, did you? Not many mothers I know walk around their home with a gun in their pocket. What happened to your ceiling? If there's one thing I've learned, it's that love is blind, greed is eternal.'

'So you're telling me you think Christos sought me out for money? I don't have any. And anyway, how did he find me? I was in the witness protection scheme – it's impossible—'

Ricky laughed and she saw the absurdity of what she was saying, standing in a Southampton alley, the prisoner of the man she had put in jail. 'Talk at the docks was that the rot went all the way to the top. You think your whereabouts couldn't be bought by a rich and powerful man? You would have been easy to find.' He put his hand on her arm and steered her back towards the car. 'He might have done it to keep you close. After all, you saw something you didn't. One day you might have woken up and realised that.' He started the engine and pulled away.

She shook her head, put her hands on top of her spinning head, shutting out his persistent quiet voice, but what he was saying was making things jump about in her mind, making connections that she'd never considered before, her mind staring down dark paths that led in directions she didn't want to see.

'Grief can make you blind. It makes you desperate for a haven, a place that shuts out some of the horrors. You need to think about whether he exploited that in you. I'm just asking you to think about it.'

They pulled up near a level crossing outside the city. A small rail station, one of the hundreds dotted across Hampshire that sucked commuters towards the riches of the capital. He turned to her as they sat in the dark car park, a fox the only wildlife to be seen. She was unbound now, sitting next to him like they were acquaintances.

They sat in silence watching the night stalker for a few moments.

'You're going to let me go.' They looked at each other, the fox running into the darkness by some bushes. 'You're prepared to take such a risk?' She couldn't keep the awe hidden. 'I could have you instantly put back in jail. Dawn would be alone again.'

He didn't answer for a long time. 'I would be lying if I said I hadn't found tonight surprising. I thought you would be harder. Meaner. I spent most of my life surrounded by bullshitters and cheats. I can tell when someone is lying. You really thought you saw me that day.' He nodded to himself. 'That's clever. That's the only way it would have worked.' He handed her back the empty gun. 'Be careful with that. It's dangerous. Not something to have round kids.'

The tears rolled in two streaks down her cheeks. 'I changed my name, my career, my home, because of a fear of what you would do . . . I don't know what to do now, I can't—'

'Go and see your mother.'

She started crying harder then, watching the fox return and dart in between the car headlight beams. 'And what are you going to do?'

'Good question. Probably nothing. Revenge doesn't help. But I want to know. We all want to know. Someone went to a lot of trouble.' He paused. 'Your husband Michael and your daughter died three months before the trial.'

She gulped in a lungful of air, staring at him. 'It was an accident.' She was pleading with him now, tears in her eyes. 'Please, I was right there, it was an accident.' She heard the clanking of the great metal chains of the Poole harbour ferry, ringing out their death knell. 'Not that. Don't try to change that.'

He made a clucking sound with his tongue on his teeth but he let it go.

From a place entirely different in her mind came a thought.

'The phone call you got at the warehouse that day. What was that about?'

'A guy wanted some stuff shifting.'

'What stuff?'

'Firearms. Shotguns, semi-automatics. Going up to Gunchester.' He rolled his eyes at her blank look. 'Manchester.'

She felt the cold metal in her lap. 'Did you see the guns?'

He shook his head. 'They were hidden, he said.'

'What were they hidden in?'

'He didn't say. He was very proud of the system he had. Said he could smuggle anything with it of almost any size. He mentioned this system a few times.'

'Who was he?'

'I don't know. I'm no fool, I smelled a rat but I was intrigued, so we arranged to meet somewhere quiet. The route there was empty – no CCTV, no one around. That was clever. No one to see me and corroborate my version of events. He never turned up. Docks are teeming with people, but only in small areas. They give the impression of being busy but there are large pockets that are empty for weeks at a time. But of course I hadn't realised he had wanted me out of the way all along.'

'So you never saw him?'

He shook his head. 'But he was probably tall. Like me.' He turned to her. 'He needed to look like me, after all.'

They both stared out of the windscreen into the night. Autumn leaves blew across the strobes of the car lights, orange flares in the light.

'I don't have the answers you want. I don't have the answers I need myself.' She wondered if grief for her lost family had blinded her to things she should have seen, to connections she should have made. She needed air, she couldn't breathe. She dragged at the car lock on the door and half fell out into the cold night.

He leaned across the seat and called after her. 'Have you got any money to get home?' He sounded like a father dropping his student daughter at the station after a visit home. He handed over a twenty from his pocket. 'If you need anything, Dawn's in the phone book. You can call me.'

He put the car in gear and did a wide circle of the empty car park before driving away. She stood for a moment then swayed and fell like a dead weight to the tarmac, sobbing her eyes out.

49

Kelly got home well after midnight and ran to her children. They were curled up asleep in the TV room because of the water damage in their bedroom. Christos wasn't home. She kept shivering and realised it was delayed shock, her emotions rollercoastering between euphoria at still being able to stoop over her children in the dark, and an overpowering emptiness. Ricky had let her go, had shown that he wasn't a danger to her, but his threat had been one of the pillars on which her new life had been constructed, and with it removed there was nothing to fill the void. She had snatched up the phone to call the witness protection officers several times on the train home, but had cut the calls before they were connected. They could be in a new place, with new identities, in just twelve hours, but Christos would still be with her. And what if what Ricky had said was true?

Kelly tried to put it together. Was it possible she had been duped? Duped into testifying to something that wasn't true? That the wrong man went to jail for all those years? That she had been a tool used by others for their own ends? But if he was telling the truth, then maybe Christos *was* involved. Maybe Christos had not met her by accident. The thought stunned her. That he had met her to keep her close, had married her for motives other than love showed he was prepared to play for very high stakes indeed. She thought back to the night she had asked for a divorce. To the violence he had inflicted. A clearer message that he would make her stay at all costs could not have been given. A husband who could do that would think nothing of sending an innocent man to jail.

She closed the children's door and opened Medea's. Her mother-in-law was snoring gently. She shut Medea's door and headed upstairs, searching the dark cupboards beyond the kitchen, the place where dried-up superglue and unused cricket bats live out their decades. Christos had come in here before firing at the ceiling. She found the box of bullets on a shelf so high up she needed a chair to reach to the back of it.

'Kelsey', Ricky had called her. Kelsey was her name. She had a flashing image of herself as a young girl in those Portakabin classrooms, the seagulls cawing and shrieking their mournful sound, the Bic with the chewed end in her small fingers, writing out her name. They say name is destiny. Christos never shut up about it, the importance of the Malamatos name. Reputation and name were the same to him, as if every action by anyone was to besmirch his family name, his legacy, the motherland, his honour and his reputation. She felt the bubbled skin on her stomach. Name had been an excuse for a lot of unspeakable behaviour. She loaded the gun and walked across the living room. She was leaving, with the children, right now. There was nothing Medea could do to stop her. Ricky had liberated her from the prison she had constructed around herself. Now it was a question of fighting.

She came down the stairs on silent feet to wake the children. She only saw the shadow of the man standing at the bottom when she was halfway down.

He stood looking up at her in the gloom, calm and assured. It was the man who had followed her to the lawyer's office. 'Why don't you get some sleep, Mrs Malamatos? Christos is worried about your state of mind, he's worried what you might do to yourself, so we're here to look after you.'

Kelly looked down the corridor and saw one of the drivers who had come to take her away from Lindsey's standing by the door. She was too late to escape. Christos was tightening the net, counting down the hours till the kids were sent away. She tried to remain calm and think through her options. She was exhausted; nothing could be done tonight so it was best to get some sleep.

'We need your phone,' the first man said. 'And just so you know, Christos has changed the code on the lifts, so it's better if you just relax and try and get some rest.'

She was trapped. Even Medea wouldn't know the new code for the lift and the stair door. She handed her phone over and walked into the TV room, lay down by her children and fell instantly asleep.

50

Kelly woke up at seven squashed awkwardly into the sofa, the gun a painful imprint on her hip where it bulged in her pocket. The kids were asleep on the floor next to her. She got up and went into her bedroom, washed her face, drank some water.

She came out into the corridor to find Medea up. 'So you're back,' began her mother-in-law. 'You decided to grace us with your presence.'

'Where's Christos?'

'He's working flat out trying to find out what happened to his employee on that ship, and to minimise the bad publicity.'

'Bad publicity? He should be here to explain to his children why he did that to our ceiling. He should be here to grovel at their feet and apologise for scaring the living daylights out of them.'

'The ceiling will be repaired today. No one will ever know what happened here.'

'You can't keep it a secret.' Their argument was interrupted by the sound of the children stirring in the TV room.

Kelly opened the door to see Florence stretching and kicking back her covers. 'It's funny waking up in here,' she said. The change of routine was a novelty, and not for a good reason.

'Did you sleep OK?'

Florence shrugged her shoulders, looking downcast. Yannis

sat up and yawned. Kelly came in the room, bent down and gave them a long hug.

'Why did Daddy do that to the pigeons?' Florence's voice was quiet.

Medea answered for her son. 'He's very stressed at the moment, what with the man falling off the *Saracen*. Though it doesn't excuse what he did. He would never hurt you.'

But what about me, thought Kelly. She came out into the corridor and looked around. The two men who were in the flat last night were still there.

Kelly turned to Medea. 'You know you can't keep me a prisoner forever.'

Medea drew herself up, indignant. 'Prisoner, what nonsense you spout. These people are here for your protection. We're worried about you.'

'I've seen what happens in this house in the middle of the night, who creeps about—'

'You see? You're getting delusions, and I'm worried.'

'You defend a man who fires off a loaded gun around his children, simply because he's your flesh and blood.' She saw embarrassment flit across Medea's face. 'That's right, I want you to feel your shame.' Kelly saw one of the men at the end of the corridor begin to walk towards them.

'Mum? What's going on? I hate it when you argue, please . . .' Florence was standing by the open door to the TV room, eyes brimming with tears.

Medea swung into action. 'Come on kids, we're going to do some painting, and help Kelly finish the masks for the Halloween party tomorrow. We'll have a lovely day here at the flat just relaxing, all of us together. I'll get all the stuff ready upstairs.'

Kelly wanted to laugh. Medea thought that a bit of playtime with the acrylics could paper over the compromises on show here.

She walked away into her bedroom again, trying to think. Ricky's revelations had only reinforced to her the danger she was in from her husband. His mother, she knew now, would stand with him through anything, defend him on every point. She came to the window and stared out at the city teeming with life below her, at the millions of lives lived in varying degrees of chaos and danger. But today she didn't feel separated from the city below her, she felt part of it, energised by it, not terrified. This morning, after the revelations of last night, she was a different person, someone who saw opportunity now.

She walked into the bathroom again, looked at her bottle of pills on the shelf, picked it up and dropped it into the bin. It was time to take responsibility, it was time to end this. First chance she got, she would escape, without the kids. One thing Ricky's tale had taught her was that tyrants don't get everything their own way. What she needed to do now was prepare for any chance she got. She felt the gun hard against her hip. And that meant at least getting some breakfast inside her.

51

The Wolf leaned forward with his elbows on his knees, rubbing his palms together. His palms made a dry, scratchy sound audible over the deep rumble of the engines. 'OK, here's what we're going to do. You need to come with me.'

She sat up straighter, ready to disagree. 'I want to stay here. I was told to stay in here.'

'That's not possible any more. You're a courier—'

'How dare you accuse me of—'

'Save it, no one's interested. Details apart, you want to get paid, more than anything else, yes? This way you'll get your money and more. Everyone's happy.'

She looked at him and he looked back. She was churning through her options, beginning to realise she didn't have many. After a moment she shrugged and struggled to her feet in the listing ship.

The storm was starting to abate, the sky that seemed to be sitting right on their heads began to lift imperceptibly as they powered northwards into the English Channel, the busiest shipping lane in the world, a great motorway of ships ploughing to their destinations. The mood on board was tense and grave; the President would be having many conversations with various agencies – coastguard, customs, police, writing reports, filling in logs, accounting for the unaccountable, trying to explain the unexplainable.

The crew was still searching the ship for the company

man, checking he hadn't got lodged somewhere, that the storm hadn't shifted something and trapped him underneath it.

The Wolf found Jonas in the ship's mess, looking nervous and morose. 'You OK? It can unsettle a man, something like this.'

Jonas shrugged. One of the Poles finished his coffee and left the room.

'Will we be delayed when we arrive?'

There he was, thought the Wolf, trying to anticipate what law enforcement would be there to greet this cursed ship when it charged into London. 'Why, got something you're keen to hide?'

'No.' He looked indignant and folded his arms over his chest.

'Come with me.' The Wolf walked out of the room, Jonas trailing behind, up the stairs to the accommodation area and stood outside Jonas's cabin. 'Open it.'

Jonas stood firm. 'Why?'

'Bring that rucksack you've got locked away in there.' He saw Jonas's eyes widen with fear. 'Bring it out here, or I'm going to order a search of your cabin.'

Jonas licked his lips, trying to calculate the risk he was running in refusing. A moment later he decided he had no option and opened the door and picked up the rucksack.

'And bring your coat.'

The Wolf led Jonas out a side door on the accommodation floor. The wind was still strong, blowing hard in their faces. Jonas shivered and pulled on his coat, his hood flapping hard against the back of his head. The rain had stopped, the grey sky beginning to be picked apart by small patches of blue.

'How many years since you've been home?' the Wolf asked as they began to walk along the side of the ship.

'You tell me,' he shot back.

The Wolf smiled. Jonas was turning into exactly the kind

of guy he liked – but he wasn't going to tell him that just yet. 'I haven't been home since you were trying to get your hand up the skirt of a girl in biology.'

'I haven't been home for five years.'

The Wolf nodded. 'So how you planning to get yourself up and running again?'

'I'll look up a few old friends.'

'Sell what's in that bag . . .' The Wolf stopped walking. 'We need to turn back, go any further than here and they'll see us from the bridge.' Jonas said nothing. 'You can work for me.'

Jonas snorted, but he was listening.

'How much you got in that bag? Come on, there's going to be a shitstorm when we dock, make no mistake. You're running a risk. There's nothing wrong in being bad, but you've got to be smart.'

Jonas was weighing up what he said.

'Chuck it overboard.'

He looked horrified. 'There's nearly a grand's worth of gear in there.'

'I'll pay you more if you do a job for me and you won't even have to do anything illegal. Chuck it over.'

'You don't know what I had to do to get it.'

'Not interested. Chuck it over.' The two of them were staring at each other, tense, Jonas making calculations. 'It's not a choice.'

'What are you offering me?'

'More than you'd make in a year.'

'A year in Bolivia or a year in—'

'Quit quibbling. And it's not a choice.'

'How long will it take?'

'Two or three days maximum. I need you to look after someone for me. You'll be a chaperone, that's all. Think of it as a triumphant return to the big smoke.' They both looked off the side of the ship. A low grey smear was forming on the horizon, their first sight of home. 'There she is. Fills your heart with joy to be back, does it?' The Wolf's fingers began to throb painfully, the waxy whiteness back again. 'Act smart, Jonas. The risks you run always need to be less than the reward.' The Wolf pulled out a bunch of hundred dollar bills and began counting them out. 'A third now, a third in the middle, the rest in three days maximum.'

Jonas looked at the money, took the old rucksack off his shoulder and tossed it over the side. They both leaned over to watch it fall, swallowed up by the churning sea.

52

Even though Georgie had grown up near the river and had been doing this job for a year, watching the big ships come in was still an event. The small dot on the horizon that grew and formed detail and grew and grew more until the great towering beast was near enough to boom out its presence. The *Saracen* had ridden out a force 9 gale, but it had been a cursed voyage. Even in these days of muster drills, GPS and fully equipped lifeboats, they had still lost a man to the vastness of the ocean.

There was a blustery wind gusting off the Thames, the remains of the tropical storm out in the Atlantic that had tipped the man overboard. It was weather to make you agitated. Some of her hair slapped her in the face and irritated her eyes. She zipped up her cagoule and turned away. Mo and she were doing onboard checks before anyone was allowed off the ship. They boarded their small boat, dwarfed in size by the huge sides of the vessel before them. They crossed the hundred feet of open water, tied up the boat and got on board.

The captain met them, his face anxious and grey.

'Not a good day at the office,' Georgie said.

He swore under his breath. 'Seventeen years I've been doing this job, never had a man overboard.' Like a Tube driver with a suicidal commuter, it was what every captain dreaded.

'Why was he on the ship?' Mo asked.

'He was coming back from a business trip to Brazil. I don't

know more than that. Malamatos employees travel for free, of course. He listened to the safety explanations, was there at the muster drill. Seemed calm, was sick, I think, but kept to his cabin most of the time. He was no problem. The crew's gathering in the galley now.'

Georgie nodded. 'We'll talk to the passengers later. Lead the way please.'

The galley was a windowless room with stainless-steel surfaces and units. Numerous stainless-steel pans hung from hooks on a central hanger over a food preparation island. They clanged and bumped together like a discordant wind chime with the slight motion of the ship. Georgie and Mo said hello and began checking passports, matching everyone up.

'When was the last time you saw the man who went over?' Georgie asked a man with a Polish name, his birthplace listed as Gdansk.

He shrugged, big shoulders moving. 'I don't think I ever saw him. He kept to his cabin most of the time.'

She nodded, moving down the line, each man she crossed off bringing her closer to Mo, who was working from the other end.

'He was sick a lot, complaining,' the next man along, with an Irish passport, added.

'When did you last see him?'

He shrugged. 'Oh, Christ. Maybe Monday? It was a difficult crossing, the storm was big, we had a lot to do. Ask the Wolf, he's a night walker, likes the danger of the open sea.' He cocked his head at the man standing next to him in line.

Georgie glanced up at the man he referred to. He was tall and broad, leaning forward on the balls of his feet. She handed the Irishman back his documents and opened up the Wolf's. 'Clyde Bonnier. Born in Liverpool . . .' She examined his passport carefully, glancing up at his face. He bared his teeth at her. 'I wouldn't do that if I were you, I'm not in a good mood.' She took a long look at his passport photo, then at the windburned face where a grin looked like it was about to explode across it, the dirty blond hair lightened from sun and salt.

'How long have you been working for Malamatos Shipping?'

'Four years.'

'What did you do before?'

'All sorts of things. We've all done something.'

'Give me an example.'

'I was a tree surgeon. Good with my hands.' He splayed them for her as if he were being helpful, doing jazz hands.

She saw Mo look over. She glanced at his muscular forearms, product of a physical job. He stood right in front of her; she wondered if he was leaning in, butting in on her personal space. 'Why'd you stop?'

'Vibration white finger. It's your body's way of saying this is the end of the road.'

She looked at his strange, waxy-looking fingers. 'You ever cut down any Brazilian rosewood?'

'Of course. Plantations are where a lot of the—'

'No – mature specimens. Amazonian forest trees.'

He looked at her for a long moment, wondering whether to frown. 'The big fellas? Magnificent, they'd be. That'd be so much fun.' He grinned at her, eager to play. 'But that would be against the law.'

He was playing with her, trying to wind her up. She closed his passport and slapped it on his chest. 'I hear you like walking around at night.'

'I find it difficult to keep still. Restless legs.'

'Were you out in the storm?'

'A force 9 in the Atlantic in the winter? Of course. Best fun to be had, that is.'

'Did you see him out there at any point?'

'It's hard to see a hand in front of your face in weather.

Real weather, I mean. Most people have never experienced
it so can't imagine what it's like. You can drown in the spray,
do you know that?'

'So you didn't see him?'

He shook his head. 'No. I didn't.'

'Born in Liverpool. Where did you grow up?'

'Me? I hardly know. Everywhere and nowhere. We're the
rootless bunch, the merchant fleet. Aren't we, lads? Making
it up as we go along.' He turned back to her, staring hard.
'Maybe you can relate to that.'

She looked away because the truth was she could. He
seemed so familiar to her, with his bravado and his magnetism.
She knew why and she was ashamed. He reminded her of
her brothers: when their darting eyes finally rested on you,
you could do nothing but glow in their momentary approval.
She found it hard to resist the pull of the dangerous ones.

She moved to the next man in line. She felt the Wolf's eyes
sliding up and down her body as she turned away.

Half an hour later the captain was showing Georgie and Mo
the cabin of the man who went overboard. 'Here's his passport, toothbrush and razor, his wallet.' He gestured at the
small pile of personal effects on the bed.

Georgie looked around the room, bigger than a prison cell,
but not by much. A small desk, a chair, a TV. A gloomy light
struggled to filter in through the two portholes but any view
was blocked by the metal wall of a dark blue container not
two feet from the window. She looked into the small bathroom.
A cream-coloured shower tray, basin and toilet. She knelt
down and looked under the bed and was greeted by a ball
of dust.

'There's nothing here,' she said to Mo and he nodded in
agreement. They got back on their tiny boat and were on
shore a little while later. She made tea for her and Mo and

waited in the customs area for the few passengers to disembark from the *Saracen*. The public customs area was visible from the office where Georgie sat and was made up of lines of dirty, scratched plastic screens and a dividing rope that looped lazily through movable metal posts, designed to corral tired arrivals into a queue. Once checked by Georgie's colleagues, they pushed through a set of double swing doors, each with a round window made of scratched Perspex. The place was sad and unkempt; the cruise ships docked further upriver now, and the operation here was strictly functional. She heard the roaring of a cleaner's polishing machine getting to work on the lino. She let herself be amazed that they still had the budget as she caught a glimpse of a figure through the scratched Perspex window on the other side of the arrivals door.

'Is that Christos?' She put her cup down.

'He's here with Sylvie,' said Mo.

Georgie stood and moved to be able to see him better. 'Who's he waiting for?' She turned round, trying to find a passenger list. 'Who's on this ship?' Mo handed her a list and she scanned the names. None of them meant anything to her.

'It's not illegal to meet someone off a ship, last time I looked,' Preston said. He lifted his shoes up on to the table, a gesture designed to irritate her.

'I want every passenger and their luggage searched.' She came out of the office and barked a series of instructions at the duty officer perched on a swivel chair.

The *Saracen* manoeuvred alongside a quay and half an hour later a thin straggle of people began to disembark with their luggage. Georgie was peering at them through the glass in the office window. She could hear Preston making a personal phone call behind her, yakking about cinema times to someone. She left the office and stood next to the customs officer. A young man with a pockmarked face shivered in the line, his backpacking clothing insufficient for a trip to northern Europe. Jonas Wyman. A man was next, then a young woman in a big parka with a fur-lined hood carrying a large plastic bag and a cushion. The customs officer was looking at her passport, inputting information into the computer from Luciana Nascimento's landing card.

The doors to the UK swung forward and back as people passed through them. Georgie occasionally caught glimpses of Christos as the doors moved.

The woman in the parka took it off and the female officer ran her hands discreetly up and down the young woman's body. Luciana put her parka back on as the officer carefully examined the cushion. She handed it back to Luciana, who stuffed the cushion down into her coat and shivered, doing her zip all the way tightly up to her chin and lifting the hood. She picked up her bag and walked away to the doors into the UK.

They turned to a man next in the line.

Twenty seconds later Georgie heard a woman screaming. She ran towards the swing doors and slammed them open. Luciana was on the floor, Sylvie on top of her pulling her hair. Jonas was shouting for them to stop and Christos was trying to pull his lover off the woman.

Georgie and Mo tried to pull the warring women apart.

Luciana was spewing Portuguese at Sylvie, who had gone puce in the face. 'This bitch assaulted me,' Luciana said, struggling to get away from Georgie.

'She just went mad, jumped on her for no reason,' Jonas added.

'Don't you fucking dare speak to me like that,' Sylvie spat at Luciana, bringing an 'oh' of shock from the gawping bystanders.

'Enough,' shouted Georgie. 'Calm down, everyone.'

Her entreaty was mirrored by Christos, who was white in the face. 'For God's sake, Sylvie, have you lost your mind?'

'First she posed as Isabella, looking pregnant. I thought it was her until she came right up to me. Then she whispered that Isabella has been harmed—'

'What a lie! Who is this Isabella?' Luciana screamed.

'Who's Isabella?' asked Georgie.

'She's fine, I spoke to the captain two minutes ago.' Christos was aghast.

Everyone started shouting again as two policemen hurried in from the building next door. The next thing Georgie knew, Sylvie had broken free of Mo's hold and swung her handbag high and fast at Luciana's head. Christos jumped forward to stop her and careered into Jonas, bringing both of them to the floor in an untidy jumble.

'That's it. Get this lot out of sight.' Georgie had had enough of the gawping crowd. She dragged Sylvie towards an interview room and shouted at Mo to take Luciana to another. The policeman took Christos by the arm and marched him into the room behind Sylvie.

Now it was Christos's turn to be livid. 'You can't keep me in here. It is critical I meet someone off this ship.'

'They can wait,' Georgie snapped. 'There are seats out there.'

'I need to phone the captain—'

'Well, your girlfriend should have thought of that before she attacked a woman for saying something she didn't like.'

They could hear Luciana's shouts from the next interview room. Preston appeared, looking like he was enjoying it all just a little too much. 'She wants to press charges.'

Sylvie sat mute, looking up at Preston with such hatred Georgie was almost scared. 'Do you know that woman?' Georgie asked her.

'I've never met the bitch.'

Georgie sighed but it was Christos who started shouting at Sylvie. 'Have you gone nuts? Isabella will have to wait now—'

'Nobody says things like that to me—'

Christos stood up from his seat and turned to go.

'Where are you going?' the policeman asked.

'I need to be out there—'

'Until I understand what's happened here, you'll have to wait.' He pulled out his notebook.

'I didn't do anything.'

'So let's get all the details and I'll decide when you can go. The maximum sentence for assault is six months. I suggest you sit down.'

53

Isabella said goodbye to the captain and thanked him. He smiled a lot and said it had been a pleasure, apologising for the weather and the rough crossing as if it were within his command to change it. He helped her off the ship and a crew member carried her bag to customs. She showed her passport and landing card to a man with milky skin speckled with moles, and showed her booking for the private hospital.

Her bag was pulled up on to a table and carefully searched by a woman customs officer. She ran her hands up and down Isabella's legs, across her back and between her breasts. She held her breath as the woman ran them across her swollen stomach. The officer asked her if she knew Christos Malamatos. Isabella gave the answer she had rehearsed with Christos: that she was a relative getting expert care in London. The customs officer put her bag down on the floor, and she wheeled it through the swing doors and into a new country.

The concourse was empty. She paused, drinking in the different signs, the different smell, the cold efficiency of the place. She became uncertain. She had expected Christos and Sylvie to meet her, they had insisted they would. Then a skinny man with bad skin hurried over.

'Isabella da Silva? Please, I have a car waiting. The Malamatoses have been held up and sent me to get you. But you'll see them soon. Very soon.'

It was good to be back on dry land, finally to feel the sickness drain away. She followed him out of the terminal.

54

It was early evening when the Wolf finally got off the ship and on to dry land. He used a phone box to dial the number for the mobile that he'd given to Jonas. Jonas picked up promptly.

'Everything OK?'

'Great, no problem at all.' Jonas sounded excited, like it was proving a far easier way to make money than he had anticipated.

'You in the hotel?'

'Yup, got the room, making my way through the mini bar – cashew nuts and those Japanese spicy things. We're ordering in a takeaway. She's found her land legs and is starving.'

'Watch that door, remember.'

'Will do. It was chaos at customs, just like you hoped. That blonde is one uptight woman. She really took Luciana to be Isabella for a few moments, and when Luciana said something provocative to her, she just thumped her right across the cheek. She fell down on the floor – madness. Officers came running from all directions.'

The Wolf smiled. Luciana fleetingly pretending to be Isabella, her provoking of Sylvie, had worked like a dream. 'Is Luciana with you now, too?'

'Yeah, she dropped the charges after a while and has just arrived.'

'OK. No one goes out, no one comes in except me. I'll be over in a while.' Christos would work out soon enough what was going on. He would be hunting in earnest for his lost courier. But he reckoned he had a few hours at least before the final act.

He slung his bag over his shoulder and like he had done many times in his life before, walked into the dark of a London evening.

55

The day of the Halloween party dawned grey and cold. Kelly had slept little, but more than the guards, who had kept their vigil all night. She was eating toast when Medea came into the kitchen. 'He wants to see you.'

'Well I'm here, obviously.'

'He's at the office, he wants you to go to him.'

Kelly felt a hint of an opportunity. 'What's it about?'

'I don't know. These men are to take you.'

She said nothing and finished her breakfast. 'I'll take the kids with me and then we're right by the Halloween party and can go there afterwards.'

Medea shook her head. 'The kids stay with me. We can finish the masks here and bring them with us in the car to the party. We'll meet you there.'

'What time are you planning to get there?'

'Three. You need to hurry, Christos wants to see you now.'

At least she would get out of the flat. 'OK, we'll meet at the play centre when the party starts.' Kelly reached out and hugged her children, a hug so tight she wanted it to last for ever.

As she headed to the service lift she saw Florence's and Yannis's weak smiles as they stood in the corridor. She forced herself to act normally. 'See you later.' One of the guards entered the new code, and they both walked either side of her into the lift. The doors clanged shut like a cell's and she felt the uncomfortable sensations of the lift plummeting to the ground.

When they reached the basement car park one man got in the passenger seat of her car, the other behind her. 'What does Christos want to see me about?'

They didn't answer and despite her best effort, her fingers shook with fear as she started the car.

It started to rain as she drove eastwards through the City and beyond, the cloud sinking on to the squat roofs of grey sixties buildings, obliterating satellite masts and TV dishes. They passed the streaked grey of cement underpasses, and Bangladeshi men hurrying past puddles, their backs bent against the rain and the wind. The wipers scraped off the dust thrown up by the lorries charging from red light to red light all the way to Essex.

She pulled into the car park by Malamatos Shipping and got out of the car. The men followed. Mary, the receptionist from Canvey Island who had manned this desk for as long as Kelly could remember and was already counting down the years until retirement took her off to Spain, looked up.

'Kelly! How are you?'

The warmth of Mary's smile was the only nice thing about the morning.

'Things have been better, and they have been worse.'

Mary nodded, showing she understood. She took no notice of the men hanging round by the door, there were always people like that coming and going at Malamatos Shipping.

'Where's Christos?'

Mary leaned across the desk towards Kelly. 'He's been here all night. He's so upset and taking it very badly. He prides himself on the safety record of his ships, as you know. I never met the man who went over' – Mary made a sideways movement with her shoulders as if she were helping to dispatch him over the railings herself – 'but terrible business, terrible.'

. Kelly nodded, scanning the office floor to the right of

Mary, a mishmash of room dividers and white plasterboard corridors, caught somewhere between modern and traditional and failing at both. She could see the closed door to Christos's office in the corner.

'Excuse me.' Mary broke off to take a call. 'Malamatos Shipping, how can I help?'

Kelly pointed towards the office but Mary held up her hand like a stop sign till she'd finished directing the call. 'He's temporarily decamped downstairs.'

'Downstairs? I didn't know there were offices down there.'

Mary lowered her voice as if what she was about to say was scandalous. 'They needed more space, I think. I'll tell him you're here.' She picked up the phone. 'Kelly's arrived.' She nodded. 'I'll bring her right down.' She got up and came round the front of the desk. 'Follow me.' She led Kelly through a double fire door by some stairs.

'I can take it from here,' Kelly suggested.

'You can't miss it anyway. The stairs only lead one way.' Mary smiled as Kelly's heart sank.

56

Kelly paused halfway down, trying to orient herself in the building. She walked to the lower level, pushed open a fire door and entered an underground chamber where heating ducts competed with wiring for space on the ceiling. Bare bulbs dangled intermittently, but the light barely penetrated into the furthest corners. The floor was dark tile and the whole place echoed. In the middle of the space were four large movable screens, creating temporary office walls. Kelly could see the wheels of several office chairs poking out from the bottom, long cords from electricity extension leads snaking away across the floor. A filing cabinet had obviously been hurriedly dragged in to help, the scrape marks still visible on the floor.

'Hello?' She called out uncertainly, her voice echoing in the dark. No one answered. She hesitantly crossed the floor towards the screens and stepped between them. Christos was sitting at one of four desks in front of a computer screen. He was unshaven, his usually pristine shirt rumpled, sleeves rolled up to his elbows. Husband and wife stared at each other over the confetti of disordered files.

'Where were you the night before last?'

She ignored him. 'You shot a gun off near our kids.'

'That's not what I asked. Where were you?'

Kelly stared down at him, the intense stare challenging her. The mouth that turned down at the corners when he was stressed. A cruel mouth on a cruel man. She sensed danger stalking her from every dark corner. 'There was no light or heating in the flat so I went for a walk and something to eat. Where have *you* been all this time?'

'Here.'

'You frightened the kids, really frightened them. You were firing a gun in the house.'

This affected him more than she thought it would. He slumped back in his chair, raked a hand through his hair. 'I'm sorry. It was the stress of the moment. I really shouldn't have done that.'

Kelly looked at her husband. She had expected him to be angry, to cover his wrongdoing with bluster and excuses, but he looked beaten, shattered. The ebb and flow of behaviour in marriage soon solidifies, how someone will react becomes set in stone, but here Christos was acting entirely at odds with what she would have expected. Fear began to crawl up her spine. Something was seriously wrong.

For the first time, Kelly took a look at the walls around her. It was like the command centre of a police investigation. The temporary partitions were pinned with blown-up photocopies of passport photos – mostly male but including some Far Eastern-looking women. Some of the faces were crossed through with heavy black marker; angry, strong strokes that in some cases had almost ripped the paper. There were lists of names with no accompanying photos but large question marks, ship sailing times, phone numbers and illegible scribbles.

'What stress?' Her voice came out as small and quiet.

She heard him get out of his chair and come round the desk as she stared at the walls. She felt his breath on her neck.

'I don't believe my man fell off the *Saracen*. I think he was pushed.'

She wheeled around to face him again, her heart beginning to beat faster. 'Why was he pushed? What was he doing on the ship?'

Christos was staring at the photos and names on the wall beyond them. His mouth was curling again. 'One of these people has taken something I want.' He spat out the words.

'What have they taken?'

He ignored her question. 'Take a look, Kelly, recognise anyone on this wall? Any names, any faces?' He was staring at her, studying her every move.

She turned back to the wall and methodically began to work through the photos and then the list of names, reading even those that had been scratched through with black marker.

'Very carefully, Kelly, don't make a mistake.'

Her eyes swivelled towards him. His face was inches from hers, his gaze never leaving her face.

Halfway down a list of names her eyes snagged on a name, but only for a second. She followed a thick black line that led from his name to a big question mark further across the board.

'Do you think I would know someone on here?'

'All these people work for me or were travelling on the *Saracen*.'

She swallowed carefully. 'But I don't know your employees, or the passengers.'

'Neither do I. When your company reaches a certain size, you cannot know everyone. It makes you vulnerable. My enemies burrow in, Kelly, like termites, plotting to undo me.'

'Why have some names not got pictures?'

'Employment records don't always include photos.'

She looked up and saw him staring at her again. She forced herself to breathe out slowly and turned back to the board. 'I don't know what I'm looking for. What is supposed to be significant?' He was examining her face, searching for something in it. 'This is connected to the customs investigation, isn't it?'

Christos's face loomed ever closer to her own. 'Recognise anyone on this wall?'

She shook her head, dragging her eyes from the wall to his. 'No. What's on that ship, Christos?'

She braced herself for a raised hand flying towards her head or a punch in the stomach, but he did something worse. He looked as if he might cry. She stepped back, her bum hitting the side of a desk. 'What have you done, Christos?'

'I've realised something as I've got older. Life has only a few moments that really matter – just a few moments when all the shit makes sense. It's when you realize what you really love, who you really love.'

Kelly stood staring at her husband, at the man she had adored with such intensity, once, such a long time ago. 'You can tell me what you've done. For the sake of our children tell me how I can help you.'

But he didn't answer, standing there among his piles of paper, staring at his estranged wife as she stared back at him.

57

With each hour that passed, Georgie felt the gnawing of something in her stomach, a twitchy feeling that something was missing. The deep rummage team were already aboard the *Saracen*, in breathing gear and protective suits, burrowing into the intestines of the ship, into smaller and smaller storage holds, into areas toxic with the build-up of oil and fumes over the years, looking for those prized triple-wrapped packages in clingfilm, a box of something that would make it on to the six o'clock news.

Preston swaggering over earlier that day saying that their tip-off had phoned again – Preston had spoken to him – claiming they needed to take a look at Southampton had also annoyed her. She wished she had got the call.

Mo was sitting at his desk beside her – and they had been arguing. She had told Mo that Kelly was from Southampton, maybe there was a connection.

'Stick to the wood trail,' he'd said sharply. 'It's what Anguish asked us to do.'

'I know, but Kelly is from Southampton.'

'She's irrelevant to this case, G.' Mo yawned.

Georgie leaned forward and began typing on the computer. 'Kelly told me she was married before, that her husband and kid died before she married Christos. Why can't I find any record of her?'

'I don't know. This is irrelevant, Georgie!'

'There are more than sixty thousand people working for Her

Majesty's Customs and Excise. I'm sure we can find someone in Southampton. I've probably got a contact on Facebook.'

Preston walked down the office, a pile of folders in his arms. 'Here's information on Malamatos ships calling at Felixstowe. For your reading pleasure.' He dumped the files on her desk and walked away.

Georgie watched as several of them slid slowly off her desk to the carpet. She was twenty-eight. Anguish was nearly fifty; his paper towers covered his entire office. Slowly but inexorably over the years she would be buried by procedure, by failures, by following the letter of the law and letting the crooks get away with it. And she didn't know how to stop it. She had no strategy to stop this bureaucracy lapping higher and higher up her neck until it drowned her with barely a whisper. Up a sheer rock face, looking straight into death's jaw, she could choose a path, use her mental and physical agility to save herself.

She felt helpless and frustrated. After everything she'd battled against with her family to get this job and it wasn't a better life, it was just a more boring one. She stood up.

'Where are you going?'

She ignored Mo and picked up her phone and walked outside and along the dock. She called Dad. 'You know anyone who ever worked at Southampton?' She watched the giant cranes unloading the containers from the *Saracen* further down the dock. And then she asked something she always swore she would never stoop to. 'Does Uncle Ed?'

It turned out they were happy to help. She turned circles on the tarmac as she listened to a lot of reminiscing about the seventies and catching up with people. She was passed from one person to the other but no one knew very much or offered any insight, until she got hold of a former union rep at Southampton docks, now retired to Torquay. He was full of life and stories and gave her a name: Ricky Welch.

He'd gone down for murder but was probably out now; it had been a very unpleasant business indeed.

Georgie wasn't convinced he could help. 'I think I really need to talk to someone who works at the docks there now.'

'That's just the thing, the way it works now is because of what happened back then, because of the hornet's nest stirred up then. If you want to glance at the underbelly, you could do worse than talk to Ricky. There was a lot of talk back then that the rot went all the way up. That people had been bought who should have known better, that Ricky was the fall guy.'

'Can you be more specific?'

He laughed. 'No, I can't.'

'Do you have a number or an address for Ricky?' Georgie asked, not very hopefully.

'Try the phone book, I would. Don't say I gave you his name,' the man counselled. 'I'm too old for any aggro.'

She hung up and saw Mo walking towards her. His anger was present in every stride. 'What the hell are you doing out here?'

'I'm just making some calls—'

'About Southampton? You've been told to stay away from that. It's a distraction.' She had rarely seen Mo so livid. 'You might fancy your boss but this is really some way to piss him off – and me.'

She was really furious with Mo now, partly because she had been caught out, her feelings for her boss had been spotted by her partner. She turned away and began striding past the warehouses, keen to hide her blushes. 'Oh that's it, march off in a huff.'

'Leave it out, Mo, I'm not doing any harm.'

They were behind some containers now. 'No, but you're wasting my time.'

She saw Lukas the Pole with the flat tyre having a cigarette.

'What makes you think I've got time to waste, eh? However hard this job is for you, it's doubly hard for me.'

Georgie had a think about that. 'OK. I'm sorry.' She tried to keep her voice low, but Lukas could hear. 'It was just an hour or so, no harm done.' She tried to change the subject by turning to Lukas. 'Hi, this is Mo, my partner. How are you?'

Lukas said nothing, he just smoked.

'Come on, let's get back to work,' said Mo and he began to walk away.

Lukas said something quiet that she couldn't quite catch.

'Excuse me?'

'You still looking for rosewood?'

Georgie took a step closer. 'Yes.'

'I heard a story in the pub a few months ago. I listen a lot in the pub.' Lukas glanced around to make sure no one was watching. 'Two dockers were laughing with a lorry driver. This driver's often hanging around looking for extra work, he has a gambling problem they say.' Mo had walked back over to them and was listening. 'The first docker is telling the other a story about this driver, about how he tries to find extra work by calling at the freight offices behind Terminal 3, asking the young girls on the desks for driving jobs. One of these girls is sexy, and the driver is trying to impress her, telling her he can maybe get her special things. She's interested, because she's thinking it's something like Chanel, a Beckham handbag, and the driver says pot-pourri. The other docker says, "What, that crap your gran puts in the khazi to hide the stink?" The dockers start laughing and the driver, he gets very defensive. He says, "But this stuff smells like real quality."' Lukas dropped his cigarette and stubbed it out, bent down and picked it up. 'Then the driver said that he did a delivery once when he could smell the pot-pourri coming from the back of the truck. It was lovely, he said. It smelled like roses.'

Georgie looked at Mo. 'Pot-pourri is always packaged, or in bags. Its smell would degrade otherwise.'

'It's unwrapped,' said Mo. 'Raw state.' They nodded at each other.

'What's this guy's name?' Georgie asked, more urgently now.

'Ian Scanlon.' Lukas turned and headed off without a backward glance.

58

Kelly walked out from behind the screens surrounding her husband. She got up the stairs somehow and through the doors back to reception. She needed air. She needed her car, because there was one place she had to go, but Christos wanted two extra sets of eyes and ears on her all day. She put a hand on the wall to steady herself and turned around quickly in case he was following.

'You OK, love? You look ill.' Mary had rounded the front desk and was coming over, bosom ready for her to fall into.

'I'm fine, I'm fine.'

Mary was pulling an eyelid out of shape, picking off a clump of mascara. Kelly saw the two guards waiting by the door. She glanced round the offices, unable to remember the layout of the building very well. 'I'm just going to the toilet.' She walked down the corridor away from the entrance. She went into the bathroom. No windows. She wheeled around and came out, headed further into the building, past Christos's normal office. She glanced into two rooms – the heads of people at desks making her move on. She saw a fire exit at the end of the corridor. Put her hand on the metal bar, then wondered if it was alarmed. She ducked into an empty office, swept files off a windowsill and opened the window. It was hinged at the middle and swung outwards at the bottom, big enough for her to slither through. She put her bum on the windowsill and lifted her legs. It would be a six-foot jump to the concrete below. She pulled the window open to the maximum and was just about to drop through when one of the guys in black rounded the corner of the building and saw her.

Kelly swore silently.

'Put your legs back in and walk out of the front door please.' She stared at him through the glass. 'We're here for your own safety.'

The situation was hopeless. She swung her legs back in and walked stiffly out of the room. She went back into the toilet, sat down and tried to think. Her urge to be rid of these two men, to get where she needed to go, was a fire growing inside her. She took her purse and her keys from her bag, stuffed them in the pocket of her coat and left her bag where it was – she could run faster without it. She came out of the toilet, said goodbye to Mary and went out of the front door. The two men walked either side of her back to the car. She took in the details of what they wore and how they moved. They were in dark suits and shiny leather shoes, heavily built and lumbering.

They all got in the car, one next to her in the passenger seat, another in the back. The one in the back made a call as she started the car.

'We're heading off now.' He turned to Kelly. 'Where are we going?'

She looked at him in the rearview mirror. 'Back into town, I have some shopping to do.'

She pulled out of the car park and made her way towards the A13, queuing on a slip road in the rain. They inched forward, bumper to bumper. She looked at the time: 9.30, the day would get eaten up in a moment. They inched forward again, the sound of horns carrying over the asphalt from the main road westwards into the city. They were coming down a hill on a bend towards the four-lane road, the east–west flow separated by the low metal rail of a fence. The traffic slowed and stopped, then sped up into second gear as a traffic light further along the road changed to green. She began to count the time between moving and stationary traffic.

The car in front moved forward. Kelly released the brake and coasted towards it, picking up speed as the car came down the hill. She opened the door and jumped out on to the verge and began to sprint down the grassy bank to the A13. She heard a grunt of surprise from the man in the passenger seat as he reached out to grab her and missed, followed by the hard crunch of the car rolling into the back of the car in front. Louder shouts carried across the wind towards her. She looked back. A big man had got out of the car in front, shoulders back and finger pointing. Only the man from the back seat was following her, slipping in his city shoes down the muddy bank.

Kelly could see the brake lights turn off on a tail of cars in the nearside lanes. She ran to the central reservation as the cars began moving behind her, facing faster-moving traffic flowing east. She went for it, jumping out with arms held high as horns honked and cars slammed on their brakes. She was across the A13 and running up a grassy mound on the other side past saplings striving skywards, encased in plastic tubes. She ran down the other side and pelted into a small estate of semi-detached brick houses. The roads were curved into closes and cul-de-sacs. She saw an alleyway edged with fencing and ran down it into another cul-de-sac. She ran on and turned a corner into a long Victorian street. She saw a woman get out of a car on the opposite side of the street and turn back into a house, leaving the front door ajar. She was in a hurry, would obviously appear again in a second or two as she hadn't turned off the ignition. Kelly could hear the car idling loudly in the mid-morning silence. She looked behind her. Christos's man was jogging down the street towards her. He looked tired, but he was keeping pace.

She had one objective: to get away. She didn't hesitate. She climbed into the idling car, slammed the door, jammed the gearstick into first and roared away up the street. Five hundred yards away was a left-hand turn. She looked in the mirror, could see the man in black sprinting fast after her. He couldn't outrun a car. She'd drive for a few minutes and dump the car when she was sure she'd lost him. She made the turn left, and then a noise made her slam on the brakes in horror.

The baby in the back car seat began to coo.

Kelly froze, staring in the mirror at the little boy in a striped hat and a blue all-in-one. His fat little arms were stretching forward, straining at his straps as he held a multicoloured toy in his hand.

Kelly's panic as he grinned at her was all-consuming. She had just kidnapped a child. In seconds the mother would come back out of her door and stand still on her path, searching for her car and, above all, her baby.

At that moment the man in black rounded the corner and stopped in confusion at seeing her parked right next to him. As he tried to grab at the door handle Kelly shoved the car into reverse and backed round the corner, flying up the road, the horrible ramifications of what she'd done mounting in her. The street was still empty, the woman had not reappeared. Kelly skidded to a halt outside the house and had just got out of the car as the woman came out of her front door, a baby gym in her arms.

Their eyes met. The driver's door was still wide open. The woman stared at her car, then at Kelly. She frowned.

Kelly smiled. 'What a beautiful baby.'

The woman's eyes slid to her baby in the back seat. Kelly could hear the slap slap of the man in black's shoes as he lumbered down the street towards her. He was a hundred metres away. The woman would notice the open door.

Remember that she'd closed it. She'd open her mouth and scream. 'They grow up so fast,' Kelly added.

The baby burbled and stretched towards his mother. The woman, ambushed by the strength of her primal bond, smiled at Kelly as the baby cooed.

'Have a nice day,' Kelly added and then she took off. She ran hard down the road away from her pursuer. He was tired after his long sprint after her in the car and she lost him as she cut through a small park and turned twice, on to a bigger road with free-flowing traffic. She jogged along for a while, cutting west, trying to find a minicab office or a black cab. She found neither, was stuck in an area of storage companies, haulage firms and low-rise offices. She saw a cement mixer rumbling along the road and on a whim stuck out her thumb. The truck coasted to a halt.

An old man sat in the cab looking down at her. She could see he was swearing behind the window glass. She opened the door to his cab. He was furious. 'What the hell do you think you're doing? Hitchhiking? If my daughter did that I'd bloody kill her.'

'I'm desperate, I really have to get to central London.'

'Desperate? That's the sorriest excuse I've ever heard. I'll give you a lift if you promise me you'll never, ever do something so bloody stupid again. Do you know the creeps and perverts out here?'

Kelly nodded and climbed in. 'I really can't thank you enough.'

'You're a stupid woman, so bloody stupid.' He shook his head and put on his indicator before pulling away, continuing to lecture her. He took her all the way to Bank, proclaiming long and loudly about the idiocy of the world and everyone in it.

59

Georgie and Mo were in a car outside a betting shop on the Bethnal Green Road, Georgie in the back seat next to Ian Scanlon, Mo in the driver's seat.

'Come on, Ian, help us here and we can help you,' Georgie said.

'I don't know nothing.'

'You pick up this delivery of pot-pourri, take it to Casson Street, and hand it on to someone else,' continued Georgie. 'Only it's not pot-pourri, is it? I looked at the paperwork for this job. These goods are listed as weighing seven tons; pot-pourri, apart from smelling awful, weighs nothing.'

Ian was staring at the black crescents under his fingernails, morose.

'Tell us where that consignment goes, and who picks it up,' said Mo.

'I don't know.'

Mo sighed. 'This can is listed as going to Leicester, but you don't take it there, you take it to Casson Street and hand it on to someone else.'

No reply.

'We're taking you to the customs office now, where you'll be booked. Unless you can come up with the names of who hired you, who you work with, you'll be left in a cell—'

'You're picking on the small guy. I just got a phone call, I'm desperate for any work I can get. It's me and that rig and that's it. If someone pays me for delivery, I'm happy. What they're shipping is none of my business.'

'What they're shipping is entirely your business. How often do you deliver to Casson Street?' asked Georgie.

'I've done it a few times. And they pay on time! I'm hustling for every job, I am. The price of diesel has crippled people like me, you pen pushers with your paid holidays and fat pensions haven't got a clue—'

'Ian, we found you in the betting shop.' Georgie shook her head. 'What's crippled you is your love of a quick buck. You're just not very good at getting cash the hard, honest way, are you? You're going to have to start naming names, Ian.'

'I just get a phone call and some instructions—'

'Who do you hand it on to?'

'Just some guy, probably working double shift like me. We don't chat or talk about the weather, we just get the can transferred and he drives off.'

'Were you due to pick up a consignment at the docks a few weeks ago?'

'They cancelled at the last minute. I was out of pocket on that job,' he huffed. 'Listen, if this is about illegal immigrants, I know nothing about that. They're a fucking disgrace—'

'Buckle up, Ian, we're taking you in.' Mo turned to face forward and started the engine.

60

Ricky was sitting in his living room armchair smoking a roll-up. His cafetiere of coffee was cooling on the small dining table. He'd shut the dogs in the kitchen for now, their jumping up on his lap whenever he tried to read was getting on his nerves. His *New Yorker* had just arrived and he wanted to dive in, read about places he would never visit, countries that were off limits to him after his conviction. He had accepted that keeping abreast of events meant doing it from this armchair. Dawn was at the supermarket buying ingredients for a paella they were going to attempt later. It was all about burning the rice apparently, which seemed counterintuitive to Ricky: damaging something to make it better. His mind flashed to what he had done to Kelly. He had scared her witless and for that he was sorry. But she had opened a Pandora's box of possibilities he was still trying to digest.

The phone rang. The customs woman on the other end of the line had the nasal twang of Essex in her voice and sounded very young. She wanted to talk about the past, about Southampton – unofficially, of course. She wanted to pay him a visit.

He ground out his roll-up in the ashtray on the arm of his chair. He had a much better idea. He would come to her. No, it was no problem at all. He would be happy to help. There was no time like the present, ex-cons tended not to be too busy. He would come to her today.

61

The Wolf had parted the net curtains and was staring down at the tarmac. Taxis were discharging passengers and picking up the well-heeled by the Savoy Hotel doors. He was looking at the only strip of road in Britain that was like the USA, taxis driving the wrong way up the street. He could hear faint laughter; it wasn't contagious. Rain was beginning to pool on the pavement. He'd forgotten how black London was – the shiny roofs of the cabs, the black lacquer of the sign above the doors, the tarmac, the umbrellas. Late October was pressing down. Only when you came home did you realise how suffocating it was.

In the suite behind him, Jonas slouched and pinged the tops off beer bottles from the minibar. He seemed happy to watch two fat ladies on the TV argue in a suburban kitchen. Luciana had her leg behind her head in a yoga pose, her yellow hot pants riding high up the crack in her arse. She'd turned the heating up so much he was sweating just standing still.

Isabella was asleep in the adjoining room. He was glad that in his past he had been aspirational and had experienced somewhere of this quality. If they were waiting in a lodging house in New Cross Isabella would have been hollering to be freed long before now. He understood that she was someone who had experienced some good things in life and expected them now she was in London.

He was edgy, time was pressing. Isabella wouldn't wait

much longer in sleepy compliance. You soon learned if you were a prisoner. Room service food and dodged questions about Christos would only keep her quiet for so long. Forty-five minutes later his vigil was rewarded. He pushed himself off the window frame and spun for the door, barking an instruction at Jonas.

Kelly came up to the reception at the Savoy in a hurry. Now she had come, she wanted it to be over quickly; something unpleasant that had to be done now for peace of mind later. The receptionist was pretty, as she would be, enough important faces flowing past her that effort might be richly rewarded. She smiled invitingly. Kelly couldn't get the name out, couldn't say it, a rare moment of superstition overwhelming her.

'Yes?' The woman smiled.

'Is Clyde Bonnier staying here?'

The woman typed on a keyboard, frowned, typed again. 'I'm sorry, there's no one here of that name.'

Kelly walked away and stood by a marble pillar. She felt a wave of nausea flow over her and closed her eyes, leaning her cheek against the cold marble. She felt a tap on her shoulder. She opened her eyes and saw a ghost.

Left foot, right foot. It was impossible, yet possible. He was holding her hand tightly and his long stride was dragging her quickly through the hotel, so she had to run to keep up. He shoulder-barged a door and they were in an empty dining room, the Thames behind them.

She stood panting, staring up at Michael. He looked shockingly older, deep grooves etched either side of his nose, his eyes more bloodshot, his hair an inch further back on his head. She grabbed his lapel. She tried to talk but three questions came out at once and it sounded like gibberish. She groaned and punched him on the arm. Then again, harder. 'Where have you been? Where have you been?' She was crying now, great sobs racking her body as he pulled her close and put those long arms of his around her. Her face was in his chest, she could smell him, the memory of him, the smell of her old life. She shoved him away. 'Where's Amber? Where is she?'

'I don't know.'

'Tell me where she is!'

He held her arms firmly, looked into her face. 'She's gone, Kelsey. She's gone. The tide was so strong it nearly ripped my life jacket off. I went right under the ferry, right underneath and out to sea. I was pulled along the coast until I found a moored boat. It's not possible she survived that.' He paused. 'I'm sorry. I'm so sorry, Kel.'

She cried anew, as if hearing the news for the first time. 'Why didn't you come back? I looked and looked for you. For so long I looked for you . . .' She moaned, the pain bubbling out. 'How could you do that to me?' She was screaming now, anger chasing the tail of her grief. 'To your daughter? You left Florence.'

'I had to.'

'Why?'

'I'll tell you everything but I haven't got long—'

'Long? You haven't got *long*? What's that supposed to mean? You've been gone eight years! Why did you have to go?' He looked uncomfortable and she got it. 'It wasn't an accident, was it? You set it up.'

He grabbed her arm, forced her to look at him. 'It was a fuck-up for sure.'

'And me? What about your family?'

'That was my greatest mistake. I saw an opportunity when we were stuck in the fog, when we went to help that drifting cruiser: I could just fall in and never come back out. I knew people who could help me start again . . . but I didn't expect Amber to come in after me—'

'You were her father – she loved you—'

'I couldn't save her. The current was so strong. I couldn't do it. And then I simply couldn't come back, after what had happened.'

'You wanted out of our marriage.'

He didn't deny it. 'I was too young, Kel, I didn't crave security and a family life like you did. But we did have good times, I know we did.' He took a step closer to her, and she could sense his strength, the magnetism in him still. She blushed. Couldn't tear her eyes away from him. 'I need to know where you heard my name, Clyde Bonnier. It's important.'

The sobs caught in her throat. 'I saw it. As part of the crew list for the ship that's just come in, the *Saracen*, that Christos—'

'That your husband was looking at?'

'My husband.' She looked at him, stricken.

'Hey, hey.' He took her chin in his hand and tipped her face up. 'I don't blame you for remarrying, you weren't to know. You were right to rebuild your life for you, for Florence. But I lived under the name Clyde Bonnier knowing you would be the only one who would understand its significance. I knew it would be something you wouldn't have told Christos.'

She blushed. She couldn't help it, even after all those years and all those experiences that battered her belief in love, she remembered. Michael and Kelsey at eighteen, up in London. Taking the flirting and the vodka and oranges in the local pubs near home to a new level. Seeing how far they could get on a £20 note. They'd scammed up on the train without paying, had hung around Covent Garden, shoplifted London tourist knick-knacks, done a runner from a Chinese restaurant on Wardour Street. Bonnie and Clyde, he'd nicknamed them. And she, who had always been a good girl, found the attraction of a bad boy like a glowing light that rushed through her soul and made her pulse with excitement.

They'd seen a sign for a talent competition outside a Covent Garden pub – a £50 prize for the winner. She had sat in the crowd and ogled glamorous women belting out their Whitney Houston tunes, their Madonna covers, watched a ventriloquist and a mime artist. When her turn came she had stood on stage and sung her Etta James number, sung quietly and tremulously about love and loss without, she realised now, understanding a word of it. But something in her performance had resonated with her audience, her belief that love could be perfect, because she had brought the place to its feet. With her first prize came drinks on the house. Later they had wheeled out, congratulations still ringing in their ears, and Michael had marched her to the Savoy, where they had booked in as Mr and Mrs Clyde Bonnier. They had paid in cash. He had pulled her up that staircase – she had never seen anything so grand – taking the steps two at a time, and that night he had taught her what love and passion could really mean. And then a few years later he had faked his own death to get away.

'You know, I would remember your voice and it sustained me. Your beautiful voice.'

She pulled his hands from her cheeks. 'I don't sing any more. Haven't sung in years.'

He paused, looking at her. 'He doesn't make you feel like singing, huh?' She looked at the floor. 'I need to know something. Are you in love with him? Are you in love with Christos?'

She got angry. 'Why the hell does it matter to you? Why have you come back now? Why now? I should bloody report you to the police.'

'There's something I need to show you. You can make a decision then.'

'Why were you on the *Saracen*?'

He took her arm and began to lead her out of the room. She hung back, protesting.

'Please, you need to know.'

He led her up the stairs, his long legs taking them two at a time. She almost had to run behind him, the memory of seventeen years before, the same stairs, catching in her throat. She followed him to an upper floor and he stopped outside a door.

Fear overtook her. 'What are you doing? What do you want? You left your daughter. She loved you and you abandoned her—'

'Please, Kel, you need to listen to a story.'

'I've had enough of lies and stories. You have no idea what I've been through.'

'I did a terrible thing, but that doesn't mean I can't atone for it. If you love your husband, then I'll walk away right now, leave you to your life.'

She didn't answer.

'But sometimes we need to be told how bad the people close to us are.'

She cried out, 'I do know how bad he is. I do!'

The Wolf shook his head. 'No you don't, Kel. You have no idea at all.' He jammed the plastic keycard in the door and it swung inwards with a squeak.

62

The room was bigger than Kelly had been expecting; she saw doors leading off on either side and realised it was a suite. She saw a big bowl of fruit and too many table lamps, and floor-length net curtains blocking the view. A man with pockmarked skin was watching telly, feet up on the coffee table, a hole visible in one sock. A beautiful young woman in hot pants and a white T-shirt was doing the downward dog by the window, her hair swishing on the carpet and flying back over her head like a Mohican halo.

The man jumped up, startled and nervous; the woman carried on obliviously.

Kelly followed Michael to a far door and through it to a bedroom. Another young woman lay on the bed, reading a magazine. She sat up as they entered, the swell of her belly visible under the fluffy hotel robe. 'Isabella, this is Kelsey.'

Isabella smiled weakly. 'Is she your twin?' she asked Kelly. 'You look so alike.'

'I'm sorry?'

Michael interrupted. 'Isabella, you know I told you on the ship that there would be a woman you would meet, and that you needed to tell your story to her, just like you told me? This is the woman.'

Isabella smiled but she looked worried. 'This is all very well, but when am I going to see them? They insisted they would meet me off the ship, I want to make sure everything's clear.'

Michael nodded. 'It will be, very soon. You met Christos in Brazil, didn't you?'

Isabella stretched her legs, banged her feet together on the bed. 'This is my first time in London. I love experiencing new places. Christos and his wife said they would pay for me to stay on for a while once the baby's born and the legal papers are signed. I'm studying art, so of course there's so much to see in London. I can't wait.'

'Christos and his *wife*?' Kelly exclaimed.

She nodded. 'They came and met me in Brazil, we talked it over. They were very clear about what they wanted. I need couples to be clear. I've done this once before, and it was great, a really life-affirming experience. I always say so. So I decided I could do it again. I met them again later at the clinic and we went through the procedures, and then a few weeks later it was all inserted and done.'

'What clinic, what procedures?'

'The fertility clinic. Unfortunately they can't have a baby. Lots of couples from Europe and America come to Brazil to find surrogates. I'm proud that I can give childless couples the baby they've always wanted. The money pays for me and my younger sister to go to college. One day I'll have my own family, but for now I'm happy to give other people a baby to love.'

'I don't understand,' Kelly said helplessly.

'With a couple normally only one person has a fertility problem, but occasionally both do. So the egg is fertilised outside the body and then inserted in the surrogate's womb.' She patted her stomach. 'So he's not mine at all, really. But he's still a miracle boy; the odds were very low, apparently.'

'This *wife* – what's her name?'

'Kelly. She's a very nice woman, but so desperate for a baby. Maybe she left it too late, maybe that was her problem.' Isabella shrugged. 'Here you have lots of money but no children. I can have the children and use the money. It's a balance that's good for everybody.'

'What did she look like, this wife?'

'Like I said: like you. Long dark hair, slim, the same age as you.'

'Why didn't they meet you off the ship?'

'They said they would, but Jonas out there' – she indicated the man watching telly – 'said they were held up and that I should wait here.' A look of worry crossed her face. 'Where are they, anyway?'

Kelly stared at Michael, realising at least some of what he had done. 'Who came with you on the *Saracen*? It's a long way to travel all on your own.'

'I had to come by ship. The airlines wouldn't take me as I was too far gone. But then we hit this awful storm and I got so sick and worried. Seasickness can bring on premature labour. The man with me was very sweet, he had medical training, but he . . . the storm . . . he went overboard.' Isabella teared up. 'It's so awful.'

Kelly stood up from the bed and reeled out of the room to the suite door, crashing into the coffee table as she went. Michael grabbed her arm when she reached the corridor.

'Kel, wait, hear me out—'

'You threw him over. Didn't you? You killed a man so you could get her, to get at him. This isn't about me, or Florence, this is about your revenge on Christos.'

He pushed her up against the wall. 'It was me or him on that ship in the storm. Remember, he was working for your husband, who thinks nothing of killing to get what he wants. That's the man you married, Kelsey.'

She pushed him away, exasperated. 'You were working for Christos in Southampton, weren't you? Christos is the man you ran from. What did he make you do, Michael? What was so bad that it was worth faking your own death for?' She pointed a finger at him, thinking she was beginning to piece some things together. 'Did you kill that old guy in Southampton? Did you make me bring that sandwich down to the docks so I would see *you* and think it was Ricky?'

'I didn't kill him, but I helped. There, I've said it, the decision that ruined my life. Christos wanted Ricky out of the way so he could take over clandestine operations at the dock, he wanted me on board. I was attracted to the idea at first, it seemed like easy money, I had a young family, mouths to feed—'

'Don't blame me for this!'

He looked pained. 'I'm not. I blame myself. But Christos was offering me opportunities I thought I couldn't get otherwise. You know I dreamed of getting out, I trained as a tree surgeon, remember, I wanted to travel . . . So it started small, and then escalated. I started hurting people, buying people off, he was testing me, seeing how far I would go.'

'But we were so happy—'

'You were happy. I couldn't tell you what was going on, it didn't fit with your image of me as a perfect husband and father. And then Christos got you involved. You came to the docks at that time, I didn't realise it was so the old guy could be got rid of and you'd see it. I was suddenly left at the back of the warehouse having to get rid of a murder weapon.' He shook his head. 'That was a step too far, way too far. Christos must have sensed my hesitation at the things he was making me do because he'd now got me to drag you into being a witness to murder and I was an accessory.

'And that's when I made my decision – the only way out was to go overboard.' He sighed. 'But Amber coming in after me' – he wiped his hand through his hair – 'that was . . . awful.'

'Who killed the old man?'

'Another of Christos's men—'

'You piece of shit.' She grabbed his T-shirt in her fists and yanked.

'Listen to me. Please. Maybe it sounds hollow but I didn't realise how Ricky would react to you as the witness at the trial, that he would make threats that caused such upheaval in your life. After I'd run, I couldn't help it, I kept tabs on you. Then you disappeared into witness protection and I lost you. I lost you for years. That was the hardest, Kel, not knowing where you were, how you were coping. And then you reappeared, married to him. And then I understood. He was being clever and strategic. He wasn't quite sure I'd really died, so keeping you and Florence close was insurance in case I ever came back. But also it was his way of showing his power – he was marrying my widow, living with my kid. People don't walk away from Christos, we both know that. And so I waited, because I feared that in the end you would need my help, and I could right some of the wrongs.'

'My mum always said you were bad, that no good would come of it.' Her eyes misted with tears. She felt empty. She had yearned for so many years for reconciliation with her lost family, and it had come like this. 'You owe me.'

'I do. You didn't deserve what happened in the Solent that afternoon in the fog. You've suffered so much and I'm truly sorry.' He took her fists in his big hands and massaged them until they relaxed. 'You're a great mother, Kel, the best. Never forget that, yeah? I know because the life of being a father, a family man, in the end, that wasn't me. Some of us are born to be parents, Kel, like you. And some of us find it harder to make the sacrifices and put in the hard work. Be proud, Kel.'

She found it within herself to nod.

'What's this story with the kid?' He motioned back at the bedroom door.

She drew herself up. 'You've got something Christos wants,

and I need to get away, away from a controlling, lying piece of shit.'

He smiled, the cheeky grin lighting his face for a flash before it was gone. 'I'll be happy to help.'

'He's looking hard for you. It won't be long until he gets photos of all the crew and makes the connection.'

'He can stop searching, I'm contacting him today. Where are you supposed to be?'

'When I'm not kept prisoner by him? There's a Halloween party this afternoon being hosted by his charity. It's at a play centre next to the docks.'

'Have you been there before?'

She nodded.

'Describe it in detail.'

Ten minutes later they had come up with a plan. Kelly turned to leave but he caught her arm. 'We can travel far, round the world and up the social strata, but sometimes only those you've known from home speak the language you do.'

She looked up at the man she had once loved, and then walked away.

She used a payphone in the lobby to phone Georgie and cursed that it went to voicemail. 'I know what's on the *Saracen*. It's not what you think. It's something that will destroy my family.' She hung up and left.

63

The Wolf was short and to the point. 'I've got your girl.'
There was a long pause and the outbreath of someone who is deciding to take the call sitting down. 'Who are you?' The voice was the same, hard and without emotion.

'The one you always feared would come back and fuck things up for you.'

'Michael, the not-dead ex-husband. Is Isabella harmed at all?'

'She's fine.'

'How much do you want?'

'What value do you put on a man's life? Each missing hour of it, each missing day. I've spent time trying to find a figure for all those lost years.'

Christos puffed with annoyance down the phone. 'Spare me the violins. I'm a businessman, not a counsellor. How much to get her back?'

'This isn't just about money.'

'Yes, it is. It's only ever about that.'

'Kelsey wasn't.' Might as well kick the elephant in the room.

'If you want a pound of flesh, you're not going to get it. But you're right, Kelly wasn't about the money. There's a pleasure in taking what others value. Your daughter calls me Daddy, hugs me every night. One day I'll walk her down the aisle, tears in my eyes. That's not going to change. Let's do this deal and you can fuck off back to your hole.'

The Wolf smiled. He was enjoying this. 'You always did

have a problem with women, Christos. You tended to get obsessed, you always wanted the women other men had, like you needed their validation. But I doubt it's going to be so easy to make Kelly play happy families when the mistress has a new baby in tow.'

'You don't have a family, so you wouldn't know.'

'You have no idea if I have a family or not.'

'Yes, I do. This takes careful planning. You have no space for anything but revenge. It's all you have, and even that won't work. I assume you've told Kelly all about our dealings back in Southampton. She's done a runner today. I suppose she came to you. Her heart will be all fired up with revenge now, I imagine.'

'I want five million.'

'I don't have that kind of money. I'll give you half.'

The Wolf cut the call immediately and stretched back in his chair. Eight minutes later he rang again. Christos answered at the first ring. 'That was a minute for every year. You've got some idea how it feels now. I'll meet you at five today at your Halloween party. I want the money in a rucksack, the rest you can figure out.'

'No one has that kind of money just lying around. It takes days to get—'

'You've had a day. You knew as soon as she went missing that you'd need money. You've got it, and we're doing this today.'

There was silence for a few moments before Christos agreed. 'You think you need to worry about me, and you would be right. But there's something you haven't considered. You need to be very, very careful around Sylvie. No one comes between a mother and her child and lives to tell the tale.'

The Wolf laughed. 'Five o'clock.' He hung up and jumped to his feet, in the room at the Savoy. 'Right, everyone. We've got a lot to do, so listen carefully.'

*   *   *

Sylvie stood behind her lover in the basement of the Malamatos Shipping offices, listening to the conversation and forced herself to stay quiet. There was no point having a three-way conversation – she had to let Christos deal with this.

She studied Christos's neck, the small bulge of skin that edged up over his collar as he held the phone to his ear. The problem was her frustration was keeping pace with her anguish. Christos hadn't tied this off. He had not been clinical enough years ago. This ex-husband of the mouse had proved to be persistent and ballsy and had exploded back into their lives with potentially devastating consequences. Christos had been weak when he needed to be strong. She watched the skin on his neck wobble. Fifty years of sun and wind had weakened its structure and made it stretch. She didn't like it.

She refused to believe that the fiasco at the customs area when they'd lost Isabella had been her fault alone. They should have got the captain to accompany Isabella personally, right into their hands. But that plant of the Wolf's had been good. Nobody talked to her like that and got away with it. No one. Women who thought they could play her needed to be taught a lesson, but her desire for the upper hand had made her take her eye off the ultimate prize.

She swallowed back tears. She felt the separation from her child as keenly as if it had been actually ripped from inside her. For the first time in years she felt weepy and flaky, almost unable to concentrate on what had to be done. Children were our undoing, she realised.

Christos turned round. 'Only a few more hours and we're back on track.'

Sylvie forced a smile and looked at her watch. She had already phoned Medea and instructed the old woman to bring the kids out to the play centre. She could look after them there. She'd relish the idea of providing care to Kelly's kids, just in case Kelly got the idea that they were hers to take. She'd done a runner from Christos's men earlier, but without her kids she wasn't going anywhere. For the first time the thought terrified Sylvie, that she was also going to succumb, like so many before her, to the biological pull of offspring. She would be left wide open by the love she had for the baby she hadn't yet even seen. She turned and headed up the stairs, having to retreat to the toilet. She forced herself to calm down, forced herself to remember what she had been told, that love allowed you to grow. It would make her stronger, this love for her child. She walked into a cubicle and shut the door, saw a handbag hanging on the hook. She opened it to see whose it was and found Kelly's driving licence inside.

And a loaded gun.

64

Kelly had given Christos everything: her love and her freedom and her self-respect and still it was not enough. Adopting Yannis, giving him a new life and a new start, wasn't enough. Their son and her child from her first marriage, whom Christos had professed to love, had been cast aside in the desire for a biological connection. She felt a fire of protectiveness towards Florence and Yannis. They were Malamatoses in everything except for the blood that pumped through their small bodies. And it turned out that to Christos, that was all that mattered. Christos wanted an heir. Like some bloated, syphilitic Henry VIII, he wouldn't stop until he got his heir.

Well, if the children weren't good enough, he didn't deserve to have them. All her guilt about separating them from their father evaporated like milk boiling dry in a pan. She stopped in the street, had to bend down to stop the bile bubbling up her throat. Sylvie wasn't just the mistress, wasn't just the lovesick other woman waiting hopefully in the wings for her lover to love her enough: she was so much more than that. A woman with a plan – a woman with a baby on the way. A woman with something Kelly could use. Kelly spun around in the street and stuck out her arm for a taxi. Sylvie had sneaked around her house in the middle of the night, revelled in getting into every corner, thinking she was clever. A black cab slowed to a halt. Tit for tat, bitch, Kelly thought as she climbed in.

* * *

Sylvie's flat was in a three-storey block in Maida Vale, set back from the main road. Kelly knew all about it; she had found out where Sylvie lived when she had discovered Christos was having an affair. She'd looked it up on Google Maps, had thought about it many times: the place where her husband's other life was lived. It was a self-effacing block with pretensions to grandeur. It didn't have a porter but it did have a small communal garden and bullying signs insisting that people couldn't park by the doors. The windows were flat modern panes with no sills, most of them with nets or venetian blinds. It was anonymous, private, made for people not planning to stay long.

She saw the CCTV camera trained on the doorway and immediately discounted it. She was an expert in surveillance, after all, she would bet it didn't even contain film, was there only as a deterrent. She rang the bell of number 9. Nothing happened. She rang again and then started on all the other doorbells and got someone on an upper floor to buzz her in. She crossed the wide lobby and took the stairs to the first floor, coming through a set of glass fire doors to a series of four plain wooden doors, each set with a spyhole.

She turned the handle on number 9 and leaned against the door. It didn't budge. The hiss of a bus's brakes and the screech of its wheels carried through the corridor window from the street. She realised she had nothing with her that she could use to force the door. She made a note of the flat numbers on this floor, retreated back down to the entrance and pressed the buzzers again. No one answered. It was the kind of place where people worked and came back late, their lives lived in more appealing places.

She walked back up to Sylvie's floor and saw a fire extinguisher hanging on the wall next to the swing doors. She unhooked it and marvelled at its weight. She stood by Sylvie's door and swung the extinguisher at the lock. A great thud rang out, and a big dent appeared in the door. She did it twice more before the flimsy door crumpled near the lock and she could shoulder-barge the door open. She hung the extinguisher back on the wall.

The door opened straight on to an open-plan living room. She closed the door as best she could behind her. There was a modern sofa in beige and a matching chair, set at right angles to the square room. The white blind cut a lot of the daylight. The coffee table was low and glass, with a celebrity magazine set neatly on top. The wall between the living room and what must be the bedroom was lined with a low bookshelf that contained a self-help manual, a fertility book and a baby care manual and a biography of a prominent businessman. There was also a photo in a silver frame – of Christos and Sylvie, her arms tight around his barrel chest. They were both laughing; it looked like it was taken at work, a world she never intruded upon.

She moved into the small kitchen, touched the curved glass of the coffee percolator – cold. She opened a kitchen cupboard. A packet of spaghetti, a drum of salt. She opened the fridge. In the door was a pint of milk, a carton of orange juice.

She opened the door to the bedroom and saw the light was still on in the bathroom beyond. It was gloomy in here, but she didn't dare turn on the light. The bed was made, the brown silk cover pooling on to the floor around it. There was a bedside table and a neutral lamp. At the bottom of the bed was a cot. Sheets and a cot bumper decorated with blue teddy bears.

She walked into the bathroom. It was cluttered with cosmetics, brushes, combs, bottles of perfume – the same perfume she wore. She opened the mirror above the basin. Her gaze fell on a lock of dark hair, like a sample hanging by the Clairol boxes in Boots. She picked it up, rubbed it with her fingers. It was real. With a flash she remembered Christos leaning over her when she was out cold after her escape attempt. He had cut off her hair. There were three boxes of hair dye under the basin in a further cupboard. She snatched at the bottles of dye; each was a varying colour of brown. Sylvie had been experimenting to find the exact matching shade to her own.

Kelly didn't attempt to stay quiet or hidden now. She went back into the bedroom in a hurry and flung open one of the wardrobe doors. There was a huge cardboard box, weighty and thumping when she pulled at it. There was a picture of a pram on the side. Sylvie was expecting to walk the streets of London with her new baby and she had posed as Kelly to get that child.

Kelly threw open another wardrobe door and saw shoes lined up neatly in the bottom of the wardrobe. They were replicas of her shoes at home. She bent down and looked at the brand names – pretty much all the same. *That* is what Christos had been writing down in the notebook and what she had filmed with the Sleepchecker. She grabbed at clothes, pulling them from the rails so they fell to the floor in an untidy cascade. Her shift dresses, pairs of black trousers, the long-sleeved black number she wore to their recent party. In the next wardrobe were Sylvie's usual clothes: gaudy skirts and pink trousers, patent shoes and flowery tights.

Two different personalities in two different wardrobes; two different people claiming the same man. Kelly found a wig, long straight dark brown hair with a fringe, cut to mirror her own.

She saw a recording machine and what looked like a projector. She pressed play and an image of herself jumped to life on the far bedroom wall. It was a recording of Kelly in her own home, taken by Christos's cameras. Walking down the corridor in the flat, from the back, images of her doing the tiniest movements that distinguish one woman from another, throwing her head back to move her hair out of her eyes, inserting a finger under her shirt by her collar bone to reposition a bra strap, twisting her hands together to adjust a wedding ring, the way she planted her feet wide as she stood at the stove, how she pushed out her bottom lip when she was irritated – and there was her glassy-eyed look as she shrank back in fear from her tyrannical husband.

All her most personal details projected life-sized on to Sylvie's wall, feeding a rival's obsession, urging a rival on. There were more photos of her in this apartment than there were of Sylvie's lover. Kelly threw things out of the wardrobe, looking for something. A few moments later she found it – a black beret, a little worn, a different brand, but just the same.

Pinned to the inside door of the wardrobe were close-up photos of her: in profile, from the back, side on. Someone who was prepared to put in that much work on a mad project to imitate a rival was someone unhinged, and very dangerous indeed. Kelly ran back into the living room, sweeping items off tables, desperate to discover how far it went. She returned to the kitchen, reopening cupboard doors that she'd shut just moments ago. Her eyes snagged on the de Cecco spaghetti. The brand she tended to buy, because Michael used to buy it and she liked the fleeting memory. She flung open the fridge again, examining the contents forensically. A packet of pancetta pieces, squidged into their plastic square, a half-finished Parmesan cheese. She whirled round, saw a line of cookbooks leaning against the microwave and picked one up. Tuscan hills and Jamie Oliver's grin. The book fell open at a recipe for spaghetti carbonara, the page splattered with oil spots and egg yolk. She picked up another book offering perfect pasta and scrabbled through the pages to spaghetti carbonara. The page was well thumbed, crispy flakes of dried Parmesan cheese like shed skin clinging to the crease.

Her children's favourite meal. Being perfected by her rival.

Suddenly, a thought came to her that made the bottom fall out of her world. She had let Sylvie look after her children. Had assumed that Sylvie wasn't a threat to them, that no one could want to harm their lover's children.

She snatched up the phone on the side table and called Medea.

'Where are the kids?'

'More to the point, where are you? You've been running across motorways, what the—'

'Are they with you?'

'Yes, they're here, but we're leaving for the party right now.'

'Wait for me. I beg you, Medea, wait for me—'

'There's no time. The driver's already here. We'll see you at the docks.'

'Hello? Anyone here?'

Kelly wheeled round. A woman hovered by the front door.

'I saw the door had been damaged. Are you OK? They've busted right in.' The woman was staring round at the disordered room. 'Can I help? When they break in it can feel like a, like a . . .'

'Personal violation.' Kelly ran out of the flat and down the stairs.

65

Georgie had had her phone on mute when Mo and she had been talking to Ian Scanlon, but she turned it back on as they drove Ian back to customs, and found a message from Kelly, claiming to know what was on the *Saracen*. *It's not what you think. It's something that will destroy my family.* She phoned Kelly back but no one answered at the house and her mobile was turned off. She cursed. She thought for a moment; she knew Kelly was going to be at the charity party this afternoon at the play centre near the docks – if she couldn't get hold of her she'd go there and talk to her. But for now she and Mo had to take Ian to the cells under the building and she left Mo to book him in and to complete the paperwork.

She was barely back at her desk before she got buzzed from reception that Ricky Welch had arrived. Mo wasn't back yet, so she went down to the lobby alone. The slim man with the long limbs didn't look like a hot-headed docker who'd done a stretch for murder. She shook his hand and brought him up to the offices and into a meeting room. This side of the building faced the Thames, and Georgie saw him glance out of the window at the miles of containers stacked on the dock.

'I guess it's changed a bit since your day,' she began, to break the ice.

He shrugged. 'We didn't check for dirty bombs in my day.'

She thanked him for coming so far at such short notice and offered him tea, which he waved away. She got straight down to it. 'We're investigating a case here that we think might have links to Southampton. If you cooperate with us we might be able to get the terms of your parole renegotiated. They'll be less onerous.'

'What are the links?'

'We're not sure at the moment.'

Ricky frowned. 'Sounds like you need to talk to someone who works at the docks today. I haven't been there in years, as you know. I haven't been anywhere much in years.'

'I'm interested in how the illegal stuff worked down there. What the processes were, the scams, if you like.'

'One thing's for certain, it will have changed now. I'm out of date. Out of the game.' He crossed his legs, took a long glance out of the window. 'Customs must be a strange job to do.'

'I don't see why.'

'To know that you only ever catch some of what's smuggled. That every success, every seizure, is actually a failure because it proves that the illegal stuff is there, and its very existence must mean that there is more, always more.'

Georgie shrugged. 'We do what we can. And we try to do it better than the criminals.'

'I hear the price of cocaine has halved in ten years.'

'And global trade has tripled. There's always a cost to success.'

'Yet I bet the numbers of people doing your job are down.'

'Which is why we rely more and more on information people like you give us.'

He pulled out his packet of tobacco and began making a roll-up.

'I'm sorry, there's no smoking in here.'

'I'll save it for outside.'

She watched him finish the roll-up and pop it in his shirt pocket. He was in no hurry. Georgie wondered if prison did that to you, made you a master at stringing out any event, to alleviate the crushing boredom. Her brother Matt had not coped well with his four months on remand. She knew she must seem impatient, eager to get results. She didn't think this was a bad thing.

'So, how did it work?'

'In the beginning, if the cans were damaged or open, we'd just help ourselves. Hardly sophisticated, but effective. We'd sell what we got, sometimes we busted them open ourselves, just for shits and giggles. I guess I got a reputation, because later I was paid to let certain containers on certain ships through, and to make others drop off the system. It was newly computerised back then and easy to make things disappear.'

'Who paid you?'

'Guys who wanted stuff done. It was never just one. What I don't think you lot – I mean customs – realise is that the more complicated the paper trail, the more checks and balances, the easier it is to make things fall through the holes. It's human nature: the more secure the system, the less people look.'

'When you went to jail, who took over? Unofficially, of course.'

He shook his head. 'I really don't know. Someone more important; someone further up.'

'But you were just saying you worked for yourself.'

'Precisely. That's why it turned out as it did.'

'I don't understand.'

'I went to jail for a murder I didn't commit.' There was silence. She sensed Ricky was used to it, the sceptical looks, the hidden sighs of disbelief, the frustration at his special pleading. 'Someone had put a lot of thought into it. About the gap that would be created after I'd gone.'

'Care to name a name?'

He shook his head. 'If it was as bent as I think it was at the bottom, it was probably that bent at the top too.' He paused. 'What's the company that you're investigating today?'

'Malamatos Shipping. Ever heard of it?'

She watched him closely, gauging his reaction. He gave a tight smile. 'It sounds familiar.'

She pressed on. 'It's run by Christos Malamatos.' His gaze was steady on her. 'Greek family originally, lives in London, got a wife called Kelly. He has a problem with illegally harvested Brazilian rosewood on one of his ships.' There seemed nothing shifty about his reaction to what she was saying.

'So what's the connection to Southampton?'

'We don't know yet. We got a tip-off, that's all. Back in the day, you ever come across any hardwood – tropical hardwood?'

Now she saw a strange look cross his face. 'I used to know someone who used to do wood . . .' He trailed off. 'But it can't be.'

Georgie was on it immediately. 'Can't be what?'

Ricky shook his head. 'No, sorry, it's nothing. The guy died a long time ago.' He paused. 'Illegally harvested hardwood? That's much more valuable than it used to be.'

'Uncut. Raw state, illegally harvested Brazilian rosewood.'

This surprised him. 'Uncut?'

'Still got the bark on it.'

'Those trees must be huge.'

'You can say that again.'

'Tropical hardwood is incredibly dense. Particularly with the bark on it. I assume you've used a detector—'

'Of course. The density comes back as uniform. There are no holes in which something's been hidden.'

He tapped the arm of his chair. 'What are they – two metres across?'

'Some of them are more.'

'Maybe the wood is thick enough to hide whatever's inside so your scanners can't pick it up. With the smell and the density, I'd say it's a possibility.'

'How do you know so much about wood?'

'I spent eight years in jail. All I did all day was read. I know a lot about the things prison governors decide are good to have in the prison library. Have you looked between the bark and the wood? You could get liquid heroin up in there.'

'We've done all the standard checks.'

'Then I'm not sure I can be much use.'

'What's the cleverest way you've ever seen to hide something?'

Ricky paused, thinking. 'In plain sight, hiding in plain sight.' He smiled, a rather sad and small smile. 'I'd really like to see that wood.'

'Let's go back to that hardwood connection you were talking about—'

Georgie was interrupted by Preston opening the door.

'He's coughed up the wood address.' Preston looked excited and she heard the commotion of other people behind him.

Mo appeared in the doorway. 'G, I need to talk to you out here.'

'Excuse me.' She got up and left the room and stood with Preston and Mo in the corridor.

'Ian Scanlon is claustrophobic. He took one look at that holding cell and started to blabber.'

'He claimed that's why he became a truck driver, to enjoy the open road,' Preston interrupted.

'The cans of wood go to Cranleigh House, a mansion in Hertfordshire,' Mo continued. 'A year ago he met the contact at Casson Street, but he had no truck with him. The guy said it had broken down and they needed to go in Ian's rig, because the delivery had to be that day. So can you believe it? He drove straight there, unloaded the can on the driveway, and he drove away.'

Angus came up to them and opened the door of the meeting room where Ricky sat. They all crowded in after him. 'You and Mo go there right now,' he said to Georgie.

'Let's go,' said Mo.

Georgie gathered her things and picked up her bag. She turned to Ricky. 'Thank you for coming all this way, but we've got to go now, something's come up. I could drop you at a station on the way and talk in the car, though.'

'Could I wait around here? Could you show me the wood when you get back?'

Mo and Preston were talking behind her, she could hear phones ringing, Mo pulling on his jacket. 'We might be hours.'

'It's no bother. I saw a shopping centre on my way in, I can kill an afternoon. I like water, the docks.'

'Georgie and Mo, get out to that house before dark.' Angus's voice was behind her in the room.

'All I can offer you is that I'll phone you when we're back,' she said to Ricky.

'Come on,' Anguish was urging, 'let's look lively now.'

She was swept down the stairs with the boss, Preston, Mo and Ricky. 'The shopping centre's that way and there's a walk you can do along the harbourside down there too.' Her colleagues were already moving away to the car pool and her last sight of Ricky was of him standing outside the customs building pulling a roll-up from the pocket of his shirt.

* * *

Georgie and Mo were in the car driving up the A1. 'Woronzow' was the name registered at the address.

'Sounds Russian,' Georgie said.

'He's Brazilian,' corrected Mo, 'with a French wife.'

The satnav directed Mo to turn off when they reached a sign to Welwyn Garden City and they passed a series of roundabouts and then drove down smaller and smaller roads, until the countryside in the grey afternoon light felt as remote as a road through the Scottish Highlands. It was the commuter belt. How Georgie would love to live out here, deep in the quiet and shadow, cycling to the train station every morning, around nice people who wanted to get on and contribute to society. She couldn't wait.

'I'd love to live out here.'

Mo shuddered. 'I *knew* you were going to say that. You're not a Home Counties' girl, Georgie.' He shook his head. 'I don't think you'll ever do it. You'll stay near your roots longer than you think. There will always be something pulling you back.'

Georgie smiled and shook her head. 'You're wrong, Mo, you're wrong.'

They followed a country road along an ancient brick wall and then slowed and came to an entrance with grand wrought-iron gates. She directed Mo to keep going for a while before she realised she'd missed it and they turned round and drove back. Mo pulled in and they saw a camera almost concealed on an ancient stone post with a doorbell. They had come to the right place. A woman answered and the gates rolled open without so much as a squeak or a rattle. They drove up a winding drive and over a slight rise. The gravel stopped in a circle of thick trees and hedges and they got out of the car. The air was cold, the smell of wood smoke drifting, the pleasing crunch of gravel underfoot. The silence was a heavy curtain around them. They walked along a stone path and came out in front of Cranleigh House. It was a substantial three-storey Georgian building with a curving front section in a honey-coloured stone. A vine travelled up one side of the big black door, set with a brass knocker and a spy hole and an expensive-looking security system.

Georgie rang the doorbell. It ding-donged pleasantly and a moment later a middle-aged woman in a maid's outfit opened the door, warm light pouring from the hallway beyond her on to the stone steps outside. Georgie and Mo showed their IDs and the woman looked a bit surprised but ushered them in, closed the door behind them and smiled, asking them to wait as she walked away.

Georgie heard Mo mutter an exclamation under his breath. The entrance hall was more than beautiful. It was stunning, like something you'd see in an interiors magazine, only here it wasn't just photos on glossy paper, it was in front of her and above her and all around her. The floor was dark wood and highly polished, covered with tasteful rugs with some kind of abstract pattern. A modern chandelier hung from the high and gleaming ceiling, casting everything in a romantic glow. There was a sofa in the hallway in some kind of soft fabric that looked like if you sat on it you'd never want to get up.

Georgie took a few steps into the house. She saw stairs leading away at an angle to the upper floors, balustrades gleaming. It wasn't stuffy or formal, it was a house to put you at ease, a house to enjoy. It even smelled beautiful. A large vase of unusual-looking flowers sat on a beaten metal table beyond the sofa, in front of an antique mirror. Georgie couldn't resist walking over and giving them a sniff. Fresh flowers in October – she knew how many thousands of miles they had been airfreighted. But they weren't giving off the smell.

The maid came back then, and they could hear a woman

calling out for them from a room off the entrance hall. They followed the voice into a large living room with a big bay window, through which were views of a large garden and beyond that a pool that was covered over for the winter. In the room pieces of sculpture stood on marble podiums.

'Hello, I'm Mrs Woronzow, however can I help you?' Mrs Woronzow was sitting on one of two huge sofas facing each other at right angles to the fireplace. She wore a blue silk bathrobe and had bare feet, her toned and tanned legs visible below the shimmering fabric. She was at least fifty, with dark hair, good skin and a sheen of wealth Georgie felt she could almost touch with her fingers. 'Come, sit. Maria, I think tea, yes? We'll take tea.' The maid left the room before Georgie or Mo could utter a refusal.

Mrs Woronzow saw Mo staring at the large picture propped on the mantelpiece. 'I see you're looking at that one. It's a Warhol. It's lovely, isn't it? A real extravagance but I justify it because I'm an interior designer, my work has to be my life. My clients live all over the world, but if they come here I want them to feel the wow.' She threw her hands up to emphasise how much 'wow' she meant.

'Is your husband here?' asked Georgie.

'He's in Basle. Back tomorrow, then it's Milan, I think.' She smiled. 'What can I help you with?'

Georgie unzipped her coat. It was hot in this room. No draughts from badly fitting windows here, no damp penetrating the hundreds-of-years-old brickwork. She walked towards the large fireplace that dominated the room. Feathery grey squiggles ran through the creamy pale marble. The fire crackled and popped pleasingly before her.

She had things to do, but she wanted to enjoy the house for just a little longer, to have something to dream about tonight, the fantasy of perfect bricks and mortar. She thought of Dad in the recliner, Ryan, Karl and Matt squished on the sofa, her more often than not lying out on the rug. Sky TV blaring, the gas fire in the lounge making condensation stream down the insides of the window from their breath, and the heat fleeing as quickly as they created it through gaps in the single-paned window. This one room was bigger than her entire house, and it was so quiet. All Georgie could think of was the empty bedrooms, the unused bathrooms, all this space and privacy. And it was much warmer than her house, too. Next to the fire was an alcove stacked neatly with logs. It was so beautiful it was like a piece of art in itself.

Georgie stepped closer to the pile. She lifted a piece of wood and put it to her nose. She closed her eyes. The aroma of roses, so rare in October. She could hear the hiss and the crackle of the fire in the Carrara marble fireplace, the immaculate pile of logs in the stylish grate burning and crumbling to ash, and smoke curling away, up into the flawlessly proportioned chimney and the cold afternoon sky.

'My God – you burn it?' She dropped the piece to the floor with a clatter and turned. 'Where's your wood store?'

Mrs Woronzow looked at her, confused. 'Outside in the barn. What's the problem?'

Georgie ran out of the front door and round the long side of the house to a weathered barn a short distance away and pulled open the door. A light came on automatically to counteract the afternoon gloom. Along one of the walls, stacked to head height and several feet deep, were hundreds of faultlessly cut logs of Brazilian rosewood. She took a step back and stared at it all, stupefied.

Mo and Mrs Woronzow came up behind her. Mrs Woronzow had pulled on a pair of wellingtons with a rim of fur at the top and thrown a pashmina over her shoulders. 'Is there a problem?'

'There's not enough. Where are the rest of the trees?'

Mrs Woronzow smiled. She stepped back outside and

pointed down the large garden. 'Come, I'll show you. Interior design these days needs to be a bespoke service, including grounds and planting. I put as much effort into the exterior as interior. We leave the large trees whole; they make a beautiful border for the west side of the lawn, a natural break with the living trees beyond. When the pale, northern light shines on the bark, it complements the dark green of the evergreen trees beyond.' She pointed. 'It really looks fantastic.'

Georgie saw, across the lawn, the natural boundary she was talking about. Three great trunks lay on their sides on the grass like fallen giants.

Georgie was incredulous. 'Do you *know* where this wood comes from?'

Mrs Woronzow frowned, and a pair of tiny, delicate lines appeared on her forehead. 'My husband imports it. His family are beef farmers, landowners. When he was a child growing up on the farm they used to burn rosewood. The trees remind him of home. Wood is a natural material, my clients are very green aware and it's important to have an emotional connection to the objects we have around us.'

'You've got no more emotional connection to those trees than I have to one of your husband's hamburgers.' Mo's voice was flat and hard. He'd had enough of her philosophy.

Mrs Woronzow pulled her cashmere closer to her, as if protecting herself from Mo's sarcasm. 'We've been very lucky. My husband's very successful, we can indulge where perhaps others can't.' She sounded defensive. 'We've been in this house twelve years now. We've worked very hard to get where we are. I want the best; this is the best. Money doesn't really come into it.' She paused, realising she needed to adjust what she had said for her audience. 'I mean, for us it's beautiful. We love beautiful things.' She looked like she was waiting for Georgie to nod.

'How much have you burned?' Georgie asked, unable to tear her eyes away from the pile of logs stacked in the barn.

Mrs Woronzow looked perplexed. 'This winter, or since we moved in?'

66

Kelly took a cab home and raced up to the flat. She grabbed a set of keys for another of the cars in the underground car park and piled what she needed into the boot. Her mind was feverish, working at a pace she hadn't needed for years. She set off for the docks and roared down Casson Street to the play centre. Her route was blocked by the catering vans and prop vans and delivery trucks overflowing on to the mud and grit of the vacant space that Georgie had been so interested in. Eventually someone reversed and she could inch into the car park. She looked around. She wouldn't have much time.

She parked in the last bay near a low wall and reversed in so that she could take off later without having to turn. She watched young women carrying large cardboard boxes of glasses in through the doors.

She got out and walked into the building. A small stage was being erected by a wall, with tables for champagne and children's party food nearby. The play structure had been draped and decorated with cobwebs and large ghouls' faces, and a witch that Kelly had made over the past month was being hung from the overhead rope walkway. It looked impressive; many hours of planning and work had been put into today's Halloween extravaganza.

Kelly saw none of it. She was checking doors for alarms, seeing whether windows opened, hunting for a back exit through the kitchen, where caterers were lining up canapés on gold trays.

The dignitaries arrived first, drawing up in chauffeur-driven cars and taxis, picking their way in high heels and cashmere coats over the grit and gravel site and into the play centre. The children and parents came after, drifting in in groups. Many of the children were already dressed up, and Kelly helped those without costumes into the masks and cloaks she had already prepared.

Jason, who Kelly made props and masks for, arrived with his two kids and came over to her.

'Glad you could come,' Kelly said, managing a smile.

'We wouldn't have missed it for the world. Look at these.' His children took the masks and put them on, pulling them up on their foreheads and waving their arms. 'It's a real production you've got here. So many people.'

'Yes. The charity's grown and grown. It was started to support the wives and children of merchant seamen lost at sea, now it mainly helps single mothers. Their men don't die now, they never return because they've got a better offer in Thailand or Cambodia or who knows where. It's easy to walk away now.' Jason was nodding. 'But for those left behind, it can be devastating.'

'Half the world is trying to escape their relationship, the other half trying to keep a hold.'

Kelly nodded, distracted. How trite he sounded. He had no idea. But that didn't mean it wasn't true. She wondered again at spending her life being attracted to the bad men instead of mild and gentle Jason. What makes us love the people we do?

'Did you decorate it too? It's amazing.'

She looked behind her as if seeing the decorations for the first time. 'No, a prop company did that, but I made the masks and some of the costumes.' She hunted for her children with her eyes, scanned the room for Christos and Sylvie.

'You OK, Kelly?'

Kelly dragged herself back to her conversation with Jason. 'Sorry. Have a drink. There's champagne and then a tour of the docks—'

He waved her away. 'I'm fine. Where are your kids?'

Her senses were on heightened alert, she felt every squeak of skin against plastic, every squeal as a child disappeared down a tube. She fancied she heard the water burbling through the pipes in the taps in the toilet, the hiss of the tea urn in the kitchen reaching boiling point.

'They're not here yet.' As she said it she saw Yannis pulling at the door to the play centre, Florence tumbling in after him, Medea bringing up the rear. 'Excuse me,' she just managed to blurt as she ran to them.

'Get off me, Mum,' said Yannis, excited and squirming free. Florence stared up at her and she was struck anew by how much she looked like her father. Kelly's hands were shaking as she handed over their costumes. She velcroed Yannis into a ghoul suit and Florence became a woodland sprite. She saw Christos and Sylvie walk across the car park towards the door. Her mouth went dry. He was carrying a black rucksack. She ushered the children away to the play structure.

Medea sat down on a chair by the door. Guard number one. She saw Christos and Sylvie, acting as if they were a couple, talking to the head of the charity and some other people, but their heads turned constantly to the doors. It was as if the whole building was waiting, holding its breath, for the explosion that was to come.

The people round Sylvie were just so much noise. Mosquitoes buzzing outside a net. Her eyes were fixed on the doors, waiting for him to arrive. She watched a taxi pull up and two people get out, the skinny runt from the arrivals hall and a tall, broad man. She knocked Christos's arm with her own.

She made an excuse to the mosquitoes, and she and Christos walked over to the entrance.

'Somewhere private,' the Wolf said. He was younger than Christos, fitter and stronger, with big arms and hams for hands.

Sylvie wondered how much comparing Kelly had done between husbands number one and two. Christos gestured towards a doorway.

'Get your mother in here too.'

Christos called Medea over. They walked into a side room and closed the door.

'Have you got the money?'

Christos held up the black rucksack in his hand, but didn't move. 'Where's Isabella?'

'She's in the hospital you chose for her. With my friend.'

Sylvie took her mobile from her pocket, stepped outside the room and dialled the hospital. She asked to be put through, and spoke to Isabella herself, asking her questions only the real Isabella would have the answers to. Confirming she was safe and in good hands, she rang off and came back into the room.

'You've seen Kelly,' Christos was saying.

The Wolf smiled, making Christos snort.

'A tearful reunion, no doubt. Women love that shit. If she knew what an arsehole you really were, what a poor choice she made, she'd not have shed them. I protected her from the real you, I never told on you, Michael.'

'I hear she doesn't sing any more. You don't make her want to sing.'

'You killed your own child. I don't know how you live with yourself.'

'You don't deserve her, you never did.'

'Neither did you.'

'If we could hurry this along . . .' Sylvie's anger was mushrooming as the men bickered over their emotional baggage. She wanted out of here, she wanted to get to Isabella and her child. The runt accompanying the Wolf came across the room for the rucksack.

'Remember, Florence is my kid,' said the Wolf. 'I can make trouble if you don't hand over the money right now.'

Christos snarled. 'If I ever see you within a mile of any of my family again, in the same country even, I'll kill you. This is a one-time offer,' he said.

The runt reached out his arm for the bag in Christos's hand. He was sweaty and nervous. He fumbled with the zip and looked in. Sylvie took a step towards him.

'Is the money in there?' the Wolf shouted.

The runt licked his lips and nodded.

My money, thought Sylvie, that's my money. I've worked fucking hard for that, keeping Christos happy, keeping him wanting more. Yeah, it's his business, his choices, his wealth, but that money has my sweat all over it. And you think you can take it from me.

The runt backed away, bag in hand. He glanced at her and she recognised a primitive instinct for self-preservation in him. He had sensed she was about to do something. She watched the Wolf step towards the door as the runt, as if looking into the eyes of a more brutal and aggressive animal, turned and ran for the door.

Sylvie pulled out the gun.

Kelly was crouched in a series of brightly coloured twisting tubes in the middle of the play structure. Yannis was wading through a pit filled waist-high with plastic balls, a level beneath her. She stared out, counting the number of Christos's men she could see. The centre was crowded with children screaming and adults drinking and laughing.

She watched Michael and the guy with the bad skin walk in, and all of them, with Medea, move into a side room. The door closed. Three guards down, just as he'd promised he'd do at the Savoy. He would give her an opportunity to get away. She set to work: she pulled a hair tie from her pocket and twisted her hair quickly into a high and tight ponytail. She knelt and pulled the waistband of her skirt over itself, shortening it by three inches. She took off her tights and shoved them into a gap in the plastic ceiling above her, pulled a differently coloured pair from her pocket and scrabbled about pulling them on. She took off her witch's mask and swapped it for another one she'd found abandoned in the ball pit.

As Florence crawled past her towards a slide, she grabbed her arm. 'Listen to me. This is very important. Go down and get Yannis to come up here. Now.' Her daughter stared at her, sensing the urgency. She slipped away down the slide and Kelly watched her as she found Yannis. A moment later the three of them climbed under a low obstacle and were together at the top of the slide. Kelly pulled off her children's masks and replaced them with two others she had in her pocket and removed Florence's wings. She held their hands and squeezed. 'Listen. You need to follow me and move very fast. This is no time for questions, this is no time for hesitation, this is time to move when I say move.' She peered out at the door behind which were both of her husbands: closed. She watched Christos's guard leaning against the large window by the fire exit door at the bottom of the slide. She could see the tarmac of the dock beyond and then the Thames. They all shuffled towards the slide.

A yell made her instinctively turn her head. The closed door was thrown open and Jonas shot through it, a black rucksack in his arms as he dodged adults and tables. Michael was hard on his heels, knocking a man out of the way, and Christos was a beat behind him. She glimpsed the flash of Sylvie's blonde hair before a hard zing rebounded off the metal of the play frame just above her head and a loud bang followed, then another, deafening in the enclosed metal space. It was gunfire.

She shoved her children's heads to the plastic floor, crouching low as the screams of mothers separated from their children began to ricochet off the ceiling. The guard by the door pushed on the fire exit and began to crawl out, setting off the door alarm. Women were charging towards the play equipment, desperately calling for their children. Champagne flutes crashed to the floor as people dived under tables and shoved each other out of the way. Jonas seemed to crumple and fell over a table, the rucksack sliding away under another. She saw Christos and Michael lunge for it as another table was overturned.

Michael had said he would provide a diversion that would allow her to get away with the kids, but she had not anticipated anything as terrifying or high risk as this. She yanked on her children's hands, trying to keep them low, and fell down the slide, her children a tangle of limbs around her. They hit the blue mats and half rolled out of the fire door.

67

Men sprinted past them as they ran with the crowd along the dock. A sobbing woman cradled a child, then Jonas ran past, limping badly until he tripped and landed heavily on the ground. Kelly tried to hug the wall that ran parallel to the water's edge. If Sylvie came out of that door she would have a clean shot at her. They were fifty metres from a corner; they had to get round that corner. Florence was ahead of her, Yannis dragging on her hand behind her. She risked a glimpse backward but couldn't see Christos. Her uneven gait with Yannis almost made her stumble. She heard the hard, urgent sounds of a heavy man sprinting behind her, then Michael came past at speed, the black rucksack on his shoulder. He overtook Florence. Ten metres. She redoubled her efforts, dragging Yannis with her. They were round the corner.

A high brick wall abutted the play centre at one end, the other end meeting a low, Victorian redbrick warehouse, ripe for demolition as the docks were redeveloped. The flats on Casson Street rose up behind the wall. To her right, a wide expanse of dock led to the Malamatos offices, warehouses and the ships. It would be a dangerous sprint in the open to safety.

Michael paused for just a moment, searching the dock for options, judging the height of the wall. He took but a moment before he ran at the wall, jumping and reaching for a pipe that ran under a ledge on the warehouse and swinging his leg on to the wall. The pipe made a groaning sound and gave way, pulling out of the weathered brick as he struggled to the top of the wall.

She ran towards him. 'Help them over!' She lifted Yannis up as high as she could and Michael grabbed his hand, dragging him in an ungainly bundle up and over the wall. Florence was easier, her light frame and trainers helping her over in a moment. Kelly heard incoherent shouts behind her as a huddle of people ran past.

Her former husband's hand was warm as she grabbed it and tried to get a foothold on the brick. She was two steps up the wall, his face straining with the effort of pulling up an adult. She saw him glance towards the river, his face betraying something. She heard the sound of heavy feet, a shout from Christos. One of her hands was on top of the wall, she had one leg nearly over.

Behind her Christos and two men were racing for the wall. 'Pull her down!'

Her eyes locked on Michael's. She had to get her knee over the wall and then she was safe. She couldn't talk, concentrating all her effort into getting over. She used to talk to him with only her eyes, or so she had thought, when they were young and in love. He frowned slightly, she could feel his hand loosening on hers, his legs tensing as he prepared to fall away on the other side. 'No!' He shook his head as if trying to free something that had snagged on his memory, and let go. He jumped down on the other side of the wall and was gone. Kelly half fell back down the bricks, Christos catching her and slamming her into the wall as he did so. Her knees gave way as she landed, a howl of pain that wasn't physical coming from deep inside her.

Christos was panting, sweating from running hard. He pulled out his phone, ordering Medea to collect the children from Casson Street. She heard the distant wail of police sirens and saw him smile.

68

Georgie, Mo and Mrs Woronzow returned to the elegant living room and the beautiful-smelling fire, the ash from the perfectly chopped logs crumbling elegantly to the bottom of the grate.

By now, Mrs Woronzow was protesting as Georgie outlined the charges against the couple. Her voice, which only moments ago had been so confident and urbane, was now high and reedy in the large room.

'I think we should have that tea now, Mrs Woronzow.'

Georgie phoned the office. There was still a lot to do, a team needed to come out here, photos needed to be taken, evidence and statements collected: all the processes that allowed a case to go to court. There was no answer on Angus's extension. She tried his mobile. Nothing. She rang the switchboard. No reply. She tried Preston. She couldn't understand why no one was answering.

Five minutes later Preston rang her back.

'Where is everyone? Why can't I get through?'

Preston sounded ill. 'There has been a shit show like you wouldn't believe. There's just been a shootout at that play centre further down the dock, where Malamatos was having his charity fundraiser—'

'A shootout? Has anyone been hurt?'

'I've no idea. Armed police have had to evacuate half the port, including our offices.'

Georgie had to sit down on the inviting sofa in the hallway. 'Where's Kelly?'

'Kelly?' Preston sounded confused. 'She's the least of our worries. Who was that guy you brought up from Southampton? He was left to wander about, wasn't he? Because he's the one the police think might be responsible. You'd better get back here right now, Georgie.'

Georgie didn't even think to tell him that they'd found the wood.

69

The Wolf watched the clean-up from the roof of an old oil storage depot. From his position flat down on his belly he could see the panicked movements of groups of people, the masks and costumes littering the dock, balloons freed from their interior home drifting skywards on the wind. The prone body of Jonas on the tarmac didn't move.

A close-run thing, but then it wouldn't be the first time. Sylvie had shot the wrong man and as he fell the Wolf had grabbed the bag. He felt the weight of the backpack heavy on his shoulders.

He had stared at Florence, looked into her pale eyes as he had pulled her over the wall. She had not recognised him. He wondered whether the tilt of her head, the line of her jaw, the way she moved, would spark some feeling in him, but they hadn't. The past really meant nothing to him. Florence could have belonged to anyone, anyone at all. He had left the bewildered children where they stood, knowing someone would be along to rescue them. But it wouldn't be their mother.

He watched as Kelly was quickly frogmarched away from the wall by Christos and some other men. Her howl of anguish at being separated from her children had carried over the wall towards him. He felt a familiar sensation, one he'd tried to dislodge for the past eight years and had never managed. He felt bad for Kelly's suffering, the bundles of cash in the rucksack not giving him the euphoria he had long dreamed of. He climbed down the metal ladder and managed to track Christos and Kelly along the dock towards the *Saracen*. He had to split then, as he heard the first of the many police cars appearing at the port.

70

Georgie and Mo drove back to the docks, a boulder lodged in Georgie's throat that expanded the closer they got to the river. She tried phoning Kelly again. It went straight to voicemail. She turned on the radio and got the first reports on the news bulletins. The situation was still confused: a shooting at a children's charity event . . . one male victim, as yet unnamed . . . It had a ghoulish melodrama to it. The head of Lost Souls, Anila, was being interviewed. By the time they drove into the car park and saw the incident vans, TV crews and the press, Georgie's world as she knew it was beginning to collapse.

In the aftermath of the shooting the police had cordoned off a large part of the docks and evacuated the customs offices, a number of warehouses and Malamatos Shipping's offices. These areas were being declared safe bit by bit and now staff were streaming back into their offices. Georgie and Mo hurried into the building, now cleared by police and operations resumed as best they could. Angus was at the top of the stairs as Georgie came up; he took her by the elbow and steered her and Mo into the stairwell.

'One question. Why were you talking to this guy from Southampton?' He looked grey and old, a spot of blood on his lip from where he'd been chewing it.

'The tip-off said there was a connection between Malamatos operations here and Southampton—'

'Why is he here? Why did you bring him up here?'

'He offered to come, he saved us a trip—'

'He offered? Mo told me that this guy's a convicted murderer, that he offered to come halfway across the country to talk to you. Is that right?'

Georgie felt the contents of her stomach begin to move unpleasantly. 'Yes, but I had no reason to assume there was a problem . . . And then we went to pursue the wood lead and we, I mean I, was going to talk to him again later.'

Angus raked his hand through his hair. 'So he was just left here at the docks?'

Georgie nodded. 'Yes. It's a public area, I don't understand—'

'This bit is very important. Did you at any time mention Christos's wife?' Georgie opened and closed her mouth. 'Because if you did, you've blown a witness protection cover. Kelly put that man who you were interviewing this morning in jail for murder. The police are all over me. If they think we led him to her, the shit is already over our heads. You know how much it costs to redo a witness protection cover? It's thousands of pounds of public money, notwithstanding the upheaval to her and her family's life.'

Georgie thought she heard Mo swear under his breath. Maybe it was a prayer.

'Give me something I can use, Georgie. Tell me you found something useful that broke this case from him coming up here.'

He was looking at her, pleading. Her boss was pleading not only for her job but for his own. And she couldn't offer a thing.

'Where did you find him? What's the trail? Tell me every I is dotted, every T is crossed on this?'

Mo and Angus were looking at her. She had been put on the trail to disaster by her family. They had laid down the crumbs in the forest, and she had pursued them as far as they led.

'Mo had nothing to do with this, it was my decision alone.'

That's when Angus got angry. 'You're not in a position to be saying that kind of thing!'

'Where's Ricky now?' asked Georgie.

'In police custody.' Angus pinched the bridge of his nose. 'They're trying to piece together what happened at the play centre. There are conflicting reports about who had a gun, and whether he was involved. They want to interview you. They're waiting in the meeting room upstairs.'

Shame lanced her. She had bathed in Angus's approval and his attention and it had been brutally removed. She had pushed the edges of what was permissible in order to impress him and had sown the seeds of her own destruction.

She turned to go but Angus gestured up the stairs. 'Go that way, it's quicker and you won't have to see anyone.' She stared up the echoing staircase, then looked back at Mo. He was staring at her helplessly. She took the stairs two at a time because she couldn't bear to be the object of that look any more. She came out on the second floor and heard the staccato chatter of a police radio from one of the meeting rooms. Her courage failed her. The police interview would signal the end of her career. There was no way back from this and she knew it. She walked right past the door without even looking in, slipped down the back stairs and out of the back door.

The wind off the river sliced through her like a scythe. She walked behind a low building to where she had chained up her bike what seemed like a million years ago now. She would delay the axe falling for that little bit longer if she could. It was human nature, after all.

She cycled away.

71

Christos hurried Kelly along, his grip on her arm a vice. People rushed past them in the other direction but they kept on. He had to half carry her, her disappointment at another failed escape stripping her of the will to fight.

They walked a long way down the dock, past the Malamatos offices and the customs block. The afternoon was still and cold, the wind had died and the sky was clear. He led her towards the *Saracen*. She tried to pause as she stared up at the huge ship, but he gripped her arm tighter and pulled her up the gangway and through the bowels of the ship, along corridors and down to a lower level until they arrived in the ship's galley, a warren of stainless-steel units and corners buttressed by fridges. He pulled a pair of handcuffs from his jacket and locked one of her wrists to the safety rail that ran round the edges of the units.

She turned to face him. 'I know about the baby. I know all about going to Brazil to buy a son.'

He didn't reply, had pulled out his phone, was scrolling through numbers.

'Christos, think of the children. The children you have *now*. You love Yannis and Florence – why can't they be enough?'

'Enough?' Christos looked up from his phone aghast, almost angry. 'Look around you, Kelly. Six hundred thousand tonnes of metal, one of the biggest fleets in western Europe, it's not a question of enough. That doesn't even come into it. You're asking the wrong question. It's about what's possible. I've told you before. *Nothing* is impossible.'

'So what happens now?' She pulled on the handcuff so that it chinked against the metal. 'You won't divorce me, so what accident am I to have? That's how you're going to get rid of me, isn't it? Me dying allows you to bring Sylvie and the new baby in. Nothing's impossible, eh?'

'A family line is not disposable.'

'You set out to meet me, didn't you? You chose me because you wanted to keep me close, because you wondered whether one day Michael might come back. You came into that restaurant where I was working, down on my luck, banished from my home town and my friends, and you knew I wouldn't be able to resist. You never loved me at all, did you?'

'That day in the restaurant wasn't the first time I saw you. I heard you sing one time in Southampton. You made an impression. And then later, after Michael and Amber were gone, I saw you sing in a pub in the Elephant and Castle. You were so vulnerable you were completely compelling, thinking of your dead child and your husband. I realised then, that if you could make space in there – in your broken heart – for me, it would be the ultimate proof of love. And I got my proof of love.'

'And this is how you treat someone you claim to love.'

'Most men are competitive, Michael and I more than most. It adds to the excitement when you win.'

'Michael's twice the man you are.'

'Here's a thing. Where is Michael now? He didn't come back for you, did he? He came back for money. He dropped you down that wall to save himself, to keep his bag of cash. Think about that, Kelly. He's a worthless piece of shit. I felt less bad about the things I've done because you were used to it.'

'You're a disgusting human being who doesn't know how to love.'

His face clouded over. 'I loved you. More than you know. We got married and you moved in, but then reality hit. I expected you to move on, but you didn't – you couldn't. Your mind was fragile, you loved and needed the kids more than me, I could tell that. And then later, you would look at me in that way, that way you're doing now. After everything I did for you, I didn't like that at all.'

'You're a sadistic, cruel—'

'Yes, I'm a perfectionist, yes, I expect and demand total dedication. I'm not going to apologise for that.'

'Bullshit,' Kelly spat. 'You love Sylvie because of how she's prepared to change herself, bend herself to your every whim. That's not a wife, that's not even a mistress – that's a living doll.'

'I want what every husband wants – attention. But yours was always elsewhere, locked in your grief and the what-ifs of the past. It was a little rebuke to me every single day of my life. However successful I was paled into insignificance next to my dying marriage.'

'Oh you've got attention all right. Sylvie creeps around our apartment at night, examining every aspect of our lives, she stands over the children – your children – in the dark. If you've ever dreamed about her, it's because she's really there.'

'I know. I like it that she's there in the flat at night.'

'She's sick, Christos, she's sick in the head—'

'She just has the guts to go all out to get what she wants. She's ballsy and fun and there are no limits to her ambition.'

'If she wants you she can have you. Let me go.'

'That's the problem, that's what you can't see. Men don't like to be made to feel it.'

'Feel what?'

'The failure. This way I'll never have to face that failure. The failure of our marriage. I won't be reminded of it.'

'What way? What way, Christos?'

'This way I'll never have to let you go.'
'Christos?'
But he turned away and walked out of the kitchen.

72

Kelly rummaged through drawers, trying to find something she could use to prise open the handcuffs. She pulled baking trays to the floor from overhead cupboards that were within her reach. She shouted for a while, until she heard footsteps on the metal of the corridor.

Sylvie appeared. She walked forward and regarded Kelly while leaning provocatively against the stainless-steel kitchen island, then used a second pair of handcuffs to chain Kelly's free hand to the safety rail. 'You know, I always wanted to be an actress,' Sylvie began. 'I got out of the 'burbs and moved to New York. I was focused, I really put a hundred per cent effort into it. And I was good, really good actually. But I had one weakness, I was told, I didn't work well with other people. I didn't like it when they stole the limelight, when I had to let them shine. The best show I ever did was a one-woman performance where the spotlight was always on me.'

'Let me go.'

'I'm a good actress because I'm good at imitating other people. I'm good at getting inside their heads. It's a challenge.'

Kelly looked at Sylvie in surprise. Her voice had suddenly changed. The American accent was gone, replaced by a flat London tone.

'I really get at what makes them who they are.'

Kelly backed up against the island as Sylvie came towards

her and began to undo the top button on Kelly's dress. Kelly squirmed, but Sylvie didn't stop. She undid the next one.

'I've studied you in detail, Kelly—'

'Tell me something I don't know,' Kelly retorted. 'Creeping round my house at night, trying on my clothes, invading the privacy of my kids, I've seen it all. You've got an obsession, things have gone too far – get off me.'

Sylvie had unlocked one of the handcuffs and was pulling Kelly's black dress over her head and down her arm, before locking her to the rail again and starting on the next handcuff.

'I've been to your flat, I've seen how much you've studied me.'

Having removed Kelly's dress, Sylvie folded it and put it on the counter. She knelt down in front of Kelly as Kelly tried to kick her. Her pump flew off as she did so. Sylvie smiled. 'One less job to do.' She grabbed Kelly's ankle and began gently to pull the tights down Kelly's thighs.

'Stop that right now.'

'I've only just begun. Of all the parts I've ever played, this is the one I think I'll relish the most.'

Kelly felt the cold of the ship seeping into her bones. 'Don't you need to be with the surrogate mother of your child? I'm sure you wouldn't want to miss the birth. Maybe once you become a mother you'll start to have some feelings.' Sylvie narrowed her eyes at that. 'You need to enjoy your last days of freedom. A new baby takes it out of you. It changes you, Sylvie. Are you ready for that?'

Sylvie smiled again. 'I like that. I really like that idea.'

Kelly snorted. 'God, you're dumb. There's something you don't know so I'll tell you, one mother to another. Christos demands total dedication. Your attention is going to be on your new baby, not on him. He won't like it. He won't like that at all. You think *I'm* standing in the way of your perfect relationship. But it's your son who's going to do that, and he's never going away.'

Sylvie dropped the tights on top of the dress.

'Did you enjoy pretending to be me? Does it give you a kick? More to the point, does it turn him on? Is that what this is? Because you'll do anything to please him, won't you?'

When Kelly was down to her bra and pants and shivering in the unheated kitchen, Sylvie came at her with a pair of scissors.

73

Georgie wanted to climb. When things got too much for her she wanted to escape. She would go home to get her kit, get to the water tower, climb the steepest, most challenging route till her muscles burned and her bones ached and she could overlay the battery acid rolling through her body with the lactic acid of physical exertion instead. Then she would get falling-down drunk. She squeezed the bike into the garage and opened the front door to find Dad and Matt crowding round her. They'd heard about the shooting at the docks on the TV news.

Their concern for her radiated out in waves. She was made to sit in a chair, she was given a cup of tea. Dad gave her a hug, his thin arms tight around her, his worry about her safety out of all proportion to the actual risk. 'If anything had happened to you I'd never have forgiven myself.'

When she saw his tired and line-cracked face, she understood his unbounded love for her, knew she would always be forgiven, and she broke down and cried, face down in his lap on the sofa, great jagged tears spilling out her frustration and her horror and her unwitting mistake.

There were exclamations all round, her dad and Matt urging her to tell them what the matter was.

'I think I've lost my job.'

'No, that can't be.'

'I've fucked up so badly. You have no idea.'

Matt patted her on the back with a kind of fatality, as if

he had always expected this outcome. 'Come to Fabric with Ryan and Shelley and me tonight. We'll have a big night out, let your hair down, it's what you need.'

She struggled out of Dad's arms and stood up. 'No, I need to think things through.'

They crowded after her into the kitchen, where she fired up the ancient computer that took up half the small workspace. She had typed Ricky's name into Google before she had phoned him, but now for the first time she read all the reports of the trial she could in detail. It was then that she found reference to a woman called Kelsey Bale, a witness whose evidence put Ricky in jail. Kelly, Kelsey. It was her, Georgie was sure. She had heard that people who changed their names often kept the same initial, it was a familiarity they found comforting, a reminder of their old selves. She turned to her dad. 'I overreached myself, I tried too hard.'

He protested loudly. 'Nonsense! You can never try too hard. You're good at your job, you love your job! Your mum would have been so proud of what you're doing, Georgie.'

She started shouting at him because she was angry at herself. 'I thought I could take short cuts, but you can't in life, there are no short cuts.' She had tried to overcompensate, to make up for deficiencies at home, and look where it had got her. The doorbell rang and for a horrid moment she thought it might be the police, chasing her down for an explanation. The irony of them coming here for her after the number of times they'd called at the house over the years was not lost on her. Matt went to answer it. 'Who's that? I can't face anyone.'

When Uncle Ed squeezed into the kitchen she rounded on him, even though deep down she knew he was not to blame. 'Your connections in Southampton sure turned up some toxic shit that's landed me in huge trouble.'

'Georgie's worried she's lost her job,' Dad said to him.

'Don't, Dad, please.'

'Just because you talked to someone?' said Uncle Ed.

'The guy I interviewed about Southampton is part of some other police case.'

Uncle Ed frowned. 'How is that your problem?'

'It doesn't matter, Ed. I'm so tired, please.'

He became defensive, which immediately put him on the offensive. 'You hear that, Matt? Your sis's tired. Don't put your white-collar stress on me. Brawn or brains, work is work, one job no better than another.'

She closed her eyes, trying to think through her shame. She phoned Kelly, but there was still no answer. She was beginning to be seriously worried about the woman's safety.

'Look at you, your little mind whirring, whirring . . . Trying to save your skin? I'll tell you something for nothing. You're not one of them.' Ed turned to her dad, nodding as if he expected him to agree. 'Human nature will out, Georgie. The looks you give your dad and me, and your brothers . . .' He let the accusation tail off.

'What are you on about?'

'Your first big case, your first time working with size, and you see how they make you pay.'

'Your conspiracy theories are boring and tedious.'

Uncle Ed narrowed his eyes, pointed a fat finger at her. 'The top is bent, G, never forget that.' It was his turn to get angry now. 'You can climb, but you can't escape. You can get educated, you can move away from your roots, marry a Hugh, but this is who you are, Georgie, this is who you are! And you should be proud.'

'Just leave me alone.'

'And remember, Georgie, all I've ever done is try to help you.'

'Help me? You're the one who got me in all this trouble in the first place!' She swore at him and marched through into the living room but he was hard on her tail, her family helpless bystanders.

He wasn't giving up. 'You'll be sorry you said that. You treat your family with respect, because you've got no one else. Debts have to be repaid. You don't get something for nothing. No one ever gets that!'

She grabbed her bag and ran from the house, slamming the door behind her.

74

Sylvie cut off Kelly's hair. Chopped it bluntly and quickly, in to the nape of her neck, short round the ears. Kelly watched the long strands of dark hair fall to the tiled floor. Then Sylvie swept it up and put it in a bin bag, opened a packet of hair dye and began to apply it to Kelly's head. The smell of ammonia invaded her nostrils. After fifteen minutes Sylvie pulled Kelly's handcuffs along the rails to the sink and used the movable arm of the catering kitchen's tap to wash the dye down the drain. She pulled a towel out of her bag and began to dry Kelly's hair. Kelly felt the new sensation of air on the back of her neck. Sylvie dumped the towel and the dye remnants in the bag, and got out a comb. Kelly could feel Sylvie running the comb in a sharp line through her hair, creating a parting where there had been none.

Now Sylvie began to undress, throwing her clothes in an untidy jumble on the floor.

'Is this how you get off? Seeing who you can fool by playing the actual wife? By switching between being two people? Is this how he wants you to be – looking like his wife but acting like a mistress? Was it your idea or his?'

'We have a connection. We came up with the idea together.' Sylvie glanced towards the door. 'Though it doesn't hurt to make a man think he was the driver.' She bent down and began to pull her own tights over Kelly's feet. 'Don't struggle.'

Kelly started to laugh. 'You're really doing all this for him? That operation you had on your nose, that wasn't for polyps, was it? It was to give you a profile like mine. You had surgery to look like me, studied me for hours and hours, imitated my every gesture, crept round my house for how many lost nights, and all for *him*? He's not worth it!' She was shouting now. 'In a few years you'll be as desperate as me to get away. Love has made you blind, you can't change him, Sylvie, you never will.'

Sylvie picked up Kelly's black dress and pulled it over her head. She did up the buttons, then picked up her own colourful dress and drew it up over Kelly's thighs. She traced a finger round the waistband of the tights, checking for bulges. 'Impressive, after two babies.'

'It won't work, Sylvie. The children will never be fooled. They know who their mother is, you can't begin to deceive them.'

Sylvie undid one handcuff and then the other, pulling the dress into position and doing up the zip. 'That's our last hope, isn't it? That the ties to our children are unbreakable. But you're wrong, and I think you know you're wrong. They're heading off to boarding school. They'll hardly ever see their mother. Women change when they have babies, don't they, Kelly? You know all about that. They are not who they were, or who they thought they'd be. When a woman has a baby, all anyone sees is the baby. The woman who carried it and cares for it is invisible.' She put on Kelly's flat black pumps and looked down her front, awe and excitement on her face. 'I never used to wear black. I look kooky!' She bent down and grabbed Kelly's foot, forcing her high heels on to Kelly's feet and doing up the straps. Then she pulled a case out of her bag and flipped open a small mirror. She put contact lenses in, then rummaged in the bag, turning away from Kelly and bending over. When she turned round a wig of long dark hair cascaded down her back and round her chin. She stood and looked fully at her. 'My name's not Sylvie. It's Kelly.'

Kelly stared, stupefied. Looks are not fixed. At that moment, staring into eyes that were exactly like her own, Kelly understood what Sylvie was doing, and why it would work. It was like looking at herself in the mirror. With the clothes, the accent, the haircut and the eye colour, the two women were indistinguishable. Sylvie had become her, had stolen her identity entirely.

Sylvie reached out, grabbed the fourth finger of Kelly's left hand and pulled off the rings. 'All mistresses want to be a little bit like wives, like the women their lovers fell for all those years ago.'

And after all, how many close friends did Kelly have, how many people who dropped round unannounced, who called her a friend, family she could rely on? There was no one, no one bar the children. Christos had isolated her so effectively it was as if she didn't exist.

'We are fascinated by our rivals. What's so strange about what I'm doing? I simply had the audacity and the desire to go further.' Sylvie bent down and pulled one last thing from the bag. A beret.

Kelly pulled and strained against the handcuffs, hollering to be freed by someone, anyone. Sylvie watched her, fascinated. 'You know, you look better like that. Think of this as the ultimate makeover. It's the favourite game of little girls, isn't it? Trying to change into those you want to be. Let me show you.'

She unclipped the handcuffs and after a brief struggle locked Kelly's hands behind her back with one pair and pushed her through the other door, away from the corridor. They entered a dining area, with a collection of bare tables and chairs. One of the walls was lined with mirrors and as Kelly turned she could see her reflection for the first time. She screamed. She didn't just look like Sylvie, with the short choppy haircut that was now blonde, she didn't just dress

Ali Knight

like Sylvie, with the distinctive bright colours and high heels, she wasn't only the same age, weight and height – she *was* Sylvie.

'The thing is, Kelly, I do you better than you do.'

And that's when Kelly understood what Christos and Sylvie were really doing, and that it would work. They were actually going to replace her. Permanently.

Kelly strained against the cuffs holding her hands. She began to shout for help.

'There's no one to hear you. Except your husband.'

Christos appeared in the doorway to the dining area with a rope in his hand.

75

Georgie phoned Kelly from the pavement outside the house. Her home phone and her mobile. When she got the answerphone she got on her bike and cycled back to the port. She coasted silently down the ramp to the car park and tied her bike to the railing. The night shift was in action further down the dock. Her leaving, her disgrace, would not cause even a ripple.

The wind had dropped and the night was cold. She walked along the dock towards the *Saracen* and stared up at the vast ship, thinking about Kelly, formerly Kelsey, about how she had done the right thing as a young woman, about her situation with Christos, about her fear for herself and her children.

What's on the Saracen *is something that will destroy my family.* Her team hadn't found anything, but that didn't mean there was nothing to find. When they had met at the sauna, Kelly had said something else. *He's going to take me out on one of his ships and put me in the world's biggest grave – the ocean.* She walked up the gangway.

The ship was silent, the giant engines quiet. She was a city child, urban in her make-up. Ships – even Christos's – were as beautiful to her as a walk in virgin forest.

She stepped inside the first door and stood for a moment, listening. The ship was huge, but its main space was for carrying cargo, the parts for the crew and any passengers smaller, compacted into a relatively cramped area. She walked across the hall to the river side of the ship and heard a faint scream from below. It came again. She walked towards the noise on silent feet.

76

'I've got the note.' Sylvie pulled out a crumpled piece of paper from her bag and kissed it. 'Just for added effect,' she said.

'Christos, you can't do this, it's mad – it will never work—'

'The last message you ever wrote.' continued Sylvie. 'I – I mean you – spent a long time getting it just right. You composed it in a moment of deep grief and despair, scribbled it down when you couldn't take it any more. When you heard that your lover and his wife were having a surrogate child, you knew he would never leave her for you, that your great love story was a lie. That the mistress trap had swallowed you – that you had waited and worked those long years for nothing. It turns out in this case it's the strong ones who are brittle, who make the dramatic gestures for unrequited love. Firing your lover's gun at his wife at the play centre, your jealousy unbounded, your pictures of Christos's wife in your flat – Christos, I think I might leave some there after we clear out the other stuff – showed how frayed your mind had become. Your heartache and remorse were too great to bear after the event.' She paused. 'You came aboard your lover's greatest ship, into the belly of his business, and took your life. It's the strong ones who, when they try, succeed in destroying themselves. I'm sure that will be mentioned at the inquest.'

Kelly watched Christos throw the length of rope over the light fitting in the ceiling, watched him tug on it, lift his body weight off the carpet. The ceiling didn't pull away. His ship was well made, after all. He placed a chair under the light fitting and together Sylvie and Christos carried her towards it.

77

From a turning on the stairs, Georgie heard Kelly shouting to be saved, the sound of a struggle. She began to run down the stairs towards the galley, a disordered room with pans on the floor. She came through the swing door from the kitchen to the dining room and stopped dead, not understanding what she was seeing. Kelly and Christos held Sylvie by the feet and shoulders, in an untidy bundle, like a carpet they were trying to move. A rope hung from the light fitting, a chair underneath it.

Sylvie saw her and began shouting at her, but she had Kelly's voice, she was shouting that they'd been in a sauna together, that there'd been a switch. Before she could understand more, Christos dropped Sylvie, grabbed a gun from a table and fired.

Georgie fell back into the kitchen through the swing door, complete surprise rendering her unable to move for what seemed like minutes but was probably less than a second. She scrabbled to her feet as Kelly's screams reverberated round the ship. She dived for the far end of the room as Christos plunged through the swing door, gun swivelling to find its target. He skidded on baking trays and fired again as she flew through the door to the corridor, the noise tremendous in the metal-encased room.

Georgie was fit and young. Climbing had honed her muscles, strengthened her sinews, given her explosive speed over short distances. But at that moment, in a ship's narrow corridor, her extreme climbing gave her something more than physical advantage, it gave her mental strength. High up a rock face, wind tearing your feet from their holds, muscles burning, fear is turned into focus, complete attention on the task at hand. Look down and take a moment to consider and you're paralysed, and then you're dead. As Georgie sprinted down the corridor to the stairs, she experienced complete involvement, a transcendental feeling of calm, the same feeling as at the most critical moment of a free climb, where the tiniest mistake leads to death.

She took the stairs three at a time, hearing the clatter of his shoes behind her, her mind jumping ahead to where she would be three moves from now. She couldn't get down the gangway without him getting a clear shot at her. She needed to stay on the ship, get distance between them, then hide and phone the police. She'd take her chances among the miles of containers.

The Wolf was at that moment by the stairwell on the *Saracen*. He had left the docks earlier to dump the rucksack in a left luggage office and had come back, wondering if there was some way he could help Kelly, but the police had cordoned off a large part of the dock and he couldn't approach the ship. When they finally removed the exclusion zone it was several hours later and dark. He heard the shots, faint but unmistakable in the night silence. Two, execution-style. He cursed, he was too late. He moved fast along the deck to a porthole that gave on to the central stairs and saw the customs officer coming up at a sprint, the clang of heavy feet behind her.

Georgie hit the top of the stairs where the exit was and turned left towards the Thames instead of right towards the dock. She began to pick up speed on the long passageway of the deck. Behind her came the sound of something heavy falling. Christos was skidding, palms splayed, face in the floor, another figure jumping on top of him.

Georgie changed direction and ran back, hunting with her eyes for the gun. The two men were tussling back and forth on the deck, slamming into the bulwark and railings. She saw the gun in a corner and ran for it at the same time as the Wolf lunged and got there before her. He turned it in Christos's face and everyone froze. Christos sat back against the railing of the ship, winded, and clutching his chest.

Georgie pulled out her phone and began to dial, but the Wolf got to his feet, snatched it from her and threw it over the side of the ship. 'Not so fast.'

'I need to phone the police—'

The Wolf gestured to Georgie. 'You too. Over there.' He was pointing the gun at both of them. Christos tried to get to his feet. 'Stay on the floor.'

Christos's eyes never left the Wolf's face. 'Now you've got the money you want to play the hero? Only a few hours ago you'd left her in the shit – again.'

'People change. And it's never just about the money.'

'We need to get downstairs,' Georgie said, increasingly desperate.

The Wolf glanced at Georgie and at that moment Christos lunged, head down, knocking the Wolf's gun arm skywards, driving him back against the wall of the ship. The Wolf was taken by surprise but he didn't drop the gun, he was stronger than that, and tried to whirl Christos and his bulk round in a circle. The two men clattered into the railing, locked together, one arm each straining high to get hold of the gun. Georgie tensed, trying to anticipate a moment where she could grab the gun and dodge a bullet.

Christos's low centre of gravity caused the taller man to bend backward at the waist over the railing. Christos landed a couple of vicious blows to his face, the Wolf bucking and writhing. The Wolf jerked his legs to try to pull Christos off him, and his raised legs caused his balance to shift. A moment later the Wolf was sliding backward over the railing, pulling Christos with him and they both disappeared over the side in a tangle of limbs.

Georgie rushed to the side and looked over to see the two bodies falling not into water but hard floor – the deck below extended out further than the one she was on. Christos landed first, smashing his neck on the railing below in his plummet downwards. The gun flew out of the Wolf's hand on impact and skittered away across the deck. Georgie hit the stairs.

When she ran out on to the level below, Christos was lying face down, unmoving, the Wolf staggering to his feet. She came to an abrupt halt. He'd got the gun. She put her hands up, went slowly over to Christos and felt for a pulse.

'I landed on top of him. Fitting, don't you think?' The Wolf spat out a mouthful of blood and staggered a bit more.

'There's no love lost, I see.'

He gave a tight smile. 'No.'

'What's come between you?'

'Money, women, kids.'

'The big stuff, huh?' Georgie needed to keep him calm; he was moving uncertainly, probably injured from the fall.

'You, you've got balls, I'll give you that. Why was he chasing you?'

'I interrupted him trying to murder his wife.'

'My wife, you mean.'

'My God – you're Michael?'

He raised the gun at her and she froze. 'Pleased to meet you. I'm glad she mentioned me.'

'So you and Christos go way back?'

He nodded.

'Did you know him in Southampton?'

'I sure did.'

'Was it you phoning us with information about his business?'

Again a nod.

'What's hidden on this ship?'

'What so many people desire, I suppose. The only thing that cannot be bought – someone who will love you unconditionally.'

She frowned. 'I don't understand.'

The Wolf spat out a glob of blood. 'Watch out, Christos is vicious and he will try to destroy you.'

'Tell me what's hidden on this ship.'

He didn't answer, dropping his gun arm and turning to Christos's prone body on the deck. 'Is he dead?'

'No.'

'Pity. I could at least have done Kel that favour.'

'Why is he so keen to keep her close to him? What happened in Southampton?'

'He set up someone so he could move in on operations down there.'

'Ricky Welch.'

He looked surprised. 'You know about that? He used Kel to do it.'

'So Ricky never killed that man.'

Again, the shake of the head.

'Do you know who did?'

The Wolf smiled and raised the gun towards her again. She took a step back, increasingly alarmed. 'Why does it matter? You need to think bigger. If you're going to take him down, you've got to think like him, think about how he got where he is today. Look around you.' He waved the gun expansively, as if taking in the river and the docks and the vastness of the city beyond, and way upriver the financial heart of the Western world. 'What's the fastest growing port in the UK? The one hiring new talent the fastest, dredging the river, building the facilities – the one keen to reassert its geographical and historical dominance? London. He wants a piece and he'll be going all out to get one.'

'How? How is he doing it?'

'Christos keeps people close. He values loyalty. Those with him have been there for a long time.' He stepped to the railing and coughed. His pain was obvious. 'I've learned something today. Only a few of us are handed moments that make us better people. Maybe this is mine. Here.'

He tossed the gun at her and she caught it and stared at him, stupefied. 'Why are you doing this?'

He shrugged. 'I'm one of the rootless ones, remember? Making it up as I go along. Maybe I'm not as hard-hearted as I thought.' Then he turned and jumped over the side of the ship, and as she raced for the railing she saw the splash far below as he plunged into the black water. The disturbance was as small as that left by an Olympic diver in a pool.

78

Kelly had felt the full force of the floor judder through her spine and up her legs when Christos dropped her to fire the gun. As he ran after Georgie, Sylvie jumped on top of her, determined to pin her to the ground. They wrestled for tense moments on the carpet, a deadly tangle of limbs and straining muscles.

Sylvie was trying to get her knees on Kelly's elbows so she could reach for the end of the rope and get it round Kelly's neck, but there was one final thing Kelly needed desperately to know. 'Why go to all this trouble?' Kelly's voice was strained as she fought to get Sylvie off her. 'You could have killed me.'

Sylvie glanced up at the door, checking who was there. 'Then I'm still playing the waiting game, hoping he'll marry me. There are always other women, other passions to pursue. This way the deal is done tonight.' Sylvie lifted her head, a hand slithering away across the carpet, pulling the rope across Kelly's throat. 'Tonight I'm reborn, I get my second act.'

Kelly tried to buck Sylvie off her. Their faces were inches from each other, Sylvie's breath on her face. 'When I insisted on a kid Christos saw that he could have the heir he so wanted. When I suggested the swap, he realised what I was prepared to sacrifice for him – he understood how dedicated I was. But don't make lazy assumptions.' Sylvie's voice was a whisper, she was conserving every ounce of energy. 'I don't want to be Christos's wife. I want to be his *widow*. I'm not as long-suffering as you. I can have it all without having to put up with him. My son will inherit everything.'

Sylvie had one knee on Kelly's elbow, her curtain of dark hair trailing across Kelly's cheek.

Kelly made a last huge effort, reared and grabbed at the strands of hair hanging either side of Sylvie's face. The movement took Sylvie by surprise and she moved her head. The wig slipped down the back of Sylvie's head and Kelly yanked. She now had her arms crossed over Sylvie's chest and her hands were pulling the wig hairs across her throat. Sylvie tried to pass the rope across Kelly's throat but Kelly's forearms were in the way.

Sylvie's face started to turn red. Her fingers were scratching urgently at Kelly's arms now, more and more frantically, as the air she needed didn't come. Kelly bucked up from under Sylvie and rolled on top of her, gripping ever harder on the locks of hair.

Georgie came down the stairs, her elbows rigid, the gun at the ready. Uncle Ed had taught her and Matt how to fire a gun in some scrabby fields in Essex, years ago. Don't tell your mum, Uncle Ed had said and winked. It was a coming-of-age present, a sign she had grown up. She had a rare moment of silently thanking him for her illegal instruction. Down the long dim corridor and into the kitchen, then across the floor, avoiding the pans. She peered through the swing door into the dining room. It looked empty.

She opened the door with her shoulder and saw the rope still hanging from the light fitting. Two tables pushed up against each other and several overturned chairs were testament to the chaos she'd glimpsed earlier.

'Kelly?' She walked further into the silent room, towards a bundle of something on the floor. She moved closer, saw it was two women, one straddling the other. The dress of the one on top had ridden high up her back, her tights low on her waist. Georgie could see a small dolphin tattoo just above her pants. It was like interrupting two lovers, sated after a bout of vigorous sex. The face of the figure underneath was partially obscured by a mass of dark hair, her arms akimbo, palms upwards as if in the moment of final surrender.

'Kelly?' The woman on top sat up slowly, as if drugged. 'Kelsey? I know what happened in Southampton.' She saw the woman who looked like Sylvie, but had Kelly's dolphin tattoo, look at the gun in her hand. 'It's OK now, they can't hurt you any more.'

Kelly staggered to her feet, swaying uncertainly in her high heels, a trancelike blankness on her features. Georgie felt the sudden rush of adrenalin leaving her limbs and she half fell against a table. The gun slid from her hand and clattered on the floor. As she bent to pick it up she heard the slow tap of high heels as Kelly walked out of the room.

79

Georgie got no sleep that night. Her statement seemed to take hours, she was up and down the stairs of the *Saracen*, indicating positions, angles and spaces to one policeman after another. The forensic team arrived and she handed over the gun. It was bagged and taken away.

She found Kelly on the deck where Christos lay, giving a statement to a policeman. She was wrapped in a blanket someone had given her, but she was shivering.

Kelly came over and gave Georgie a hug. 'Thank you,' Kelly said, her voice a whisper. They stared down the deck at the paramedics trying to stabilise Christos.

'Tell me, did you see Ricky Welch earlier today?'

Kelly frowned. 'Ricky? No.'

'He wasn't at the play centre?'

Kelly shook her head.

'Your witness protection will have to be redone. I'm really sorry.'

Kelly's answer surprised her. 'Ricky is no threat to me. I'm through with hiding.'

'The police might disagree.'

'They can't force me.' She was already gaining strength, reasserting herself.

'Tell me, the message you left me – what's on the *Saracen*, what was it that was going to destroy your family?'

A look Georgie couldn't interpret flitted across Kelly's face.

'Nothing that matters now. Just family stuff.' They paused as the paramedics walked past, carrying Christos away.

'Michael saved my life tonight,' Georgie said. Kelly looked sharply at her. 'Before he jumped overboard he said maybe he wasn't so hard-hearted after all.'

She watched Kelly take a step forward, lean over the railing and stare into the black water. The staccato stop-start of the motorboat revving back and forth, searching for the man who had dived in, carried over the night air. She saw Kelly do a small shake of her head, as if trying to dislodge something that might have flown into her hair, and then she saw her smile. The first time, Georgie realised, she had ever seen her do so. She had a very good smile.

As dawn broke Georgie took a walk and had breakfast in a greasy spoon popular with the night shift. She ate a lot, she was ravenous. She wondered whether she was stuffing herself to block up the feeling of emptiness inside. At nine o'clock she headed back to the office.

Angus was already at his desk, a steaming coffee and bacon roll hiding in the fortress of his papers. He waved her in, got up and told her he'd heard all about the drama on the *Saracen*. 'Some days in this job are quiet, and some defy all reason.' He shook his head and then looked up as a woman stood in the doorway. 'Tina, come in, come in.'

Georgie stood up as the head of HR walked in.

'The PR's downstairs,' she said.

Angus nodded. He pointed a finger at Georgie. 'You are one talented woman. I want Tina to do everything possible to keep you here.'

'There'll have to be an investigation though,' Tina said.

'Have you talked to the police about Ricky Welch yet?' Angus continued.

Georgie shook her head.

'Get it over with and then maybe we'll know where we stand.' He ran a hand through his hair. 'Is the car here?'

Tina pointed at the door. 'Mo and Preston are downstairs.'

'We're going to do a press conference at the Woronzows' about the wood. We'll probably have to stand in the road to do it – the wife's got all lawyered up and that's already causing problems, as you can imagine. We're unlikely to be allowed back on the property. The husband's in Switzerland. At least he'll have to stay there, he can't come back here. He's not welcome.' He rolled up a piece of A4 and pointed it at the piles of paper on the desk. 'Just more paperwork.' Angus sighed and Georgie understood. Partial victories were often the outcome.

'I'm sorry you can't come with us, Georgie, but until this situation is clear—'

Tina interrupted him, wobbling from side to side on her kitten heels. 'Until we know if there is any blowback on the department, it's best to keep you away from anything to do with Malamatos Shipping.'

Georgie said nothing.

Tina smiled. 'This case is being seen as an example of international cooperation to protect the Amazon, one of the world's most unique and important habitats. The Brazilians are claiming just as much credit as we are.'

'I need to run to the little boy's room and then we can ship,' Angus said.

Tina nodded as he flicked the roll of paper across the keyboard on his desk, as if knocking out stray breadcrumbs from between the keys. Georgie leaned forward, ears straining.

Angus looked at her. 'You OK? You've had a hell of a night. Go home and get some rest.' He flicked the paper across the keyboard again. Harder this time, then watched something small fall to the floor.

Georgie stared at him. That noise. It was the rattling, scraping sound from the end of the message on Christos's phone, that Ryan had recorded, that she had sat in Joel's recording studio trying to unpick. A tick, a personal tick as individual as pulling an eyebrow or twisting a lock of hair.

Angus smiled and stood up, dropping the baton of paper in the waste bin. 'Am I ready for my close-up now?' He laughed softly, smiling down at Georgie in her chair. Tina followed him out of the office.

Georgie didn't think she was able to stand. She took three deep breaths, looking around Angus's office. On the noticeboard behind his desk there was a photo of the department, the day she'd first started: Angus with the new recruits. The new generation, building the best port in Britain, a twenty-first-century trade hub for a twenty-first-century city. She ripped it off the wall and shoved it in her pocket. She could hear voices approaching in the corridor, the sound of Preston laughing. She walked out of Angus's office and, for the second time in two days, slipped down the back stairs.

80

Ricky was back in a jail cell. Once you were fucked you tended to be fucked again and again in life, he'd begun to realise. The young woman who had invited him up to London had not come to see him again. He'd rung Dawn; that had been the hardest part, to hear her hopes of a normal life dashed again. The rational side of his brain told him he couldn't be kept here. But life kept repeating itself on the same spool, the same story retold over and over. He hadn't been at the warehouse at that moment on that day either, and look where he'd spent the next eight years.

He sat very still, trying to stay calm. It had been convenient then, was too convenient now. He wondered about the young customs woman. She had called the shots, even though he had invited himself up. Youth didn't keep you clean, didn't keep you at arm's length from corruption.

Ricky waited for breakfast; they were later than he had expected in bringing it to him. The coffee would be appalling. He had a flash of his strong, thick brew in his cafetiere back home. He tried to take something positive from all this. He must be close. For him to have ended up back in here, he was close to finding out who had set him up.

He heard voices outside the cell, then the door slid open and a policeman led him to an interview room. Georgie Bell was already there. The policeman left them alone and closed the door.

'How tall are you?' she asked. She wasn't wasting any time.

'Six one.'

She pulled a photo from her pocket and placed it on the table. 'Recognise anyone in this picture?'

She was panicking, an urgency and a fire in her eyes that he didn't think was a good thing for her. He sat back. 'You need to be careful. I ended up back in here—'

'Do you recognise anyone in this picture?'

He looked closely.

'That's your colleague.' He was pointing at Preston. 'And this Indian-looking guy here.' He touched Mo's face.

'Yes. Anyone else?'

He shook his head, then looked at her wonderingly. 'You're hunting someone on the inside, or you're trying to get evidence to get someone on the inside.' He looked back at the photo. 'The only one old enough to have a past is this guy.' He tapped his finger on Angus's face. 'But I don't know him.'

'You sure?'

'Yes. Who is he?'

She was frowning now, as if she had expected him to have a different answer. 'OK. What was kept out of your trial? Every criminal trial has information that is never submitted, for various reasons.'

He thought for a moment. 'I had a previous conviction for assault, there was a lot of argument about that in pre-trial hearings. There was a tattoo. Kelly saw a tattoo on the murderer's arm, but she contradicted herself as to what the design was.' He pulled up his shirtsleeve and there above the elbow on his bicep was a faded Celtic cross, blue-green with age against his skin. 'She said it was a cross, then she wasn't sure. It never ended up as evidence, which my counsel said was good for me.' He shrugged, to show that it hadn't been.

'How did you end up in here this time?'

'Christos Malamatos phoned the police and said he saw

me outside the play centre. But that can't be true, because I wasn't even there, I was in the shopping centre. Only a little while later they get calls saying there's been a shooting.'

'How does he know what you look like?'

'His wife may have shown him pictures, or I've been set up.'

'I don't think you had anything to do with it. You'll be out of here later today. The CCTV at the shopping centre will clear you most likely.'

'On the contrary. I want to make sure I'm in here for as long as possible. I need a rock-solid alibi in case anything happens to you.' She stared back at him. 'You're trying to work backward. Filling in the blanks because you've got information you can't reveal yet. That works for me, but be careful. Be very careful.'

81

The light had faded on another day by the time Georgie pulled up outside Angus's house. She was in the Kent commuter belt in Ryan's car, in a large village with big houses set back from the road and surprisingly high levels of traffic. The house was single-storey and wide, grander than she had been expecting, with a large garden and a gravel drive. She pulled in and parked by his dark-coloured saloon.

She rang the doorbell and a few moments later Angus opened the door. 'Sorry for wanting to come out to see you here, but in the light of what's happened, I felt better talking away from work.' The tiredness was beginning to overwhelm her, thirty-six hours with no sleep was taking its toll.

He was wearing a white linen shirt rolled up to the elbows, jeans and socks. He'd changed since getting home. He looked more dishevelled out of the office. He nodded and looked a bit distracted, but ushered her in.

'Are your family here?' She knew he had two sons, and a wife whose name she couldn't remember.

'They're all out. Come through.'

She followed him into the kitchen at the back. The house had a seventies vibe, pine kitchen units and cork squares on the floor, surfaces cluttered with paper and cookery books and a knife block. She saw a rugby kit balled in a corner by a pair of trainers. It was a masculine space, a house where the toilet seats were always up.

'Do you want a drink?'

Georgie shook her head.

He was nervous, moving around the kitchen with no purpose, fiddling with a fruit bowl with a dried-up lemon in it, spinning a coin. 'You still haven't talked to the police about this witness protection issue. You need to see them right now. They are going to get seriously pissed off.'

'What does 1824 mean?'

Angus frowned. 'What?'

'What does it mean? It's a code you use for shipments, isn't it?'

'I don't know what you're talking about.'

'"1824 is no". You were warning him that a can would have to be given up.' There was a tense silence. 'You knew him at school, didn't you?'

'Who?'

'Christos. You've known each other all your lives. I wondered where the connection came from. It's something Kelly's first husband told me: he keeps people close, he knows them for a long time. I checked the records and you're the same age. That got me thinking. Same year, it had to be school.' Angus was staring at her, his expression impossible to read. 'But you went your separate ways for a while, you to the south coast – I checked your employment file, you worked in Southampton, it's where you cut your teeth, before you requested a transfer back to London. What were you prepared to do, to keep in with him? Ricky didn't know you, but that didn't mean you didn't know Ricky. There were thousands of employees at the docks in Southampton, but I bet you made sure you knew the one you were going to impersonate. Tell me, you got a tattoo up your sleeve?'

Angus's face was draining of colour. 'You've lost your mind. You've got no evidence whatsoever, this will never stand up.'

'Internal affairs will take a look, though, a long hard look. You sure love your paperwork. Well, I finally looked at the paperwork, at the volumes of trades. Malamatos Shipping began using the port of Southampton the year you started working there. After the Ricky Welch trial the volumes down there trebled. When you moved back to London, guess what? His volumes here grew exponentially.'

Angus scowled. 'It's academic now, he's in a coma and probably won't be waking up. The company will be broken up, he'll die and I'll get my life back. Unlike you.'

He lunged at the knife block, pulling out a carving knife and hurling it hard and fast at her. Georgie threw herself behind the kitchen table as the knife clattered away across the floor. 'Ryan!' She screamed as loud and as hard as she could and that's when her brother kicked in the glass in the back door and, with Uncle Ed in tow, jumped on her boss.

Georgie got to her feet in a hurry. 'I happened on Ricky by chance, but when he turned up in London you saw a golden opportunity: a way of getting rid of me and him in one go. You could kill my career and put him back in jail.'

Angus couldn't talk because Uncle Ed had twisted back his arm and he was in too much pain. Georgie pulled up the sleeve on his right arm. There was no tattoo, but the faintest outline of one that had been removed. She could just make out the shape of a Celtic cross.

82

Three Weeks Later

Kelly stood in her high heels looking down at Christos. He lay beneath a tangle of wires and beeping machinery. A ventilator worked his chest up and down, a monitor was attached to his finger. His eyes were open, deep purple bruising under them refusing to fade. He stared back at her, blinking occasionally. It was hot in the room and she saw a trickle of sweat move down the side of his face. She wondered if he could feel its crawling, irritating passage. She lifted the sheet off his legs, exposing his feet that hung sideways at an odd angle. The forest of black hairs stood out against his waxy skin. She pinched his big toe. Nothing. She ran a nail across his instep. He produced not the merest flicker.

The doctor appeared at the door to the room. 'Mrs Malamatos, perhaps we can talk outside.'

She turned away from her prone husband and followed the doctor into an office.

'I can't sugarcoat it, Mrs Malamatos, your husband's condition is very serious. The trauma to the head was severe. He has been stabilised but he has also subsequently suffered a stroke.' Kelly felt the cold, hard seat below her thighs, the floor through the soles of her feet. 'We'll just have to take it day by day.' The doctor picked up a rubber band and began absent-mindedly twisting it in his fingers, performing the complicated, unconscious movements and coordination of muscles, bones, tendons and nerves that were entirely beyond her husband. 'We need to wait for the swelling in his brain to reduce to see the extent of the nerve damage before we can work out what movement he may regain. I need to warn you that it might be extremely little. At present he can only blink. This is a sign though, that he hears and understands what is being said around him.'

The intonation in his voice didn't indicate that this was a good thing. He paused, waiting for her reaction. 'I'm sure you've got lots of questions.'

She leaned back, crossed her legs the other way. 'Can I get the 29 bus to the ponds on Hampstead Heath from here?'

A team from internal affairs was clearing out Angus's office, overseeing the removal of a man's career, the dismantling of the piles of paper. It was all going into clear plastic bags and being labelled with a series of letters, numbers and slashes. Georgie, Mo and Preston stood watching from outside the door until Tina from personnel arrived and tried to shoo them away with pleas to let the team get on with their job.

They dragged themselves away, like reluctant bystanders from a car crash.

'What, not even a little tear? I always thought you quite fancied him.' Preston nudged Georgie in the ribs.

She gave him her best flying daggers look.

He grinned and shook his head in wonder. 'You know what scares me a bit about you, Georgie? You don't give a shit. I thought *I* was hard-hearted, but you . . .' He tailed off. 'You're in a different class.'

Mo came up between them. 'Anyone seen the stand-in boss yet? Cos I have. He drives a Toyota Prius.' Georgie heard Preston groan.

'Your information is only partly correct,' she added. '*She* also rides a motorbike. A Moto Guzzi.'

'It's nearly five, there's nothing to be done here now, it's time to go.' Mo leaned over and picked up his coat. 'East End girl, goodnight.' He held up a palm to Preston, who gave him a lazy high five. 'I'll see you all in the morning. Same shit, different day.'

Georgie picked up her bag, hearing the comforting clunk of the karabiners sinking to the bottom, and walked out of the door. She saw a shadow across the car park, indistinct in the bright lights being thrown from the customs building. She narrowed her eyes and tried to see through the darkness. A figure in a three-quarter-length coat stepped into a pool of light. It was Uncle Ed, standing and waiting. They looked at each other across the car park. She owed him, and he knew it. How he intended to exploit this situation to his advantage still wasn't clear. But one day his demand would come.

Out on the Thames the deafening roar of a ship's horn rumbled across the water, borne towards them on the tide. She could feel the ground shake with the vibrations as it made its way to port, bringing its secrets with it. Her climbing equipment rattled together in her canvas bag.

Uncle Ed smiled, his whitened teeth a hard line in his mouth.

83

The Wolf watched Luciana pad across the roasting sand to the bar. The heat haze made the banana leaves on the roofs of the long line of bars at the top of the beach shimmer. Luciana passed a small blond boy who was pointlessly running round and round while his mother glugged from a bottle of overpriced mineral water. Luciana put her hand out and tried to tousle the boy's hair. It struck the Wolf, watching Luciana watching the boy, that she talked too much about children, thought too much about them, wanted them too much. He watched her watch the boy scamper away.

The deckchair was giving him backache. The beer Luciana was going to queue for would give him a headache. He felt a fag butt squish between his toes. A family with white skin going pink trailed past, bickering loudly, the father angrily swatting his ankles, grains of sand flying in the flat, hard light. It was January, supposedly a new year, a new start. It didn't feel like it.

He stood up suddenly, the whines of children from around the world cutting out the sound of the Indian Ocean. He picked up his rucksack, threw it over his shoulder and walked away.

84

Eight Months Later

The nurse who came every day was filling in the notes on the forms she had, resting her paperwork on the small side table in the hallway of the terraced house. 'He's stable, same as before. I'll give him a bath tomorrow.'

'OK. I'm sure he'd like that.'

'We can make sure that sore on his thigh is healing.' They both looked up at the snuffling noise coming from the kitchen.

'Oh, Joe's awake.'

The nurse followed Kelly into the kitchen. The back door was open and warm summer air drifted in from the garden. Kelly bent down to the Moses basket and picked up the sleepy baby. His head dropped on her shoulder.

The nurse leaned forward and stroked his cheek. 'Such a poppet. What a sweetie.'

'I know. He's adorable. Thanks for coming,' Kelly said as they walked together to the front door.

'It's my job, remember,' the nurse replied, shutting her bag with a click and pulling it up under her arm. 'I was going to tell you yesterday but I forgot: there's a support group over near the precinct for those caring for severely disabled family members, if you feel you need that. You've got such a lot on your plate.' She nodded at the baby just to emphasise the point.

Kelly smiled. 'Oh, thanks for telling me but I'm managing just fine.'

The nurse looked approving. 'I tell everyone back at the clinic that you're an example to us all.'

'Well, you've got to remember Christos's no bother.'

They both laughed. 'Shush,' said the nurse, lowering her voice and looking guilty.

'Why are you whispering?'

'Well, do you think he can hear anything?'

Kelly turned towards the half-open living room door, patting Joe's back as she did so. She could feel the warmth of his vital body beneath his babygro. 'I'm convinced he hears everything. It's why I always include him in family life. In my life.'

The nurse nodded. 'And he can see his gorgeous son. That must help, even in a small way. It's always better if patients can stay in their own homes. I'm sure he gets some comfort from the familiar. I'll see you tomorrow, same time, same place.'

They said their goodbyes and Kelly shut the door. She walked back into the front room. The house had had to undergo substantial renovations since Kelly bought it, and this room was now Christos's bedroom, with an ensuite bathroom with a hoist. The back of the house had a small living room and a kitchen that gave on to the garden, where the children played for hours on end, or scrabbled through the hedge to use next door's trampoline. When they first came round the neighbours' kids had been apprehensive of the high-backed wheelchair with the man in it who was twisted at a funny angle, and the machine that made the rattling noise every time he breathed in, but now they no longer paid him any attention. 'He's my very quiet daddy,' Yannis was used to saying.

She opened the bay window. It was important to keep the place well aired, to enjoy the summer breeze. She sat on the windowsill for a moment and watched the nurse's car pull away from the pavement outside. Her lips brushed the fresh softness of Joe's fuzz on the top of his head. His hair was dark, like his father's, but his eyes were blue – a hint of his mother. He nuzzled her neck, his little nose wet like a puppy's. She held him high above her head as he giggled and stretched his little hands towards her, his face and heart wide open for his mother's love. She looked up at the perfect child, her love for him exploding through every pore. She had asked Isabella at the hospital after he was born what her favourite name was. It was a tiny thanks for the great gift she had bestowed on the Malamatos family. Isabella had smiled and said, 'Joe.'

Kelly sat him on the floor in a sunbeam and rubbed her bare neck, exploring the feeling of her fingers on skin. She'd kept her hair short and got her hairdresser to give her a more subtle blonde colour. She'd ditched the dark colours and lost the beret. Sylvie had been right about some things, it turned out. Now she preferred brights, she liked high heels. She stretched lazily and glanced at Christos in the wheelchair, parked to be out of the sun. A small dribble had formed on his immobile lips, she'd wipe that away later. The chair was motorised using a remote control, so she didn't even have to push him. She sometimes changed his position, put him where she wanted him.

'Christos, Joe and I are going out for a walk on the beach, then I'll collect the kids from school and we'll all come back later, OK?'

His eyes stared back at her. 'Oh, and I think Medea is coming to visit on Saturday. You know how she loves to see the grandchildren.' She often talked to him, playing out her dilemmas and her choices, making sure he knew what she was doing. Making sure he knew where she was taking the children, the decisions she was making for them.

Once the truth was revealed to Medea, the depths to which her son had gone to try to do away with his wife, she was stunned, and ashamed. She hadn't known about the surrogate child, but the child was still her flesh and blood. She knew how valuable a grandmother could be to a family and her love for her son's children, all three of them, was real. She had come to visit, her home cooking left behind this time. Seeing her playing with the kids softened Kelly's heart to her former enemy. Medea had looked at her broken son, his head lolling uselessly in the wheelchair, tears in her eyes. 'I have no

right to expect anything, but I am here to help, if you need it. The more hands to raise children, the better. Kelly, you are this family, and under your guidance and protection may it continue.'

Her own mother was back in her life – Kelly's new house was near her mum's. They had taken long walks on the beach together, filling in the lost years, rebuilding the trust that had been lost.

Kelly felt the summer warmth on her back, relaxing and liberating, full of possibilities. There were obligations to being married. She had signed up to a duty of care. When word spread in the quiet street that she was caring for a husband who was 'locked in' after a terrible head injury, her new neighbours rallied round, invited her out, offered all kinds of help for her children and new baby.

'You don't understand,' she'd say. 'I feel blessed. Being together with a young family is the most wonderful thing. Christos used to say to me that he would never let me go. It was his vow to me. And so I felt it was only fair that I do the same for him.'

Her old friend Lindsey had come to stay with her kids, shaking her head in wonder at her commitment, a glass of wine in one hand, a fag in the other. 'That's what real love is, Kel.' And she had raised her glass in her garden chair.

She picked Joe up again and he squirmed in her arms,

wriggling and cooing. Love made the world a better place, for every member of her family. She watched a seagull land on the birdbath in the small front garden, its huge wings concertinaing as it snuggled in and bathed, droplets of water flying from its feathers like diamonds in the sunlight. She smiled as she watched it take off and soar away into the blue. Free.

Acknowledgements

With thanks to Craig Sears for the sea tales, Andy Tomlinson for showing me what really lies at the top of St Pancras and how beautiful it is, Mandy Perry and the wonderful women who introduced me to wild swimming, editor Francesca Best and all the team at Hodder for their advice and guidance, my agent Peter Straus, and above all, Stephen Upstone, for putting up with me through it all, and for being able to fell trees.

Read on for an extract from the first psychological thriller by

Ali Knight

WINK MURDER

Kate Forman has an enviable life: a loving family and a
perfect husband, Paul. But late one night Paul comes home
drunk and covered in blood, mumbling about having killed
something – or someone.

When an attractive young woman who works for Paul
is found murdered, Kate's suspicions about what he has really
done send her on an increasingly desperate search for the
truth that threatens to smash her carefully constructed life.

Doing the right thing should seem obvious, but as the lies
multiply, the truth is not as straightforward as it seems.
How well do you know the person you're married to?

Out now in paperback and ebook

HODDER

I

I snap my eyes open in the dark, sensing something is not right. The room is instantly familiar, coming into focus with the help of the city light that sneaks past the roman blinds. Tasteful prints hang on the wall, armchairs guard the fireplace opposite, one has Paul's clothes piled on it in a disordered mountain, the other cradles my dressing gown, neatly folded. I'm in our bedroom, a place of safety, a haven from life. The other side of the king-size is empty, the pillow fluffed. Paul is not home. I hold my breath because there is the noise again, a shuffly scraping that's coming from everywhere and nowhere. My heart pounds in my ears. The clock clicks to 3.32 a.m. as I hear a crash downstairs. It might wake the children and this thought alone forces me out from under the comforting warmth of the duvet. I am a mother; point one on the job description is to protect them, at all costs. My movements are slow and deliberate as I try to steel myself for what I'm about to do. I pick up my mobile and turn the handle on the bedroom door hard to ensure it opens without a sound. Someone is groaning in the hallway and it doesn't sound like Paul.

I have mentally rehearsed what happens next quite often because Paul is away for work a lot at the moment and I think it's important to know how I would fight for the only thing that really matters to me – my family. I like to be prepared. So, as if I'm a fire warden at work, I'm putting it all into action. I take a deep breath, punch 999 into the keypad but don't press the green button, turn on the light and run for the stairs, shouting as loudly as I can into the night silence 'Get out of my house!', phone aloft like a burning spear.

I thump loudly down the stairs and use my gathering momentum to swing round the swirly circle at the bottom of the banister as a shape heaves itself across the kitchen at the end of the hall. 'Get out, get out! The police are outside!' I flood my world with light at the flick of a switch as the dark bundle clatters to the floor with a chair. I pull a cricket bat from the coat stand and feel its comforting weight in my palm and am in the kitchen in a second, the weapon close to my chest. 'Get out of my house!' He has his face on my kitchen tiles but as I raise the bat the shape turns to me and I see my husband, staring up at me from the floor.

It is my husband, but not as I have ever seen him before. He is crying, taking great gulps of air, snot running down to his mouth. I toss the phone on the table and drop the bat to the floor. 'Paul, what on earth's the matter?'

He doesn't answer, because he can't. He looks up at me and my former fear for myself is replaced by a more acute worry for him. I try to pull him upright but he is like a dead weight in my arms; he's folded over and crushed, his demeanour transformed. That was why I didn't recognise him from behind, he is not the man he used to be. 'What's happened?'

Paul smashes his fist into the side of his head and groans again. 'Kate, Kate—'

'Oh my God, what's going on?'

He gets to his knees, shaking, leaving the car key on the floor. Paul is a big man; he's tall, with wide palms, and shoulders you can fall asleep on, it was one of the many things about him that I fell in love with all those years ago. He made me feel protected. 'Kate, oh help me—'

His hands are caked with blood.

'You're bleeding!'

He looks down at them in disgust. He staggers to his feet and I pull limply at his coat, he must be cut somewhere under the thick wool. 'Are you hurt?'

'I . . . I, oh God, it's come to this.'

'What?' He closes his eyes and sniffs, swaying. 'What has happened?' He shakes his head and drags himself into the downstairs toilet and starts washing his hands, flakes of blood and brown water swirling away down the plughole. 'Paul!'

He wipes his face on his shoulder and nods his head. 'I killed her . . .'

He shakes the water off his hands and I slap him, hard. 'Tell me what is going on!'

My husband looks at me, his arresting brown eyes blood-shot from his tears. 'What a mess, what a stupid load of . . .' He sighs from deep within. 'Oh fuck, Kate, I love you so much.' And with that he falls right past me on to the hallway floor in a faint no manner of prods, shoves and screams will wake him from.

Something at least becomes clear to me: Paul is pissed. He must be completely rat-arsed. There are probably many things I should do at this moment but first I must pee. I sit on the toilet and stare at the long body of my husband passed out on the floor, his feet turned inwards, his palms up as if he's indulging in a spot of yoga. I am shivering with anger that he could get in a car and drive home in such a state. I shake his shoulders but he doesn't move. I am not a spontaneous person, I need to plan things, to think; I have never imag-ined a situation like this before and I am at a loss, paralysed in the face of so much that needs to be discovered. After a lot of pushing and heaving I manage to turn Paul over on to his back and pull his coat apart checking everywhere for a wound. When I find nothing I am pathetically thankful – blood makes me faint. I sit back on my heels and stare. The hard planes of his handsome face have dissolved into a puffy mess, his strong jaw has receded into his neck. Paul is snoring, his chest rising and falling. The house is silent, my children slumber on unaware. The kitchen clock accompanies him with its staccato beat. The fridge hums and a window rattles. The house settles back into its night-time rhythm. At 3.50 a.m. I get to my feet, tiredness moving over me in waves. I can think of nothing better to do than go to bed. He'll wake up in the end.

2

What seems like a second later a small hand pokes me in the stomach. 'Ava! Stop that!' My daughter is squirming over me in bed.

'Mummy, let me get in,' she pleads, letting blasts of cold air into the warm fug under the covers. Normally my four-year-old wriggling in for an early-morning cuddle is one of my greatest pleasures, her soft, flawless skin so close, cold little feet pressing into my back, but it's 7.10 a.m., my head is pounding, my eyes scratchy. Paul is not here and the flashing memory of last night pulls me sharply upright, my heart banging in my chest. 'Mummy, I'm cold, Mummy . . .' I cannot believe I slept, that I could leave my husband in such a state on the floor. Horrible images of his dead body being casually stepped over by Josh on his way to turn on the cartoons hurry me out of bed. '. . . Daddy's on the sofa hiding under a blanky.'

I stumble from bed, pulling on my dressing gown. Ava scratches her blonde head. 'Mummy, can Phoebe come and play?' I ignore her as I busy towards the bedroom door. It's time to get the truth about last night.

Paul isn't in the front room. I find him in the kitchen leaning against the counter, a cup of tea in one hand and a slice of toast in the other. He is dressed and shaved and talking at Josh, who's bent over a cereal bowl. My husband looks completely normal. 'Here, I made you one.' He holds up a steaming cup and smiles. I don't smile back but cross my arms in a "try me" gesture. He puts the tea down, packs his grin away.

'What happened last—?'

'Nothing.'

'That was *nothing*?'

'I got drunk and maudlin, that's all.' He shrugs as if trying to make light of it.

My eyes narrow in sceptical disbelief. 'But you were saying you . . .' We both look at Josh's head to see if it's moved. I don't need to use the word. I'm not even sure I can say 'killed', it seems so bizarre and melodramatic with the sun shining in the window and talk of congestion on the M25 coming over the radio.

'Don't be daft.'

'So what happened?'

'Nothing!'

'Who were you talking about?' Josh begins to sense something different from the normal morning pattern and like a tortoise emerging from a long hibernation lifts his head from his bowl, blinking at his parents.

Paul glares at me. 'No one.' I hold up my hands and wave them at him sarcastically. He knows I'm referring to the blood.

'I ran over a dog.'

'What's "ran over"?' Ava skips into the kitchen in a policeman's hat.

'I can't believe you drove in that state!'

'Kate, please! I'm contrite enough, I've got an awful hangover.' We lock eyes.

'Shreddies or toast, Ava?' I ask crisply, moving to the cupboard.

'Krispies. I want Krispies.' I reach for a bowl and spoon.

'A dog?'

'Yeah. I felt I had to move it and I got covered in . . . you know.'

Blood. Your hands had blood on them, Paul, is what I want to say, but I hold back. 'What kind of dog?'

'What?'

'What kind of dog was it?'

'Labrador cross, I think.' He looks at his feet. 'I had to drag it, I got upset.'

I stare at my husband as he stands in the kitchen, the beating heart of our home, his progeny around him. I know him better than he knows himself. He often tells me that. And I know that when he looks at his feet he's lying.

'You know what breed, but you don't know what sex.' Paul looks blank. 'Last night this dog was a "she". This morning it's an "it".'

He shrugs, his face revealing nothing. 'It all seemed more real last night, I suppose. Dogs can seem like people when they're hurt.' He drains the last of his tea and brushes crumbs off his suit. 'I've got to go.' He moves towards me and gives me a long, tight hug, rocking me slowly from side to side and planting an affectionate kiss in the middle of my forehead. 'Oh, Eggy, you're always looking out for my welfare.'

I have a high forehead, which I've always hated. Almost as soon as I started hanging out with Paul and his crowd, lovesick and in awe of him, to my severe mortification he made his friends laugh by calling me Egghead. But as the months went on and I started to dream that he was falling for me, I became Eggy, and of all his endearments it's the one I love the most. He smiles weakly at me as we walk arm in arm to the front door. I help him into his coat as he hunts around for his scarf and work bag.

'Mum, Ava's spilled milk on my comic!' There are screams and shouts from the kitchen.

'You'd better go,' Paul says, opening the door.

'Are you OK?' I cling on to him for a bit longer, trying

to massage away the dissatisfaction from my unresolved questioning. He nods, pulling my arms away. 'Are you sure?'

'Never better,' he says, but he looks sad as he walks down the path.

'Mum!' I wander into the living room, Ava's scream rising through the octaves. I see a screwed-up blanket under which he spent the night, the indentations of his body are still visible in the cushions. He must have been up early to wash away the effects of last night. When we talked there was something I couldn't bear to ask him, the lid on a box of emotions I was too scared to lift. What could have made him weep on our kitchen floor like that? Five years ago Paul's father died of a sudden stroke. I never thought any man could show such grief as he had then – until last night.

3

My name is Kate Forman and I am very lucky. I have been told this often enough by friends and family and I truly believe it. My successes are many: I have been married for eight years to the most wonderful man on the planet, we have two beautiful, healthy children and a house far bigger and grander than I ever imagined I would live in. I'm thirty-seven years old, I don't have to dye my hair and I can still wear the clothes I bought before Ava was born (though not Josh; motherhood takes it's toll on us all, however much we pretend otherwise). Accident, design, hard work or chance, I don't really care; I am happy and so is Paul, and that is all that counts.

I know that Paul is happy, because he admitted to me recently that he thought he loved me more than our children. He asked me if I thought that was wrong, and I laughed and shook my head. I sometimes think I don't deserve Paul. His family is much grander than mine, he went to a top public school, his mum lives in a manor house in a nice bit of countryside, he grew up with a tennis court, lots of brothers and sisters, first editions on the shelves and paintings that may or may not be valuable, nobody seems to know or care. It's all much more impressive and romantic than my mum and stepdad's sterile box on a suburban estate, photos of mine and my sister Lynda's graduation hung proudly on the lounge wall.

I met Paul on my first day at university. I was Katy Brown

then. In fact, he was the very first person I met after I'd left home. I arrived at the station with my bike; Mum was bringing my stuff up in the car and was meeting me on campus. Paul was the third-year student driving the van ferrying strays and cyclists to our accommodation. I was the only one he picked up on that run and I fell in love with him instantly. He was deeply tanned and ridiculously fit after a long summer break somewhere in Europe. He drove one-handed with his elbow jutting out of the rolled-down window, the late-summer heat bringing a pleasing other-worldliness to our journey. As we careered round huge roundabouts and sped down the dual carriageways of a big and unknown city, I felt an unadulterated joy at what life held, sensed excitements that have been hard to recapture since. He was two years older than me and teased me not unkindly for being a fresher. He was flirting and I lapped it up. He had big brown eyes and dark hair that sat up in tufts, which he would rub distractedly. He still has all his hair today. As he lifted my bike out of the back of the van I couldn't believe that university would be so full of such gorgeous, exciting men. Needless to say, it wasn't. In the next few weeks I scanned the campus but caught only brief glimpses of him. He waved at me a couple of times through the crowd that surrounded him, and that's as far as it went. I made new friends, threw myself into first-year university life, got distracted by other relationships. I came to London after graduation giving him barely a thought. Five years later my friend Jessie started dating Pug, and besides having a ridiculous name Pug hung out with Paul.

Paul was married to Eloide then. At first I thought Paul must have said Eloise, but no, even her name had to be different – and difficult. She was a natural blonde. I'm not proud of what happened a year later, but they had no children, thank God, which made things cleaner. We just had a connection that couldn't be denied. The first night we spent together was one of the most supreme moments of my life. It goes without saying that the sex we had was . . . I have no words to properly describe the intensity, the honesty of it. I got pregnant two months after his divorce came through.

Our story doesn't end there, it just gets better and better. Paul proposed on a weekend in Paris when I was seven months gone, we were married when Josh was one. Our baby looked so cute on our wedding, wriggling in his little white sailor suit with blue trim. My mum jiggled him all through the service in the pretty rural church. Afterwards she cried and told me I'd done very well.

We've moved house three times since we've been together; from the flat to a pretty Victorian terrace to our imposing three-storey near the park. Paul runs a TV production company and has been very successful. We've traded up. If things stay as they are, who knows what we might acquire or how soon Paul can retire. I don't work full-time any more. Before I met Paul I worked in market research analysing consumer behaviour – 'poking our noses in and getting paid for it' we used to say over the water cooler – but after I had Josh my interests dovetailed with Paul's and I got my break as a TV researcher, which I've been doing ever since. I now work on *Crime Time*, a tabloid-style weekly show that relies heavily on CCTV footage and viewers' mobile phone videos to catch criminals, from petty thieves to murderers. Even though I work three days a week, Paul still says that I'm 'dabbling'. While sometimes that annoys me, it's also fair to say that my sphere is the home, Paul's is work, and we unite in the middle, like a neat Venn diagram.

This morning should be like any other, fiddling with packed lunches before hustling Josh and Ava off to school. Normally I can take almost anything in my stride but today the children's bickering shoots right to my irritation vein. There is milk all over the kitchen table and chair, Josh is flicking a sodden magazine so splatters hit the paintwork. My children are spoiled, and guilt steals over me at how I overindulge them, overcompensate for what was lacking in my own childhood. Paul doesn't mind though, he's very forgiving.

I step through the kitchen chaos and pick up Paul's cricket bat, untouched and ignored by his unsporty son, and return it to its place in the hall. I'm suddenly struck by how close I came to really battering him with it, and he doesn't even know. Roll on 12.30 and lunch with Jessie. Today I'm drinking wine.

Ali Knight

THE FIRST CUT

A best friend murdered.
A marriage going nowhere.
A deadly obsession.

Nicky's had more than her share of heartache. So when she
meets a hot young stranger she thinks a little flirting can help
her forget the past. She's married, but it's innocent enough.

Except what starts as fun leads to a terrible ordeal,
and a dark secret.

Nicky's about to discover that the scars of love
can last a lifetime.

Out now in paperback and ebook

HODDER

In the best books, the ending often comes as a shock.
Not just because of that one last twist in the tale,
but because you have been so absorbed in their world,
that coming back to the harsh light of reality is a jolt.

If that describes you now, then perhaps you should track down
some new leads, and find new suspense in other worlds.

Join us at www.hodder.co.uk, or follow us on
Twitter @hodderbooks, and you can tap in to a
community of fellow thrill-seekers.

Whether you want to find out more about this book,
or a particular author, watch trailers and interviews, have
the chance to win early limited editions, or simply browse
our expert readers' selection of the very best books,
we think you'll find what you're looking for.

And if you don't, that's the place to tell us what's missing.

We love what we do, and we'd love you to be part of it.

www.hodder.co.uk

@hodderbooks

HodderBooks

HodderBooks